Eliza Allen Starr

Patron Saints

Eliza Allen Starr

Patron Saints

ISBN/EAN: 9783741183843

Manufactured in Europe, USA, Canada, Australia, Japa

Cover: Foto ©Andreas Hilbeck / pixelio.de

Manufactured and distributed by brebook publishing software (www.brebook.com)

Eliza Allen Starr

Patron Saints

PATRON SAINTS.

BY

ELIZA ALLEN STARR.

Golden vials full of odours which
are the prayers of the saints.

APOCALYPSE v. 8.

BALTIMORE:
JOHN B. PIET & CO.
No. 174 W. Baltimore St.
1883

DEDICATION.

TO

THE FAITHFUL

YOUTH

OF THE CATHOLIC CHURCH IN AMERICA,

TO WHOSE INTERESTS I AM PROUD TO DEVOTE MY LIFE.

CONTENTS.

ILLUSTRATIONS.

INTRODUCTION.

FATHER R———, under the influence of whose æsthetic yet thoroughly practical mind these sketches of Patron Saints have, from time to time, been written, always insists that "Children's books are not, necessarily, childish." I have applied this rule to the matter, as well as to the style, of these sketches; for I have found that children can understand books which they cannot read for themselves. At my elbow, as I write, stands a lively example of this well-known fact. Master Bertie, who has reached his eighth year, will lie on the floor, or perch himself on a chair in a position utterly unattainable by any one but a rope-dancer or a child with bones as lithe as willow-rods, and listen by the hour to "Sister Nellie," only two years older than himself, while she reads Hawthorne's "Wonder Book for Children," or Ruskin's "King of the Golden River," "written," as he tells us, "for a very young lady."

Any child, intelligent enough to listen with pleasure to a well written fairy tale, is capable of understanding, and appreciating, the story of nearly every saint whose name appears in the Calendar; and if boys and girls do not enjoy reading the Lives of the Saints as generally written, it is because they do not readily take in a closely printed page of condensed facts. The same facts, dilated upon with even ordinary enthusiasm, such as one hears in conversation, would seize upon their imagination, and interest their affections.

It is one of the misfortunes of abridged histories for children, that they give the dry facts, without any of those pleasing digressions that sustain the interest of the adult reader in the perusal of the original work. It is like feeding on condensed meats, which, however nutritious, fail to give the relish of the usual dishes of beef and mutton.

There is a singular forgetfulness, also, of another fact, very noticeable among children, and this is, the readiness with which they grasp the wonderful in nature and the miraculous in the history of humanity. Robinson Crusoe and the Arabian Nights will never lose their hold upon the young of any generation; and for this reason—they recognize the power of the youthful imagination and trust themselves to the sympathies of their young readers. The early Christians did not attempt to gratify this love of the marvellous, and this capacity for sympathizing with the most extraordinary relations, by putting before their children fictitious narratives; but they did what was far more direct, and far more effectual—they gave them the Acts of the Martyrs, and the sublime history of Christianity in the midst of persecution. They did not fill their libraries with exciting stories of lion-hunts or adventures with elephants, and tigers, in the jungles of India, but they told them the story of a St. Pancratius, inviting the leopard to open to him the gates of the martyr's heaven; of a St. Agnes, playfully dropping over her childish hands the manacles ordered for her by the harsh Roman Prefect; of a St. Dorothea, smilingly promising to her pagan lover, turned accuser, fresh apples from Paradise, as she was on her way to execution; and, however worldly wisdom or pagan learning or cynical philosophy may sneer at these beautiful traditions, a guileless child has never yet been known to smile with incredulity, or to carp with cautiously worded phrases at these miraculous Acts of the darlings of Christian literature. Put the lives of the saints into the language of colloquial narrative; let them appeal to the ready sympathies, the noble sensibility to the highest code of honor, of the children of to-day; connect them with the sports and the studies, the trials and the temptations of the child, living at this moment in America, in the United States; and the saint will prove a dangerous rival to the fairy, and the true Acts of the Martyrs will triumph over the juvenile fictions that now prepare the mind of the youngest reader to crave only the high-seasoned, sensational novel. Protestantism may indeed pause before admitting the Lives of the early Christian Martyrs, or the thrilling narrative of many a Catholic priest or courageous nun among the barbarians of all nations and of all climes, into their Sunday School libraries; but Catholicity recognizes these narratives as the natural and appropriate literature of the Christian child as well as of the Christian adult; and, by so doing, shows the rare quality of her maternal instinct, and gives a sublime testimony to her confidence in the intellectual vigor and spiritual discernment of even "babes in Christ."

To one who stands only on the thrèshold of Catholic literature how precious and how varied do its treasures appear; how inviting the safe and duly guarded paths of learning; how ennobling the types of virtue presented to the admiration of the "children of light!" But if this is the experience of those standing only upon the threshold, how grand are the spectacles, how ravishing the vistas, opening to the eyes of the really ardent student and the profound scholar! Those who blame Catholics for "confining themselves to their own literature," know little of the celestial spaces open to their intellectual telescope.

And shall we, who have entered upon this inheritance, consent to forget the supernatural traditions of the heroic ages of faith, and, mingling in the tide of naturalism setting off from these sublime shores, seek our recreation only at the common level of mortal interests? Shall we, moreover, condemn our youth and little children to find their entertainment in the fictitious narratives of the day, instead of presenting to their enthusiastic admiration the inspiring examples of real personages and genuine heroes; or, presenting to them these glorious types of Christianity, shall we do so after the dry and concise manner of Gazetteers and books of dates? Or shall we dilate upon the attractive points of our narrative, and show, as we can now so well do, how the saints have been the true civilizers and teachers of the world, the true men of letters, of science, and of wisdom, as well as the inspiration of true genius in all Christian ages? It is by showing to children, the inquisitive boys and the impressible girls, how the saints have been the practical working men, as well as the crowning glory of their age, that we are to rouse within them a sincere veneration for the Saints of God; a veneration too deep for the finger of a malignant scepticism to blight, too lofty for the poisoned arrow of a paganized philosophy to wound. Let us not trust, in this age of extraordinary dangers, to ordinary means of safety. Let us not be contented with the mere learning "by rote," and by "reason of custom," the history of the Church and of her saints; but, with the first dawn of understanding, let the vision of Christian virgins, of spotless confessors, of triumphant martyrs, take possession of the infant imagination; and thus shall that "sweet hour of prime," which comes to the young of all nations, find them consecrated to the loftiest ideals of human excellence, and, it may be, of supernatural sanctity.

But the principle upon which I have based the choice of subjects for this volume of Patron Saints, is no less true when applied to Art than to Literature. It is not because the children around us are incapable of appreciating the great works of religious art, that they are not made familiar with them. The real truth of the matter is, that children comprehend these sublime productions much better than they do those of an inferior or less exalted order. Set before any intelligent child, instructed in the dogmas of the Christian religion, a tolerable representation of the two most renowned pictures of "The Last Judgment," the one by Andrea Orgagna on the walls of the Campo Santo at Pisa, and that by Michael Angelo in the Sistine Chapel at Rome, and we shall find the sympathies of the child sustaining the preference given, by the most accomplished critics of art, in favor of Andrea Orgagna. Again: let any innocent child, of ordinary sensibility, be familiar with the angels painted by that holy monk, Fra Angelico of Fiesoli; and then put before him the flippant, erratic beings fluttering about the sacred personages in many a picture called religious, and the profound instinct of the child will be on the side of the Angelical Brother. There is no child who does not hang enraptured over Correggio's "Nativity," "*La Notte*," of the Dresden gallery; and although it may not understand the enthusiastic praises of Frederic von Schlegel over this wonder of religious art, the silent joy of the child is one and the same with that which prompted the eulogium of the great German critic.

It is not, then, because children are incapable of appreciating these works of art, in the noblest sense of appreciation, that they are not made acquainted with them; but rather because of the indifference to the highest excellence of such works in the minds of those who are responsible for the mental and spiritual culture of the young. It is not the child, who is indifferent, but the parent; and very much of this indifference is the result of circumstances, until a vitiated taste unfits a generation to appreciate what, under other circumstances, would excite the most delightful enthusiasm. We have all heard of children, removed very early from their parents and country, who have lost the knowledge of their mother tongue, and although they may regain it more easily than others may acquire it, for them it is, practically, a foreign language. This seems to apply in a special manner to ideas of religious art, and the appreciation of its most exalted types, among Catholics cut off from communication with the sources of true criticism, and separated, also, from those traditions that keep alive the feeling for true religious art. In this country, until photographs multiplied in the cheapest form the works of the great masters, by far the greater number of our American people had really no opportunity of forming any correct judgment in regard to religious art; and now, unfortunately, too many sentimental and utterly spurious conceptions have been palmed off upon the Catholic child to allow him to think or feel with the candid accuracy of first impressions. Many a child, who, if its tastes had never been injured by exaggerated or puerile representations of sacred subjects, would have evinced a taste creditable to the most æsthetic culture, now turns from the celestial grace of a Fra Angelico, or a Perugino, or a Lionardo da Vinci, or even of a Raphael, to the sentimental, untheological, bedizened caricatures of religious emotion to be found on every side. It devolves upon those of the present day, who have in their hands the forming of the popular taste, to restore the ancient traditions, and to encourage such representations as shall aid, and not hinder, a clear understanding of the dogmas of the Christian faith.

In France, such men as Count Montalembert and M. Rio have pleaded the cause of the purest types of religious art against the corruptions of popular taste; and it is, certainly, not derogating from us as a nation, at such a distance from the centres of Christian traditions, if some words of entreaty are offered in behalf of the highest types of religious art as found in the choice collections of Europe, and brought to our shores, against the degenerate types and unwitting innovations that prevail among us.

To sincere persons who may attach only a secondary importance to the purity of artistic types in religious art, it will throw a new light on this subject to quote the opinions expressed, ages ago, by those who held themselves responsible, before God and the Church, for everything connected with the Divine worship and Christian civilization.

If we go back to the ages when Christianity was still an underground religion, compelled to practice its sacred rites amid the gloom of the Catacombs, we shall learn what were the types of sacred art sanctioned by those standing within the halo of the first Christian traditions; and it is to be remarked, that in these subterranean chapels, occupied by a generation whose blood was called for as the seed of the future Church, we find all solemn, indeed, but ineffably serene; with an air of tender simplicity and even supernatural buoyancy, expressing beatitude rather than happiness, and full of the celestial triumph of the heavenly Jerusalem. The head of our Lord, found on the ceiling of the fourth chamber of the Catacombs of St. Calixtus on the Via Appia, beneath the Church of St. Sebastian, could not be misunderstood, wherever found, and is worthy of being considered the prototype of those heads of the Redeemer still to be seen in the most perfect examples of Christian art.

But as time went on it became customary for even such teachers as St. Cyril, to dwell upon the humiliations of our Lord as foretold by the Prophet, who describes Him as "An abject among the people, a worm and no man," until the popular taste declared that He should be represented, in works of art, as without comeliness; and during His passion as hideous by reason of His anguish. Happily for the safety of doctrine as well as the truth of art, this view was combated by the three Latin Fathers, St. Ambrose, St. Augustine and St. Jerome, and, in the East, by St. John Chrysostom and St. Gregory of Nyssa, all living so early as the fourth and fifth centuries. When the question was revived in the eighth century, St. John of Damascus, and Pope Adrian I., so far from countenancing, or even treating with indifference, this innovation upon the traditions of sacred art, boldly declared the Redeemer, "A new Adam, and a model of perfection in form;" while no less in the twelfth century, when the meagre type of the Byzantine artists was in a measure thrust upon Christendom, the voice of St. Bernard was raised in defence of the original pictorial traditions of Christianity.*

Nor will this surprise us, when we remember the

*See M. Rio's De l'Art Chrétien. Page 9.

place occupied by the artist in the eyes of the Church. St. Bede, writing in the eighth century, describing the pictures brought by St. Bennet Biscop for the decoration of his twin churches, St. Peter and St. Paul, says, "Those, therefore, who knew not how to read, entering these churches, found on all sides agreeable and instructive objects, representing Christ and His saints, and recalling to their memory the grace of His incarnation and the terrors of the last judgment." The Synod of Arras, held in 1205, declared, that "Painting is the book of the ignorant, who know not how to read in any other." And an inscription, formerly legible, over the principal doorway of St. Nixier at Troyes, expresses the desire of its pastor to familiarize the faithful with the facts and dogmas of religion; "for which reason," he says, "I have caused to be painted three windows, to serve as a catechism of instruction to the people."

It was not, then, merely as a decorative art that painting was encouraged, or so carefully defended from any essential variations; but as a powerful appeal to the will and the understanding of the Christian world, through the sense of sight; and, as such, to be encouraged and guarded. According to the spirit which then belonged to art, or rather vivified art, as the soul gives life to the body, there was not a dogma of the faith "committed to the saints," not an incident, either in the Old Testament or the New, bearing in any way upon these greatly venerated and beloved dogmas, that was neglected by the pious artists of those ages of faith; and as the literature of those ages was made up, in great part, of works on Theology, or of works bearing upon the eternal interests of man, so the pictures that glorified those ages, as they are found in the churches, in the ancient chapels of devotion, especially at Assisi, on the walls of the Campo Santo, and, later still, on the ceiling of the Sistine Chapel, may be called grand compendiums of the history of the world from Adam to the Christian Era, through the childhood, ministry, death, and glorified life of our Redeemer, the establishment of the Apostolic Church and its miraculous growth, to those events marking the spiritual rank of the generations by which they were executed; and then, winging an eagle flight beyond time, and sense, and things known to the mind of man by experience, the forecasting imagination of the artist depicted the sublime issues of the final judgment and the beatitude of the elect. The pictures of these ages, of which we are speaking, might be treated, collectively, as pictures of devotion, and had their places, as all perceive, very suitably, in those sacred edifices created for the most sublime necessities of the human soul. It belonged to a later period, when the admixture of worldly learning and the exactions of wealth and luxury in the Christian world had turned art aside from its supernatural end, checked the celestial flight of its sanctified aspirations, and claimed for mortal interests a share, at least, in what had been, hitherto, dedicated to eternity, to draw distinctions, only too well deserved, between the sacred historical picture even and the devotional. It is now the task of all writers upon religious art to draw, clearly and delicately, the dividing line, and to judge of sacred pictures, not so much by the personages delineated in them, as by the motive animating these pictures as conceptions. There is a naturalistic school in sacred art, as well as in Theology, which seeks to bring within the range of natural motives, and natural conditions, the most supernatural incidents of the Old and New Revelation; and there is also an historical sacred art, as different from the most exalted conceptions of devotional art as the historical books of the Old Testament are different from the Psalms, the Canticle of Canticles, or the transcendent Revelation of St. John of Patmos.

We might take, as an example, the Crucifixion, that sublime scene which the devout imagination of every Christian has again and again depicted to itself, especially during the time of daily meditation. Nothing can exceed the intensity of dramatic action, the richness of costume of the Roman soldiery and the centurion on the one hand, and of the scribes and Pharisees on the other, introduced into many of the celebrated Crucifixions that are to be found, in every country, from the hands of the masters of art in the fifteenth and sixteenth centuries. They seemed to vie with each other in producing the sensible contrast between the pageantry of a blind, cruel, and unbelieving world and the abjection and sorrow of the Lamb of God. While looking at these pictures one almost hears the blasphemous taunt, and the merciless orders of the richly attired officials given in a tone of haughty dictation that overpowers the sigh of the devoted and afflicted Magdalene; while the waving of plumes, the glitter of lances, the dazzling array of military power, and the crush of eager and insulting multitudes, hardly leave room for the drooping figure of the Mother of Sorrows; or, if the Blessed Virgin is given any prominence, it is no longer as the example of fortitude in suffering—"standing," as the Evangelist expressly mentions, "by the cross;" but as a mother, overcome by the anguish of her son, and fainting in the arms of her friends. Without commenting on the theological inaccuracy of the last mentioned action of the Mother of God, we can say, that such pictures, although gorgeous, and powerfully attracting the admiration of every generation, must still be classed with the historical Crucifixions only; as not, in any sense, conforming to, or developing, the central idea of the sacrifice on

Calvary; nor that transcendent excellence of our Divine Redeemer, that gave, even to the horrors of that deicidal scene, a pathetic beauty which the total eclipse of the sun itself could not wholly obscure.

This central idea of the bloody and actual sacrifice on Mount Calvary and this inextinguishable loveliness of the second Adam, together with His inseparable Divine nature, supplies that type, or devotional ideal, which occurs to the mind most readily during the morning hour of meditation. The historical type, especially under some mental conditions, might indeed occur to a person during this meditation, but it is not the one most conducive to those affections called the *fruit* of meditation. The historical type, save in some very exceptional instances, is the worldly, the exterior, the realistic, if not naturalistic, view of the mystery of Redemption and its closing scene. The devout Crucifixion is quite, quite different. In this there are no Roman guards close to the cross of the Man-God. Instead, we find the Mother of Dolors, standing with the fortitude possible only to the Mother of God, beside the cross of this victim of Love; opposite her is the Beloved Disciple; between them, and embracing the cross, is the holy penitent, St. Mary Magdalene, while the other holy women are sometimes seen in the distance. It is pre-eminently the sacrifice of Mount Calvary as repeated in the mass, that is represented in these truly sacred, truly devotional pictures. There is no torturing agony of position, no restless anguish, no movement; but the adorable Body hangs upon the three nails in the droop of unutterable, Divine patience, the arms nearly horizontal, the head bowed gently upon the breast that never heaved with a turbulent emotion. It is the suffering of a self-offered Holocaust; and the soul melts, like glass, before the tranquil ardors of this furnace of Omnipotent Love.

Perfectly parallel instances of these different conceptions of the same event, are found in the "Descent from the Cross," and in the "Entombment." Take the Descent from the Cross by Rubens, in the Cathedral at Antwerp, and we have all the qualities that belong to the graphic, historical picture of sacred events, vividly and powerfully conceived. One fears, while looking at it, lest one of those busy hands may slip from the sacred body; and we sympathize with the involuntary action of the Blessed Virgin, who puts forth a hand, as if to take the place of the one that may fail.

But if we turn to the devotional rendering of this scene, how different are the emotions excited! In that most tender and expressive picture by Duccio, we see the maternal instinct of the Blessed Virgin, but in an action how pathetic! The venerated and beloved body is not yet wholly detached from the cross, for the faithful Nicodemus is carefully drawing the nails from the feet; but already, as the body is gently lowered from the sacred "tree," the maternal arms of the Blessed Virgin have received Him, and she presses on His lifeless lips the kiss of adoring love.

There is another picture of the "Descent from the Cross," by Fra Angelico, a description of which, in the "History of Our Lord," as begun by Mrs. Jameson and continued by Lady Eastlake, touches directly upon this point.

"No more Christian conception of the subject, and no more probable setting forth of the scene, can perhaps be attained. All is holy sorrow, calm and still; the figures move gently and speak in whispers. No one is too excited to help, or not to hinder. Joseph and Nicodemus, known by their glories, are highest in the scale of reverential beings who people the ladder, and make it look as if it lost itself, like Jacob's, in heaven. They each hold an arm close to the shoulder. Another disciple sustains the body as he sits on the ladder, a fourth receives it under the knees; and St. John, a figure of the highest beauty of expression, lifts his hands and offers his shoulder to the precious burden, where in another moment it will safely and tenderly repose. The figure itself is ineffably graceful with pathetic helplessness, but "Corona Gloriæ," victory over the old enemy, surrounds a head of Divine peace. * * * * In this picture it is as if the pious artist had sought first the kingdom of God, and all things, even in art, had been added unto him. * * * * Pious carefulness and earnest decorum here do even this hard work better than the most ostentatious display of anatomical knowledge and physical strength." Lady Eastlake has given in her drawing only the centre group, "leaving out," as she remarks, "the sorrowing women on the right, with the Mother piously kneeling with folded hands, as if in this attitude alone she could worthily take back that sacred form."

In the Deposition or Entombment, we find that only those masters who lose themselves and their art in the adoring love and sorrow that must have filled every heart in that little group of mourners, that procession of worshipful grief, have succeeded in touching the innermost spring of exquisitely tender feeling, to which this scene must ever appeal. Even Raphael, while producing, on this subject, a masterpiece of art, failed to express, or appeal to, the sentiment that would have made it a devotional picture in its highest sense; and the winding sheet tells us why. It is not held, as in deeply devotional pictures, at its full length, thus giving expression to the venerating awe that the lifeless humanity of the world's Redeemer must have inspired in the least of those privileged to bear it to the "new tomb" reserved for it, but the youthful energy and zealous action is suited rather to some incident in Mythology. It is not the recollection of Christians, who would esteem the too near contact with that adorable Body as sacrilege, that we see in this picture, but the vigor of youthful athletes bearing one of their own number to the tomb.

But if we turn from Raphael, in these pictures of the passion and death of our Redeemer, to those of a more contemplative school, we must still refer to his inspired genius some of the most exalted types of the Incarnation. The "Madonna del Sisto," or the "Dresden Madonna," as it is frequently called, marks the faith of Raphael in the most sublime dogmas concerning the Holy Infancy.* Much as the picture suffers in many engravings, it can never lose the supernatural majesty, the ineffable solemnity, that seals this sublime picture as consecrated, in its most secret motive, to the mysterious dogma of the Incarnation. What the *Et Homo factus est* (And was made man) must ever be in the music of the Creed, all devotional pictures of the Holy Infancy must be in the world of art. There can be no lightly tripping measure when the mysterious clause concerning the "Word made flesh" is treated either by voice or instrument; but the mystery sends the notes, far, far off into the eternal spaces, and the knees of the multitude bend simultaneously, like rushes before the wind. There may be charming pictures painted from some other motive; but no picture of the Holy Childhood that is not the offspring of meditation upon the Incarnation can ever meet the devout necessities of the Christian soul.

To let one's eye run over any collection of Raphael's Madonnas is to realize this distinction in the works of

---

*See account of the conversion of *Rumohr*. Épilogue a l'Art Chrétien, M. Rio. Vol. II, Page 112.

this great artist, who has painted every shade of maternal feeling, from the admiring veneration mingled with tenderness that characterizes several of his most popular works, and makes them the delight of many a mother as she hangs over the crib of her infant, to the supernatural exaltation of the Dresden Madonna, in which is expressed all the mysterious sublimity of the event of the Incarnation, and the awful grandeur of "the woman clothed with the sun." The two angels at the foot of this group, standing, as it were, in some rift of mundane clouds, and giving us a glimpse of heaven and its glories, are not, as they are so often represented, chubby babies looking smilingly upon the baby above; but magnificent cherubs, with the superhuman knowledge of their angelic rank expressed in their adoring gaze upon the Mother of God and her Divine Son; their wings dipped in the colors of the rainbow, and their entire being rapt in the contemplation of that mystery from which springs the whole glorious panorama of Christian doctrine and of Christian art.

If any one, judging from the preference given in these pages to the "Mystical School of Art," should draw an inference in favor of pre-Raphaelite theories, as they are understood in this country, I would say that nothing could be further from my own intention. If I do not mistake the idea of the best expressions of the, so called, pre-Raphaelite movement, it is a return to those purely religious motives that inspired the noblest schools of Christian art, before pagan art had tainted the imagination of Christendom, and before mere human motives, or motives below the human as it exists under Christianity, were supposed to form proper subjects for the brush or chisel. Thus far, the pre-Raphaelite movement is on the side of truth, and of truth under its noblest aspects. But the moment art is spoken of in regard to a period of time, and not in regard to its spirit, the moment that artistic skill is despised, and meagre forms and childish perspective, and worse than childish ignorance, at this age of the world, are claimed to be the distinctive marks of religious art, that moment the movement becomes a retrograde one, and in no way to be tolerated. I have never supposed this extreme view of pre-Raphaelitism to be worthy of a moment's consideration; and the throwing upon the whole movement this puerile accusation, and combating it upon this ground, has always seemed to me a proof of superficial and altogether inadequate views of its real merits.

Let us suppose that Demetrius, the silversmith spoken of in the Acts of the Apostles, had, instead of rejecting Christianity, received it by the mouth of St. Paul, and had used his craft, not to multiply statues of the "Diana of the Ephesians," for idolatrous worship, but of the Blessed Virgin, the Mother of Jesus, to satisfy the veneration of the faithful. We cannot suppose that he would, under such circumstances, reproduce his Diana with a few changes in the dress or position, and call it the Blessed Virgin; neither can we suppose that, having the skill of a cunning artificer, he would feel himself bound to forget this skill, and make only a rude, ugly image of the Mother of Christ and the Mother of Christians. It is only reasonable to suppose that he would bring to his conception of the Blessed Virgin, all the veneration of a true believer, and all the skill of the cunning workman. This case of Demetrius illustrates the true relation between devotional art and human learning. To insist upon robbing devotional art of the aids of human learning, is to return to a worse than Byzantine bondage; whereas the naturalistic freedom, of substituting human for Divine personages, has something worse than paganism in its errors; since it is a sin against knowledge that we have no authority for expecting will be "winked at."

While I am writing, the venerable Overbeck works, in his Roman studio, with a sanctified enthusiasm that places him at the head of living Christian artists. With the learning of all the glorious schools of more favored epochs at his hand, he uses this learning only as the means of securing the most perfect expression of religious ideas and emotions. Among the "Forty Illustrations of the Four Gospels," by this truly Christian master, is "The Visit of Jesus to Bethany"—to the house of Mary and Martha and the risen Lazarus. Our Lord is represented as just entering the door of this abode, so often and so singularly favored, and both Mary and Martha bow to the very ground before Him, while the benignant hand of this Omnipotent Friend and Guest is raised in blessing. This act of prostration is, evidently, not intended for the form of salutation common in the East; but it expresses, and is intended to express, the very same faith in the real presence of Jesus which animates every one who bows, or genuflects, before the altar on which He resides.

The works of Overbeck,* who is now more than eighty years of age, are full of consolation; proving, as they do, the possibility of a modern school of religious art. This possibility is founded upon the indestructible nature of the Church herself, to whom art is an auxiliary; and the history of the Church is very likely to be the history of art. The occasional errors and feebleness of religious pictures, both in early and later times, have sprung, not from an exhausted treasury, but from those imperfections incident to our mortal state; and her rejuvenations have come, not from those,

*The death of Overbeck was announced soon after this page was written.

who, esteeming her dead or powerless, have sought to enthrone an art merely natural, in her stead, but from a vivifying of her own immortal powers, and a re-kindling of that religious fervor and simplicity of faith that inspired the pencil of Fra Angelico and his brother monks, Lionardo da Vinci, Michael Angelo, Raphael and Correggio, in their most sublime compositions. Christian Art is the true Art, the one sublime Art, in all Christian ages; and the Church, so long as she is the Church, will not cease to fructify, to inspire, and to reform, if need be, the pictorial types of the Christian world.

I cannot refrain from describing a small Düsseldorf print in my possession, representing our Blessed Lady sitting at the foot of the cross from which her Divine Son has been taken, and contemplating the crown of thorns and the three nails beside her upon the ground. Between her and the city of Jerusalem in the back-ground, there is only a part of the upright length of the cross to be seen. She is quite alone. The mantle covers her head, rests on the bowed shoulders, on one of which shines a mystical star, and is then laid in ample folds over her knees. One hand touches her cheek, the other is raised slightly, with a sorrowful gesture, while the eyes rest, with an intense, meditative pain, upon the crown of thorns and the three gross nails. Nothing could be more simple or more direct than the motive of this picture; yet it is an epitome of the science and the practice of meditation. The most learned treatise upon meditation might fail to impart the one idea that is needed to teach the uninitiated the practice of this difficult devotional exercise; but what the most explicit instruction, by written or spoken word, might fail to impart, is here pictured forth to the comprehension of the most simple or the most ignorant. The wildest Indian careering over the plains and declivities of the Rocky Mountains, if a Catholic, could learn from this picture how to meditate; and the Carmelite nun, persevering in the strict silence and severe recollection enjoined by her rule, would prize the lesson given by the lay brother of the holy Order of St. Dominic, Fra Angelico of Fiesole.

Religious art is the blossom of religious dogma, and is its pictorial exponent. It is no more possible to have a religious art without dogmas, than to have a religious worship without faith. From this faith in a revealed dogma, will spring, with more or less perfection and vigor, every work bearing, in the most remote manner, upon religious events and emotions; and, not from the bare belief, but from the glowing, sanctified inspiration of devout affection, holy desire and adoring faith, have sprung, in every age, those conceptions of heavenly things that appeal to the sympathies of modern as well as of ancient Christendom.

Under the influence of this conviction, that the Art of the Church must be subject, like the Church herself in her exterior relation, to efflorescence and decadence, yet must remain ever the same in motive, ever appeal to the same interior sense of divine things, ever contain the germs of the same eternal dogmas, I have selected the illustrations for this volume, from the works of comparatively modern, as well as of ancient artists, and even from those of the present generation. But I need not go beyond the neighborhood in which I am writing for a proof of this. Over the altar of our church of the Immaculate Conception is a picture of the "Virgin Conceived without Sin," of a type so pure, so exalted, that it deserves to be named on these pages devoted to religious art. It was produced under circumstances that fully explain its extraordinary claims upon the devoted hearts of the faithful who kneel before it in the small church, that, when this picture was painted, stood on the edge of the prairie into which the city fades; and these circumstances exemplify the point upon which all modern religious art unquestionably turns.

The pastor of the Immaculate Conception had so far finished his church that the High Altar was to be erected; but where was the altar-piece to come from? It was then anything but a rich congregation, made up of families each owning its small lot and house, but neither, in general, fully paid for. For him that desires ardently enough, the mountains will move from their foundations; and who can set a bound to the desire of the Christian pastor for the religious decoration of his church? "Some truly pious picture," he said, "that should be painted from devotion and paid for from the treasury of Heaven." This was not a tempting offer to most artists; but among his congregation was one to whom this appeal had a special charm; and the only obstacle was a diffidence of his own powers. "It was one thing to paint for the world, quite another to paint for the Altar of God;" but this diffidence was overcome by the promise of such aids as only the Altar can procure. A Novena was begun, and on the last day Holy Communion was received with special devotion. The type chosen for this picture was the statue of the Immaculate Conception, modeled in Rome during the year in which the dogma was defined, and which not only received, in the studio of the artist, the verbal criticisms of the Holy Father, but the modeling stick was used by him to indicate a change in some folds of the drapery to secure its perfection. In this picture there is no studied pose of the figure. The white drapery falls to the feet, one of which is placed, with unaffected composure, upon the head of the serpent which it was promised she should crush. The blue mantle covers the head and drops serenely over the white robe. The head is not bent, but a certain modesty, an indefinable delicacy, inclines it without suffering it to droop; while the hands touch serenely at the tips of the fingers in an attitude of ineffable worship. It is not difficult to believe that when, on the Feast of the Immaculate Conception, this picture, begun as a work of devotion, continued and finished as such, appeared in its place over the High Altar, there were few whose hearts were not consumed with a more ardent devotion, and few eyes that did not moisten with more tranquil tears of holy confidence in the prayers of the Immaculate Mother of God. Time has only added to its mild splendors the charm of sacred associations, and I now turn from the Immaculate Conception of a Guido or a Murillo, to the calm beauty, the tender modesty, the absolutely virginal sanctity, of this picture over the altar of a church on the edge of our western prairies.

As it is my intention to dedicate these sketches of Patron Saints to the youth of the Catholic Church in America, I will dedicate this Introduction to the Catholic parents of these children. No interests can lie so near the hearts of good parents as those centering in the spiritual integrity of their offspring. They do not expect their children to become saints; very few indeed desire such perfection in their children, esteeming saintship as a pearl of too great price; but there is a certain staunch and positive adherence to the customs of faith, as well as to its dogmas, that no one could see dying out of Catholic generations without something deeper than a sigh. Many an "Old Country" Catholic, born among the traditions of Mother Church, near some "Holy Well," accustomed to hear of pilgrimages to favored shrines, reared within the shadow of some noble Abbey, whose ruins stand as silent witnesses to the faith of former generations, and where the All Hallow's Eve, and the Holiday of Obligation, are odorous with pious observance—many a Catholic of this favored sort comes to our country, tries the life, it may be, of a pioneer, or of some dweller in a district of scattered homesteads, where a mass is never, never said, excepting irregularly, in some farm house larger than the others, or miles away in some lonely chapel where the Blessed Sacrament never can remain for a single night; where there is no Sunday School, no instruction in Catechism, no confraternities, no special devotions; where Sundays and Holidays of Obligation are with difficulty distinguished from other days—or, if residing in a town or city, finding the Catholic Church insignificant in the sight of the community, if not actually despised; Catholic notions of morality ignored, Catholic devotions, processions, missions, novenas, miracles, treated as superstitious nonsense—under all these disadvantages he brings up a family of boys and girls, quick in perceptions, impressible in temperament, and then wonders, with a wonder full of painful anxiety, why these boys and girls, who are (thanks to the grace of God!), firm Catholics, are still not enthusiastic Catholics; wonders that they are so poor in sentiments of religious veneration, and lacking almost utterly, the charm of a tender piety in their daily actions—forgetting how these emotions, in himself, were fed by the very air he breathed in childhood, by the conversation, and even gossip, of the neighborhood in which he was born, and by all that routine of life under the conditions of faith, which grows up unconsciously, like a hedge, around a Catholic family in a Catholic country, village, or city. It is time, alone, that can supply many of the lost links of religious association in a country like America; but still, a great deal can be done by reflecting people to weld anew these associations out of the practices of Catholic faith.

It is to supply some of the minor conditions of a happy Catholic community that I have endeavored to connect incidents related in the lives of the saints with the events of the present day; to take up some thread, by which it can be shown that to-day is of the same woof as yesterday in the loom of Divine grace; that in the generations of the Catholic Church epochs pass into each other, overlap each other, so that the devotions of one century descend to another, in such a manner as to prove that their changes are only developments of the same motive, of the same spiritual necessity.

There is no doubt that the lives of the saints thus conceived, are capable of an almost infinite development of interesting associations for the scholar, the poet and the artist, as well as for the Theologian and the Religious. No better proofs of this can be given than the St. Elizabeth of Hungary and St. Columba of Ireland, by Montalembert, and the short, but charming, Legend of Glastonbury, by Anderdon. In fact it is precisely to this development of the influence of a saint upon society and its ideals, that we are indebted for the religious art of the thirteenth, fourteenth, fifteenth and even sixteenth centuries; and for the poetry of those ages, of which the "Divina Commedia" of Dante, and all those sublime hymns which make so large a part of the sacred office for the ecclesiastical year, are the living efflorescence. Neither imagination nor devotion can feed upon the recital of bare facts, however sublime in themselves. That the saints may be to us what they were to the people of the "Ages of Faith," inspirations—inspirations to piety, to holy living and to devout genius—they must come to us surrounded by all the moving associations of their times and all the venerable and noble traditions which have gathered around them in succeeding times, like an atmosphere of glory.

Whatever helps the Catholic parent to preserve Catholic traditions, Catholic customs, and a Catholic sentiment, in his family, will bring a blessing upon any house; and for this reason I beg of you Catholic fathers and Catholic mothers to keep on your walls such pictures, such representations of the Divine mysteries of the sacraments and of the saints, as will encourage a truly Christian spirit of devotion in your families. Let these pictures be such as will prove "catechisms of instruction" to the young, as well as incentives to devotion for the adult; and, insensibly, they will excite the desire in the minds of your children to know something of the traditions that inspired them; until, by one of those unexpected graces that succeed to years of prayer, the dormant dispositions of faith will be roused and their eyes will be quickened to perceive the celestial relations between man and his Maker, man and his Redeemer. Every hour of serious work in this direction tells upon the future. The time may not be far distant when America may be called the "Land of Saints;" and we may see companies of pious pilgrims to some shrine, or spot of extraordinary devotion, taking the place of those pleasure parties which now set no limit to their ambition save such as the oceans, on either side of this vast continent, may compel. Let us remember that the seed must be cast into the soil, or the sunshine and dew of God's mercies will be in vain; and, casting in the seed with a believing hand, we may trust to God to perfect His own glorious work for the future generations of faithful Catholics in America.

No claim for originality can be set up by any one writing about the saints. The ancient Acts of the Saints have been, and must be, the sources from which every one draws his narrative, directly or indirectly, concerning these heroes of the Church of God, and the true heroes of humanity. But however just it might be to refer my readers to the precise pages on which I have found these facts, there is a serious objection to cumbering juvenile pages with references. I will therefore state briefly, that, first, Rev. Alban Butler's invaluable "Lives of the Saints," is the work upon which I have principally relied; then, Dr. Lingard's "Antiquities of the Anglo Saxon Church;" Count Montalembert's "Monks of the West;" also, "Christian Schools and Scholars." For the pictorial additions to the book, I am largely indebted to the "Düsseldorf Series of Religious Prints;" and both as to the text and illustrations, to Mrs. Jameson's works upon Christian Art, and to Kuglers "Hand-book of Painting." The admirable writings of M. Rio have fallen into my possession too recently to enrich my pages, as I could wish, from his choice treasury. But in his "Poetry of Christian Art," as in "Vandalism and Christian Art," and "The Actual State of Religious Art in France," by Count Montalembert, I have found nothing but confirmation of the ideas advanced in this unpretending volume. The unrivaled works of those great men in Europe who, like Frederic Rumohr, A. F. Rio and Count Montalembert, have consecrated their ripe learning and exalted genius to the cause of æsthetic Christian art, so far from discouraging my efforts have rather stimulated them, by throwing a new and extraordinary light upon the path I have chosen. I trust that the time is very near when the Catholic children of America, as well as of France, of Germany and of Italy, will not be driven to books of, at least, doubtful Catholic tendencies for the key to their own treasures of devotional art, but will have free access to the knowledge they will more and more crave on this subject, without danger to faith or to piety.

Following, then, with cheerful humility, in such august footsteps, I present my little book upon "Patron Saints" to the Catholic public of the United States, as a token of my gratitude for all the solace and the ever-increasing delight I have received from the study of Catholic Art, as well as from the sublime records of her canonized Saints, whose prayers have been my defence, whose friendship has been my consolation, and whose aid I hope to invoke in the hour of death.

ST. JOSEPH'S COTTAGE.

Vigil of All Saints, 1869.

SAINT PETER

ST. PETER AND ST. PAUL.

If you have ever so small a map of Palestine, or the Holy Land, look over it carefully until you find the Sea of Galilee, or, as it is otherwise called, Lake Genesareth and the Sea of Tiberias. If you have any pictures of the Holy Land, be sure to look those over also, and see if among them is not a view of this beautiful lake, set among the mountains of Judea, its shores studded with fair cities and towns, on its waters the frail barks of the Galilean fishermen, and on its beach the fishermen's nets spread out to dry. Still, it is not for the beauty of the lake nor of its shores, that I ask you to do this, but because upon this lake and upon its shores and within its towns, took place some of the most wonderful and important events in the life of our Lord. Among these important events were the several calls, given by Him to His service, of the rude fishermen of the neighborhood, and, foremost among these, was the choice of Simon, called Peter.

Let us turn to the simple account given by St.

Matthew, in chapter iv, verse 18, of his gospel, of the calling of St. Peter.

"And Jesus walking by the Sea of Galilee, saw two brothers, Simon who is called Peter, and Andrew his brother, casting a net into the sea (for they were fishers). And He saith to them: Come ye after me, and I will make you fishers of men. And immediately, leaving their nets, they followed Him."

Try to picture to yourselves the Redeemer of men as He walked on the pleasant shore of the Sea of Galilee, the blue sky of Asia above Him, before Him the waters of the lake and the little boat of the two brothers, Simon Peter and Andrew; try to picture that face of Divine beauty, whose look, it would seem, no candid soul could resist; try to catch the tones of that voice whose invitations, so simple and so brief, drew the fisher from his nets, and the publican from his receipts of custom, and you will no longer wonder at anything but the hesitating of people, now-a-days, as to whether they will follow this same Jesus, or not.

To read the Four Gospels is to read the story of Jesus Christ and of His apostles, disciples and friends; and, especially of St. Peter, who had so large a place in all the scenes of the three years ministry of his Master. Peter was one of the three selected by Him to witness His transfiguration; he was, also, one of the three who went with our Lord to the Garden of Gethsemane, and he was one of those who *ran* to the sepulchre when he heard the first news of His resurrection. How little those who stood on the shore of the Sea of Galilee that morning—within hearing, it may be, of the voice of Jesus of Nazareth, and who saw the two brothers leave their nets and follow Him—how little any of those bystanders, and how little St. Peter, himself, realized to what he had been called! And, to this call of St. Peter, what a contrast is presented in the call, by the same Jesus of Nazareth, to Saul of Tarsus, from that time called Paul! The first, in the tranquil freshness of morning, or the pensive stillness of evening, on the breezy lake shore; the last, at noonday, on the burning sands of the road to Damascus, towards which Saul, attended by armed horsemen, was traveling with hot speed. To Peter, Jesus calls out with a voice of gracious invitation, "Follow me, and I will make you a fisher of men." To Saul of Tarsus that same voice speaks, in tones of awful reproach, "Saul, Saul, why persecutest thou me?"

I shall not attempt to give you so much as the bare facts of the lives of these great apostles, both, by the direct voice of Jesus Himself, called to His most sublime service, as you can refresh your memory of them by a careful reading of the Four Gospels and the Acts of the Apostles; but I shall begin this book, intended for your instruction and pleasure, by giving you some idea of them both in one sketch, since no list of Patron Saints would be complete without the names of these two grand pillars of the Church of Christ, St. Peter and St. Paul. We find their festivals making glad every season of the ecclesiastical year; and so closely are they united in the mind of the Church, that the

Office read by every priest on the feast of one, always includes a commemoration of the other. The new year opens with the Feast of the See of Peter, or, as it is called, the "Feast of St. Peter's Chair at Rome;" and, a few days after, we celebrate the festival of "The Conversion of St. Paul."

On the pile of loose papers at my right hand lies a paper-weight, which you would notice on account of its elegance of form, the variety of colored marbles of which it is made, and, also, for a likeness of the Holy Father, Pius IX., very carefully cut out of the piece of pure white marble on the top. In the wooden box, in which this paper-weight was brought from Rome, and in which it is, still, often placed for safety, is a bit of rock from the prison in which St. Peter and St. Paul were kept for eight months. This prison was no other than the frightful Mamertine Prison, a dungeon deep under ground, from which the most cunning, or the most desperate, prisoner could never hope to escape. It is hewn out of the solid rock, and is, in truth, two prisons in one; for the upper prison opens into the lower one by a large hole, through which the unfortunate persons, condemned to live in it, were let down by ropes or chains, and were raised from it in the same manner.

Such was this specimen of the prisons of pagan Rome! The horrors of this dark well or cavern, shut out from the light of day, are not to be imagined; but we read that to St. Peter and St. Paul it was a place rich in consolation; for they had the holy satisfaction of converting, by their teachings and their example, Processus and Martinian, the captains of their guard, and forty-seven others, to the Christian faith. Tradition tells us, that having no water in the prison with which to baptize their disciples, at the prayer of St. Peter a fountain sprang up from the stone floor; and this fountain is to be seen, to the wonder of all travelers, to this day. A commemoration of SS. Processus and Martinian, as martyrs for the same faith as SS. Peter and Paul, is made on the second day of July; by which we can see what sort of converts they proved to be, who were baptized in this miraculous fountain.

From this living tomb of the Mamertine Prison, the two great and holy apostles were led forth, on the same day—the venerable St. Peter to be crucified, and, at his own request, with his head downward, declaring it too great an honor to die the same death as his Divine Master, and St. Paul to be beheaded. Their martyrdoms, sealing their preaching with the testimony of their blood, took place on the 29th of June; and on this day they are honored, the world over, as the chiefest of the apostles.

There is another feast called the "Feast of St. Peter's Chains," celebrated on the 1st of August, to commemorate the deliverance of St. Peter, the Prince of the Apostles, from Herod's prison by the hand of an angel, as related in chapter xii of the Acts of the Apostles. A watch-guard is commonly worn in Rome, even by Protestants, called St. Peter's Chains, in which one sees, on a very small scale of course, the chain that fell from the limbs of St. Peter, when they were touched by the angel, with the manacles for the hands, and the fetters for the feet, and the cross with the head hanging downward, upon which St. Peter suffered death.

To Catholics, who wear this watch-guard in a spirit of faith, and with proper dispositions of piety and virtue, an indulgence has been granted; and, to such Catholics, no chain of gold can ever seem so precious as this rude semblance of St. Peter's Chains.

You may think that I have forgotten about the paper-weight, with its delicately cut likeness of Pius IX., and about the "Feast of St. Peter's Chair at Rome," or that I had no special reason for speaking of them together. But I have not forgotten any of them; and you will see why the Roman paper-weight and the Roman Feast, and the Roman Pontiff are all associated in my mind, as I wish them to be in yours.

Learned writers like Cardinal Baronius and Thomassin, show, by many examples, that it was an ancient custom with the churches to celebrate every year an anniversary festival in honor of the consecration of their bishops. If you look over the "Ordo," or ecclesiastical almanac, for 1869, you will find at least five of these festivals celebrated in the United States during this year. If, at the present day, when there are so many bishops that one might suppose it possible to omit these anniversaries without danger, we still see them so carefully observed, how much more should we expect to see them noticed during those first ages of Christianity, when it was of the greatest importance to mark every event of this kind.

The "Feast of St. Peter's Chair at Rome" is spoken of in very ancient Lives of the Saints (or Martyrologies as they were formerly called, since nearly all the early saints were martyrs or suffered what equalled a martyrdom, like St. John the Evangelist), and thus gives us the best proof possible that St. Peter was actually the first Bishop of Rome. We say, "The Chair of St. Peter," because our word chair is taken from a Latinized Greek word *cathedra*, which means a seat or a chair. The church in which the bishop of a diocese has his canopied chair is called the cathedral; and the "Feast of St. Peter's Chair at Rome," is simply the festival commemorating St. Peter's taking charge of the Roman diocese, or, of taking his seat in the rude chair of the first Bishop of Rome.

I do not think any of my young readers would be surprised if they should be told, that the early Christians had such love and respect for St. Peter that the very chair on which he sat was of priceless value in their eyes; or, that they kept this chair so carefully, with so much veneration, that in after ages it was beautifully covered with choice woods, and materials far more costly than the chair itself, which in this way has come down to the present time, and stands in the great church of St. Peter in Rome.

Still, it is not in honor of this chair, however venerated, that the feast is kept, from age to age, with so much solemnity and devotion; but to honor the office and the authority of St. Peter as Bishop of Rome, and vicegerent of Jesus Christ Himself as the head of His Church; thus making the See or diocese of Rome one with the See or diocese of Peter. The present Pope, Pius IX., is the successor of St. Peter as Bishop of Rome, and, like St. Peter, represents our Lord Himself, as the head of the Church. Devotion to Pius IX. is devotion to St. Peter, and is a grateful acknowledgment of the goodness of Jesus Christ, not only in appointing a visible head for His Church during the life time of St. Peter, but in appointing successors to St. Peter, whose duty it should be, like that of St. Peter, to "feed the sheep," "feed the lambs," of His flock; who should hold, like St. Peter, the "keys of the kingdom of Heaven," with the power to do for us in all things as St. Peter did for the first Christians, and who should prove himself to be the "Rock," on which the Church stands securely in every age—so securely, that, as our Lord declared, "The gates of hell shall not prevail against it."

St. John was called the "Beloved Disciple." It was St. John who sat next to our Lord at the Last Supper, and leaned his head on the breast of his Master with such a familiar tenderness. Unlike St. Peter who denied Him; denied, as he stood warming himself by the fire in the hall of the Roman governor, that he was a disciple of Jesus Christ, or that he even knew Him; unlike the other disciples, who all fled from Him when they saw Him betrayed by Judas and in the hands of the rough soldiers, St. John stood, with the Blessed Virgin and St. Mary Magdalene, beside the ignominious cross of this same Master and Lord, and received His dying requests. All this might, very naturally, lead us to think that St. John would be appointed the "Chief of the Apostles," if for no other reason than his affectionate fidelity to his Master, and to His cause. But, we find, instead, the keys given to St. Peter, with this very remarkable charge: "And thou, when thou art converted, confirm thy brethren;" as if the grace of perseverance would be given to them through Peter. St. Paul tells us that after his miraculous conversion, by which he was divinely instructed in the faith of Christ, he "saw none of the apostles save Peter only;" thus acknowledging that St. Peter, alone, as the head of the Church, had the authority to set upon him the seal of a teacher sent from God.

In this authority, or supremacy, of St. Peter over all the other apostles, we find the reason why the present Bishop of Rome, or the Pope, Pius IX., who is the successor of St. Peter, and invested with the same rights, has authority over all the other bishops in the world. To deny this authority, is to deny that our Lord left a head to His Church, or that there is any voice in the world that can tell us what is truth or what is error, what is right or what is wrong; and this is why a belief in the Pope as the successor of St. Peter, and with the same authority as St. Peter, is the one mark by which we know the true religion from the false religion, the true reformer from the false reformer. So long as a religion acknowledges Peter as the head of the Church, and is ready to be reproved by Peter if it errs—so long as a reformer is ready to stand still, to go back, or to go forward, as Peter, the head of the Church, shall decide—so long that religion and that reformer is safe. Fidelity to Peter as the Pastor of Christians, submission to Peter in all things that belong to religion and to morals, is the crowning glory of a people and of a nation; it is the only safety of bishops and of priests, as well as of every lay-man and of every lay-woman; none of us are safe unless we are good and devout children of St. Peter and the See of Rome. Nothing, also, is told more plainly in the history of Christian nations than this—that the happiest time a nation has ever had, the "Golden Age" of that nation, the age of which the people are most proud, the age about which historians like, most of all, to write, and poets to sing, and artists to paint, was that age in which the people were most delighted to honor Jesus Christ by honoring His Vicar, the Bishop of Rome, the Father of the Faithful; in which the people and their rulers were guided by the same sublime rules of universal justice that have guided the Roman Pontiffs in all generations, and in which their freedom was the holy freedom of obedience—obedience to the laws of God and the laws of Christian society as taught by the Church.

It is with this grand and universal fact before my eyes that, on the very first pages of this book which invites the children of America to read, and learn by heart, why they should love and revere the saints of God, I have placed the glorious names of St. Peter and St. Paul; in the hope that these same young readers, when they are men and women, will make a Golden Age for their country; will so love their Church, and so practice its holy instructions, as to crown their patriotism by their faith.

But if this is true of nations and of governments, it is much more easily seen to be true of the Church herself. It is not by declaring ourselves independent of the See of Peter, that we are to reform abuses or repair wrongs; it is not by declaring ourselves independent of the See of Peter, that we can display our strength. "Union is strength;" and to weaken or break any of those holy, and mysteriously powerful links, which unite the Church, in all countries, to its centre, the See of Peter, is like breaking some of those wonderful little bones, or sinews, or bands that wind round and round the curious joints in these bodies of ours. You have sometimes seen a child lame for life, and all because some of these little bones or muscles had been injured. It is in the same way that people who try to live without the authority of Rome, or who do things against the spirit of the Church if not against the letter, make the Church lame, and feeble, and even lukewarm, in some portions of a Catholic country. People may not become heretics in such a community, but they are very far from being really good Catholics; and all because they have fancied they knew better than the Vicar of Christ and the successor of St. Peter. It is by attaching ourselves more and more closely, to the See of Peter, that the Church will be stronger, more venerable, and more beautiful, not only in Rome, but at home. Let us cultivate then, my dear children, a very lively and devoted affection to our Holy Father, the dear and most venerable Pius IX.; let us feel a deep interest in every word that the Holy Father speaks to the great Christian family in whatever part of the world it may be. Remember that he speaks to us in America, just as much as to the people in Europe; remember that we are as dear to him as they are, and, indeed, one would sometimes think even dearer, so many and so fatherly are the marks of his interest in all that concerns us.

I remember one very touching story about the kind heart of Pius IX. It is the custom of the Holy Father on certain days to see and speak with all who may desire to see and speak with him, from all parts of the world. There was, some years ago, a rich American family visiting Rome, and they had with them a good negro waiting-woman, and this good waiting-woman was a Catholic. Margaret, this was her name, heard so many people talking about the dear "Papa," as the Italians call him, that she had, every day, a stronger and stronger desire to see him; not only as she did sometimes when she was riding with her mistress, and they would say, "O, there is the Pope!" and she would catch a glimpse of a dear old gentleman dressed in a woolen soutane and broad-brimmed hat like a priest, with this one difference, that everything he wore was white, walking briskly over the road leading on to the country around Rome called the Campagna—she not only wished to see him in this way, but she wished, this poor Margaret, to see him, and speak to him, and get his blessing, all to herself? You may think this a great piece of presumption in the poor slave woman Margaret, and so, my dear children, it certainly would have been if the Holy Father had been merely a king or an emperor; but being, as he is, the Father of the Christian world, poor Margaret was as much his child as the princesses of Italy or the empress of France. Poor Margaret longed for this until she found courage to stand, with all the others who were waiting, in one of the great halls in the palace of the Vatican, until the Holy Father should come into the hall. At last he came in at one side of the hall, and came slowly down that same side to the very end, speaking, as a gentleman in waiting would tell him their names, with each person; and this happy person would kneel down and kiss the ring of the Holy Father, and get his blessing. Margaret saw a great many noble-looking ladies with their beautiful, fair-haired children, waiting patiently; and she saw the Holy Father, as he came to them, take each of these little children by the hand; and it seemed to her that he gave to them a tenderer blessing, even, than to their mothers. She was so interested that she forgot to be afraid; and there was something too in the face of this good Pope that gave her courage, and she felt happy just to watch every motion, and every look that he gave to those whom he saluted as he came towards her. At last the gentleman who had all their names, called out, "Margaret." Margaret! only Margaret! There was no Madame, no Mademoiselle, nor even Mrs. or Miss to this name of Margaret. Very likely many who waited near her were astonished to see her there, only they remembered in Rome what they are very apt to forget at home, that before the Vicar of Christ all men and all women are of one blood. As I have said, this single name of Margaret was called out; and then how shall we describe poor Margaret's feelings? For the hundredth part of a second she was humbled to the dust, at what seemed her boldness; but the next thought that went, like lightning, through her mind was one of joy; and so poor Margaret bowed with her soul full of love and veneration at the feet of the Holy Father. She did not dare to press her dark lips to the ring on his hand, still less to kiss that hand, as so many had done before her, not knowing that it was the *ring* which they should kiss. O no, she did none of these things, but seemed rather to wish to kiss the floor under his shining feet. But the Holy Father, who had shown so much benignity to the beautiful, fair-haired children, had a deeper and a tenderer benignity in store for the poor slave woman, Margaret. He lifted her from the floor, on which she had sunk in an ecstacy of happy humility; raised her up, spoke to her in her own tongue, asked her to tell him her story and also the story of her people in America. How long it took to hear all that he wanted poor Margaret to tell him! No one in all that vast hall seemed to interest the good Pope like poor Margaret, and when she had answered all his questions, he gently told her to kiss his ring and kneel for his blessing, "not only for herself but for all her people in bondage." Do you, can you imagine how happy a heart, how comforted a spirit, poor Margaret carried in her dark bosom, as she flew, rather than walked, away from the Vatican palace that day, and how, instead of going straight to her kind mistress, (for she was a kind one,) she stopped at the first church door, and poured out her joy at the foot of some altar where the little lamp told her Jesus was waiting to receive her thanksgiving!

It is to kindle in your young hearts a single spark of personal affection to this holy old man, this venerable priest, this Bishop of Bishops, that I have told you this story of poor Margaret; and it is for the same purpose, that is, to keep alive the love of Catholics for their chief Bishop, that the Church has gathered around her, at Rome, schools or colleges, where students from every part of the world are educated under the eye, and at the knee, of the Vicar of Christ. You have all heard of the American College at Rome, where the pious youth of our own country, who wish to become priests, Roman priests, find themselves perfectly at home. You have also heard of the College of the Propaganda, to which Italians are not admitted, while it welcomes to its noble halls, to its magnificent course of studies, to the teachings of its great professors, the elegant Greek, the ardent Celt, the enthusiastic American, the mild East Indian and even the black Ethiopian, who has inherited from his barbarous ancestors the very gait of the lion, that untamed king of the desert—all are found within the walls of the College of the Propaganda, and all are welcomed in their native tongue, and all so instructed as to be able to carry to distant countries, the ripe learning, the solid piety and the profound love for the See of Peter, which are best learned under the smile of the benignant Pontiff himself. One of these students of the Propaganda, who wished to bring away such a memento of his college life as only a student of the Propaganda could ever possess, asked from each of his companions a copy of the Lord's Prayer written in his own language. One hundred and ten different languages and dialects were thus collected, and taken with him, as a prize, to his home in a foreign land. Another student brought with him, to America, two photographed groups, in which were the Rector and Prefects of the college and several of his companions, and in both these groups were pure Africans, one of whom was leaning, affectionately, on the shoulder of a handsome Greek.

No student in one of the national colleges, or in the college of the Propaganda, would leave Rome without an interview with the Holy Father and getting his special blessing, and, very often, certain privileges that a priest prizes above all others; nor is he ever allowed to leave the Holy Father without some gift, as a memento of that never to be forgotten interview, with the universal Bishop of the Catholic Priest; and the simple gift with the name of the Roman Pontiff written by his own hand, more than all the blessing, drops into his heart as a seed of devotion to the See of Peter; nor can the labors, the sorrows, and too often, the sore disappointments and humiliations of his missionary life, extinguish the flames of love lighted up in the soul of the Roman priest, who often renders, in his least acts, a fealty to the See of Peter as graceful as it is sincere.

Will, then, any of my young readers fail to mark the "Feast of St. Peter's Chair at Rome," on the 18th of January, as one especially dear to an American Catholic?

There is a tradition about St. Peter, and repeated by no less a person than St. Ambrose of Milan, that all my young friends will like to remember, for it tells a great deal, in a few words, of that fervent and very dear old apostle, whose imperfections have a charm about them like the imperfections of your very, very little brothers and sisters ; and this is, the charm of unaffected simplicity, or of perfect honesty. Dear St. Peter! The world has always held up its hands in horror at his denial of his Master, in contempt at his cowardice, for he was afraid of a poor maid-servant in the house of the Roman governor! And yet the world goes on denying Jesus day after day! and seldom, alas! like St. Peter, hears the cock crow, or weeps one bitter tear of contrition; while St. Peter, not only "went out and wept bitterly" in that early twilight of Good Friday morning, but he wept his life long for this one hour of weakness; wept until the tears ploughed deep furrows down his good, honest cheeks, browned with travel, and hardships, and labors, in the service of the Master he once "swore that he knew not."

This is the tradition, or the story, told about St. Peter, by those who knew him, and told by those who heard it to the Christians they knew, until it came down, in the fourth century, to that great doctor and father of the Church, St. Ambrose.

Nero, that most cruel of all the cruel Roman emperors, had begun his terrible persecution of the Christains; and the little flock of lambs among the raging pagan wolves, trembling at the idea of losing their beloved Bishop, begged him to fly from Rome, if only for a little while. St. Peter at last told them he would do as they wished; and, when night came, he took a crooked way among narrow and dark streets, until he came out on the road called the "Appian Way." Then he walked very fast, and expected to be soon out of the reach of his fierce persecutors. But as he was hurrying along, he was met about two miles from the city gate, by his Lord—the dear Lord and Master he had served so long and so faithfully, and so ardently—traveling towards the Rome that St. Peter had just left in such haste. Struck with amazement, poor Peter cried out, "Lord, whither art thou going?" To which his Master, looking at St. Peter with his old, sorrowful look of loving reproach, answered: "I am going to Rome to be crucified again;" and then vanished, was quite gone. Poor St. Peter! He was young when he said to his Lord, who wanted to wash his feet, "Nay, Lord, Thou shalt never wash my feet;" and when his Master said, "If I do not wash thy feet thou hast no part with me," St. Peter cried out, "Lord, not my feet only, but also my hands and my head." St. Peter was young then; but now, when his Master met him on the Appian Way at night, flying from Rome, he was old; his short curling hair was white with years, and troubles, and hardships; his face had deep wrinkles in it, and, as I have said, two furrows had been ploughed down his cheeks by his tears of repentance for one hour of weakness; his limbs, too, were stiff with age, and the pains of age; but, although he was old in body, the soul, the mind, the heart, were all as full of life, and of feeling—fuller, a thousand times, of love for Jesus—as on that night of the last supper. How that look of tender reproach pierced his heart! How it took away from him the fear of Nero, and even the fear of leaving his little flock orphans! St. Peter knew, then, that Jesus would take care both of the sheep and the lambs, and he turned, turned without a moment's delay, toward the great, wicked, cruel, blood-thirsty city of Rome; thirsting always for blood, but above all else for Christian blood; turned towards Rome and entered again the great gate of the city, and, being seen by some cruel spy on the watch for Christians, was seized, and thrust down into the lowest and darkest chamber of that frightful Mamertine Prison that I have told you about, where he and St. Paul spent eight months together, and from which he came out to be crucified for his Master.

Michael Angelo made a statue representing Jesus Christ as He appeared to St. Peter on the Appian Way; and a copy of it is in the small church built on the spot made sacred by this mysterious meeting.

If you think for a moment, how wonderful seem those eight months spent together by St. Peter and St. Paul in the dark Mamertine Prison! Two such heroic souls, crowned by such heavenly graces of fortitude, of love for God, of love for their fellow men! How great must have been the comfort that each gave the other, and what conversations they must have had about the Redeemer for whom they were ready to lay down, or take up again, their lives! The picture of St. Paul that I have selected for you, represents him addressing St. Peter in prison, upon some of those sublime occasions when the darkness of their dungeon was changed to more than the brightness of day by the angels who attended upon them, and who brought to them, in place of the worldly comforts for which men are ready to give away Heaven and the hope of seeing God, the holy delights of the saints in glory.

But it is time to say something of St. Paul, the Apostle. Nothing in the Sacred Scriptures is told with a grander simplicity than the story of the conversion of St. Paul, as you will find it in the Acts of the Apostles. The fiery, but honest, zeal of Saul in persecuting the first Christians; his standing by and

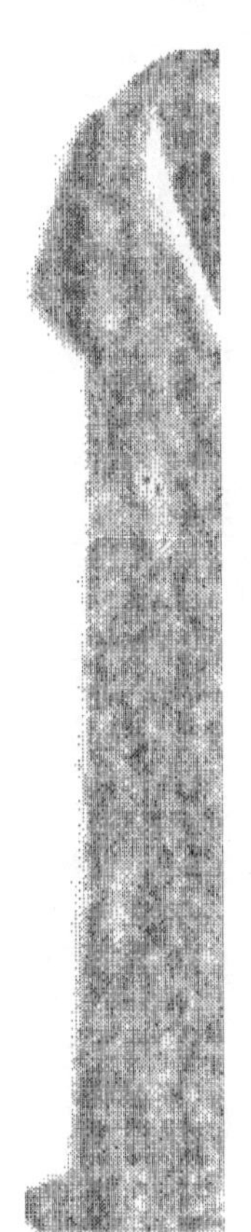

SAINT PAUL.

consenting to the death of the holy deacon, St. Stephen; the awful brightness of the heavenly vision that met him on the way to Damascus, before which the noon-day sun was like a twilight or an eclipse, and which so dazzled the eyes of the proud Jew who had learned philosophy at the feet of the grave Gamaliel, that he entered Damascus, not as the bold defender of the Jewish synagogue and the Jewish law, but as a helpless blind man, led by the hand through the streets of that sunny oriental city; led past all the groves of olives and figs, all the pleasant gardens and rainbow-tinted fountains of beautiful Damascus, to a quiet lodging in the "street called Straight, at the house of one Simon, a tanner;" the three days of penitential fast, during which he tasted neither bread nor water, his great soul bowed down under the new sense of having despised, rejected and persecuted, not a mere man, however good, but the Eternal Son of the Eternal Father; for Saul, having been divinely instructed by the vision, now knew that this Jesus, whom he had persecuted, was no other than the Lord who would, one day, judge him; the visit to Saul of the aged Christian, Ananias, who, at the command of God, laid his hands on the blinded eyes of the once proud persecutor, now the meek disciple of Jesus crucified; the falling, at the touch of Ananias, of thick scales from his eyes, like those scales of pride, of prejudice, and of worldliness that made him "kick against the pricks," or evidences of God's truth, and which fell from the eyes of his mind at the touch of faith;

and, when his sight had been thus restored, the joy of his baptism; after which he rose up, and took food, and was strong again; his going out into the streets of Damascus, no longer the Jew, Saul of Tarsus, but Paul, Paul the Christian, Paul the Apostle to the Gentiles—all these wonders and miracles are told to us by St. Luke, in the Acts of the Apostles, in such a manner as to make one certain that they could only have been learned from the lips of St. Paul himself.

In the whole wonderful history of the triumphs of Christianity over the powers of this world, there is not one so startling, and so magnificent, as the conversion of St. Paul; not one that was wrought so directly by the visible power of God; nor has there been, in all the eighteen hundred years since the ascension of our Lord, a convert who has been more ready to say, "Lord, what wilt thou have me to do?" or more prompt in obeying that will when it has been made known. This readiness on the part of St. Paul, is what we call, "the grace of correspondence," or the grace of a will corresponding, or agreeing, with the will of God; the grace to desire what God desires, to will what God wills. Once, too, a Christian, St. Paul did not pause to count how much his sacrifice had cost him. Instead of this, he tells us that "I counted all things as loss that I might gain Christ." Once a Christian, he remembered, that "although many run, one gaineth the prize;" and "therefore," he tells us, "I chastised myself, lest, while preaching to others, I myself, should be a castaway." Once, a Christian, once converted to the spirit of Christ's Church, not merely conformed to its outward practices or duties, "neither principalities nor powers, nor things present nor things to come, nor height nor depth," could separate him from Jesus, and Jesus crucified. To him scourging had lost the sting of disgrace; and the judgment halls of kings and of Roman governors, the hill of Mars in the midst of the polished and learned people of Athens, and the dungeon at midnight, when the earthquake of God's anger opened the prison doors, and loosed the fetters of this suffering confessor to His truth, were so many pulpits, from which he preached Jesus crucified, until multitudes were persuaded to be, not like Felix the governor "almost," but, like St. Paul himself, "altogether" Christians.

Yet neither his sacred office as an apostle, nor his sanctity as a true saint, ever hid the qualities peculiar to him as a man. He tells us in his epistles, that he labored with his hands that he might not burden the churches with his support. While he was converting thousands by his preaching, he practiced industriously the trade, which, according to the Jewish custom of teaching some handicraft to every boy, he had learned in his youth, and made tents to supply himself with the necessaries of life. We can also see, very plainly, that although St. Peter was chosen while an illiterate fisherman, to be the Prince of the Apostles, St. Paul did not think that he must forget the learning which fell to his lot as a youth and young man, in order to be like St. Peter; but he uses this worldly knowledge, learned at the feet of the greatest doctors of his day, to convert the most cultivated and elegant nations of the world. God, who made use of the simplicity of St. Peter to confound the wise, made use of the learning of St Paul to the same end. Humility is not, necessarily, the companion of ignorance; for ignorance is often arrogant; while ripe learning is, quite as often, patient and gentle towards the unlettered and dull of understanding. It is, also, very plain, that St. Paul did not think it against sanctity to claim his rights as a Roman citizen. He was born in Tarsus, a city to which the Roman emperors had granted many privileges. These privileges St. Paul did not consider it necessary to give up in order to be humble. Many saints have given up the privileges of their rank or position, and their motives have been purely supernatural motives, and very pleasing to God and very much praised by all good men. But St. Paul, who was enlightened in a special manner upon all things relating to Christian precept, claimed his rights as a Roman citizen; and he did so from motives honorable to him as an apostle of Jesus Christ.

God has created us with reason, and sensibility, or a feeling of propriety; and if we look attentively at the lives and actions of the saints, we shall find that they acted, in every instance, with admirable prudence, and a most delicate regard to all the circumstances of their state in life. It is safe to say that the saints did not commit blunders, for blunders always show carelessness, somewhere, or the overlooking of some important fact; and the saints were wonderfully circumspect. There is something very noble, and very courageous, and very edifying, in the protest of St. Paul against the cowardly cruelty of his countrymen who accused him, and of the Jewish tribunal which condemned him to be scourged, as no Roman citizen could lawfully be, and, finally, in his appeal from the time-serving Roman 'governors to Cæsar himself; and this example of holy courage should banish forever from Christian souls, the pretended meekness that is only base cowardice. The meekness of the saints is a meekness full of courage. It never yields to injustice, as injustice, but as to God, who may allow the unjust decree to injure us for a time. The saints never "called evil good;" they suffered injuries and wrongs and insults, and the persecutions which they could not avoid; but they never mistook injustice for justice, nor felt obliged to do so from a false notion of charity.

Again: many persons, when reading the life of a favorite saint, by trying to copy, literally, the actions of this saint, have made sad mistakes. Never imitate as one machine imitates the work of another machine, the actions even of a saint. God, who made the saint you admire, also made you, and made you a little unlike any other being in the world; as much so as one leaf differs from every other leaf even on its own tree. God respects this individuality, that makes you a little different from everybody else in the world, and His Church respects it, and he wishes you to respect it in yourself. St. Paul tells us that "one star differs from another star in glory;" and no two saints of God are, or can be, exactly alike, because the saints are all very honest people, very sincere people, very simple or single minded people. Instead, therefore, of being scandalized, as I have heard people speak of being scandalized, at the peculiarities of St. Peter or of St. Paul, you should look upon them as proofs of that honesty, without which people cannot be real saints. There is no such thing possible as a deceitful, make-believe saint, or one who performs his actions to be seen of men. The saints perform their actions as if standing in the sight of God, who cannot be deceived; and it is the doing of our actions for this All-seeing Eye that keeps them single, honest, without guile.

You will see that I have left you to read over in the Four Gospels and in the Acts of the Apostles, many events in the lives of these great saints. I should be sorry to see any book taking the place of the sublime narratives in the Holy Scriptures; and all other books, if properly written, will add to our enjoyment of the sacred writings.

The Feast of the Conversion of St. Paul is on the 25th of January; and no one who has, like St. Paul, received the grace of conversion to the true faith, can fail on that day to pray with the Universal Church, that he who was "a vessel of election, holy Paul the Apostle, will intercede for us to God who chose him."

As we look back, through eighteen hundred years, to that glorious morning of Christianity, when the Apostles and Evangelists, and the first saints of the

Church, to whom God gave such shining marks of favor, stood before the whole world crowned with supernatural faith, hope and charity, "rejoicing like strong men to run the race" of perfection, how puny seem all our own feeble efforts to serve that Divine Master, who is our Master as well as theirs! And we are ready, for an instant, to let go our hold upon the plough, losing the courage that is necessary for perseverance. But true humility, true faith, hope, charity, look only to seeing God's plans succeed, and think of their own only so far as they help on, or are a part of, the plans of God. The words of the poet,

"They also serve who only stand and wait,"

may console many a hidden saint, who offers to Jesus Christ the homage of his supreme love; not privileged, indeed, like the burning thurible, to swing before the altar, sending up clouds of fragrant incense; but, like night-blooming flowers, permitted to sanctify by the perfume of humble virtues the solitary places, and make glad the wildernesses of human life.

St. Peter is always known in pictures by the keys in his hand, symbolising his spiritual power as Chief of the Apostles, or by the cross planted with the head downward. There is a picture of his crucifixion by so early a painter as Giotto, and one of Perugino's most beautiful pictures, as well as one of Raphael's, represents him receiving the keys from our Lord. Every event of his apostolic life has been the subject of some work of art by the greatest masters in painting, sculpture and mosaic; but by none with more feeling than by the Dominican monk, Fra Angelico, who painted that scene, after the Last Supper, of the washing of the feet, when St. Peter exclaimed, in an ecstacy of love and worship, "Lord, not my feet only, but also my hands and my head!" It was at such times that St. Peter breathed forth the first flames of that ardent devotion which characterised his life as an apostle. The Rock, and at the same time the timid disciple; the life-long penitent and the Head of the Church—such is St. Peter, than whom none of the apostles has more claims upon our love, our veneration, and our gratitude.

The picture of St. Peter which you will see as you read these pages, is drawn after a picture by Overbeck, the greatest of living artists. Overbeck, now more than eighty years of age,* lives in Rome, and has, ever since his conversion to the Catholic faith, devoted himself to painting religious pictures. This venerable man receives visitors at his studio every Sunday afternoon, and takes the trouble to explain these paintings, and drawings in charcoal, on his easel and upon the walls. A series of pictures by him, called, "Forty Illustrations of the Four Gospels," is a wonder of religious art in our own day. Sitting in the shadow of St. Peter's Chair at Rome, the works of his pencil

*Between the writing of these pages and their going to the press, the death of this Christian Artist has been announced to the world.

and brush breathe forth the choicest aroma of piety and of faith.

The picture of St. Paul, was chosen from a great number, as giving a sublime idea of the great Preacher and Doctor of the Gentiles; and, also, as a votive offering to the Patron Saint of the "Order of St. Paul the Apostle," in the United States of America.

Let us close this sketch by repeating the collect used by the Church in addressing both these glorious saints, St. Peter and St. Paul:

"Protect thy people O Lord, and preserve, by Thy continual defence, those who confide in the patronage of the Apostles Peter and Paul!"

SAINT AGNES.

IN that grand old city, Rome, while its beautiful temples, now used for the worship of the one true God, were given up to the idolatrous worship of gods and goddesses unworthy of the love or respect of one good man, woman, or child; while the rich, and the learned, and the noble, laughed at the few Christians, who, they supposed, lived among them as fools, or vagabonds, or worse still, as knaves and deceivers; while the emperors, who dressed in purple and gold and jewels, when they gave banquets and festivals, knew that the sport which would most please the Roman people was to give a few Christians to the lions or the panthers, or to wild cows; while Rome was this corrupt, pagan Rome, instead of what it now is, "The Holy City" of the world—at this time, this dark time as it seemed for the persecuted Church of God, lived, in this very Rome, a lovely girl whose name was Agnes.

The parents of Agnes were of ancient and noble family, so ancient and so noble that no one supposed

SAINT AGNES.

they could belong to the despised followers of a crucified Jew; but ancient and noble as the house was from which they came, they prized, above all this worldly distinction, the holy and venerable name of Christian. The little Agnes grew up a flower of Christian grace, an example of Christian virtue. You must remember, my dear children, that when Agnes lived in Rome, Christians could have no grand churches, no processions, no choirs or singers, no Christmas and Easter days, that would attract any attention from the pagan world around them. It was not even safe to have one's nearest friend know one to be a Christian; for to be known as a Christian was to be thrown to wild beasts, or beheaded, or burned to death. The Church, therefore, watching then, as now, with a supernatural prudence over the welfare of her children, advised all Christians to avoid the least display of their religion; to live quietly; to attend the Holy Sacrifice of the mass, not in public places, but in the houses of those nobles, who, like the parents of St. Agnes, could easily receive large numbers into their houses without exciting suspicion; or, in still darker days of persecution, they assisted at the Holy Mass in Catacombs, rooms dug under ground, with large apartments and galleries leading into each other. In the walls of these underground apartments were deposited the venerated bodies of Christian martyrs; and the ranks of the martyrs included nearly all the faithful departed in those days, since few, comparatively, died natural deaths; and thus while mass was celebrating, instead of having five relics in the altar-stone as every priest must now have when he says mass, there were hundreds of relics all around; bodies, and bones, and phials full of the blood of martyred saints. O, my dear children, with what fervor, with what devotion, must not the Christians of that time have assisted at the Holy Sacrifice, seeing so much to remind them that they too, at any moment, might be called upon to die for Him, who had first died for them! How precious must that religion have become to them for which they had seen so many willingly give up rank, wealth, friendship, family love, and even life!

In such a school of devotion was reared the little Agnes. The only child of a noble family, she was often obliged to appear at the luxurious banquets of her relatives and friends. But it was not for such scenes of revelry and splendor that Agnes ever pined. She loved better (Oh, how infinitely better!) that early gathering around the altar in her father's palace, or among the dark chambers of a Catacomb, where, long before daybreak, some good priest, at the risk of life, consecrated the Host and distributed to the faithful—who at the same risk had flocked around their pastor—this "Bread of the Strong," this Body broken and this Blood shed for sinners. May we not believe that among these worshippers none received more frequently, or with greater eagerness, this "Holy Food" than the gentle Agnes?

The companions of our Agnes dressed in rich stuffs, wore jewels beyond price, (as we should think), and used costly perfumes, devoting the greater part of their time to decking their persons. But the noble Agnes followed none of their vain customs. She always appeared at their gay banquets, among the richly attired guests, in a plain robe of white; a mystery to her pagan friends, but easily understood by a Christian as the white robe of the child-spouse of Christ Jesus. She never wore jewels. Jesus was her jewel, her crown. No diamond, no sapphire, no emerald, ever shone to her eyes as the face of her Beloved; no opal in its changing beauty, no pearl in its soft loveliness, could rival the mild look of her Redeemer, who seemed to be ever at her side or above her as a vision—the present beatitude, as He was to be the eternal joy, of the blessed child Agnes. No wonder, then, if when the time came for the sweet sacrifice of that unspotted life, if when a motive of chagrin, or envy, or hatred of extraordinary goodness, moved some reckless, wicked pagan to dog her quiet footsteps under the suspicion of her being a Christian until he could prove her to be so, and then report the only daughter of a noble Roman house as a follower of the lowly Nazarene, crucified between two thieves—no wonder if when that time came, it came to her not as a trial but as a triumph. It was not the tender girl, torn rudely from a sheltering home, from doting parents, to be given over to the dungeon and to the torturers; but the exile, at last setting sail for her native land; the bride, going forth to meet an eternal Spouse.

The bloody command of the Roman emperor, Diocletian, against the Christians, appeared in March, 303; and the next year, on the 21st of January, the name of St. Agnes was added to the list of Christ's martyrs. The "Acts" of this darling saint, this cherished virgin martyr, who has been, ever since the year 304, the admiration of Christendom, were written by no less a person than the learned doctor, the holy confessor, and renowned bishop of Milan, St. Ambrose. These wonderful Acts of St. Agnes prove how dearly our Lord prized the innocence of this holy child, since an angel defended her from the sinful approaches of wicked men. They also prove what courage is given to the most tender and timid when Jesus calls on them to suffer for Him. The noble and delicate maiden shrinks from the blasphemous crowd, until she finds herself, like her Master, in the hands of a furious rabble, and for His sake. She faints at the sight of racks, and hot pincers, and horrid instruments of cruelty, until she is told they are intended for her, as a Christian; knowing, as she does, that through these torments lies her way to God. St. Agnes was only thirteen years old when she was taken before the Roman tribunal to answer to the single accusation of being a Christian; and if we wish to know how the little ones of the household of Christ can look their torturers in the face, we may study the Acts of this young girl, Agnes.

As I have said, she was only thirteen years old; and the night before that morning in January, when she appeared before the dreadful tribunal, had been spent partly in prison, partly in the midst of human beings worse even, one would think, than the demons themselves. Yet when she comes before the judge her face has lost none of its serenity, none of its celestial beauty. We are told that a murmur of displeasure ran through the crowd when this mere child was brought in between armed guards; but the harsh prefect, who had steeled his heart against all pity, seeing that her hands were free ordered them to be put in irons. The jailor took the smallest pair of manacles, and put them on her slender wrists, but she playfully dropped her hands and the cruel irons fell to the floor. With a face deeply moved, we may believe with a heart far more so, the jailor said to the prefect, "Such infant wrists deserve other bracelets." Finding that she could not be put in irons on account of her extreme delicacy, the prefect showed his severity by his rough questions, to which she returned only celestial answers in praise of her Heavenly Bridegroom; he then commanded her to offer incense to the gods; but she could not be compelled to move her hand, slight as it was, excepting to make the blessed sign of the cross, until, exasperated by her courage and constancy, he ordered her to be beheaded. Agnes, transported with joy at this sentence, still more at the sight of the headsman, "went to the place of execution," says St. Ambrose, "more cheerfully than others go their wedding." Every means was tried to break her noble resolution of suffering for Christ, but in vain, and having made a short prayer she bowed her beautiful young head to the stroke of the sword, to be united forever in heaven to her Divine Spouse.

Her body, that innocent body which had been "the temple of the Holy Ghost," and which might well be looked upon as a venerated relic, was buried at a short distance from Rome, on the road called the "Nomentan Way." On the very spot where she was buried a church was built, which, in 625, was an ancient edifice and was, at that time, repaired. A statue of St. Agnes stands over the high altar; beneath the altar is a sarcophagus containing her relics; relics so well authenticated that the most unwilling must admit them to be the bones of St. Agnes. In this church, also, is a mosaic (or picture made of bits of colored marble, curiously set in cement), representing her as standing, crowned, with a book in her hand; out of the earth spring flowers and a sword lies at her feet. Every year this church is visited by the Holy Father with great devotion; he is accompanied by the cardinals, and other ecclesiastical dignitaries, and also by the students of the Propaganda. At one of these ceremonies, several years ago, the floor of the ancient church gave way; yet no one was killed, nor, in the end, seriously hurt. The exclamation of the devout Pontiff, as he saw the danger, was, "Immaculate Mother, pray for us!" This church gives title to a cardinal; and every year on the feast of St. Agnes the abbot of St. Peter's *ad Vincula* (or "St. Peter's Chains"), blesses in it, at high mass, two lambs, which are thence carried to the Pope who blesses them again. After this they are sent to the Capuchin nuns of St. Lawrence, who make of their wool "Palliums," or small white tippets, decorated with plain Roman crosses in black wool, which the Pope blesses and sends to archbishops, in all parts of the world, as an emblem of the meekness and spotless purity that should adorn their sacred office.

There is another church bearing the name of St. Agnes, within the walls of Rome, on the west side of the Piazza Navona, on the spot to which she was dragged by the soldiers and exposed to the insults of wicked men. The chamber, which for her preservation was filled with the heavenly light that blinds the eyes of the corrupt, has become, by the changes in the level of the city, an underground cell, and is now a chapel of peculiar sanctity, into which visitors descend by torchlight. On the floor of this chapel is a very ancient mosaic, and on the walls is a bas-relief (sculptured in marble like figures on a medal), representing St. Agnes with clasped hands, her long hair falling over her person, and driven onward by furious soldiers. The upper church is very beautiful, rich in precious marbles and columns. It is a custom with the Roman people to strew the floor of this church with evergreen box on her festival; and for many years I have had a sprig, picked up by a friend from one of the aisles on the joyous feast of St. Agnes of Rome.

Next to the representations of the Apostles and Evangelists there is no saint who appears in pictures as early as St. Agnes, so early, and so enthusiastic, was the veneration paid to this dear child. Her picture (or effigy) is found on the glass and earthern ware vessels used by the Christians in the fourth century, with her name inscribed, so as to leave no doubt of her identity. She carries in one hand the palm of the martyr, in these early pictures, and is sometimes crowned with olive. In later pictures she is always represented with a lamb, beside her or in her arms, and she is distinguished in this way among the virgin martyrs in the "Coronation of the Blessed Virgin," by Fra Angelico. The lamb is called the symbol of St. Agnes. Her name, which signifies chaste in Greek, and lamb in Latin, is found in the Canon of the Mass, and in the Litany of the Saints, and is thus invoked by every priest celebrating mass; also on solemn occasions, such as the ordination of priests, on Holy Saturday, and on all days of special prayer.

The feast of St. Agnes was formerly a holy day for women in England, as appears from the council of Worcester, held in 1240. St. Jerome, writing in the fourth century, the same in which St. Agnes "sealed her faith with her blood," tells us that the fame of St. Agnes had spread among all nations, and that hymns, and praises both in prose and verse, had been written of her in all languages. Not only St. Ambrose, but St. Augustine, another father and doctor of the Church, wrote the praises of St. Agnes; and centuries after, Thomas à Kempis, whose "Imitation," or "Following of Christ," is read by every person, as a book next to the inspired words of wisdom, honored her in a special manner, and he speaks of many miracles wrought, and graces received, through her intercession. St. Martin of Tours, also, was very devout to St. Agnes; and to this day there are few, even among those denying the power of her prayers, who do not love the name of Agnes, and many give it to their little daughters with the silent intention of winning her friendship and protection for the dear child of their hearts.

If every boy should love St. Stanislaus and St. Aloysius, every little girl, the world over, should love St. Agnes, the Virgin Martyr. Never let a day of your life pass without invoking the aid of her sweet prayers, that you may imitate her purity, her devotion to Jesus, and her holy courage in suffering for Him. Her feast is on the 21st day of January, and on the octave, or eighth day after the principal festival, a second Office celebrates the consoling apparition of St. Agnes to her parents, accompanied by a lamb "whiter than the driven snow," and assuring them of her perfect happiness. Invoke her specially on these days, and do not, in your petitions, forget her who writes this as a tribute of love to her patron saint.

SAINT BENEDICT AND SAINT SCHOLASTICA.

IN the town of Norcia, in the ancient See, or diocese, of Umbria, in Italy, about 480 years after the birth of our Divine Lord, lived a Roman family of note. Very likely, my dear children, the members of this distinguished Roman family were the envy of many less fortunate, as the world calls people fortunate; and their wealth and position, and all the pleasures and honors that came with them, were talked about by their neighbors and their countrymen. But it was, after all, not their wealth, nor their position, which handed their names down to us so many hundred years after their dust had mingled with the dust of their graves; not their bravery in war, nor their wisdom in statesmanship; but the fact that in this family the Church had found two of her saints; had canonized them, had put upon them the solemn seal of God's approbation, and had placed them before the world as worthy to be imitated, and powerful to help us by their prayers.

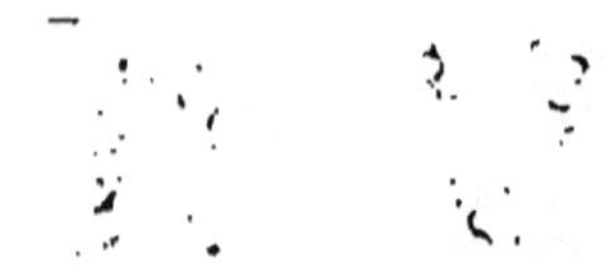

SAINT BENEDICT AND SAINT SCHOLASTICA.

There is no worldly distinction, no rank, no pride of place, which in the hour of death, and certainly at the Day of Judgment, will not seem of less value than a grain of sand; whereas the glory, the joy of a saint, or the glory and the joy of the worthy father or mother of a saint, is never known until that day of general judgment, when the choice made by the children of the world in favor of a high position, great wealth, noble titles, of foolish or wicked pleasures, will be seen to have been all a mistake; and the choice of the children of God on the side of holy poverty, scrupulous innocence, self-denial, humble contrition, and faithful obedience, will be approved by the whole world, and will be called the wise choice, even by the wicked. In that day it will be seen how truly blessed, and how much to be envied, were the parents of these two holy children, St. Benedict and St. Scholastica.

This name of Benedict, by which the young Roman nobleman was baptized, means, *well said*, or *blessed.* When this truly blessed child, was fitted for the higher studies of a noble, or patrician, his father sent him to Rome and placed him in the public schools. It was not, at that time, easy for a Christian parent to find a thoroughly Christian school for his son as he can now do; but, to obtain an education such as Eutropias naturally desired for the young Benedict, he was obliged to send him where the sons of those rich Romans were educated who had despised Christianity, and who were, still, pagans in their hearts. Thrown among these half heathen boys, and compelled to have them for companions, this innocent youth, who "knew not what vice was, and trembled at the very shadow of sin," no sooner came to the threshold of the world, than, shocked by its wickedness, he resolved to leave it forever. Remember, my dear children, it was not the vices of grown up people that so shocked the young Benedict, but the vices of young boys; their profane talk, their immodest actions and words, their disobedience and rudeness of temper. If the boys of this generation, or of this country, are better than the Roman boys in the fifth century, it is because Christianity has made them so. There is no grandeur of noble birth, no splendor of a palace, no elegance of learning, even, that will tame the fierce passions of our fallen nature: it is Christianity which not only makes them harmless, but yokes them to the plough of usefulness, or trains them, like swift Arabian horses, to add to the pleasure and happiness of man and of society.

But, as I have said, the Roman boys of the fifth century had not been trained under Christian Brothers, nor in any of those religious schools in which the boys who read this book have learned their Christian doctrine, and good Christian conduct; and the only way in which the young Benedict could keep his innocence was to fly from their company forever. This noble resolution, so full of the heroism of the children of God, St. Benedict took when only fourteen years of age. He left Rome without telling any one, but was followed by his faithful old nurse, Cyrilla, who loved him most tenderly. How well her affection was returned will be seen by the following story, told by St. Gregory the Great in his life of St. Benedict.

When the young Benedict and his good nurse had traveled as far from Rome as Enfide, they stopped at this place for awhile, and found themselves among many pious people who, from choice, lived near the church of St. Peter. The nurse Cyrilla, was, no doubt, on very good terms with these neighbors, for we are told that she borrowed from one of them a sieve to clean her wheat. This sieve, in the time of St. Benedict, and for ages after, was made of clay, and had holes in the bottom of it through which the chaff was shaken, as we now sift meal and flour, while the clean kernels of wheat were left in it. The same sieve is still in use for winnowing wheat, but is made of wood. I can hardly imagine how such a thing should have happened to a woman like Cyrilla, for I must believe that she was very careful of anything belonging to another, but so it was; Cyrilla, on going out of the room, left the clay sieve on the table in such a way that it fell on the floor and was broken in two parts. On her return what was poor Cyrilla's mortification and distress to see the borrowed sieve broken through her carelessness! How, she said to herself, can I ever be excused for so great a blunder, and how shall I ever make good the loss, because this neighbor will not allow me to pay her for the sieve? Thinking of all this she began to cry bitterly. But Benedict, the religious and mild boy, when he saw his nurse weeping, took her grief to heart, and carrying the two pieces of the broken sieve to his room, he gave himself, with weeping, to the most earnest prayer. When he rose from his knees he found the broken sieve so perfectly restored to its former state that no sign of a break or crack was any more to be found in it. On seeing this his delight was very great, and he hastened to his good Cyrilla, lovingly consoling her, and handing back to her the sieve whole, which he had taken from her broken.

This wonder became known to every body in Enfide, and was thought so much of that they hung the sieve in the church, that the people of that generation, and of all generations to come, might see what perfect grace was with Benedict at the very beginning of his life.

Notwithstanding this tender affection for Cyrilla, shown by the miracle he was allowed to work for her, when they came to Afilium, thirty miles from Rome, he found a way to leave behind him even this dear attendant, and went further on among the wild rocks, the dark and awful mountain gorges, of the desert of Subiaco. Here he was met by a monk named Romanus, who gave him a hair-cloth shirt, and a monk's dress made of skins. But Benedict did not stop with Romanus, for he was full of the holy ambition to find God as he was found in these solitudes by the Fathers of the desert; and he went on further and further still, until, coming to the middle of a high and very steep rock, facing the south and overlooking the swiftly running waters of the river Anio, he found a dark and narrow cave, a sort of den, into which the sun never shone. Here the boy Benedict found what he liked; and here he lived for three years, unknown to any one but the good old monk. Romanus was not light of foot, like his young friend, and could neither climb up, nor down, nor into, in any way, this strange home of a mere boy, who had resolved to love God above all things. But although he could not, himself, take the remains of his scanty meal to Benedict, he found a way to give it to him; a way so ingenious that only his love for the innocent youth could have put it into his mind. He tied the food to a cord, and with it he also tied a little bell, and these he carefully dropped down the steep rocks until they reached the opening to Benedict's dark cave. The little bell told Benedict when his kind friend had sent him his food, which he took exactly as it was sent to him, without any dainty fault finding, and with such gratitude as the saints feel for the daily bread that God alone really provides for any of us. It was God who put it into the heart of the aged monk, Romanus, to provide for the youthful hermit in a neighboring cavern; but it is God, also, who puts it into the heart of the parent, like an instinct, to provide for the tender child, and afterwards raises up guardians and friends to give him all that he needs for comfort and happiness.

The life led by St. Benedict in the desert of Subiaco lets a bright sunbeam into the mystery of the lives led by so many of the Fathers of the desert, since it is above nature for a boy to choose such a life. It helps us to realize what extraordinary courage God gives to those who really wish to serve Him with their whole heart. We live weak and cowardly lives, intent only upon our comfort, dainty food, nice clothing; or else upon our games, our frolics with our school mates, our selfish ambition to be the first in every thing, often enjoying our prizes altogether, or for the most part, because we "do not like to be beaten!" and we forget that God has made us capable of actions so heroic in self-denial, so beautiful with a holy enthusiasm, that before the achievements of many a youthful saint the self-denial and courage of the greatest conquerors look poor, and shorn of all their glory.

But although our young Benedict was thus, as people imagined, buried to the world, and no longer of use in it, Almighty God was bestowing the choicest graces upon this dear child, this holy youth. Lost to the eye of man, the eye of God watched, with delight, his growing sanctity in the solitude of the desert; like some beautiful flower which blooms amid the loneliest haunts of nature, and thus gives glory to its Maker where the foot of man has never trod, nor the knee of man ever bent to give Him homage.

The time at length came, when, accustomed to guard his senses, thoughts, imagination, and to curb the natural desire of the youthful heart for novelties and pleasures, our Saint of Subiaco was called forth from his beloved solitude to help other souls, seeking, like himself, to give to God the undivided homage of their hearts and lives. The shepherds who found him in this cell, built by the hand of nature, took him at first for a wild beast; but the holy words in which he addressed them, and the pains he took to give them religious instruction, soon made these good rustics see, beneath his dress of wild skins, a true servant of the living God. That delightful historian, Count Montalembert, whose "Monks of the West" I hope you will sometime read, says, that he "pities any Christian who has not seen this grotto of St. Benedict, this nest of the eagle and of the dove; or, who ever having seen it, has not prostrated himself with tender respect before the sanctuary from which came that flower of Christian civilization, "*The Rule of St. Benedict.*"

After he was found by the shepherds his fame went abroad, and some monks in the neighborhood asked him to be their superior. But they were soon disgusted with his perfect life, and ended by hating one whose holiness was a reproof to their own careless lives. They even went so far in this hatred as to mix poison with his wine; but the saint, having made over it, as was his custom, the sign of the cross before drinking, the glass shivered as if a stone had fallen upon it. "God forgive you, brethren," said the saint with his usual meekness and tranquility. Finding that he could do them no good, but rather provoked them to do wicked things, he left these unhappy monks and went back to his beloved cave, to live joyfully again by himself. But this could not be. Crowds of pious people came to him to be instructed in the way to become perfect, and as he must give them shelter, he was obliged to build, one after another, twelve monasteries, each taken care of by twelve monks; and in this way he became the superior of a large community of religious. Priests and layman, Romans and Barbarians, flocked around him as they heard of his virtues and his miracles. At his command Roman nobles, and savage Goths, took axes and hatchets, and used their strong arms to cut down, and root out, the brushwood from the soil, which since the time of Nero, that cruel persecutor of the Christians, had again become a wilderness. The painters of the noble ages of Christian art have left us many pictures representing the following scene as described by St. Gregory.

A Goth, who had become a Christian at Subiaco, and who was a zealous but clumsy workman, dropped his tool to the bottom of the lake. The rude wood-cutter was very much grieved over the loss. St. Benedict, seeing the simplicity of heart under this regret, by a miracle raised the lost tool to the top of the water, and then said to his rough but good son in Christ, "Take thy tool—take it, work, and be comforted."

Among the noble youths who joined St. Benedict were two who are often his companions in pictures; Maurus, whom Benedict made his assistant, and Placidus, whose father was lord of Subiaco; which did not, however, make his son any the less humble; for he was happy in doing the meanest of the work in the monastery, and even drew water for the community from the lake once made by the slaves of Nero. One day while Placidus was drawing water, his pitcher proved too heavy for him and he fell into the lake. St. Benedict ordered Maurus, his faithful disciple, to run quickly and draw the child out. At this sudden call of his superior, Maurus went, without a minute's hesitation, and full of the spirit of obedience, intent only upon doing what he had been told to do, walked out upon the water as safely as upon the ground, and drew his fellow disciple, Placidus, from the lake. St. Gregory says it is hard to say if the miracle was wrought by the command of the abbot, St Benedict, or, by the obedience of the young monk, St. Maurus; and Bossuet, the great preacher, says, that "obedience had grace given to it to obey the command, and the command had grace given to it to make the obedience safe:" and thus we have a lesson in obedience as the secret of success.

But the great fame of St. Benedict excited in the heart of a reckless man a desire to ruin our saint, by corrupting his spiritual children; and he tried to do this by sending wicked persons among the monks, as they labored in the fields, to tempt them to sin. When St. Benedict saw these wicked persons among his good monks, he knew that it was done out of hatred to himself; and to save his good monks from such awful temptations, he determined to disarm this bitter hatred by leaving his beloved desert of Subiaco. He placed wise superiors over his twelve monasteries, and went, a voluntary exile, from the place where he had lived for thirty-five years, and where he could say, if man ever could, that all the beauty, and order, and piety around him, was the fruit of his own labors, of his own zeal for God's interests. Traveling southward he came to a valley, surrounded by steep and wild rocks; and from the centre of this valley rose a high and lonely hill, that overlooked a beautiful river, woods and valleys, and, far off the blue waters of the Mediterranean sea. This lonely hill was Monte Cassino, which the memory of St. Benedict has made a place of pilgrimage and of sacred renown. At the foot of this mountain, which is in the kingdom of Naples, Benedict found the ruins of an old Roman town, and among these ruins he made his home with his few disciples. But while the Christian saint was at the foot of the mountain, very near its rocky summit stood a pagan temple, in which the Apollo of ancient Greece was worshipped as a god by uninstructed peasants. St. Benedict no sooner heard of these idolaters in the midst of a Christian country, than he set out for their neighborhood, and instructed them so gently and so fervently in the Christian faith, and his preaching was made so powerful by the miracles which he performed, that he persuaded them to break their idol, to destroy their false altar, and to cut down the grove, lest it should be to them the occasion of falling again into their old sin of idolatry. Upon the ruins of this temple he built two chapels, in honor of the true God and the true faith; one dedicated to St. John Baptist, the first Christian monk, the other to the great St. Martin of Tours, the same who divided his cloak with a beggar. Higher still than these chapels, on the very summit of the mountain, he built his monastery of Monte Cassino, from which "piety flowed," as a Pope, Urban II., once said, "as from a fountain head of Paradise."

There is so much in St. Benedict's rule of life at Monte Cassino which it would be useful for you to know, and besides, so many wonderful miracles attended this life, that I shall give you what is written about it in some of the best histories of those times, as they have come down to us through the writers of our own day who are ripe scholars and wise men.

St. Benedict, who had learned to subdue every feeling and wish that was contrary to perfection, had also the gift of reading the souls of others; of reading their very thoughts. He used this gift for the benefit of his monks, especially the young monks, with whom he worked in the fields or in the building of the houses of the community, sharing all their labors; and he used it not only when present with them, but when they were journeying, and praised them or reproved them on their return according as they had deserved.

By this supernatural knowledge he knew when they were troubled by temptations; when they were discouraged or faint hearted, or when the world looked very pleasant to them and the monastery looked very gloomy, and its labors very heavy—all this he would see; and he would say something to them, or better still say something to God for them, and they would be happy, and at peace again. One instance is told of this reading of the secret thought of a young monk that is indeed wonderful, and shows what insight God sometimes gives to those who have the care of souls. It should also remind us, that if it would trouble us to have a fellow mortal read our thoughts, God reads them always; for nothing is, or can be, hidden from His All-Seeing Eye.

Many rich and noble youths came to St. Benedict at Monte Cassino, as they did when he was at Subiaco, to put themselves under his direction; and many were also confided to him by wise parents, who prized his instructions, and his rule of life, more than worldly advantages. These patrician youths, born to command, labored with the brothers of the monastery on the farms or on the buildings, and followed the same rule in all things. St. Gregory tells us, that among them was the son of the first magistrate of the province. One evening when it was his turn to hold the candle at supper for the Abbot Benedict, pride rose up in his heart, and he said to himself, "What is this man that I should thus stand before him while he eats, with a candle in my hand like a slave? Am I then made to be his slave?" Immediately, as if he had spoken his proud thought aloud, St. Benedict reproved him sharply for this movement of pride, gave the candle to another, and sent him to his cell dismayed to find his most secret thought read and reproved. It was in such ways that St. Benedict curbed, as with a skillful horseman's bit and bridle, the proud spirit of the rich and noble-born young men who were sent to him;

and who, having been born and pampered in luxury, knew not that any one had rights but themselves.

While St. Benedict was thus preaching, by precept and example, to his large family in the monastery, he did not forget the people living in the neighborhood; nor did he content himself with preaching to them the doctrines of faith; he healed the sick, cured even lepers of their dreadful disease, and those unhappy persons possessed by evil spirits were delivered from them; he provided for the hungry and the shivering poor; he paid the debts of honest men who were oppressed by those whom they owed, and gave to them the corn, and wine, and cloth, sent to him by the rich Christians. A great famine afflicting the neighboring province of Campania in 539, he gave out to the poor all the provisions of the monastery until, one day, there were only five loaves on which to feed the whole community.

The monks were frightened at seeing their food given out of their mouths, and were very melancholy. But Benedict reproached them for their want of faith, saying, "You have not enough to-day, but you shall have too much to-morrow." And so it proved; for the next morning they found at the gates of the monastery two hundred bushels of flour, given by some unknown hand.

We shall now see how this patriarch could meet the cruel conquerors of his native land. I have told you that there were some of the barbarian Goths, who had invaded Italy, in the monastery of Monte Cassino, and these helped in restoring to fertility the soil which their ancestors had laid waste. But there were others who hated the Italians, and, above all, hated the monks. One especially, named Galla, went the country over, mocking at, and even killing, the priests and monks whom he met, and torturing the poor peasants, or the people whom he supposed to have money, until they gave up everything to him. An unfortunate peasant, exhausted by the torments that Galla had put upon him without mercy, had this idea come into his mind, to tell his tormentor that he had given everything he owned to the Abbot Benedict. When Galla heard this he stopped his cruel tortures, but bound the arms of the helpless peasant with ropes, pushed him rudely before his horse and told him to lead the way to this Abbot Benedict. In this savage style they came to Monte Cassino. When they reached the top of the high mountain they saw the abbot seated alone, reading at the door of the monastery; "Behold," said the poor peasant, "there is the Father Benedict of whom I told thee!" The Goth, believing that here, as elsewhere, he should compel everyone to do his bidding through terror, called out in a furious tone to the saint, "Up, up, and give me what has been stored with thee by this peasant." At these fierce words the man of God raised his eyes from his book, and, without speaking, turned them slowly from the barbarian on horseback to the poor, abused peasant, bound before him. "Under the light," says the historian, "of that powerful gaze, the cords which tied his poor arms loosed of themselves, and the innocent victim of the proud oppressor stood upright and free, while the cruel Galla fell to the ground, trembling and beside himself, and there remained, at the feet of Benedict, begging the saint to pray for him. Without interrupting his reading, Benedict called to the brothers to carry the fainting Goth into the monastery and give him some blessed bread. When he had come to himself, the abbot told him how unjust, how cruel he had been, and exhorted him to act differently for the future."

But a greater man than the savage Galla was subdued by the holy grandeur of our saint. Totila, the greatest conqueror of his times, after his great victories, made a march of triumph through Italy, and when on his way to Naples, seized with a desire to see this Benedict, who was everywhere called a prophet, he turned aside to Monte Cassino, and sent word to Benedict that he would visit him. The saint answered that he would be welcome. But Totila, wishing to prove if he was really the prophet that he was called, dressed the captain of his guard in the royal robes and purple boots, which were the marks of royalty, gave him a numerous escort commanded by the three counts who usually guarded his own person, and then told him to present himself to the abbot as the king. The moment St. Benedict saw the captain, thus dressed like the king, he said, "My son, put off the dress you wear; it is not yours." The officer threw himself on the ground, terrified at having tried to deceive such a man. Neither he nor his escort dared to approach the abbot, but went back at full speed to the king, to tell him how immediately their base trick had been discovered. Totila himself then climbed the steep mountain on which the monastery stood; but when he reached the top, and saw from a distance the abbot, seated, and waiting for him, the conqueror of the Romans, and the master of Italy, was afraid. He dared not go forward, but threw himself on his face before this servant of Christ. Benedict said to him, three times, "Rise." But at last, seeing his fear, the monk rose from his seat and raised him up. During this interview Benedict reproved him for all his wrong-doing and told him what would happen to him; all of which came to pass. The king was deeply moved, and begging his prayers he left him; but not without carrying away with him a wholesome lesson for all his future life. Although victorious he was never again cruel, and his barbarian nature was changed.

St. Benedict founded his monastery at Monte Cassino in the forty-eighth year of his age, or in 529. The visit of king Totila took place in 543, the year before the death of St. Benedict, who forsaw all the terrible ruin that would come upon his country from the barbarians, and that would finally sweep over his dear children of Monte Cassino. He was found one day, by a noble friend, weeping at the coming sorrows that God had revealed to him.

During all these long years of which you have been reading, there was one person who was as dear to St. Benedict as his own soul. When he left Rome, and while he was hidden in that cave among the rocks of

Subiaco; when he left this dear retreat and took up his abode on that mountain overlooking the river and the woods and, far beyond all these, the blue waters of the Mediterranean Sea—during all this time he never forgot his beloved sister, his twin sister Scholastica, born on the same day as himself and with whom he had passed his most innocent childhood. One day, after he had settled his monastery on that rocky height, this sister climbed up the steep ascent of Monte Cassino, and the stone is still shown to visitors where this dear sister stopped to rest, stopped to take breath before she hastened on to see this beloved brother.

You may have heard wonderful stories of twins, who have been not only very much attached to each other, but have always done the same things at the same time, even when at great distances from each other; if one is sick, the other is sure to be sick, too; and I have in my mind's eye, twins who have entered the novitiate of a religious house together. Such persons are twins in mind and heart, as well as by the fact of having been born on the same day, of the same mother. St. Benedict and St. Scholastica seem to have been united in this mysterious manner, for we are told of St. Scholastica that she became a nun, quite as soon as St. Benedict became a monk. After St. Benedict had established his community at Monte Cassino, St. Scholastica came, with her nuns, to Plombariola, five miles south of her brother's monastery; and, following the same rule, the brother and sister ran side by side the race of Christian perfection.

After so many sorrows, so many persecutions, so many and so great labors, what consolation must not St. Benedict have enjoyed in this near neighborhood to a sister so dear, so perfectly one with himself; and St. Scholastica—what joy, what safety, what increase of devotion, must she not have found in this neighborhood to a brother so holy, so wise, and so faithful to her best interests! Yet they seldom met; so seldom that you might think they cared very little for one another; but those who love each other as Benedict and Scholastica loved each other, are not weaned by absence; they enjoy knowing that they are near one another, breathing the same air, seeing the same sky, the same mountains and valleys, and, above all, living under one rule and plan of life. They may not see each other, but they make each other happy for all that. Once a year, only, Benedict and Scholastica left their convents, each with a companion, to meet in a house at a short distance from the monastery. Here they would spend the whole day together, talking of what lay nearest the hearts of both, God, virtue, heaven; and in this sweet and holy intercourse the hours passed swiftly until the sun told them it was time to return to their convents, when they would tranquilly separate, to walk more carefully than ever before, the narrow path to heaven. Lovely affection, uniting so closely and so tenderly these holy souls, without once turning their eyes or their wills from God, to whom they owed the first and the last beat of their hearts! Shall we not ask them to obtain for us, by their prayers, the same tranquil and holy affection for our nearest and dearest friends; so loving them as not to forget God; so loving each other as to help each other to love Him supremely to whom we, of right, belong! St. Francis de Sales tells us that "Our hearts should be clean as ivory, cleaving to nothing." It is when we cleave to our friends rather than to God, that our best friends become snares. It is the loving God above all things, that prevents this great mistake.

St. Gregory, who wrote the life of this brother and sister, has given an account of the last visit which St. Scholastica paid to St. Benedict at their place of meeting. They had passed the day as usual in heavenly conversation, such as angels might have shared; had sung together the psalms for the "Canonical hours," and sat down to their simple evening repast. When it was over, St. Scholastica, foreknowing, it may be, that this would be their last visit together in this world, or wishing for some further instruction or consolation, asked her brother to remain all night, and they would spend it as they had already spent the day, in conversing upon heavenly things and praising God. St. Benedict, unwilling to break the rule of the monastery which forbade the monks to spend a night outside the gates, unless on a journey, asked her not to press this affectionate request. Scholastica, finding him resolved to return home, laid her joined hands upon the table, bowed her head on them, and, with many tears, begged of Almighty God to grant her this desire of her heart. Her prayer was scarcely ended, the silent wish of this loving and beloved sister had but pierced the Heavens, when there broke from the peaceful sky such a storm of wind and rain, thunder and lightning, that neither St. Benedict nor his companion could set foot out of doors. Knowing that this sudden storm must have come in answer to some prayer of his sister's, he complained to her gently, saying, "God forgive you, sister; what have you done?" She replied, "I asked a favor of you, my brother, and you refused it; I asked the same favor of God, and He granted it to me."* St. Benedict was no longer unwilling to stay, for he saw that it was the will of God that he should do so; and they spent the whole night in delightful conversation, chiefly on the felicity of the saints in heaven; of the angels and archangels, the cherubim and seraphim who stand forever before the face of the Father, and of the Queen of angels and of saints, who sits within the glory that surrounds her Divine Son; these made up the subjects of their conversation, with a filial and pious remembrance of their good parents and ancestors who had gone before them

* The house in which St. Benedict and St. Scholastica were accustomed to meet is now a chapel. The bed of a brook, dry in summer, lies between the chapel and the monastery; but the sudden rains which fall in this region, often, in a few minutes, fill the dry bed of the brook and send a fierce current between the chapel and the monastery, even overflowing the banks, and making it impossible to ford the stream. It was such a storm that followed the prayer of St. Scholastica. These interesting facts, with many others showing the veneration still felt at Monte Cassino for every spot associated with the memory of St. Benedict, were told to me by Father B——, a Benedictine monk who had lived, for many years, in this celebrated monastery.

into the eternal world, and to the enjoyment of those delights for which they longed more than the children of the world long for its most costly pleasures. How quickly must the midnight have come, and the hours for the Divine Office, which they recited together, and how quickly, too, the cool grey dawn must have looked in upon the room where they sat, and which was the signal for them to break off this happy meeting! With the morning they parted, and three days after St. Scholastica died; died before the joy of that last meeting with her saintly brother had faded from her heart, before the tones of his voice had ceased to vibrate, like the echoes of some strain of holy music, on her ears. Can we not believe that the desire she felt to prolong the visit, a desire so tender and so strong that it was noticed by God, and indulged, can we not believe that this desire came from some feeling that it would be their last on earth? Nor will it seem very strange, after these wonders that we have been reading about, if St. Benedict was allowed to know of the death of his sister before the messenger could be sent to Monte Cassino. We have all of us heard of the death of some friend at a distance from us, and, looking back, we have perhaps found that at the very moment this dear friend was breathing his last breath we were engaged in all sorts of worldly plans, gaities and enjoyments; and we may have felt shocked that we could have been so insensible as not to feel something in the very air which would have told us our dear friend was dying. But what is denied to the fondest natural affection, God often grants to the saints who have left all their friends to follow Him. At the very moment St. Scholastica was giving up her soul to God, St. Benedict, rapt in religious contemplation in his convent on Monte Cassino, had his eyes supernaturally opened to see the soul of his sister ascending to heaven in the shape of a white dove. "Filled with joy at her happy passage from earth to heaven," as we are told, he gave thanks for it to God and declared her death to his brethren; he also sent some of his monks to bring her body to Monte Cassino, and ordered the tomb which he had prepared for himself to be opened to receive her dear remains, that even in the grave their dust should not be divided.

The death of St. Scholastica was the signal for the death of her brother, the patriarch of his Order, one of the shining lights of that distracted century. The great St. Benedict died only forty days after seeing, in a vision, the soul of his sister ascending to God. It would seem as if their holy conversation on the joys of heaven had loosed the only tie that bound St. Scholastica to earth, and that her brother, on seeing her ascending to it, had no longer any hold on mortal things, but was free to follow her celestial flight. He foretold his death to several of his monks then at a distance from Monte Cassino. A violent fever seized him, and on the sixth day of his fever he asked to be carried into the chapel of St. John Baptist. He had already ordered the tomb in which his sister was lying to be opened. In the presence of that open tomb, and before the altar, he received the Holy Viaticum, and then, placing himself at the side of the tomb and at the foot of the altar, with his arms raised towards heaven, he died, standing, while murmuring a last prayer. Can you imagine anything more grand than such a death for a saint like Benedict!

He was buried by the side of his sister Scholastica, in a tomb made on the very spot where the heathen altar to Apollo stood, which he had persuaded the pagans to pull down. The feast of St. Scholastica is kept on the 10th of February; that of St. Benedict on the 21st of March.

From the Düsseldorf prints, of which I shall often speak, I have selected one representing the last interview between St. Benedict and St. Scholastica. You will see the lamp, as it swings from the ceiling, casting a halo of light on the head of the venerable abbot, whose raised hand is pointing heavenward as he speaks of the joys of Paradise. The young monk who stands behind him, and the aged nun who accompanied Scholastica, are devout listeners; while before him is his sister, rapt in an ecstacy of joy by his words, her eyes carried, by his heavenly discourse, beyond even her saintly brother to Him who is the King of saints, as He is their everlasting delight. At the upper corners of this picture are two very small ones; that on the right hand representing St. Benedict alone, in contemplation; that on the left hand representing him kneeling beside St. Scholastica on her bier, her hand pressing the crucifix to her bosom, while above her, in

a stream of heavenly light, hovers a white dove. The spot on which St. Benedict was favored by this vision, is still shown in the upper room of one of the turrets of the monastery on Monte Cassino.

I have a rose bud and leaves gathered by a friend from the garden of St. Benedict's monastery at Subiaco. This garden is a sort of triangular plat of ground that stands out on the side of the rock a little in front of, and below, the grotto that sheltered St. Benedict. The rose has been plucked many years, but still keeps its graceful stem, and mild perfume, and, almost, its beauty of color. It is said, that while St. Benedict was still a youth at Subiaco, he overcame a great temptation by throwing himself into a hedge of rose bushes and rolling on this thorny bed until the infernal temptation had left him. Seven hundred years after, St. Francis of Assisi came, to visit the wild desert where Benedict received such graces, and prostrated himself before the thicket of thorns where the virtue of Benedict triumphed over the weakness of fallen nature. After bathing with his tears the soil of this battlefield of youthful virtue, he planted there two rose-trees. The roses of St. Francis grew, and have outlived the briars of St. Benedict, and from these rose-trees I think my rose bud came. After this example of courageous virtue, can any youth say it is impossible for him to keep his innocence?

You can tell which is St. Benedict, in pictures where many saints are represented, by a broken cup standing on his book, or by a serpent darting from it to commemorate his miraculous escape from the attempts to poison him. The thorn-bush, too, is found in pictures of St. Benedict, to remind us how his virtue triumphed; and in a beautiful little picture by Perugino, in the gallery of the Vatican, Rome, he is seen with his monk's cowl over his head, and an asperges, or holy water sprinkler, in his hand, to symbolize his holiness of life.

I cannot close this sketch, my dear children, without giving you one of those facts by which history, even when written by those who scoff at the Church and her Orders of monks, gives testimony to the good which the world owes to this same Church and her despised monks.

When Rome, after being many times threatened by her barbarian enemies, was at last given over to them by the avenging justice of God, and was besieged, burned and plundered, no magnificence of her temples, no treasure of art, was of any more value in their eyes than a handful of dust. They set to work like demons, and the labors of thousands of years were distroyed in a few days. When they at last left the city to its fate, Rome was absolutely a desert. Rome, as it was when the innocent Agnes died at the hands of an executioner, would not have believed that such an awful punishment was in store for her. As she then drained the cup of wicked and cruel pleasures, so she was, afterwards, forced to drain the cup of retribution. During forty days not a human being stood within her vast boundary. Foxes made their holes in the palaces of her Cæsars, serpents crawled, unmolested, among her sumptuous baths ,and the banqueting halls of her nobles. Wild animals, no longer awed by the presence of man, came from the mountains and deserts of the neighborhood, and met the fierce beasts of India crawling out of their open dens under the Coliseum, prowling among its beautiful arches and gamboling at will on the floor of that amphitheatre where they had been trained, by a cruel nation, to sport with Christian victims, and thus make the frantic "Joy of a Roman holiday." Pagan Rome was dead, trampled on, utterly lifeless. God's judgments against her for these horrible cruelties had been fulfilled. But to Rome, unlike Babylon of old, had been given a priceless treasure, a sacred deposit; and this was the blood of Christian martyrs, and, especially, the blood of St. Peter and of St. Paul.

This blood was to be the seed of a new life. God had chosen the city of Rome for Himself, and for His Church, and He remembered mercy in the midst of justice. After forty days there was heard amid the awful silence of this "abomination of desolation"—not the cry of an army, not the huzzas of a multitude returning to take posession of their old homes, but the holy and peaceful chant of a religious procession, which had come, with prayers, and hymns, and penitential litanies, to take possession of the desolated city in the name of God and of His Church. That little band, my dear children, was a company of monks from the monasteries of St. Benedict! The kings of the world, the learned in art and science, left Rome to her fate; but the humble, laborious Benedictines, raising her up in the name of Jesus and his holy apostles St. Peter and St. Paul, poured oil into her wounds, and put wine to her lips, and Rome lived; lived no longer as pagan, but as Christian Rome! That we still have Rome, with her galleries of pictures and statues, her Pantheon dedicated to the worship of the true God, and even the naked pillars of her Forum preserved for the admiration of the world, that we still have her noble Christian Basilicas, her holy shrines, her martyr's relics, we owe, not to the deceitful powers of this world, nor to any wisdom of civil rulers nor of civil governments, but to the undying power of God in His Church. Remember this; and when ignorant or prejudiced men would make you believe that the Church, the Spouse of Christ, is the mother of darkness, not of light; of ignorance, not of knowledge; of barbarism, not of civilization; of slavery, not of freedom; you can remind them, that as the Rome of to-day, which they enjoy so much, is the foundling of the Church, supported in her arms, revived by her care, fostered by her magnanimity, so all the boasted learning of our age, the triumphs of civilization, the delights of literature, the majesty of sweet music, the wonders of art in architecture, sculpture, painting, and mosaic, have come to us, with Rome, through the Church and the successors of St. Peter.

SAINT DOROTHEA.

ST. DOROTHEA.

ON my table, lies a large, well-worn, worm-eaten copy of the Lives of the Saints. Beside this book, and almost as necessary to me, is a portfolio of pictures of the saints. Most of these pictures belong to a wonderfully beautiful series of religious prints, the "*Düsseldorf Series*," of which one may say, that not only the painters of such pictures must have been religious men, but also the engravers; so delicate, so expressive, so faithful is every line of flesh and drapery. One need not be a Catholic to linger with affection over these pictures; much less can one with a spark of devotion for martyrs, virgins, confessors, look quietly at them for a quarter of an hour, without feeling a sincere shame at one's mean love of one's self, in place of their generous, hearty love of God and their fellow creatures; or without begging of them, with a sigh of contrition, to obtain for one, by their sweet and prevailing prayers, more of that love of God and

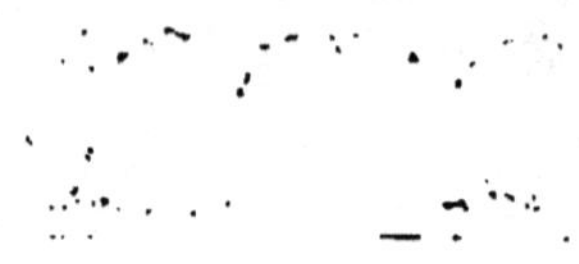

SAINT DOROTHEA.

one's neighbor, which was, really, the secret of their being saints.

I am sometimes puzzled which of the saints in the worm-eaten book, or among the pictures in the black leather portfolio, to choose for my young readers, so admirable, so wonderful, so worthy of imitation in our humble way, are all the saints. The saint that I have selected for this month of February, is St. Dorothea, for she looks so lovely in the picture that I cannot resist the wish to tell you something about her. Then, too, she has that peculiar charm, that attraction, which belongs to a virgin martyr.

St. Dorothea was a young and beautiful girl in the city of Cæsarea, in the province of Cappadocia, Asia Minor. The Church in the early age in which St. Dorothea lived, did not approve, any more than the Church does now, of mixed marriages; that is, of a Catholic marrying an unbeliever. The young and beautiful Dorothea was a true Catholic, and a faithful child of the Church; therefore, when Theophilus, a rich and handsome young pagan, fell in love with her and wished to marry her, she excused herself, because he was a pagan and she was a Christian.

You will wonder, my dear children, how anyone pretending to love a good and beautiful girl, could, in one moment, become her cruel enemy; but this may convince you how little we can trust to the affection of those who love us only for themselves. No sooner did this pagan lover feel sure that Dorothea would not marry him, for all his beauty and riches, than he resolved to be revenged upon her. It was very easy in those days of bloody persecution to be revenged upon any Christian, however noble or powerful he might be, or however innocent. The lover, now turned to hater, had only to tell Fabritius, the cruel and persecuting governor of Cæsarea, that Dorothea would neither marry a pagan nor sacrifice to the idols, because she was a Christian, to have her seized by a rough guard and taken to a dungeon, and then brought before the tribunal, or court, where the governor would ask her if she was a Christian.

You may be sure that when St. Dorothea, though so young, was asked this question by the governor, she did not hesitate, nor try to excuse herself for being one; but lifting her innocent face to heaven she thanked God that she was indeed a Christian, although knowing that for this alone she would be sentenced to some dreadful death—perhaps to be thrown to wild beasts, or to be stretched on a rack until she died from the torture of bones, and sinews, and nerves breaking all over her delicate body, or perhaps to be burned at the stake—all dreadful to think of! But while any, and all, of these might be her portion, the young maiden had not a thought of denying her Lord, her only lover and spouse. We are told that when the governor ordered her to be brought before him, she came with her mantle folded on her bosom and her eyes meekly cast down. The governor asked, "Who art thou?" and she replied, "I am Dorothea, a virgin, and a servant of Jesus Christ." He said, "Thou must serve our gods or die." She answered mildly, "Be it so; the sooner shall I stand in the presence of Him whom I most desire to behold." Then the governor asked her, "Whom dost thou mean?" She replied, "I mean the Son of God, Christ mine espoused! His dwelling is Paradise; by His side are eternal joys; and in His garden grow celestial fruits and roses that never fade."

Her eloquence and Christian loveliness so subdued the cruel governor, that he commanded her to be carried back to her dungeon; and, in order to overcome her holy fidelity to her Lord, he sent to her two sisters, named Calista and Christeta, who had once been Christians, but who, from terror of the torments with which they had been threatened, had denied their faith, had become apostates, were no longer of the one fold of Christ Jesus. The governor promised a large reward to these unhappy sisters, if they would persuade Dorothea to deny her faith, as they had done; and they, full of self-conceit, boldly entered her prison. But how different was the end of this visit from what all had expected! Instead of terrifying Dorothea with the picture of the torments that stood ready for her if she refused to offer incense to the gods of the pagans, they no sooner entered her cell than she began to reprove them, like one who had authority, and drew such a picture of the joys of heaven, which they had, in their weakness and cowardice, allowed to drop from their unworthy hands, that they fell at her feet, saying, "O blessed Dorothea, pray for us, that our cowardly sin may be forgiven and our repentance accepted!" And Dorothea did so, and they left the dungeon to proclaim aloud that they were Christians.

Then the governor, furious at such a result, commanded that the two sisters should be burned, and that Dorothea should stand by and see their torments. Very likely this cruel governor, who could be very brave when he was sending two helpless women to death by the hands of an armed guard, imagined that Dorothea would be as afraid of fire as he would be himself; for you may believe such people as Fabritius are very great cowards. But, although Dorothea knew that she would feel, herself, the very same torments, she not only stood by, but encouraged these sisters to suffer bravely for Christ, saying, "O my sisters, fear not! suffer to the end! for these short pains will be followed by eternal joys!" Thus encouraged by Dorothea they died, and the saint was condemned to be cruelly tortured, and then beheaded. The torture she endured with holy courage, and her execution—but before I tell you about that we must go back to the tribunal of Fabritius, the governor, and to Theophilus, who had brought upon Dorothea all these sufferings. He had stood in the court room while the governor was questioning Dorothea, and when she made that beautiful reply about her spouse, Jesus Christ, "By whose side are eternal joys, and in whose garden grow celestial fruits and roses that never fade;" and when they were leading her to execution whom should she see among the cruel rabble, waiting to see her suffer, but Theophilus, who taunted her with her refusal of him and with the revenge he had taken; and then added, in bitter mockery, "Ha! fair maiden, goest thou to join thy bridegroom? Send me, I pray thee, some of the fruits and flowers in his garden, of which you boasted to Fabritius; I would fain taste them!"

Perhaps some, I hope all, of my young readers feel sure they would never, even to save themselves from death, deny their holy religion; but few, I fear, can hear a school-fellow taunt or insult them for being Catholics, without a reddening of the cheek or a flash of the eye, or a proud and resentful answer. Yet it was exactly this grace, to bear an insult not only with meekness but with joy, which made our Dorothea fit to be a martyr for so meek a master as Jesus Christ. She remembered, remembered not only with her mind but with her heart, how the rabble insulted her Divine Master, her Celestial Spouse; how they blindfolded Him and spat upon Him; how they taunted Him on His way to Calvary; and, without one shade of anger, or even one look of pain, on her beautiful and open face, she looked upon Theophilus, inclined her head with a gentle smile, and said, "Within an hour I will send you apples from Paradise."

The guilty young man tried to utter a laugh of scorn and derision, but the laugh died away in his throat. He did not, as he intended, go to see Dorothea beheaded, but asked some of his pagan companions to go and eat and drink with him, hoping to drown the remorse which he felt coming over him for his wickedness to Dorothea. It was not an hour after this—St. Dorothea had not been an hour before the smiling face of her God, not an hour in the full joy of the Beatific Vision, which makes the rapture of angel and archangel, of saint and martyr, and of Mary our Blessed Mother—when a radiant youth entered the room where the young men sat feasting and rioting. The youth bore in his hand a dish of precious gold, curiously wrought, and in the dish were apples, more ruddy and more perfect than the young men had ever seen before; and, the wonder was, at that season no one had ever heard of apples in Cappadocia. The heart of Theophilus smote him, but he said boldly; "How is it that you bring us apples?" "The Christian martyr, Dorothea," said the shining one, "sends you these apples from Paradise."

The poor young pagan turned pale, deadly pale, and, leaving his companions to finish the feast, went directly to the governor who had, that very morning, condemned Dorothea, declared himself a Christian, and, before the sun set, he too was a martyr, and stood before God baptized in his own blood.

Dear children, as none of us have shared, or ever can share, the counsels of Almighty God, none of us can know what the future may have in store for us to suffer for Christ, for His Church, and for our dear old religion.

Among the converts to the same religion for which St. Dorothea died, was, several years ago, a young lady, who afterwards went with her brother, a rich Boston merchant, and his family to China. This gentleman was very fond of his sister, and loaded her with beautiful and costly presents. When, after two or three years, he was preparing to return to America, what was his surprise to hear his sister say, she had decided to remain in China as a Sister of Charity.

Once he would not have given his consent to her becoming a Sister of Charity anywhere; but now, in his distress, he said, "You shall be a Sister of Charity, only, return with us to our friends; there I will give you land, a house; endow it; all you can wish for I will give; but return with me to Boston; there, if you wish, be a Sister of Charity."

But the heroic girl, hearing a voice, "In China I will have you serve me," much as she loved her brother, saw the ship bear him away to all she held dear on earth, and turned to her humble duty as a Sister of Charity among the idolaters of China. Often and often, when fearful tales come to my ears of martyrs in China, I think of the young Boston convert and Sister of Charity, and wonder if I shall ever hear her name among those of the Chinese martyrs. I am certain she would gladly suffer death for her Saviour; for, long before she was a Sister of Charity she had learned to bear insult with the meek joy of a St. Agnes or a St. Dorothea. God only knows if some young reader of these pages may not one day hear that same sweet voice of Jesus, saying, "As for thee, follow thou me," and you will follow Him, I am sure, if it be to the giving of your life to idolatrous China or Japan, or the Cannibal Islands of the South Sea; and it may be that on the list of martyrs will yet shine the name of some faithful little reader of this story of St. Dorothea, on whose feast-day priests will offer up the Holy Sacrifice in blood-red vestments, thanking God that America, and the United States, has given a martyr to Christ. This may all be; but one thing we know; all of us will have many taunts, and jeers, and calumnies, to bear for our holy faith. Let us learn to bear them with such a smile as St. Dorothea gave to her cruel lover and accuser, and we shall bear a testimony for God and for His truth, which God, and His truth-loving Church, will not forget.

I have taken out the picture of St. Dorothea to look at it once more. How tenderly, and how joyfully too, she looks out from the picture; her meek eyes raised to heaven, in her right hand is the palm she won with her virgin blood shed for Christ, in her left is a basket of apples with their fresh leaves, while at her side lies the sword by which she suffered, and triumphed. Dear, joyful St. Dorothea, pray for us!

St. Dorothea won her crown and palm as a virgin martyr, on the 6th day of February, 303 years after the birth of Christ, or one year before St. Agnes of Rome. She suffered under the same emperor, Dioclesian. Her body is kept in the celebrated church that bears her name, beyond the Tiber in Rome. She is spoken of in St. Jerome's martyrology, and St. Aldhelm, an

English saint and doctor of the Church, writes the story of her martyrdom.

St. Justin has said, "We are slain with the sword, but we increase and multiply; the more we are persecuted and destroyed, the more are added to our numbers. As a vine, by being pruned and cut close, shoots forth new suckers, and bears more fruit, so it is with us."

Christianity is the same now as in the days of St. Justin, as in the days of St. Dorothea; let none of us try to escape our cross, or our martyrdom whether by word or by the sword.

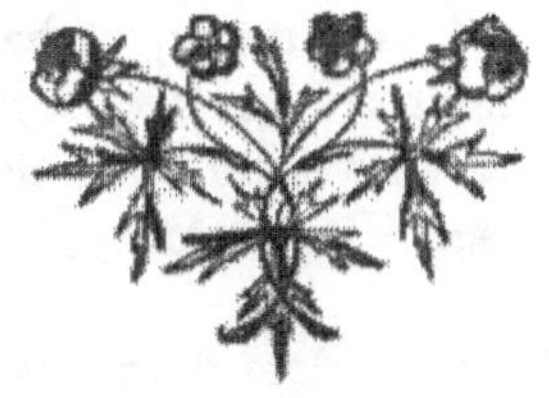

ST. JOSEPH.

SHALL we look over the Calendar, dear children, and find our saint for March? Many bright names shine on the page for this month. St. Francesca of Rome, whose life, as written by lady Fullerton, should be familiar to every child; her feast comes on the 9th of March; and on the 17th is the feast of St. Patrick, the apostle, not only of Ireland, but really of America. Yet, my dear children, I shall run the risk of disappointing some of you, indeed, very many, perhaps, and choose the saint whose feast comes two days later, on the 19th of March, and who is no other than St. Joseph, spouse of the Blessed Virgin Mary, and foster-father of Jesus Christ.

I could not tell you, in less than a large volume, all the reasons I have for wishing to interest you in St. Joseph; but I hope when you have read this brief tribute to that "model of all pure and humble souls," you will feel your hearts so drawn toward this just man, by your admiration for his virtues, that you will make it the study of your life to copy them, and that you will never allow one day of your life to come to an end without practising some regular devotion to St. Joseph.

A great many Protestants have said to me, "The Bible says very little about the Blessed Virgin; why is it that you Catholics speak of her so much?" Almost as often as this remark has been made to me, I have replied, was there ever, in all the books of the world, so much said of any woman as of the Blessed Virgin, in the second chapter of St. Luke's Gospel? Of what other woman could it be said that an angel was sent to her, not only to tell her that she should bear a son, but, that this son should also be the Son of the Most High, the Emmanuel, or, "God with us," and the Messias who had been promised by God to to His people; and promised, not alone through His prophets, but, by His own mouth, to Adam and Eve before they were banished from the Garden of Eden? Of what other woman was it ever prophesied, as it was of the Blessed Virgin, that all these things should come to pass? It is not the number of pages written about a person which makes us esteem him; it is rather the lofty excellence and merit of the facts of his life. Many larger books than all the Four Gospels put together, containing, as they do, the greatest and most important facts of the life of our Lord, have been written about very ordinary people; and more pages, a hundred thousand times over, have been written about these Four Gospels, than they contain; which proves what I have said, that it is not the number of pages, nor of chapters, nor of volumes, written about a person, which tells whether he is truly great or not, but the grandeur and excellence of the events of his life. In this sense we may truly say that a great deal has been said in the Bible about the Blessed Virgin, and about her spouse, St. Joseph.

The evangelist tells us, in a few words, that St. Joseph was a descendent of David, that greatest of all the kings of Judah; the sweet Psalmist of Israel; and, also, a saint, who was not contented with being a saint himself, but has done more than any other poet in the world, to help others to become saints. It was from such a royal house as the house of David, that our meek friend, St. Joseph, was descended.

You have all listened very sharply, when your father and mother, and other friends, speaking of some person whom you know, have said that he was the son, or grandson, or nephew, of some very distinguished man; and if a descendent of some of those noble Catholic kings, of whom you have all read so much, were to come to this country and settle down in your neighborhood, what a peculiar respect you would feel for him. He might not be any richer than his neighbors, he might even be poorer than most of them, but he would have a claim on your regard, such as no mere riches could give, for he would possess what money cannot buy, a drop of the blood of a noble Christian sovereign running through his veins; and, if any one were to write the life of this neighbor, one of the first things he would say, would be, that he was "descended from such or such a distinguished, or virtuous, king or prince;" and you would think a great deal had been told in these few words. But certainly, no more could be said of one's lineage than what St. Matthew said of St. Joseph, that "he was of the house of David;" and St. Matthew even takes the trouble to tell the name of every one of his ancestors, so far back as Abraham.

The second great fact, mentioned by St. Luke as well as by St. Matthew, is, that St. Joseph was espoused to a virgin whose name was Mary; and in the same breath we are told that to this virgin came the angel Gabriel, from his shining place before the throne of God, to make known to her the glorious part she was to take in the redemption of the world. Yet this part was not forced upon her; she was not obliged to become the mother of the Messiah; but the angel paused, after he had told her of the great honor intended for her, until she should give her consent. To such a wife had Joseph been espoused; and is not this a great deal to say of any man however honorable in himself?

But although Mary had given her consent to be the Mother of the world's Redeemer, God did not forget His faithful servant, St. Joseph, who had respected the desire of his holy wife, the Virgin Mary, to remain always a virgin, dedicated to God. Observe, God did not forget St. Joseph; but when He found that St. Joseph was troubled by events which he could not understand, He sent an angel to him in his sleep, who said, "Joseph, son of David, fear not to take unto thee Mary thy wife, for that which is conceived in her is of the Holy Ghost. And she will bring forth a Son; and thou shalt call His name Jesus, for He will save His people from their sins." I think every one of my young readers will say that this one event, is, of itself, enough to make any person's history a very interesting one, even if told in a few words.

If you dwell a moment, on this wonderful story of the marriage of the Blessed Virgin and of St. Joseph, and of the Incarnation of the Son of God, which took place under the humble roof of St. Joseph, you will realize how great a trust was committed to St. Joseph by the Lord of Heaven and of earth. For, not only was the Immaculate Virgin put under his care, but God Himself, the Second Person of the most Holy Trinity, took refuge in this good man's home.

If one of your friends, my dear children, should be appointed by the government of the United States as the guardian of some great treasure, like the public papers, such as the treaties between this nation and other nations, or the boundary lines between this and neighboring countries, you would say that it was a great honor to have such a trust put into his hands; and if, after his death, it should be written of him that not only was this trust committed to him, but that he fulfilled it most faithfully, you would say, "This is better than volumes of empty praise; this is a fact that speaks louder than words." We shall now see how

St. Joseph fulfilled the unheard of trust committed to his care.

We read that when the decree of Cæsar was made known, which commanded the tribes of the Hebrew nation to go, each to its own city, to have every name enrolled, in order that the Roman Emperor might be able to tax every Jew in Judea, Joseph, obedient to the laws of man, took his innocent and beloved wife with him to Bethlehem. It was winter, and we can imagine the distress of St. Joseph in being obliged to expose Mary to such hardships. But what must not that distress have been when he found "no room for them in the inns" of Bethlehem! Every room, and every corner, had been taken up; and the only place of shelter which they could find was a stable, where the ox and the ass had a claim even before themselves. It was here that the Son of God was born, and His crib was the rough manger with the hay and the straw for a bed and a pillow.

We can, perhaps, imagine how cheerless and uncomfortable that stable must have seemed to this tenderly attached pair, the Blessed Virgin and St. Joseph, not only for each other, but for that celestial Being who had chosen them as His protectors; but we cannot imagine the joy, nor the glory, exceeding all human rapture and magnificence, which filled that lowly stable on the night of the Nativity, which every Christmas celebrates, and, next to the Virgin Mother herself, St. Joseph was the first one who ever took the Holy Infant into his arms.

My dear children, let us pause a moment, and consider what it was to receive into his arms, to hold on his breast, to caress with a venerating, worshipful tenderness, beyond any affection that a father can ever bestow upon a child, the Incarnate Son of God! We can never hope to describe this happiness, this beatitude; still less to express it fully in our poor, cold words, our forms of mortal speech; but we can imagine something of it, especially you, happy child, who have been admitted to your first Communion. Remember, when the privilege of receiving Holy Communion is again granted you, that you are favored, more intimately than even St. Joseph, with the immediate presence of your Saviour and your God, and humble yourself profoundly under a grace so little deserved.

If we followed the simple gospel narrative, (remember—I am telling you nothing which every one does not read in his Bible), we find that St. Joseph was with the Blessed Virgin when she received the visit of the shepherds, on the very night of our Saviour's birth, and when the three wise kings came, with their gold, frankincense, and myrrh, to adore the King of kings, and the source of all wisdom; and he was also her companion when she presented her Divine Son in the Temple, as all the Hebrew mothers were commanded to do. Nothing can be such a rebuke to our spirit of disobedience, our wish to escape every obligation, as this act of pure obedience to the law of their nation, on the part of the Blessed Virgin and of

St. Joseph. They might well have considered themselves excused from keeping such a law, intended for very different persons from themselves; but, instead, we see them going up to the temple with the simple offering allowed to the poor, which was two turtle doves. But although they came, so humbly, and so quietly, into the temple, doing nothing to attract attention, not even displaying the Divine Infant which must have made all other infants seem, suddenly, to lose their beauty, two persons were waiting for them, had been waiting for them many a long year. St. Luke tells us that "when His parents brought in the child Jesus to do for Him according to the custom of the law,"Simeon, who had come, by the inspiration of the Holy Spirit, into the temple, met them, took the Infant into his arms, and blessed God, saying, "Now, O Lord dost thou dismiss Thy servant in peace;" with the rest of that beautiful anthem which the Church takes good care that we shall all remember. St. Joseph also heard that prophecy of sorrow concerning the Blessed Virgin, when Simeon said, in the midst of great promises, "And a sword shall pierce thine own soul;" and we can understand how it must have given a still deeper tenderness to his love for Mary, to know that sorrows were to be her portion, sorrows from which even his love could not save her. And not only was Simeon inspired to go to the temple on that day, but also Anna, the devout prophetess, who declared the little Jesus to be the Messias, and "spoke of Him to all who looked for the redemption of Israel.". St. Luke tells us that both the Blessed Virgin and St. Joseph were filled with a holy and devout wonder at these events.

But the sorrow and the joy of the presentation in the temple, were still fresh in their hearts, when another of those great events, which were crowded into their lives, took place. If you turn to the first chapter of St. Matthew's Gospel, you will see how cunning a trap the wicked Herod thought he had laid for the baby Messias, the promised King of the Jews, who, he fancied, would turn him and his family from the throne. He charged the three wise kings to return to him, and tell him where he should find this little king, that "he too might adore him;" whereas he only wished to destroy him. Can you think of anything more horrible than such a feeling toward any little infant, and above all to the infant whom Herod, with all the Jewish nation, had been expecting for thousands of years! And all for the sake of a few years of empty pomp as a king! But the evangelist tells us that the wise men were warned by God in a dream, not to return to this wicked Herod, and thus for a time he seemed cheated of his prey. But the sinful purpose, once indulged, never sleeps. The more Herod thought about this little infant, the more he hated it and the more he determined to kill it. He therefore ordered all the male children of two years old and under, to be murdered! When this dreadful order was put forth, who could suppose the helpless infant in the stable of Bethlehem would escape? But that angel who had already visited Joseph in his peaceful slumber, was again sent to him, to tell him, "Take the young child and his mother and fly into Egypt, for Herod will seek the young child to destroy him." St. Joseph had become accustomed to the visits of angels; he knew their voices; he was not afraid to obey them; nor did he wait for morning, but roused the Blessed Virgin gently from her light sleep, told her of the command given to him by the angel, and, without a moment's hesitation, made ready his meek, but sure-footed ass, to carry the Lord of Heaven and earth, and his Immaculate Mother, into the land of Egypt. How many persons whom you know, and very good persons too, would do like St. Joseph, leave behind him country, friends, all his affairs, to carry the Son of the Most High, far away from the wicked plottings of the very men He came to redeem? Almost every body leaves God to take care of Himself, instead of owning, with devout gratitude, that He has allowed us to take care of some of His dearest interests, and, especially of His dearest treasure, which is no other than His own beloved Son. St. Joseph, however, was noble enough to believe that God's interests were his interests, God's safety his safety, God's affairs his affairs, and, moreover, that he could not have any interests, nor any affairs, important enough to make him neglect those which belonged to God.

There are few pictures, in the world, more touching than those which represent this Flight into Egypt. Sometimes the Holy Family is seen sitting under a palm tree, the Infant resting on the lap of His Mother, and angels adoring Him; while St. Joseph is leaning on his staff, and contemplating, as he might well do, this happy group. A cave is still shown in which they once took refuge on this long journey, made without any of those conveniences which are thought necessary for a mother and her little infant. Innumerable pretty and touching legends, also, are tôld of this Flight into Egypt, so that poetry and art owe some of their loveliest flowers to this flight from a murderous king. But, as I wish to confine myself to what the Bible tells us of St. Joseph, I shall leave these legends for another time, or for you to read when you are old enough to consult more learned books.

For seven years, then, or until the death of Herod, St. Joseph was a willing exile from his native land. For seven miserable years on a throne, Herod had been willing to kill hundreds and hundreds of innocent little ones, and, in intention, to kill the Messias of his nation! But after all he was obliged to die; and the little one, safe with His Virgin Mother and St. Joseph, in the land of Egypt, was brought, at the command of an angel, and by the same careful hands, to Nazareth. The meek descendent of the royal house of David returned, as promptly as he had departed, at the word of this angel; returns to his country, to the little town of Nazareth, to the humble cottage where the mystery of the Incarnation had taken place, and to his trade as a carpenter; and, in his workshop is the Child Jesus.

If we think it a privilege to live in the same house with a very learned or wise person, remember with whom St. Joseph lived intimately for thirty years. There are few pictures more attractive than those which place before us the boy, Jesus, in the workshop of St. Joseph. He helps His foster-father saw the heavy timbers, planes the thin boards, picks up the sticks and shavings that nothing may be wasted, and performs, with the most winning sweetness, all those small labors which so many children consider hard or disagreeable, and, perhaps they are even so proud as to think, degrading. To such children I would say, look long and often at the frontispiece of this volume, and you will soon be ashamed of your selfish, dainty indolence.

We will read a little further in our Bibles, dear children. The evangelist, St. Luke, tells us how Jesus, when He was twelve years old, went up to the temple at Jerusalem with His parents, and, purposely remaining there after they had left it in order to return to Nazareth, He was sought by them with the greatest agony of anxiety, and found, on the third day, disputing with the learned doctors of the Jewish law. When Mary sees her beloved son, she forgets everything in her maternal devotion, and says, "Son, why hast Thou done so to us; thy father and I have sought Thee sorrowing." You see, my dear children, how the Blessed Virgin urges, as one of her most affectionate reproaches, that He has given anxiety to St. Joseph. How tenderly this sounds through the 1857 years since it was spoken—"Thy father and I have sought Thee, sorrowing." I think you will never again, my dear children, feel that it makes no difference with Jesus and with Mary how you treat St. Joseph. I think, indeed, I am certain, that they are very much hurt when dear St. Joseph is at all neglected; and, on the contrary, are very much pleased—take it, even, as a respect paid to themselves—when St. Joseph is honored, or in any way noticed.

We must not take this affectionate complaint of the Blessed Virgin to her Son, on finding Him in the temple, as a reproof. So far from this, it was only her sorrowful way of showing her adoring affection for Him. Many of the saints have indulged in these fond complaints to Jesus, when they have been deprived of His dear society, or of the consolations which they generally receive from Him. At such times they say affectionately reproachful things to Jesus, and tell Him how much they have suffered from His absence; and our Lord has made known, to several of the saints, how much He prizes these fond complaints of His dear friends. How could the Blessed Virgin have said anything to Jesus which would tell Him how much, or rather how infinitely, she loved Him, better than, "Son, why hast Thou done so to us? Thy father and I have sought Thee sorrowing." Try, my dear children, to have tender, affectionate ways with your sweetest of friends, Jesus. Do not act as if He were only a very slight acquaintance, or a friend very seldom seen; but treat Him as your dearest, your nearest, your most intimate of all friends. The stiff, stately way people have towards Jesus, does not come from love; but, from the want of it. Jesus never complains of the familiarity of His friends—their loving, tender familiarity—but of their neglect, their forgetfulness, their cold, hard, selfish way of loving Him. Jesus understood His dear mother; and her tender reproach was sweeter to His ears than the unloving, whispered praise of the proud doctors of the law.

After this touching scene in the temple, we are told that Jesus returned with Mary and Joseph to Nazareth, "and was subject to them." What a lesson, my dear children, in that docility with which a child should be subject to the will of its parents! How many boys and girls grow proud, and impatient of control, as soon as they find themselves growing tall, or strong, or handsome! Is it not mortifying to think that children, after having been nursed, and tended through all the sicknesses and helplessness of infancy and childhood, should use their first reason, and strength, and improvement of every sort, in resisting the wish, the will, and the command of their parents? As much as to say, you may take care of me when I cannot take care of myself; you may nurse me when nobody else will take the trouble to do so; you can support me, feed and clothe, and educate me, because if you do not, no one will; but, as soon as I can, I will disobey you, please myself, and act according to my own ideas. Is not this very shocking when put into words? But it is more shocking to see it acted before one's eyes, every day of the year, by some proud, perverse, unhappy child.

From the time of this return to Nazareth and the peace of its dear cottage, St. Joseph is not spoken of in the Four Gospels. But the Church, the Mother of the gospels, and of the epistles, and, ever since they were written, their faithful guardian and wise interpreter, has preserved many precious traditions concerning this highly favored saint. St. John tells us at the end of his gospel, that the whole world would not contain the books that could be written about Jesus of Nazareth; and we must therefore conclude, that we are to go to the same fountain from which the gospels flowed, that is, the Church, for whatever has been left unsaid or unwritten in her sacred books. Let us, then, take our places, like good children, at the knee of our divinely instructed Mother, the Church of God, who has not only books, written and printed books, for us to read, but has her memory stored with the choicest recollections, the most endearing reminiscences, which she guards as a holy deposit. Where is the child who could forget its parents, its nurse, its early playmates? No more could the Church, with her supernatural memory, forget her Lord and Master, His Blessed Mother or His foster-father St. Joseph.

We have now come to *our* part of the veneration due to St. Joseph. If we wish to know how much we ought to love him, how much we ought to venerate him, let us go, first to Nazareth, then to the stable of Bethlehem, and to Egypt during those seven years of exile, and again to Nazareth during the peaceful, hidden life of our dear Lord in the home of St. Joseph. Let us see how he was loved, how he was esteemed, by Him who knew what was in the hearts of men, and who is to be, one day, the Judge, and the everlasting reward, of that just man, St. Joseph. If we do this, my dear children, instead of fearing that we shall esteem, and venerate, and love St. Joseph too much, we shall be very much ashamed that one, who was so highly honored by Jesus Christ, has been treated with so little respect by us.

The first and best way to honor St Joseph, is to imitate his virtues; his uprightness, his fidelity to the trust confided to him by God, his readiness to obey every command of God, no matter how much trouble it might cost him. These are great virtues, and to practice them we are often obliged to make a great effort; but if we persevere, as St. Joseph did, we shall gain that most excellent of all habits—the habit of virtue. Let us, also, be humble like St. Joseph; pure and innocent like St Joseph; devout like St. Joseph; which means, simply, the loving God above all things, as St. Joseph did. This is the honor which St. Joseph likes to receive, and to obtain the grace to honor St. Joseph in this manner, let us try some of those simple ways so well known to pious people.

We all believe in the intercession of saints; let us, then, be sure to ask St. Joseph to pray for us, that we may obtain those graces, and practice those virtues, which made him so dear to the heart of Jesus.

St. Joseph is the special patron of all priests. The life of this holy spouse of an Immaculate Virgin, and the protector of Jesus while a child upon earth, is considered the model which is to be copied by those who handle the adorable Body of Christ in the Blessed Sacrament; and, that they may be able to copy his life, there are special prayers, by which priests, before and after mass, implore the intercession of St. Joseph. Remember, then, that the first simple way to make sure of the help of St. Joseph, is to *ask* for it.

You will never see a nun, or a sister of any Order, who has not a profound respect for St. Joseph, and a very great and sincere confidence in his prayers. A venerable Sister of Charity told me, only a few days ago, that three hospitals had been given to them immediately after the novena to St. Joseph which they always make before his feast. "I know where a hospital is sadly needed," some one said, on hearing the sister tell this; "can you not move the hearts of some of these rich people around us to give, at least, the ground for a hospital?" "Wait until after the Feast of St. Joseph," was her reply.

I should hardly dare to tell you how many convents, schools, asylums for every sickness of soul and body, have been started, and carried on successfully, among really poor Catholics, under the protection of St. Joseph. And not only priests, and nuns, but all persons sincerely devoted to St. Joseph, and humble in their wishes, will find St. Joseph ready to help them in all their necessities. St. Joseph was himself a poor man. He was not a merchant-prince, who could buy pearls, and precious stones, either to sell again or to give to his spouse, the Blessed Virgin; he kept neither horses nor chariots; he had no servants, neither did he live on dainty food. He was a carpenter, and worked patiently at his trade. We cannot, therefore, expect St. Joseph to obtain a life of indolence and luxury for us; but we may expect him to pray that all our necessities will be supplied, and that we shall be able to pay all our just debts This humble life of St. Joseph, of the Blessed Virgin, and of our Divine Lord, ought to make us ashamed to ask St. Joseph for riches and luxuries, as I have said; but we can ask him to give us a home as comfortable as he had himself; and to add to his own comforts what will be good for us. Many persons are disappointed because St. Joseph does not make them prosperous in their business, which means that they shall make a great deal of money. Remember that money and prosperity are, sometimes, very bad for all of us; but straitness and humility are very wholesome. The spirit of the Holy Family in the cottage at Nazareth was a very humble spirit, and unless we have this spirit we certainly cannot expect St. Joseph to help us—help us, perhaps, to ruin our souls. But I must tell you how St. Joseph did, really, build a house for one of his friends. This person had long been asking St. Joseph to assist her in finding a little house of her own, a home humble but peaceable. She had no money to buy nor to build this little home, but she still believed that, if it were best for her to have it, it would be provided for her. A Sister of Mercy said to her one day, "St. Joseph will not only build your little house, but he will furnish it." The prediction of the good cheery sister, came true, and in a way that astonished even those who had a sincere faith in the prayers of St. Joseph. Would you not think this person utterly ungrateful if she could ever forget this, or, if she could ever fail to make known to others how much St. Joseph will do for his friends, for his sincere and affectionate friends? And, would you not also think it very ungrateful in her, if she should, by and by, complain that St. Joseph did not give her a larger house? The spirit of the Holy Family was a very humble and contented spirit, and those who expect St. Joseph to help them, must have this same humility and contentment, which made the Holy Family so happy in their home among the hills of the little town of Nazareth.

There is one more necessity in which we must try to have St. Joseph for our special friend and patron; and, this is, our extreme necessity at the hour of death. The friend who can help us in that awful hour is indeed a friend to honor and to love. The gospels do not tell us that St, Joseph died; but I suppose no one doubts that he did die. The gospels do not tell us that he died before our Lord was crucified; but we have no reason to think that He would have left the Blessed Virgin to the care of St. John, had St. Joseph been still living. The Church, as I have said before, has a memory for all these blessed facts, and she tells us that

St. Joseph died a most peaceful and happy death, attended by Jesus and Mary. What a calm and holy death must not that have been! The Blessed Virgin near him to give him the help of her prayers, and his foster-son—who was also his Creator, and whom he had protected and supported by his hard labor during His infancy—holding him in His omnipotent arms! In return for such a happy death, St. Joseph is ready to ask the same holy privilege for us, of having Jesus and Mary beside us at our last hour; and, whether on our beds, in our own homes, among our beloved friends, or among strangers, or on the broad wintry ocean, or alone in the deep forests, St. Joseph will then come, and bring with him Jesus and Mary to be our unspeakable comfort. Therefore we are taught to say often, "Jesus! Mary! Joseph!" to make sure of a happy death; and no sweeter ejaculations can sound in the ears of the dying than these:

"Jesus! Mary! Joseph! I give you my heart, my soul, my life!

"Jesus! Mary! Joseph! assist us in our last agony! Jesus! Mary! Joseph! grant that we may die in peace in your holy company.'

Overbeck has drawn a number of pictures, illustrating the life of St. Joseph, and the one representing his death would make any Christian wish to die under his patronage; to lead, if need be, a life as humble and laborious as that which St. Joseph led, if its end could be as peaceful and as sure of heaven. The frontispiece of this volume is taken from these illustrations of the life of St. Joseph by Overbeck, and represents the interior of the Holy House of Nazareth. St. Joseph is busy with his joiner's tools; the young Jesus, with a face of heavenly contentment, is sweeping up the shavings scattered on the floor, while the Blessed Virgin, just entering the room, looks at her son with a gesture of worship, as well as of love and admiration at His humility. Below this picture I have placed one from Correggio, as a *predella*, or pendant picture, representing St. Joseph holding the Divine Infant in his arms, as he must so often have done, with a rapture surpassing all the joy that a parent can feel in caressing his most beloved child. It is a rapture like that of the good priest, when he holds in his hands the consecrated Host, and adores it with unutterable devotion; a silent rapture which makes him willing to give up all other privileges for this—the privilege of calling Jesus down to the altar, holding Him in his hands and offering Him up as a sacrifice for himself and his people! The good priest may meet with many sorrows and crosses, many hardships and disappointments; but so long as he has this privilege he can well afford to leave sceptres to kings, great nations to their rulers, armies to their generals, and navies to their admirals. He may be despised by men, but he is powerful with God; and all the happiness of the world, in comparison with it, is but as a little clay.

I told you, my dear children, that I had so many reasons for wishing to interest you in St. Joseph, that a volume would not contain them if written down.

SAINT JEROME.

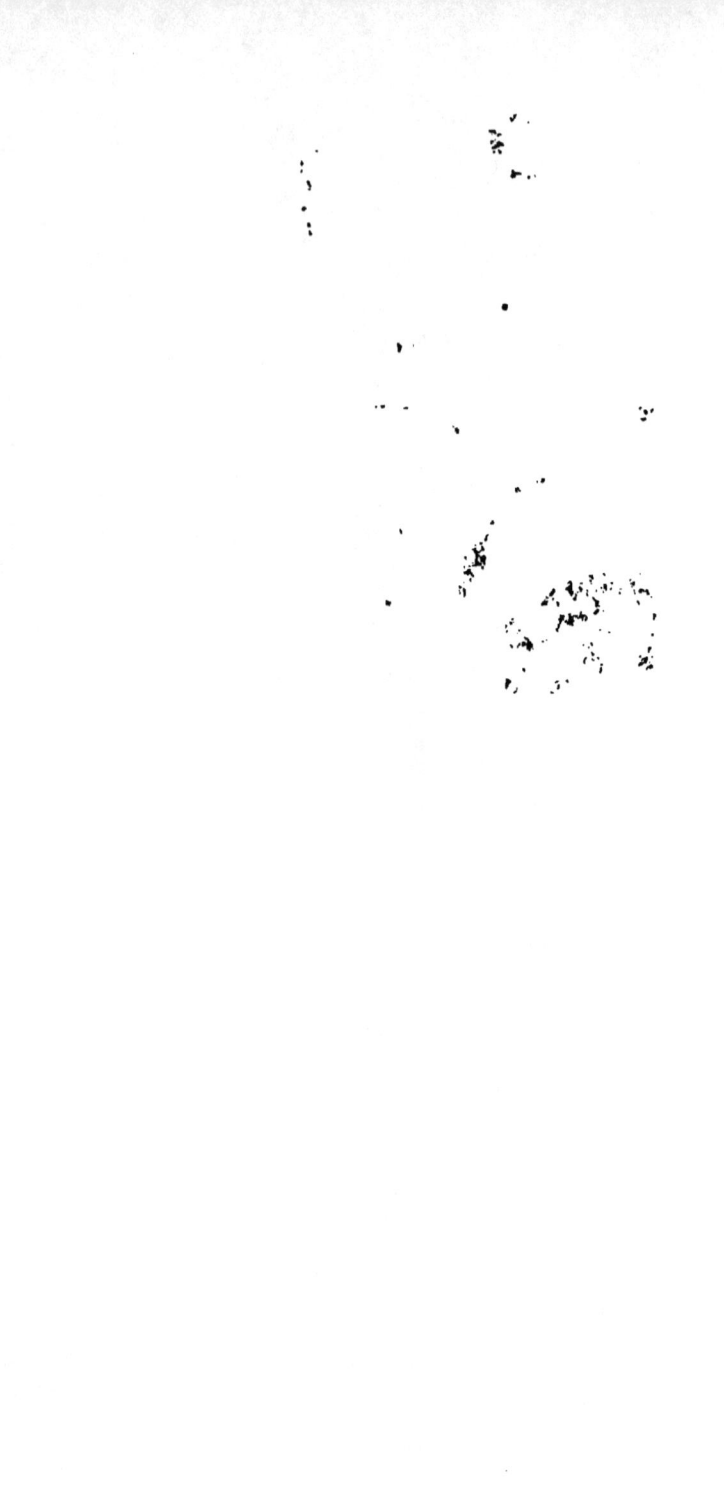

I have one very special reason, however; which is, to have every one of my readers repeat, once, the ejaculations I have given above to obtain a happy death, for an intention so near to my heart, so necessary to its happiness, that, after my own salvation, none can be so near. Can any child refuse me this favor?

ST. FRANCIS DE PAULA.

ON the second day of April, the Church honors the holy confessor, St. Francis de Paula, founder of the reformed Franciscan Order of the Minims. Francis was born about the year 1416, at Paola, or Paula, a little city in Calabria, Italy, between Naples and Reggio. His parents though very poor, were industrious, and happy in their humble condition, directing their whole lives to the one purpose of serving God faithfully. They did not say, like so many people, "We will get rich, and then we will serve God with our riches; we will then build churches and be kind to the poor; at present it will not do to be too pious." O, no! the parents of our saint said always, "We will serve God now; we will be pious and devout now; we will be charitable now, dividing our slender means with fellow creatures poorer than ourselves."

The reward which this humble pair received, for thus loving God and serving Him faithfully, would not, perhaps, be coveted by many people who are called good, but it was one which they prized above all consolations, for God gave them a saint for a son. This son was given to them after many prayers, and, as his parents believed, at the intercession of St. Francis of Assisi for whom he was named; and he was consecrated to God from his birth.

Many parents, even pious ones, would say, if they had but one child, and that a son, "God does not ask us to make such a sacrifice; if we had two sons we might give one to God; but this only one we must keep for the consolation and support of our old age, or to bear up the family name." All this may be very well, but humble James Martotille and his wife did what was far better, far nobler, far more magnanimous; they gave their only child, and that a son, to God, to serve him as a poor religious. This showed the generous quality of their love for God; and, while we blame none who keep their only children for themselves, we cannot but admire these parents, who could so far rise above the affections of nature. They did not love their son less than other parents love their sons, only they loved God a great deal more. And how strangely did God take by surprise these hidden virtues of His poor servants, and crown them before all the world; for while they never thought of their family name as worth preserving, they still live by it on the pages of history! Many an ambitious parent, who has withheld a child from God that he might bear up his name, has seen, during his life, the last of his race die before his eyes.

The little Francis was reared in the holy sentiments of his father and mother, and solitude and prayer were his delight. Instead of craving dainties, like the children we see, he took every possible opportunity to deny himself these indulgences, and was never so well pleased as when the food was plainer even than usual. At thirteen years of age his father placed him with the Franciscan Friars at St. Mark's, where he learned to read, and laid the foundation of that severely holy life which he ever afterwards led.

You can imagine how lonely the poor little cottage of James Martotille and his wife seemed to them, after their amiable child had left it—left it, not to return after a few months or even years at school, but, as they knew, for their lifetime. There were many dreary days and long evenings to look forward to, which hitherto had been cheered by their beloved boy, but neither of them would hold back from God what they had promised to Him; and besides, they knew their son would be happy in his vocation, and they also knew, that if he persevered, he would obtain many spiritual comforts and blessings for them which he could not while living with them in the world. There was but one indulgence of their fondness for this dear child, which they allowed to themselves, and this one was still a matter of devotion. I have told you that the parents of little Francis believed that St. Francis of Assisi had obtained this child for them from the hand of God, and before he had left them altogether, before they had given up their natural claim upon him, they wished to visit the spots made sacred by the seraphic piety of their dear patron, and to thank him for his kindness to them. They took with them the young boy, Francis, and thus the three made together the pilgrimage to Assisi, and to the humble church, called by the Benedictine Monks of Subiaco, to whom it once belonged, Portiuncula, and dedicated to the holy angels, in which St. Francis received so many graces, which was, on that account so dear to him, and which has been, ever since his death, a place of special devotion. When this act of thanksgiving had been performed, Francis, with the full consent of his parents, retired to a lonely place about half a mile from his native town; but finding, even there, too many things to distract him at his prayers, he made for himself a small cave on the sea shore, where, at the age of fifteen, he lived the peaceful, and sublime life of a hermit. He had no other bed than the rock itself, no other food than the herbs and berries which grew in a wood near by. Before he was twenty years old, two other persons joined him, desiring to lead the same life of prayer. The neighbors built three cells for them, and a little chapel in which they sung the praises of God, and where a priest from a neighboring parish sometimes said mass for them.

This was in 1436. Seventeen years after, the number of his disciples had become so large that the archbishop of Cosenza allowed them to build a large church, and monastery, on the same spot. So great was the love and veneration felt for these good monks, that the whole country joined to help them, and even noblemen claimed the honor of carrying burdens for the workmen.

While this building was going on, our saint performed several miracles, as appeared when the process for canonization, as it is called, compelled persons to speak, under oath, of the wonders they had seen. This process of canonization, dear children, is one which I wish you to understand very clearly. You must, first, remember that the Church does not *make* saints, any more than she makes dogmas or doctrines of belief. When a person dies who is esteemed very holy, so holy that every one speaks of his or her wonderful virtue, and piety, and also of his or her extraordinary gifts, either of miracles or of supernatural practices of devotion, the Church, although she may not appear to notice these expressions of admiration, takes very careful notice of them; and, when she finds that they really are extraordinary, she appoints some wise and prudent priests to collect the facts in this person's life, and these facts are given under oath, that is, in the most solemn manner, and in such a way as to prevent any mistakes. Besides those who are so ready to tell all the wonders done by this good man or woman, there are persons who are very ready to tell all the bad, or imperfect things, which this good person has ever done. The one appointed to hear, and to report, all these bad, or imperfect, acts of this good person's life, is called the *Devil's Advocate*, because Satan is always ready to tell our shortcomings and imperfections to our Divine Judge. Satan praises us to our faces, but he says very hard things of us to God; and while he is always excusing us to ourselves, he is our unpitying accuser at the bar of judgment. You see by this how the Church sifts the actions of her saints, as men sift wheat, when they wish to know if it is good wheat. After all these testimonies of living eye witnesses have been taken, as carefully as in a court of justice, the Church lays them quite one side, and waits until this generation, of perhaps partial friends or personal enemies, have all died; then she takes up the life of this good person again, looks at it carefully; and if she decides that this life is above the ordinary, and even the extraordinary, goodness of the faithful, she very cautiously calls this person Blessed, or, as she expresses it, she *beatifies* him. It is not until several generations after this, that she declares him to be a saint, and solemnly puts his name on the list or *canon* of the Church, from which time he is called a *canonized* saint.

An honest-minded man, who had been taught in his youth to look upon all the wonderful acts of the saints as imaginations of pious friends, was one day repeating some extraordinary piece of news; and a Catholic friend said to him, "Do you really believe that to be true?" "How can I doubt it," said the first, "when it has been told by such clear-headed witnesses, who could have no motive to deceive or exaggerate." "You then consider that testimony sufficient, however wonderful the fact may be?" "Certainly," said the honest-minded man. "And yet," said his friend, "you will not believe one of the miracles of the saints, although the wisest, and most honest, men of their generation were eye-witnesses to their miracles." After a good deal of talking the honest man owned, that he should allow to be good testimony what the Church rejects, when she is sifting the life of a saint; and should, also, call that a miracle, which the Church has, often and often, proved to be a delusion or a fancy. You see by this, my dear children, that the Church does not make saints, but only tells us when a good person is found to be so good, so extraordinarily and supernaturally good, as to be worthy to be placed on the list of those who are known to be saints, whose Office is read by every priest on their festival, on which day, also, they are honored in the Holy Sacrifice of the mass.

It was while the life of St. Francis was under this microscope of the Church, that the miracles which he performed during the building of his church and monastery, were made known.

When the buildings were completed, St. Francis set about regulating everything within and without; and, above all, labored to give to his monks such a rule as would enable them to attain to a very high degree of Christian perfection. *Charity* was the watchword of his order; and humility was so necessary to its life, in the eyes of St. Francis, that he begged the Pope to give them the name of Minims, to signify that they were the least in the house of God.

From this time we hear of many wonders performed by our saint; but, as we find with all the saints, the greatest of the wonders which he performed was the practice, the daily, hourly practice and habit, of a supernatural, miraculous humility, charity and self-denial. When I say a supernatural, miraculous humility, charity and self-denial, I do not mean one that is against, or contrary, to the nature of man; but one which is above the power of any of us to practice by our own strength, or, which is simply above nature. The supernatural and miraculous, then, is not against our human nature, but above it; and there are certain very perfect dispositions which we cannot have, unless God gives us something which is above, and beyond, our natural strength. Both Adam and Eve were created with supernatural graces. When they lost their innocence, they lost these supernatural graces, and all their children and descendants, even down to ourselves, are born, not like Adam and Eve in a state of supernatural grace, but as Adam and Eve were after their fall; or, in a state of nature. The saints, by the use of those supernatural graces stored with the Church, and given to us in the sacraments, climbed above the state of nature into the supernatural state, in which miracles are as easy to them as the common actions of life are to us; and their supernatural humility, charity and self-denial, show how high they climbed on the way to perfection. Remember, always, this noble and blessed difference between nature and grace; and ask of God to give you, not the power to work miracles, but the grace of a supernatural charity, humility and self-denial, and your life will then be one perpetual miracle.

We are told that Ferdinand, king of Naples, was provoked with Francis for some very plain, but very necessary, advice given to him by St. Francis; and, pretending that the saint had built monasteries without his permission, ordered him to be seized, and brought to Naples as a prisoner. But when the officer who was sent to arrest him came into the presence of this meek servant of God, he was so moved by the readiness of the saint in preparing to go with him to Naples, that he was filled with awe, went back to the king without Francis, and persuaded him not to injure this good man.

Besides healing the sick, and even bringing the departed soul back to the body, by the power of his prayers, St. Francis was allowed to see into the future, and tell what would happen to his country and to his sovereigns; and almost numberless facts of this sort are told about him.

When we say that St. Francis cured the sick, that he made the lame to walk, or that he called the soul back to the body by his touch or by his ardent way of imploring God to do so, for His own greater glory, we mean something very different from the wonders and juggleries and mesmerisms performed, even at the present day, and in our own neighborhoods, for people who call themselves very wise. The children of the Catholic Church have only to study their catechism, to know the sin of consulting such persons, either for the curing of their sicknesses, or to know what is to happen to them in the future. Let them leave false prophets to those, who, denying the miracles of God's saints, and even of Jesus Christ Himself, are ready to believe every juggler's trick, and to throw aside their crutches at the word of a blasphemer.

In 1469, the Pope, Paul II, sent one of his chamberlains to learn if Francis was indeed the saint which so many called him. When the chamberlain arrived at Paula, Francis, as usual, was among the masons, at work on his church; but seeing two strangers coming towards him, he left his work and met them, bowing very low to them. The chamberlain had disguised himself, so as not to appear like a person of rank, nor even to be known as a priest; and when Francis met him with such humble courtesy he was equally humble, and attempted to kiss the hand of Francis, brown and hard with toil. But Francis would not allow this, and, falling on his knees, said he was himself bound to kiss the hands which God had consecrated during the thirty years he had said mass. The chamberlain was greatly surprised to hear a perfect stranger thus tell the number of years he had been a priest; but he said nothing, wishing to talk with Francis in his convent, aside from his companions. The chamberlain was a very eloquent man, and he tried to convince Francis, by a long discourse, that his rule was too severe, and also of the dangers to which a person is exposed who pretends to miraculous gifts, or who lives in any way differently from other good Christians; and urged him to leave all his extraordinary self-denials. Francis heard him patiently, and answered him with great humility; but, finding that the mind of his visitor was not changed, he took from the fire some burning coals, and holding them for a long time in his hand, said, "All creatures obey those who serve God with a perfect heart." These golden words were repeated by Pope Leo X. in the bill of his canonization. The chamberlain returned to the archbishop of Cosenza, and to the Holy Father at Rome, and told them that the sanctity of Francis was greater than his fame in the world.

The generous offering of an only child, and son, to God, seems to have been followed by a reward, even in this life, to the humble parents of our saint; for we afterwards hear of his sister, and of the miraculous consolation given to her by her brother. A youth, the nephew of the saint, having died, his mother, the saint's own sister, came to him for comfort, and filled his room with sounds of lamentation. After the mass had been said for the repose of this youth's soul, St. Francis ordered the body to be carried from the church to his cell, where he ceased not to pray, until, to the astonishment of the mother, St. Francis presented her son to her alive, and in perfect health.

But the miracle, which, among all the miracles of St. Francis, dwells deepest in my memory, and rouses my most lively gratitude, is one not impossible to many a hidden saint of God in our own day, in our own society, and in the very state, or town, or village in which we live.

Louis XI, king of France, a prince as tyrannical, as jealous of his own authority, and as impatient of everything that crossed his wishes, as any who ever wore a crown, after a fit of apoplexy fell into a slow decline. In his sickness he desired nothing so much as health, and dreaded nothing so much as death. He gave his physician ten thousand crowns every month, so long as he should preserve his life; and, under the feeling that this fellow-mortal could shorten or prolong his existence, he was not only obedient to every command that he gave him, but stood in the greatest awe of him; while towards every one else he was so perverse, so fretful, and even cruel, that his noblest subjects dreaded to go near him, and nothing could tempt them to ask of this powerful king the smallest favor. The wise Thomas à Kempis, in his Imitation of Christ, tells us that "Few are improved by sickness;" and so true was this of the poor, sick, unhappy king, Louis XI, that he shut himself up in one of his strongest castles, Plessis-les-Tours, near the city of Tours, not like a hermit who flies to some lonely wild where he finds but one comfort, the comfort of serving God and conversing with Him, but like some great polar bear, who sits in his den to growl at every one who comes near him, unless at his own command and to amuse him. Here, in order to divert his mind, he had jesters, dancers, all sorts of entertainments; but his peevishness and melancholy were all the same. At the very time, too, that he was thus trying to satisfy his restless wishes by what, any Christian knows, can never satisfy, never truly console, he was greedy for prayers, and ordered processions and pilgrimages for his health, and even against the north-wind, which he found increased his pains, and called for holy relics to be brought to his room. It may seem very strange to you, dear children, that a man, like Louis, could be so profane, and, at the same time, have so much faith in holy things; could act as if this world were all he needed for his happiness one moment, and the next moment show a superstitious faith, instead of the sound and reasonable faith of a good Christian, in the supernatural means which God has allowed us to use in our extreme need. But sin makes men very inconsistent, and above all men the instructed Catholic, who knows what sin is, and yet commits it with his eyes wide open.

While Louis was thus showing to the world the foolishness of a sinful Christian, and while his sickness continued to increase, in spite of physicians and pious prayers, he remembered having heard, in his days of dissipation and prosperity, of the holy hermit of Calabria, who had done so many wonders in behalf of the suffering; and he sent immediately one of his embassadors to beg this humble man, Francis de Paula, to come to his castle, and cure him of his malady; making the greatest promises to serve both him and his Order. We can all understand how a saint, like Francis, would not be moved by any promises to himself; but we might think when a great king offered to befriend his young Order, to give it lands and houses, and to make it an honorable Order, that even Francis would think this a providence and not to be slighted. But the saints esteem as very little, what the world will go upon its hands and knees, and lick the dust, to make its own. St. Francis knew that it was not the man who could make the most money for his Order who would be its greatest benefactor; but the one who should bring into that Order, most of the spirit of God. St. Francis of Assisi would not allow his religious to put up grand buildings, nor increase, in any way, the riches and possessions of his Order; and St. Francis of Paula knew that the money of an impenitent king, like Louis XI, would not do his Order of Minims any good. He therefore declined this great honor of curing the king by a miracle; which Louis no sooner found out, than he entreated Ferdinand, the king of Naples, to send his humble subject, Francis, to him. But Francis told king Ferdinand that he could not tempt God, nor would he travel a thousand miles to work a miracle which was asked from low and selfish motives.

The king, being thus denied, desired, more than ever, what had been refused to him, and begged the Pope, Sixtus IV.,to use his power in his behalf. Sixtus, no doubt, saw in this anxiety of the king to secure the saint, some sign of grace, for he commanded Francis to go to the French king by two formal writings. St. Francis immediately obeyed, by setting out for France.

He passed through Naples, where Ferdinand honored him with marks of the greatest respect. He also took Rome in his way, and the Pope and cardinals lavished upon him tokens of favor and regard. He set sail from Ostia, and landed in France, healing many persons sick of the plague along the road. The king, overwhelmed with joy, and believing that his own relief from ills and pains was near at hand, gave a purse of two thousand crowns to the one who brought the first news of the saint's arrival in his dominions, and sent his eldest son, the Dauphin, to meet the saint at Amboise and bring him to his palace. On the 24th of April, 1482, St. Francis arrived at Plessis. The king, with all his court, went out to meet him, and falling on his knees implored him to obtain of God a prolongation of his life. St. Francis told him, no wise man ought to desire this; adding, that the lives of kings had their appointed time to end like the lives of their meanest subjects, that the will of God was not to be changed, and that there remained for his majesty only to make an act of resignation to the Divine will, and to prepare himself for a happy death.

The king, who had no doubt expected quite a different answer, was not angry with him, as he would have been with any one else, but ordered that he should be led to a room in the palace near the chapel, and that an interpreter should be sent to him; for our saint, with all his heavenly wisdom, could not speak French. St. Francis, thus lodged near the king, had many opportunities to speak to Louis, both alone, and before his courtiers, all of whom were persuaded that Francis spoke from the inspiration of God. The physician who had been so long deferred to by the king, and who had told him that he should, some day, be sent away like all the others who had served this cruel tyrant, but that the king would not live eight days after he had left him, was furious against St. Francis, and did all he could to destroy his influence with Louis; but the unhappy king was faithful to his saintly friend, and corresponded to the grace which he had obtained of having this holy man by his side. And, for this fidelity, he received his reward; not, indeed, the recovery of his health, nor the prolongation of his miserable life, but the grace of a perfect change of heart, and desire, and purpose. When he found his end approaching he no longer repined, but sending for his saintly friend received all the sacraments, commended his three children to his care, and expired peacefully, in the arms of St. Francis, on the 30th of August, 1483.

St. Francis, who had performed countless miracles for the relief of the poor and the humble, refused to work the one desired by a powerful monarch, not out of a lack of respect for a ruler, but because he knew the miracle would only confirm Louis in his wickedness; and, also, because he wished to obtain a far better answer to his prayers than a long life in this world; which was, a happy death for this monarch, who had merited a very unhappy one.

We can also learn, my dear children, how much

God esteems sincere faith, even when other virtues are lacking; for He allows it very often to go in advance, and to procure other graces, which, at length, make a soul acceptable to Him. It seems that the faith of Louis, imperfect as it was, had something in it pleasing to God, for He permitted it to obtain the best and highest answer; whereas, many persons who practice the natural virtues of kindness, justice and temperance, yet scoff at the objects of supernatural faith, fail of those graces which God bestows at the prayer of faith, however imperfect. He who asks, "nothing doubting," is sure of some answer, perhaps better than the one he craves.

We are told that the Dauphin, when he became king Charles VIII, honored St. Francis even more than his father had done, considering him his wisest counsellor, and visiting him every day as long as he stayed at Plessis. St. Francis stood as god-father for his eldest son, to whom his name was given; and the young king built a beautiful convent for our saint in the park of Plessis, in a place called Montils, and another at Amboise, on the very spot where he met St. Francis when he was Dauphin; and in 1495, when he made a triumphal entrance into Rome, and was saluted by Pope Alexander VI. as emperor of Constantinople, he built in Rome, on Mount Pincio, a stately monastery for the Order of Minims, under the name of the Blessed Trinity, to which none but Frenchmen can be admitted as monks. During the reign of this same king, St. Francis founded the convent of Nigeon, near

Paris; and at this time two doctors, who had opposed the Order of Minims before the bishop of Paris, were so moved by the sight of the saint at Plessis, that they entered the Order in 1506. King Charles died in 1498, and Louis XII, succeeded him. At first he allowed the saint to return to Italy, but he soon showed so much anxiety for his return that St. Francis came back to Plessis, which God had blessed by his presence.

Again at Plessis, he was the centre of piety, until, warned by his great age to prepare for death, he lived in his cell, for three months, the hermit life which he had loved as a boy on the sea-shore of Calabria, denying himself to every one, that nothing might divert his thoughts from God and eternity. He fell sick of a fever on Palm Sunday, 1506. On Holy Thursday he called all his monks into the sacristy, exhorted them to love God, each other, and all mankind, and to observe their rule punctually. This great saint, who had performed so many miracles, then made his confession and received Holy Communion barefoot, with a cord about his neck, as is the custom of his Order. He died on the 2d of April, 1508, being ninety-one years old. The mother of Francis I, prepared his winding sheet with her own hands, and he was canonized by Leo X. in 1519. His body remained uncorrupted in the church of Plessis-les-Tours until 1562, when the Huguenots broke open the shrine and found it whole and perfect, fifty-five years after his death. They then dragged it about the streets, and burned it in a fire made with the wood of a large crucifix, which they had hewed to pieces. Some of his bones were recovered, and are kept in several monasteries of his Order, at Plessis, Nigeon, Paris, Aix, Naples, Paula, and Madrid.

The best pictures of St. Francis de Paula, are by the great Spanish artist, Murillo. He is represented as a very old man, with a long white beard. He wears a dark brown tunic and the cord of St. Francis of Assisi. His habit differs from others in the short scapular, or piece hanging over the shoulders, reaching a little below the girdle, and rounded at the ends; at the back of this scapular is sewed a hood that is drawn over the head. In pictures of St. Francis the word "Charity," is generally found in the glory above, or carried on a scroll by an angel.

A picture painted by Lavinia Fontana, who was one of the best portrait painters of her time, represents the Duchess d'Angouleme, the same one who prepared his winding-sheet, kneeling, with four maids of honor, at the feet of St. Francis, and presenting to him her infant child, his god-son, afterwards king Francis I.

Plessis-les-Tours still cherishes the memory of Francis de Paula; and a descendant of the noble house of Plessis, told me, only a few days ago, of the picture which represents the Daulphin Charles meeting the saint. Through the holy prayers of St. Francis, Plessis has become a shrine, instead of the hated retreat of a sick tyrant; and the representatives of the house of Plessis carry with them, as their choicest claim upon the love of Christians, the holy memory of the son of the humble peasant, James Martotille, of Calabria.

Pray for *us*, O holy St. Francis, that our death may be, like thine, the gate to a blissful eternity with God, and His angels and saints; since that life is indeed lost, worse than useless, which does not close with a good death! To the soul at peace with God, the thought of death brings no melancholy, but rather a peaceful looking forward to a perfect joy, unmixed with evil. "How sweet," exclaimed a saint, "to close one's eyes on this sorrowful, uncertain, unsatisfactory life, and open them in an instant on God, and the assurance of eternal bliss!" Again, then, let us say, "Holy St. Francis pray for us!" and repeat our Hail Mary, closing ever with that powerful request, "Pray for us now, and at the hour of our death!"

SAINT BEDE.

DO you ever, my dear children, when admiring a noble landscape, stop to think how much the beauty of one part of this landscape depends upon the beauty of some other part of it; how the loveliness of the meadow is made all the lovelier by its winding brooks, its swiftly-flowing river, or, by a single majestic elm, standing, as I remember to have seen one in my native valley, amid the verdure and the sunshine, its graceful branches lifted and swayed by the lightest breeze of summer, and holding the eye, at every turn, by its beauty and grandeur—how the sublimity of mountain-ranges takes a new glory from the atmosphere of some placid lake, as the Adirondacks are seen across Lake Champlain from Burlington, steeped from base to summit in violet-tinted mists, with all the kindling splendors of a summer sunset, burning, shifting, and then fading away, above them—do you ever, I repeat, stop to think how much the meadow and the river and the elm, how much the mountains, the lake and the sunset, owe to each other? You could not paint one without painting the other; you never remember one without remembering the other; and, through all the changing years of your life, the meadow and the mountains will live in your memory, glorified by the graceful majesty of the elm, by the purple mists of distance, and the shifting and flushing hues of sunrise and sunset.

History and the lives of great men illustrate, and are illustrated by, each other. To know the saint, to have a clear picture of him before your mind's eye, you must know something of the country and the generation in which he lived; and although the people of these days may pretend to despise, or, may honestly despise, through ignorance or inherited prejudice, the saints of God, yet these saints belonged to the times in which they lived in such a manner, that no true history of those times can be written without noticing them; and sometimes a saint stands out, among the men and the events of his day, as the elm stands out on the "north meadow" of old Deerfield, giving, by its singleness and its perfection, a majesty to the landscape altogether its own. Of no saint can this be said with more justice than of St. Bede, or, Venerable Bede, as he is generally called. An "Anglo-Saxon, born at one extreme limit of the Christian world, and of a race only half a century before plunged in the darkness of idolatry," he stands before us now, after so many centuries, as the most learned man of his time, as the father of English history and the actual founder of history in the middle ages; for, by the precision of his language and by the accuracy of his narrative, he laid a foundation upon which later writers could build the edifice of a true and noble history of succeeding generations. No one, therefore, can separate the life of St. Bede from the annals of England, and no one can banish him from his true place among the choicest scholars of that, or of any other, time.

It was in 673, while St. Benedict Biscop was bishop of Northumbria, one of the four ancient kingdoms of England, that on one of the estates belonging to the monastery of St. Peter, founded by St. Benedict Biscop at the mouth of the river Wear, a boy was born named Beda (which in Saxon means *prayer*,) or as we call it Bede. We know nothing of his family, excepting that he was given by his relatives, at the age of seven years into the care of St. Benedict, (or Bennet, as he is sometimes called,) and that St. Bennet confided him to his friend, Ceolfrid, who took him in 680 as one of of his colony of twenty monks, "tonsured and untonsured," who went with him to lay the foundations of another monastery about five miles from that of St. Peter's and called, very properly, St. Paul. There, at St. Paul's, was our little friend, Beda, in the year 686, when a terrible pestilence swept off all the monks of St. Paul's but the good "Abbot Ceolfrid, and," as the annals read even to this day," one little boy." Beda must have been one of the brave little boys, for we read that the abbot contrived, with his help, to chant the canonical hours, which they did in the midst of their sighs, and tears, and heart-rending sorrows, until other monks joined them in their desolated retreat.

It is plain that Ceolfrid had no notion of leaving his monastery, of St. Paul's at Jarrow, on account of this misfortune; and it is also plain that the boy, Beda, had no notion of leaving the good abbot. This was his home; and of all the pictures which the writing of these pleasant lives of the saints has brought before me, few have had so tender a charm as that of the abbot and his little novice, singing, amid the desolation at Jarrow, the praises of God at the canonical hours —matins, lauds, prime, terce, sext, none, vespers, compline—the very same as when the stalls, (or seats of the monks in the convent chapel,) were filled by their good brothers in the pleasant days gone by, instead of being empty; the very sight of these empty seats making the chapel lonelier to the only two living, out of the twenty who had left Wearmouth, for Jarrow-on-the-Tyne, with so light a step six years before.

Before we go any further I must be sure that my very youngest reader, or listener, understands about the "tonsure" of our friends, the monks of Jarrow. If you look at the picture of St. Laurence, in this book, you will see a perfect Roman tonsure, such as was worn by the monks of that day. In the picture of St. Benedict, too, you will see a young monk with a perfect tonsure, *i. e.*, the hair is shaved on the top of the head so as to leave a wreath, or circlet, of hair only.

St. Benedict has lost some of his tonsure by reason of age, so that the circle is not perfect; but this, you must remember is a *Roman* tonsure, and was the sign of a professed monk, or one who had made his full vows. Little Beda could not have boasted of a tonsure when he sung the Hours, alone, with the abbot; but we hear that six years after, when he was only nineteen years old, he was made a deacon, like St. Laurence, and then, we may presume, he was a tonsured monk.

You will be surprised to hear that, although St. Bede was so learned as to be called the first scholar of his age in the whole world, he never traveled out of his own country, not even to Rome, the desire of all Christian pilgrims. He lived always at Jarrow, and in one of his books, "The Records of the Fathers of Wearmouth and Jarrow," he dwells, with delight, on the memory of the many happy years he himself passed within its walls, and on the thought that none of them had been spent in idleness. "All my life," he says, "I have spent in this monastery, giving my whole attention to the study of the Holy Scriptures; and in the intervals between the hours of regular discipline, and the duties of church psalmody, I ever took delight in either learning, or teaching, or writing." He was exact to the minute in the observance of his rule, and although its duties often interrupted his favorite studies, he never sought to be excused from any of them; and never, especially, from attendance in choir. "If the angels did not find me there among my brethren," he would say, "would they not ask, "Where is Bede?

why comes he not to worship at the appointed hour with the others?" His disciple, Cuthbert, says of him, "I can declare with truth, that never saw I with my eyes, or heard I with my ears, of any man so unwearied in giving thanks to God." Pious writers tell us, that, as of the ten lepers spoken of in the Gospel who were healed of their leprosy by the power of Jesus Christ, "only one returned to give thanks," so it is with Christians who pray with great zeal that they may obtain blessings, but seldom remember to thank God for His favors when received. St. Bede, it seems, was very careful to make thanksgivings, and loved the praises of God, which "were ever in his mouth."

But you will ask, perhaps, how St. Bede, if he never traveled, became so learned? To answer this very sensible question, we must go back, not only to St. Bennet, but to the great Pope, St. Gregory, under whose inspiration the new era of Christian letters began, even in Italy. From the new foundations of learning and piety laid by him, he sent the Apostle of England, St. Augustine, to convert that nation fully to Christianity. A monastery, dedicated to SS. Peter and Paul, was founded at Canterbury by St. Augustine, and this monastery was under the care of St. Gregory himself. A catalogue of the library that St. Augustine and his companions brought with them to England, is preserved at Trinity College, Cambridge. It consisted of "A Bible in two volumes, a Psalter and a book of the Gospels, a Martyrology, the Apocryphal Lives of the Apostles, and the Exposition of certain

Epistles and Gospels." The short catalogue closes with these few words: "These are the foundation, or beginning, of the library of the whole English Church, A. D. 601." The writer from whom I have taken these facts, adds, "We may well linger with delight over this short list, that displays to us as the foundation stone of all our knowledge, the Sacred Scriptures; these were the books sent by a Pope to be the beginning of a national library, and from them St. Augustine began to teach the English." It was St. Gregory who watched carefully over all the necessities of the young Church, and sent to it, not only sacred vessels, vestments, church ornaments and holy relics, but "many books." From the schools starting up under such powerful encouragement came the scholar, St. Bennet Biscop, whose journey to Rome, in company with St. Wilfrid, fixed one purpose deep in his heart; to devote his life and his great energies to the founding of a noble seat of learning in his native land, and to fit himself to do his work well before beginning it.

In order to do this, he gave up the governing of his monastery to a still greater scholar, named Adrian, and spent two years in studying under him as under a master. It was when such pupils as Bennet were ready to study under such teachers as Adrian, that the love of art, and of science, and, above all, of sacred letters, inflamed the minds and hearts of the noblest men of that age. After studying at Canterbury under Adrian, and that learned Greek, Archbishop Theodore, Bennet planned a fourth visit to Rome, purchasing, and begging, books all the way, and returned to England loaded with treasures, that were afterwards stored in the two monasteries of SS. Peter and Paul, where our Bede was placed, like a bee among the blooming clover-fields. There was no need that he should travel, for the riches of the world's best minds had been placed by Bennet in the libraries he had founded with such a holy enthusiasm. And not only books, but fine arts, unknown to his countrymen, were brought by this ardent scholar and saint, Bennet Biscop, to the rough Britons. The French artisans were called over to England to give beauty and strength to his stone edifice, and glass-makers, the first ever seen in England, were invited to put in the windows. On his fifth visit to Rome, in company with the abbot, Ceolfrid, he brought back, not only books and relics, but pictures. At the end of the Church of St. Peter he placed pictures of our Lady and the twelve Apostles; on the south wall were scenes from the Gospels; and on the north the visions of the Apocalypse. The pictures placed in St. Paul's were so arranged as to show the connection between the Old and New Testament; a picture of Isaac, bearing on his shoulders the wood of the sacrifice, standing beside one of our Lord bending under the wood of His cross; a picture of the brazen serpent which God commanded Moses to raise in the sight of the plague-stricken Israelites, that all who looked upon it might live, beside a picture of the Crucifixion of our Lord and Saviour Jesus Christ. "Those, therefore," says St. Bede, "who knew not how to read, entering these churches, found objects representing Jesus Christ and His saints, and recalling to their memory the grace of His Incarnation, and the terrors of the last judgment." St. Bennet also brought back with him, John the Venerable, abbot of St. Martin's, and arch-chanter of St. Peter's, that he might teach in the English churches the method of singing, throughout the year, as it was practiced in St. Peter's at Rome, and "this he did for Wearmouth and for all the monasteries of that province, and many invited him to teach in other places."

Nothing could give us a more correct notion of the value which the Church places upon decorum and beauty in the ordering of her sacred ceremonies, than the zeal of St. Bennet in bringing from Rome, to his monasteries at Wearmouth and Jarrow, this venerable teacher of the chant approved by the Church. We can believe that there were very few quavers and semi-quavers in the music taught by this holy ecclesiastic; but lest you should imagine this simplicity to be a sign of rudeness and ignorance, I will remind you that the Gregorian Chant which you hear every Sunday when the priest sings the first clause of the *Credo*, the *Gloria in excelsis Deo*, the *Preface* and the *Pater noster*, is the chant which the great St. Gregory, the special friend and protector of the Church in England, had himself arranged for the sacred Offices. The music sung by the priest at the altar is the same in all countries; and the Church watches very strictly over this part of the Divine worship, in order that no light or worldly music may be sung in her sanctuary, and, also, that the voice of her priest may have that solemnity, that sweetness, and that holy accuracy, which alone is worthy of his sacred place at the altar of God. But if the Church shows such care for the music within the sanctuary, can we suppose her indifferent to the music sung by the choir? So far from being indifferent, she has claimed the noblest music, ever composed by man, for her choirs; and when the leaders of choirs, or the choirs themselves, turn from these treasures of sacred song to the music of the most perfect operas, presuming to sing in the Divine honor what has been composed to express human affection, they not only profane the worship of the Church, but show a depraved taste, and a mind and heart incapable of enjoying the celestial harmonies to which the Church has given a voice. The highest praise that can be given to any choir is, that it sings religious music in a religious spirit.

When we read the descriptions, given us by St. Bede, of the swiftness with which this love of learning, like fire on our western prairies, spread over a whole nation, we sigh over the lukewarm indolence of our own generation, when "good society" seems to be cloyed with its shallow learning, and careless of the honors which true scholarship should win in every civilized community. Yet the hunger and thirst for knowledge which then distinguished the Christians of Britain, was accompanied by a simplicity of manners, to be seen no where in its most charming perfection, as it is when united with profound learning, excepting in monasteries. These men, who were devoting their lives to establishing seminaries of learning on the wild shores of England, might, every day, be seen in the kitchen and farm-yard. Abbot Easterwine, once a courtier of king Egfrid's, who filled the place of abbot during the absence of St. Bennet, delighted in winnowing the corn, giving milk to the young calves, working at the mill or forge, and helping in the bakehouse. It is thus that he is described by St. Bede, who also tells us of the "spiritual beauty of the abbot's transparent countenance, his musical voice, and gentle temper, and how, being seized with his last illness, he came out into the open air, and sitting down, called for his weeping brethren, and then, after the manner of his tender nature, gave them all the kiss of peace and died at night as they were singing lauds."

It was in such an atmosphere of zeal for God and for all that could beautify the service of man towards his Creator, that St. Bede was nurtured; and the sanctified juices thus sent, like the sweet vernal sap, through his whole being, he returned to the world, and perpetuated in it, by his works.

We have said that St. Bede was most exact in fulfilling all the duties commanded by his rule of life as a monk. Besides these duties he was both mass-priest and professor in the schools. By the rule of the first, he was obliged to administer the sacraments, visit the sick, and preach on Sundays and festivals; by the second, to teach to others the learning he had himself acquired. Even before his ordination, the monastic school was placed under his direction, and he gave instruction to 600 monks of Jarrow, as well as to pupils flocking from all parts of England.

You could hardly recognize in this picture of St. Bede, or, Venerable Bede, any likeness to the "lazy monks," so often quoted for the benefit of boys and girls, who do not know how many of the most common blessings of civilization we owe to the laborious monks.

It was in the midst of such various labors that his numerous works were composed, written and copied by himself alone, as he tells us; and in the list that he made of them before his death he names forty-five, of which he was the author. Among these books are discourses and commentaries on Holy Scripture, treatises on grammar, astronomy, the logic of Aristotle, music, geography, arithmetic, orthography, versification, the computum, (or the table of time for movable feasts), and natural philosophy. His Ecclesiastical History and Lives of the Fathers are like deep wells, not to be drawn dry of their carefully filtered facts, and are, and always must be, delightful in their unaffected way of telling their story of men and their times. St. Bede was also skilled in the Latin, Greek and Hebrew tongues.

The one special debt of gratitude, however, that we, English speaking people, owe to St. Bede, was earned by his labors to perfect the English language, by establishing grammatical rules. My young readers, perhaps, find their English grammar a very dull study, they may grow weary over its adverbs and adjectives, its singular and plural, and, above all, its verbs, and the agreement between them and the nouns and pronouns. They may never have thought much about the way in which this grammar has been classified and simplified until almost any child, after it has learned to read, can study a grammar, the rules of which may be taught us as soon as we talk at all. Still less have they thought how many great scholars have used their choicest learning to assist us in doing what seems, no doubt, to my young readers, the most natural thing in the world for any body to do—speak good English. These scholars were, almost without exception, monks, and, barbarous as any language might be, it could not resist the persevering efforts of our friends, the monks, to bring it into order and shapes of beauty. St. Bede is known to have preached to the people in English, and he translated, for the instruction of his flock, both the Psalter and the Four Gospels. To understand the labor necessary to accomplish all this, you must remember, that before their conversion to Christianity, the Anglo-Saxons—who are now so proud of their learning, and boast of it as if it had come to their race by natural inheritance—had no *written* compositions of any sort; their poetry, even, consisted of songs, and narratives, that were preserved solely in the memory of their bards, who made additions as their genius prompted them. This poetry was not written down until the time of King

Alfred in the ninth century, and then only very imperfectly. It was to bring this rude, but rich, language into a form capable of expressing every sentiment of the heart and soul of man, as we see it afterwards used by Shakespeare in his immortal plays and tragedies, that St. Bede used his knowledge of those already perfected languages, the Latin, and, especially the Greek, that most perfect of all the languages ever spoken or written by man. To St. Bede belongs the glory of having, first, applied himself to this noble task, and we find that his reason for so doing was worthy of a Christian scholar; for, writing, in 735, a long letter to his dearest friend, Egbert, archbishop of York, he urges him to appoint priests to the rural districts who would be earnest in teaching to the peasantry the doctrines and the practice of their religion, and, especially, to teach them to repeat the *Creed* and the *Our Father* in their native tongue, "which," he adds, "I have myself translated into English to assist those priests who are not familiar with the native tongue."

The respect felt by this great scholar for his native language even in its rude state, may be a lesson to many, even at this day, when we have such reason to love and honor it. Our love of country, and of our native tongue, is sometimes deeply hurt to see how eager people are to learn to speak many languages, while the charms of the rich and noble language they are allowed to claim as their own with all its treasures of history, the lives of its heroes, the ballads and romance of its youthful ages, the noble poetry of its later times, is quite overlooked. The greatest pains is taken to have mere children learn to speak French and German, while they are allowed to speak and write their own language very imperfectly; and are so ignorant of the principles on which it is founded as not to be able to distinguish between a glaring corruption of their mother tongue, or a base importation from another, and good English; and some are even so lost to self respect, as to prefer a very commonplace French phrase to a noble Anglo-Saxon one. It should be the pride of every child to speak, and write, his native tongue with absolute correctness, and, with as much elegance as circumstances will allow. Every child, therefore, born to speak the Anglo-Saxon, or English tongue, should feel a just pride and a lofty enthusiasm, measured only by his love of his country and of his race, in preserving all the richness, strength and harmony of his native language; and, to consider that the purity of that language is one of the tests of the civilization, and refinement, and also of the sterling excellence, of his nation. Whatever may be your reason for learning other languages well, remember there are ten-fold stronger and better reasons, for learning your own perfectly; and if you have never studied any language but your own, do not feel ashamed; only take the more pains to study that in such a manner as to honor it both by your spoken and your written word. A pure accent, perfectly grammatical expressions, and correct spelling, are accomplishments of which one has reason to be proud; while for the absence of these, no smattering of a dozen modern or ancient tongues can ever atone. Besides these very solid acquirements, all children, whether boys or girls, should, as they grow up, become acquainted with the works of the best authors in the English language. You should not be satisfied with reading every new novel, nor even with reading every new history, or poem, that is published, but you should go back to the old poets, to the old historians, who have been tried by generations and have been found very nearly perfect; and thus your taste and judgment will be formed upon the best models, and your ear so trained that it will be offended by any inaccuracy, or by any words that are against the spirit, and genius of our language. You will never, probably, speak French, German, Italian or Spanish, with the purity of a native of any one of those countries; but do not disgrace yourself by speaking English like a foreigner. A Parisian or a Florentine is proud of the purity of his accent. Emulate them, not by cultivating the Parisian or Florentine accent, but by the purity of your English accent and of your English diction. St. Bede would commend you, I am very certain, for such a patriotic and decorous emulation.

I have spoken of the list, written out by St. Bede himself, of his works. At the end of this list, is a prayer, which my young friends will read with tender interest, for it will give them a deep look into the sanctified heart and mind of St. Bede. "Oh, good

Jesus, who hast deigned to refresh my soul with the sweet streams of knowledge, grant to me that I may one day mount to Thee, who art the source of all wisdom, and remain forever in Thy divine presence."

Such was the modesty of this great man, that we are told by one who does not speak without knowledge of the subject, that if St. Bede had been left to his own will, his name and his learning would have been lost to us. But in 703, having been made priest, both his bishop and his abbot commanded him to write for the welfare of his countrymen. He obeyed, and for thirty years his pen was never idle. The great plan of writing an Ecclesiastical History of the Anglo-Saxons, was spoken of to him by the abbot of St. Augustine's in Canterbury, himself a disciple of St. Theodore and Adrian. All the English prelates approved of the plan, and were not slow in communicating to St. Bede all the information within their reach; and Pope Gregory III. allowed the records of the Holy See to be examined to aid St. Bede in his work. When finished it was received with applause by the public; succeeding generations preserved it as a memorial of the virtues of their ancestors; and Alfred the Great translated it into the Anglo-Saxon tongue, for the benefit of those who could not read it in the original Latin.

We must now come, however unwillingly, with St. Bede to that narrow gate through which all must pass, sooner or later, the learned and the unlearned, the faithful and the careless, the pious and the lukewarm. To us it is sad, even in imagination, to stand by the death-bed of this lovely Christian scholar; but we must believe, that, to St. Bede, it was a thought full of joy to find himself coming, nearer and nearer every day, to this narrow gate of death. What terrors could death have for one whose baptismal innocence had never been sullied by rude contact with a wicked world, and who, in the holy peace of a cloister, had kept himself unspotted even from the ambition that is said to be "the last infirmity of noble minds!" His character is thus given in the breviary lesson for his feast: "He was easily kindled, and moved to compunction by study, and whether reading or teaching often wept abundantly. And after study he always applied himself to prayer, well knowing that the knowledge of the Sacred Scriptures is to be gained rather by the grace of God than by our own efforts. He had many scholars, all of whom he inspired with extraordinary love of learning, and what is more, he infused into them the holy virtue of religion; he was most affable to the good, but terrible to the proud and negligent; sweet in countenance, with a musical voice, and an aspect at once cheerful and grave."

The translation of the Four Gospels was the work on which he was employed when the summons came for him to put aside all labors, however holy, and forever unite himself with God. We shall see how St. Bede spent the last days of his life, and this will help us to understand how sacred a thing learning is in the eyes of a saint.

The particulars which I shall copy for you are quoted, by all who have written about St. Bede, from a letter written by his pupil, Cuthbert, to a schoolfellow, Cuthwin, and this letter shows how much more touching is a simple narrative of facts than any studied eulogy. Little did the young man, Cuthbert, think, that this letter, written with a swelling heart and tearful eyes for his fellow-student, who loved St. Bede as he did himself, would find its way to the children of the nineteenth century, living in a country undreamed of by the holy and learned monks of Jarrow-on-the-Tyne. I shall quote it entire, that my readers may have a specimen of a letter written, by one young monk to another, in the eighth century, more than one thousand years ago.

"To his most beloved in God, and fellow-reader Cuthwin, Cuthbert, his fellow-pupil, wisheth health in God forever.

"I received with pleasure the present that you sent me, and perused with satisfaction the letter of your devout reverence. For it informed me of that which I most earnestly hoped for—that masses and holy prayers are diligently performed in your monastery for Beda, the beloved of God, the father and master of us both. I feel then the greater pleasure, on account of my love for him, to describe briefly, and to the best of my ability, in what manner he departed this life; the more so, as this is what you particularly request.

"About a fortnight before the feast of Easter, (April 17), he was reduced to a state of great debility with difficulty of breathing, but without much pain; and in that condition he lasted till the day of the Lord's Ascension, the seventh before the calends of June, (May 26). This time he passed cheerfully and joyfully, giving thanks to Almighty God both by day and night, or rather at all hours of the day and night. He continued to deliver lessons to us daily, spending the rest of his time in psalmody, and the night also in joy and thanksgiving, unless he were interrupted by a short sleep; and yet, even then, the moment he awoke he began again, and never ceased with outstretched hands to return thanks to God. I can declare with truth, that I never saw with my eyes, nor heard with my ears, of any man who was so unwearied in giving thanks to the living God.

"O truly happy man! He chanted the passage from the blessed Apostle Paul—'It is a dreadful thing to fall into the hands of the living God,' (Heb. x, 31), and several other passages from Holy Writ, warning us to throw off all torpor of soul in consideration of our last hour. And being conversant with Anglo-Saxon poetry, he repeated several passages, and composed the following lines in our tongue:

"'Before our forced departure no man is more wise than he needs to be; no man knows how much he ought to search, before leaving this world, what shall be the judgment of the soul for good or evil, after the day of death.'

"He also chanted the antiphons according to his and our custom. One of these is, 'O king of glory, Lord of hosts, who on this day didst ascend in triumph above all the heavens, leave us not orphans, but send upon us the spirit of truth, the promised of the Father. Alleluia.' When he came to the words, 'leave us not orphans,' he burst into tears and wept much; and after a while he resumed where he had broken off, and we, who heard him, wept with him. We wept and studied by turns; or rather wept all the time that we studied.

"Thus we passed in joy the fifty days till the festival of the Ascension, and he rejoiced greatly and gave thanks to God for the infirmities under which he suffered, often repeating 'God scourgeth every son whom He receiveth,' (Heb. xii, 6), with other passages of Scripture, and the saying of St. Ambrose, 'I have not lived so as to be ashamed to live among you, nor do I fear to die, for we have a gracious God.'

"During these days besides the lessons which he gave us, and the chant of the psalms, he undertook the composition of two memorable works, that is he translated into our language the Gospel of St. John as far as 'But what are these among so many?' etc., (John vi, 9), and made a collection of extracts from the notes of Isidore, the bishop, saying, 'I will not suffer my pupils to read falsehoods, and to labor without profit in that book, after my death.' But on the Tuesday before the Ascension, his difficulty of breathing began to distress him exceedingly, and a slight swelling appeared in his feet. He spent the whole day, and dictated to us with cheerfulness, saying occasionally, 'Lose no time. I know not how long I may last. Perhaps in a very short time my Maker may take me.' In fact, it seemed to us that he knew the time of his death. He lay awake the whole night praising God; and at dawn, on the Wednesday morning, ordered us to write quickly, which we did, till the hour of terce, (nine o'clock). At that hour we walked in procession with the relics, as the rubric for the day prescribed; but one of us remained to wait on him, and said to him, 'Dearest master, there still remains one chapter unwritten. Will it fatigue you if I ask more questions?' 'No,' said Beda, 'take your pen, and mend it, and write quickly.' This he did.

"At none, (three in the afternoon), he said to me, 'I have some valuables in my little chest—pepper, handkerchiefs, and incense. Run quickly and bring the priests of the monastery to me, that I may make to them such presents as God hath given to me. The rich of this world give gold and silver, and other things of value; I will give to my brethren what God hath given to me, and will give it with love and pleasure.' I shuddered, but did as he had bidden. He spoke to each one in his turn, reminding and entreating them to celebrate masses, and to pray diligently for him, which all readily promised to do.

"When they heard him say that they should see him no more in this world, all burst into tears; but their tears were tempered with joy, when he said, 'It is time that I return to Him who made me out of nothing. I have lived long, and kindly hath my merciful Judge forecast the course of my life for me. The time of my dissolution is at hand. I wish to be released and to be with Christ.'

"In this way he continued to speak cheerfully till sunset, when the forementioned youth said, 'Beloved master, there is still one sentence unwritten.' 'Then write quickly,' said Beda. In a few minutes the youth said, 'It is finished.' 'Thou hast spoken truly,' replied Beda, 'take my head between thy hands, for it is my delight to sit opposite to that holy place in which I used to pray; let me sit and invoke my Father.' Sitting thus on the pavement of his cell, and repeating, 'Glory be to the Father, and to the Son, and to the Holy Ghost,' as he finished the word 'Ghost,' he breathed his last, and took his departure for heaven. All who saw him die declare that they never beheld any man close his life in so devout and tranquil a frame of mind; for as long as the breath was in his body, he never ceased to repeat the *Gloria Patri*, with other religious expressions, nor to give praise with extended hands to the true and living God. Know, however, beloved brother, that I have much more to relate of him, but my want of skill in composition obliges me to be brief. I intend, however, at some future time to write more fully what I have seen with my eyes and heard with my ears."

Thus died St. Bede, a little after sunset, May 26th, of the year 735, on the eve of the Feast of our Lord's Ascension, celebrating that joyful festival, we may believe, among the heavenly hosts, and those saints made perfect, who, like St. Bede, never tire of the

Divine praises; their ever dilating knowledge of the perfections of the Deity exciting them, continually, to new songs of love and jubilation.

We hope many a Catholic schoolboy will take the holy Beda for his patron, invoking him when he feels his ardor for study, or his perseverance in the paths of learning, beginning to fail; and like St. Beda, inflaming anew the sacred fire by consecrating to God, and to His most sweet and gentle service, whatever of mind or heart has been bestowed upon him; not forgetting to say, Holy St. Bede pray for me, that like you I may live and die to the praise of the Father and of the Son and of the Holy Ghost. Amen!

St. Bede is spoken of in the Roman martyrology on the 26th of May. His Office, however, is celebrated in England on the 29th of October, on account of some translation of the relics, it may be. This last date makes him the patron of a dear boy who died, I believe, in a state of innocence that must have made him dear to the heart of St. Bede, and he certainly made St. Bede very dear to my own. I beg for this dear child, who was laid, long ago in his early grave, a "Rest in peace," from every one of my readers.

SAINT DUNSTAN.

MONG the illustrated books that were the delight of my childhood, was one containing a picture of St. Dunstan, archbishop of Canterbury and primate of the Church in England. He was represented as of most venerable aspect, and writing with a style, or ancient pen. An account of this great man's life was also given with the picture; and besides the praise given to his fervent piety, his profound learning, his prudence and holy wisdom, he was said to have been an illuminator, as well as an accomplished transcriber or copyist, of sacred books. The volume containing all this was not a Catholic one, merely a popular magazine for children, scattered all over New England. I have often wondered if the other children in the neighborhood liked this picture as well as I did; if they remembered it; and if it was to them, as to me, a point of attraction, around which gathered, in after years, noble traditions and generous sentiments.

St. Dunstan was a native of Glastonbury, "That holiest spot," it has been said, "in all England;" for there the faith was first planted by a person no less honorable than St. Joseph of Arimathea, that "rich man" and "noble counsellor," as he is called in the gospels, who assisted with his devout hands to take down the body of his Divine Lord from the cross, and, wrapping it in fine linen and the most costly spices, laid it in his own new tomb. Thirty years after he had earned, by this act of love, a place in the heart of every Christian, flying from the persecutions of his countrymen and taking with him, as his only treasure, a few drops of the Blood of his Redeemer, he landed on the western shore of England and found a peaceful asylum on an island surrounded by marshes. This island was called by the Britons, Avallona, or Isle-of-apples, because it abounded with apple-trees; and we are told that every year the island still blushes with the delicate bloom of its orchards. It is from the Britons themselves that we inherit the tradition of the landing of St. Joseph of Arimathea with his twelve companions; and of the drops of Precious Blood that he brought with him, preserved in the same chalice that was used by Jesus Christ at the Last Supper, when he instituted the Holy Eucharist. This tradition of the chalice and its sacred contents, was kept alive in those poems celebrating the virtues of the "Knights of the Round Table" in King Arthur's time, all of whom ardently desired to possess this holy relic, called the *Saint Graal*, or "Holy Cup." To the

Britons themselves, also, we trace back the lovely legend of the first miracle on British soil, performed by St. Joseph of Arimathea to save the souls of a few simple-minded savages, and thus laying deep in the national heart the seed of Christian faith which he had come to plant on that distant shore. Received with kindness by the Britons, he chose the first moment in which he saw them hesitating to believe what he was telling them of Christ and his religion, to confirm their faith by a miracle. Planting his pilgrim staff, cut from the same thorn tree of Palestine from which the Roman soldiers had gathered the thorns that crowned the head of Jesus in His sorrowful passion, into the unblessed, pagan soil, lo! the dry staff quickened at the prayer of this lover of souls, and sent forth leaf-buds into the cold December air; at sight of which the poor pagans fell at the feet of the messenger of the Prince of Peace, and were converted, listening with docility to the word he had come to preach to them. And not only did the thorn send out its tender leaf-buds, but it struck roots, strong and healthy roots, into the fresh British soil, blossoming, during fifteen hundred years, for the edification of the faithful, and is still to be seen by the pilgrim to the shrine of Glastonbury. Here, too, this same Joseph of Arimathea built a chapel out of the twisted and interlaced branches of the willow, and consecrated it to the Blessed Virgin; that Mother of Sorrows, to whose supernatural grief and supernatural fortitude he was an eye-witness, and which he must have carried in his memory, as a fountain of devotion, to his death.

Such was the beginning of the great abbey of Glastonbury; and tradition tells us that within its walls lies the dust of that spotless Christian knight, King Arthur; for, having been mortally wounded in one of those long battles between the Britons and their Saxon invaders which lasted three days and nights, he was carried to the good and faithful monks at Glastonbury, died with them, and was there secretly buried.

At Glastonbury, then, we might look for a saint; and it was in this old Christian town, sanctified by such precious memories, that St. Dunstan was born. The exact date of his birth does not seem to be known, but it was probably before 940, or in that tenth century, which has been called the darkest century of the Christian Church. Here, then, at Glastonbury, he was offered by his parents at the altar of Our Lady, and as soon as he could prattle was given over by them to the care of some Irish monks who settled in the deserted abbey, earning the bare necessaries of life by teaching the children of the neighborhood. Of these good monks he learned the doctrines of the Christian Church, and also the elements of sound scholarship. Centuries before the time of St. Dunstan there was a great school at Glastonbury. Students from Ireland and Scotland and France, as well as from England itself, came to Glastonbury to drink at its full fountain of learning. But Glastonbury had shared the fate of many other noble retreats for learning and piety during the invasions of the barbarians from the north of Europe; and what, in the time of Venerable Bede, as you have already seen in his life, was a centre of civilization and learning, being under the protection of a great religious community, was, at the time of St. Dunstan's birth, a melancholy home for a few monks, who showed their love for learning by teaching it to the young children around them. Most happy, however, were those "excellent masters of the sciences," those few monks at Glastonbury, for to them the providence of God committed the training of one of His noblest saints on the list of the British Isles. His extraordinary genius soon showed itself, and he outstripped his companions in every branch of study which had any interest for him. Thus accomplished in the learning of his age, and enjoying the advantages of his noble birth, he was taken to the court of the good king, Athelstan, by his uncle, Athelmus, archbishop of Canterbury. Athelstan, who was a lover of virtue and of learning, honored Dunstan with a regard above that which he gave to any other person at the court, which so excited the envy and jealousy of the ambitious courtiers that they did not hesitate to invent all sorts of malicious lies, charging Dunstan, even to the king, with the practice of sorcery; a foolish story founded upon his musical skill, by which he was said to bewitch the king; and they also accused him of a heathenish regard for the poetry of the old Saxon bards. After a short struggle to keep his high place at court against such enemies, he retired to the house of his relative, the bishop of Winchester. Here he had leisure to meditate upon the fleeting honors of a life in the world, and to lay out a holy plan for the future. The good providence of God did not forsake him under these misfortunes. His life had been one of singular devotion and purity, and although he was not willing to be driven from an honorable place near the king, to which his birth, his genius, and his learning gave him a just claim, he was far from any worldly habit of mind. While in these good dispositions a long and severe illness showed to him, as nothing else can, the nothingness of all earthly goods compared with heavenly ones; and on his recovery he offered himself to the bishop for the service of God. The habit of a monk in the order of priesthood was given to him, and he was sent to the very church in which he was baptized, and to the abbey where he had lived, as a child and a youth, with his old friends, the learned Irish monks of Glastonbury.

Before he left this school of religion and of letters, of science and of art, his skill in music, painting, engraving and working in metals, had won for him a wide-spread and just fame. Some of my readers may be surprised that a young man in the "Dark Ages," should have been encouraged to aspire to such a varied and noble culture, especially as he did not appear to have a vocation for a priestly or monastic life. We often hear people saying, that in those ages none but priests were allowed to be scholars; yet here is a young and elegant courtier coveting every accomplishment that could grace his rank at the present day. It was after he had learned, at the court of the good king, Athelstan, that "all is vanity" outside the service of God—which indeed none learn so well as those who have had enough of the pleasures and grandeurs of the world to know how hollow are all the appearances of such happiness, how far short of the desires of the human heart are all the contrivances of society for enjoyment—that Dunstan was ready to bring to the service of God, and to the service of the Church, the treasures he had received from his pious instructors. In the retirement of his monastic life at Glastonbury, we find him embellishing the Sacred Books with all the zeal, and patience, and industry, peculiar to the student-monk and ecclesiastic, of that period. He could, without wrong to any one, apply himself to the studies he so much loved, and to that art of the illuminator which was then devoted, in all its freshness and perfection, to the beautifying of the sacred text. The canonical books of the Bible, were, in those ages, laboriously written out by hand on vellum or parchment. The work of a copyist was considered a very responsible one, as the correctness of the sacred text was so easily impaired. To copy, perfectly, was a great merit; but, in addition to this, to design, and execute in the most brilliant and lasting colors, pictures illustrating the great events in the Old or New Testaments, was, in those ages of faith, looked upon as a labor receiving the choicest blessing of Heaven as its great, its only reward. At the present time, there is a general turning of amateur pencils and brushes to the imitating of these beautiful remains of the devotional art of the middle ages; but these feeble attempts have not the aim of those good monks to inspire them. Much as the nineteenth century boasts of its love for the Bible, it has never produced such decorations for the holy text as were executed, under the greatest inconveniences, by a set of men, whom the Reformation has branded as "ignorant of the Bible." Many of these mediæval artists were simple monks, peaceful, patient, laborious; but besides these, (who have not left an initial letter by which their works might be known, much less their names remembered), we find that more than one bishop of the Church was honored, as an illuminator of Scripture. In every convent were skillful masters of the pen and pencil, and a copy of the gospels is still preserved in the British Museum, with an inscription, telling us that it was "written by the hands of Eadfrith, that Bishop Ethelwald added the illuminations, whilst Bilfrid, the ankret, bound it in sheets of silver-gilt, and set it with jewels, and the priest Alfrid furnished the Anglo-Saxon Gloss" (*i. e.*, explanations or comments). As I have said, Dunstan, the profound scholar, the holy ecclesiastic, the companion of princes, the favorite of a good and learned king, had this praise added to the list of his many virtues, that he "*excelled* in illumination." In a manuscript in the Oxford Library there is a drawing from his hand, a figure of Jesus Christ appearing to Dunstan who is adoring at his feet. So enthusiastic was the regard entertained for these works of the devout illuminators, that, after death, the right hand which had wrought such glowing devices to illustrate the Word of God was often carefully embalmed.

But not in painting, alone, was Dunstan famous as an artist; he was also skilled in the working of precious metals for the sacred vessels, in designing embroideries for chasubles, and even in the casting of bells. In reading the delightful annals of that century —delightful in spite of many sorrowful irregularities, since faith was still recognized and still lived out by Christians in all parts of Europe,—we often come upon passages that tell us of the priestly gifts of exquisitely wrought gold and silver altar ornaments, sent by Dunstan as the work of his own hands to some missionary friend in a wild country. It is said, that of the four large bells that afterwards adorned the new abbey church at Abingdon, two were cast by the hands of the abbot, and two, yet larger ones, were the handiwork of St. Dunstan. It was one of his delights, also, to carve in wood, to mould figures in clay and wax, and to engrave. Mention is made of a vestment embroiderd by a royal lady, Ethelfreda, for which St. Dunstan made the design. Indeed the art of designing, as well as the labor of the artistic workman, was encouraged in those ages by priests and monks of all ranks, as it gave them the recreation which every one needs, and also saved them from the dangers of idleness.

In these peaceful and holy labors Dunstan passed his monastic life at Glastonbury, when the death of King Athelstan, and the coming to the throne of his brother Edmund, again drew him from his seclusion. Edmund's palace of Chedder was only nine miles from Glastonbury, and he often visited its old church with singular devotion. In this way he became acquainted with the sanctity of St. Dunstan, and, calling him back to the court, made him his chief counsellor, and gave him the territory of Glastonbury that he might be able to restore the abbey to its former splendor. Dunstan immediately collected a community, giving it the rule of St. Benedict; and, in doing this, he became the restorer of order, and the reviver of learning, in his native country.

Nothing could exceed the prudent zeal with which Dunstan brought back among the people the schools that had been destroyed by public calamities, and revived the seminaries for the education of priests in the new abbeys, springing up under his wise and vigorous government; and in these schools and seminaries some of the most famous ecclesiastics of that century received their education. St. Dunstan allowed the reading of the Latin poets, because, as he said, it polished the mind and improved the style; he also encouraged the study of Anglo-Saxon poetry, that his preachers might speak, eloquently, their native tongue. Science was not forgotten, and arithmetic, geometry, astronomy, and music were carefully cultivated by his pupils, while many of them excelled in the art of painting, so especially beloved by their master. In the time of good King Alfred, who mourned over the low state of knowledge in his age, monks were despised, and few but ignorant and rude persons could be persuaded to wear a cowl. St. Dunstan turned the tide, and Glastonbury could soon found other houses and other schools from the ranks of its own well taught scholars. Among these scholars was Ethelwold, whose name is found, so often and so pleasantly, on the same page with St. Dunstan's, that we never see one without expecting to see the other. Ethelwold, too, was the abbot whose bells chimed in so sweetly with the bells of St. Dunstan from the towers of the new abbey. One of the graces for which the writers of that age tell us he was distinguished, was a peculiar charm of manner that drew to him the hearts of the young. To any one who is devoting a lifetime to the instruction of youth, nothing can be more gratifying than the honor and love manifested towards their teachers by the young of those distant, and (as we are so apt to believe) rude, times.

King Edmund reigned but six years and a half, and his two sons, Edwy and Edgar, being too young to govern, his nephew Edred was called to the throne, and his veneration for St. Dunstan was even greater than the veneration of his uncle, Edmund. To Edred succeeded the unworthy Edwy, a profligate youth, who on the very day of his coronation insulted the noble guests at his table. It was the courageous reproof given to him on that day by his royal father's old counsellor and dear friend, St. Dunstan, which the wicked Edwy could never forgive. St. Dunstan was obliged to escape to Flanders, and the two abbeys of Glastonbury and Abingdon, governed by Dunstan, were broken up, and the monks scattered by the order of the king. But his exile only served to spread abroad the sweet odor of his sanctity. At the church of St. Peter's, at Ghent, a vestment is still shown that was worn by St. Dunstan. As to Edwy, his people soon threw off the hateful hand of the tyrant, and set upon the throne his brother Edgar, who immediately called home our saint and promoted him to the same post of confidence that he had filled under his father and his uncle. He was soon made bishop of Worcester; two years later he was made primate, and going to Rome to receive the Pallium,* was sent home to England as the Apostolic Legate.

He was now in a position to carry out all his noble plans for the reformation of abuses, and the establishment of schools and seminaries. Everywhere new monasteries were springing up; the old abbeys of Ely, Peterborough, Malmsbury and Thorney, rose out of their ruins; and such was the eagerness of the king and of his people, that more than forty abbeys were founded or restored while St. Dunstan was primate. Can you believe that we are talking about a saint in the "Dark Ages?"

Besides these grand and imposing works he revived

---

* See *Pallium* in the life of St. Agnes.

the parochial schools, required the priests to preach every Sunday to their flocks, and, in their schools, to teach their parish children grammar, the church-chant, and some useful trade. Do you think, my dear young readers, that these "Middle Age" children under the protection of the good primate, St. Dunstan, need much pity even from the children of the present day and in the United States?

It was during the life of St. Dunstan that the wishes of the good king, Alfred, or Alfred the Great as he is called, were really carried out, for in St. Dunstan's time, under his encouragement and that of his friend Ethelwold, everything was done to instruct the people in their own language. Besides translating several of the books of Scripture, Ælfric, one of Ethelwold's scholars, devoted to English literature, composed a Latin and English grammar, and other school-books, for the use of beginners. I cannot so much as name all the good works, to encourage learning and solid piety, performed, or inspired, by St. Dunstan. Good schools arose in every part of the kingdom, and the annals of Ramsey Abbey would interest my youngest reader, or—listener; for, many a little boy and girl who cannot yet read fast enough to read these pages for themselves, will, I hope, hear them read by some older child in the family. One pretty incident may touch the fancy of some good-hearted little rogue who is perhaps charged with all the mischief done in the house, and, sometimes is told that he is the naughtiest boy in the world and that every body despairs of him.

If such a little boy gets hold of this book let him read for his comfort about four little fellows in the school of Ramsey Abbey.

"Four little boys, named Oswald, Etheric, Ædnoth and Athelstan, had been placed in the school by St. Oswald (a dear friend of St. Dunstan's), all being sons of powerful Saxon *thanes*, or lords. They were received before they were seven years old, and were of innocent manners and beautiful countenances. At certain times they were suffered by their master to go and play outside the cloister walls. One day, being thus sent out by themselves, they ran to the great west tower, and laying hold of the bell-rope, rang with all their might, but so unskilfully that one of the bells was cracked by the unusual motion. The mischief becoming known, the culprits were threatened with a sound flogging; a threat which occasioned abundance of tears. At last, remembering the sentence they had so often heard read from the rule of St. Benedict, 'If any one shall lose or break anything, let him hasten without delay to accuse himself of it,' they ran to the abbot, and, weeping bitterly, told him all that had happened. The good abbot pitied their distress, and calling the brethren together who were disposed to treat the matter rather severely, he said to them, 'These little innocents have committed a fault, but with no evil intention; they ought, therefore, to be spared, and when they grow up to be men it will be easy for them to make good the damage they have done.' Then dismissing the monks, he secretly admonished the boys how to disarm their anger; and they, following his directions, entered the church with bare feet, and there made their vow; and when they grew up to manhood and were raised to wealth and honor, they remembered what they had promised, and bestowed great benefits on the Church."

No doubt my little friends have often been told not to conceal any mischief they may have done, however grave, or, however unintentional; but they may not have supposed that St. Benedict would provide for accidents in a rule for monasteries. I hope the knowing this, and the success of the four little boys in the old abbey ofRamsey in escaping a whipping by obeying this rule, will fix it so tightly in the memory of every child who hears about it, that none of you will ever fail to accuse yourselves of all your mischief, and bear, bravely, your punishment, if you cannot get rid of it, rather than be a skulking coward of a child, to grow up into a mean, cowardly man, or a deceitful, cowardly woman, ready to tell all sorts of lies in order to cover up a poor little mistake, as well as some great blunder. Own up to all your mistakes and blunders, but never be a coward and, almost of course, a liar. I shudder when I remember all the misery, injustice, and heart-break, that has come on families, neighborhoods, and countries, by some cowardly act to save one's self from deserved blame. One hardly knows whether most to pity or to despise the person who can allow another, innocent, person, to suffer for his sin or his blunder. Of one thing, however, I am certain; St. Benedict pitied and despised such conduct as much as we possibly can, or he would never have made that splendid rule, "*Make haste* to accuse yourself if you have lost or have broken anything." Remember this as long as you live, and act upon it, and you will not suffer in purgatory for some mean sin of concealment, that perhaps seemed small, but which drew after it such consequences as make death-beds hard. Be good, courageous, noble-hearted Christian boys and girls, if you expect to look our dear Lord full in the face at your private, individual judgment; and though you may be obliged to stay awhile in purgatory, you will remember, all through its great pains, the dear, dear look in the eyes of your kind Judge, who hated lies and told who was the father of them.

You have, no doubt, conceived a high regard for King Edgar, under whose powerful protection St. Dunstan performed such prodigies of goodness and wisdom. I must now tell you of a great misfortune that befell Edgar. You may fancy that I shall tell you that an army of barbarians invaded his kingdom; or that some one of his household was treacherous; or that he lost his children. Any, or all, of these dreadful misfortunes might have come upon Edgar and it would not have been so terrible as this one—for he was so unfortunate as to fall into a terrible sin. I say, he was so unfortunate; because we cannot suppose that Edgar intended to commit such a crime, until his passions had blinded him to its enormity. In those early days of Christian civilization there were fewer social restraints upon the untamed passions of men, and especially of kings, than at present, when the laws of the land and of society have all been modeled, for many centuries, on the principles of Christian morality. Therefore the Christians of those days, and especially the kings, were more in danger of surprises, and were more exposed to falling into scandalous sins. King Edgar, then, as I have said, was surprised by a great temptation and he yielded to it. St. Dunstan immediately sought him out, and, with all the boldness of the prophet Nathan before King David, he remonstrated with him on his sin. The king, struck with remorse, begged, with many tears, that a suitable penance might be laid upon him, and St. Dunstan gave him a penance for seven years. During this time he was never to wear his crown, was to fast twice every week, and give large alms. He was also bound to build an extensive nunnery, in which Christian virgins might be consecrated to the service of God. These conditions the king faithfully kept, and founded a rich convent for nuns at Shaftsbury. When the seven years of his penance were over, St. Dunstan, in a public assembly of the lords and prelates, set the crown again upon his head, and thus gave, to the entire kingdom, an example against sin in high places.

We know that many persons, in this age of the world, would prefer to have a wicked king or ruler go on committing wickedness, to allowing the priests and bishops of the Church to have so great an influence over him. But in England at that time all were glad that there was a spiritual power respected even by kings, and we, certainly, need not wish that Edgar had despised St. Dunstan or his counsels.

Notwithstanding the great labors connected with such a life as that of the holy archbishop of Canterbury, we read that he frequently visited the churches in all parts of the kingdom. Those who live in large cities, surrounded by the luxuries of religion, often forget the privations and irregularities suffered by those who live in some far off corner of a diocese or province; and also forget the pleasure felt by the pastors and inhabitants, of these lonely districts, when they find themselves, and their interests, affectionately remembered by their superiors. It puts new heart and life into their labors, and they meet with courage, after such a visit, what before overwhelmed them. On these pastoral visits St. Dunstan preached often and with great eloquence; and few were so hardened as to resist his appeals. He employed all his revenues for the relief of the poor, and no heart in all England was more tender towards the suffering than that of its great primate. But neither the care of the churches, the monasteries, the schools, nor the attendance upon the king, nor even the necessities of the poor, ever made him neglect his prayers and meditations; and after the occupations of his crowded day were over, he watched late into the night in communion with God. Glastonbury was his dearest solitude, and thither he would often retire from the world to give himself up to heavenly contemplation. When at Canterbury it was his custom, even in the coldest weather, to visit the church of St. Austin (or St. Augustine, apostle of England), outside the walls, and that of the Blessed Virgin adjoining it.

We must now see how this good man died. 'In 988 St. Dunstan had grown very feeble, and the feast of the Ascension in that year was the last day on which his voice was heard in the solemnities of his cathedral. On that day, after the reading of the gospel, he walked in state from the vestry to the pulpit, and preached with surpassing energy on the Incarnation of Jesus Christ, the redemption of man and the bliss of heaven. He then went on with the mass until the end of the *Pater Noster* when he again turned to his people, exhorting them to follow their head and leader to the realms of happiness, and pronounced over them the episcopal benediction. After the kiss of peace he addressed them a third time, as if his heart yearned towards them, and begged them to remember him when he was gone; for he felt that his hour of death was very near, and that he should see them no more in this world. The tears of the clergy and of the people proved their affection for this venerable saint, to whom they all owed so much. He concluded the mass and had sufficient strength to take his usual place at the table in the hall for the festal banquet. After dinner he returned to the church, pointed out the spot in which he was to be buried, and then withdrew to his chamber, where he spent that day and the next in acts of devotion, and in advising and consoling those who visited him. On the Saturday after the Ascension, mass was celebrated in his room by his own order, and as soon as he had received the communion he burst into the following prayer: "Glory be to thee, Almighty Father, that hast given the bread of life from heaven to those who fear thee; that we may be mindful of thy wonderful mercy to man in the Incarnation of thine only-begotten Son, born of the Virgin. To thee Holy Father, for that when we were not thou didst give to us a being, and when we were sinners didst grant to us a Redeemer, we give due thanks through the same thy Son, our Lord and God, who, with thee and the Holy Ghost, maketh all things, governeth all things, and liveth through ages and ages, without end." Soon after this, on the 19th of May, the day on which the Church still honors him in her office, he calmly expired, it being the sixty-fourth, or the sixty-fifth, year of his age, and the twenty-seventh of his life as archbishop.' He was buried in his own cathedral, in the place he had appointed, though it is probable that some part of his relics were taken to his beloved Glastonbury.

In St. Dunstan we see the model of a monk, priest, bishop. The goods of this world, which he always possessed in abundance, were used for the highest and noblest interests of the Church, of God, and of the laity who make up so large a part of that Church. Our Lord said, "He that would be greatest among you let him be the servant of all;" and it was by his right royal service towards the necessities of the Church and the people, that St. Dunstan became "a great priest, who in his day served God, and none was found like to him who kept the law of the Most High."

Let us then invoke, with deep devotion, the revered name of that saint whose holy life we have been following, saying with humility, "Pray for us, holy St. Dunstan, that we may be made worthy of the promises of Christ;" that we too may be faithful servants in our day and generation and win, by that service, the "Well done, good and faithful servant." Then, my dear children, whether, as the years go on, you belong to the flocks, or to the pastors, or to the bishops, of the Church of God, whatever afflictions or disappointments may await you here, you may be sure of a crown of glory and the everlasting peace of the faithful servants of God, and of His Church.

THE BELLS OF ABINGDON.

Ting—ting—yet never a tinkle;
  Ring—ring—yet never a sound
Stirs the beds of periwinkle,
  Stirs the ivy climbing round
The belfry-tower of well-hewn stone,
Where, ages ago, at Abingdon,

Saint Dunstan's bells, with Saint Ethelwold's hung;
Hung and swung;
Swung and rung;
Rung,
Each with its marvellous choral tongue,
Matins and Lauds, and the hour of Prime,
Terce, Sext, and None, till the Vesper hymn
Was heard from the monks in their stalls so dim;
Then lent their chime
To the solemn chorus of Compline time.
And blessed was he, or yeoman or lord,
Who, with stout bow armed or with goodly sword,
Heard, at the hour,
Those wonderful bells of sweetness and power;
And, crossing himself with the sign of peace,
Had his Pater and Ave said at their cease.

Ting—ting—yet never a tinkle;
Ring—ring—yet never a sound
Stirs the beds of periwinkle,
Stirs the ivy creeping round,
Creeping, creeping, over the ground,
As if to hide
From the eye of man his own rapine and pride.
Matins, and Lauds, and the hour of Prime;
Terce, Sext, None, Vespers, and Compline time,
Unrung,
Unsung;
The bells and the friars
Alike in their graves; and the tangled briers

Bud in May, blush with blossoms in June,
Where the bells, that once were all in tune,
Moulder beneath the ivy vines;
Only, as summer day declines,
The peasants hear,
With pious fear,
Ting—ting—yet never a tinkle,
Ring—ring—yet never a sound,
Where, in their beds of periwinkle,
And ivy close to the ground,
Saint Dunstan's bells, with Saint Ethelwold's, keep
A silent tongue while the good monks sleep.

SAINT ANTHONY.

ST. ANTHONY OF PADUA.

MANY, I hope most, of my little readers have heard of St. Anthony of Padua. I say, I hope; for he was not only a very lovely, but a very powerful saint; by which I mean that he has obtained many great blessings for those who have been faithful to ask his prayers.

St. Anthony was born at Lisbon, Portugal, in the year 1195. He became a monk of the Order of Friars Minor, founded by St. Francis of Assisi, in Padua, Italy, and died near that city, June 13, 1231. In this city of Padua, where his relics are still kept with great care, and piously honored, were wrought the most splendid miracles of St. Anthony after his death. A few of these I have selected for this sketch, but by far the greater number must be left for you to gather, with delight, from the Lives of the Saints by Alban Butler, or from still more charming and complete biographies of this dear saint of happy Padua.

Happy Padua! Have you ever thought, dear children, how happy that city must be, in which such miracles are worked as the curing of sick people whom no physician can help, the recovery of lame, blind and paralyzed persons, and, what is far more wonderful, the curing of great sinners; for sin is the worst of all diseases, the saddest of all sicknesses.

But what I have at heart to-day in writing about St. Anthony, is this; to let you know that St. Anthony is not only the benefactor of Padua, but of all who ask him for his prayers faithfully and affectionately. Remember, *affectionately*. I am quite sure that St. Anthony likes to have us ask him for favors in this way, and I have a notion that most of the saints feel on this point like St. Anthony. It is not courteous for us to say, "Saint So-and-so, get us this, or that, or the other, blessing we want," like a boor, or an ill-natured person, who wishes us to do something for him. The saints really wish to have us love them, not for their own satisfaction, but because they, being the friends of God, sincerely love Him, and desire to see Him loved by others; and if we love the friends of God we shall soon come to loving God Himself, which is exactly what the saints want. It is because love, love for God, and for His friends, is the disposition which brings with it peculiar and great blessings, that St. Anthony, and all the saints I have ever heard of, like to have us ask them to pray for us, and get blessings and mercies, and saving graces for us, as we would ask our dear friends to help us or please us; to say "*Dear* St. Anthony," or "Dear St. Agnes," or "Dear St. Elizabeth," or "Dear St. Aloysius;" and, if we have a medal or a picture of the saint, to kiss it with affectionate veneration. At such signs of love on our part, they are very likely to be moved to great tenderness towards us, and we are pretty sure to get what we ask for.

I believe, little children, that I have given you a very good rule as to the spirit, and manner, in which you are to ask favors of the saints, those kind and powerful friends of God, and of us poor "sinners in this valley of tears."

I will now give you an example, not very far from home, of the success of this way of asking for favors through the prayers of the saints.

More than fifteen years ago, (it does not seem so long ago, so fresh is all I remember of her in my mind,) there lived, in the city of Philadelphia, a little girl, hardly ten years old. I might tell you of the many charming qualities of my little friend, her amiability, her winning ways, her gifts of mind and heart, but, most of all, her tender, practical piety. She had learned from the saints, and from the saint who was her confessor, a bishop and a great theologian, how to love God; and in return for this help which they had given her, she dearly loved her friends, the saints of God. Among these friends her special friend was, as she used to call him, "*Dear* St. Anthony of Padua," that old, old saint, who lived so long ago as 1195. What could such an old saint care about our little girl, only ten years old, living, not in Padua, but in the United States, and in that Quaker city, Philadelphia? Yet little Mary not only loved St. Anthony, but St. Anthony dearly loved little Mary, as was proved by the ready way he had of getting her everything she asked for.

When I say, everything, you must remember that our little Mary was a child who asked only for such things as God would wish her, or her friends, to have, and asked for them only for the supernatural reason of bringing, in the end, glory to God and to His saints. Therefore, when her little brother said to her, "Now, Mary, pray to St. Anthony to find the penny I have lost," she reproved him, saying, "Your penny is not necessary for you, and perhaps you will be better without it."

One blessing little Mary was always begging of St. Anthony, which was, to find lost souls, the souls of sinful or of unbelieving people, and especially of Catholics who believed but did not practice their religion. Many such souls were saved by the prayers of St. Anthony, urged on by the prayers of little Mary.

Now comes a wonderful part of this devotion practiced by our little friend. She only lived to one month of thirteen years, dying in the odor of youthful sanctity, her holy confessor declaring, that he "believed she passed straight from earth to the immediate presence of God," the object of her love. To her parents and friends she left her devotion to St. Anthony; and the Novena of Nine Tuesdays to this saint, and a medal in his honor, have, through them, come into general use. Favors and blessings beyond counting have been given, in answer to the faithful practice of this Novena, to those who ask St. Anthony to find, not only lost watches, lost health, lost good of all sorts, but, above all, lost souls. Bishops, priests, monks, and nuns, have caught a new love for St. Anthony, and a fresh confidence in the intercession of saints, from the example of this little girl, to whom St. Anthony has shown so many favors even since her death.

Remember, my dear children. that the great saints you read of are as powerful to-day as they were ages ago; and that if you are not oftener helped by their prayers, it is because you forget to ask for them, or ask for them but coldly, and with but little faith.

One more American story of St. Anthony. The late Bishop Neumann, of Philadelphia, a most holy man, some years before his death, lost, in an unaccountable way, not only a very choice collection of theological books, but a great number of precious relics. The good prelate was very much grieved, especially for the loss of the relics, and immediately began a Novena to St. Anthony of Padua. He also promised, that, if these treasures were found, he would have a picture painted in honor of St. Anthony. Hardly were the Nine Tuesdays of the Novena over, when the books and relics were restored to him as mysteriously as they had disappeared. The bishop, who knew how to be grateful for favors, as well as how to ask for them, kept, to the end of his life, an affectionate devotion to St. Anthony, and I have, still, one of the pictures of our saint which he brought, himself, from Padua. I have also a medal of St. Anthony, brought from Padua by a Protestant lady, who visited that city almost solely out of respect to St. Anthony; also, a Jerusalem medal of St. Anthony, the head of the saint being rudely carved in the soft, pearl-tinted gypsum of the Holy Land.

Bishop Neumann and little Mary learned the lessons of faith on different continents, but the devotion was as earnest and sincere in one as in the other. The learned bishop, learned, not only in theology but in science, was, like the little girl, simple-hearted enough to believe in the prayers of our saint.

You may like to know how St. Anthony, who was born in Portugal and lived there until he was more than twenty, should have spent the most wonderful years of his life in Italy. Prince Pedro, of Portugal, brought over from Morocco the relics of five Franciscans who had found a martyr's crown in that barbarous country, which so touched the heart of our saint, that he wished only to be a martyr. Very soon after, some Franciscan friars came to the convent where he was, to beg an alms. He told these poor friars what was his holy ambition, and they encouraged him to join their Order, which was more severe than the one he was then in. After a long time his prior consented to this change, and he took the poor habit of St. Francis, with the cord, and had leave given him to go to Africa to preach the Gospel to the Moors, where it might be, he would get his dear wish—to die a martyr. But sickness obliged him to return to Spain, and on his way back contrary winds drove him to Messina, on the Island of Sicily, where he heard that St. Francis was at Assisi. Weak and sick as he was, he could not resist his desire to see this living saint, the founder of his chosen Order. When he had once seen St. Francis he wished to be always near him, and thus his sanctity and learning became known to St. Francis, who appointed him to the study, and afterwards to the teaching, of theology. The wisdom of St. Francis was acknowledged by every one who ever listened to the preaching of St. Anthony, for he was eloquent, not only according to the eloquence of this world and the judgment of men, but according to that other and higher sense, in which eloquence draws sinners from the love of perishable good and vanities, to the love of eternal good; it was in this sense, as well as in a worldly one, that St. Anthony was called, by all the men of his generation, a most eloquent preacher.

Many of St. Anthony's sermons were illustrated by images drawn from the beautiful world around him; for, like St. Francis, he was a man of tender heart, that overflowed with love even for inanimate things, since they were made by the finger of God Himself. Our Blessed Saviour stopped in one of His sermons to praise the "lilies of the field," and we read that St. Mary Magdalene of Pazzi was rapt to an ecstacy by the beauty of a flower. St. Anthony not only loved these delicate beauties of nature, but he loved animals, especially those animals common among men. To this day the domestic animals in Italy are blessed, in honor of St. Anthony. The whiteness and the gentleness of the swans, the kindness of those strange birds, the storks, to each other, roused his admiration, and the very fishes drew him to the shores and river banks by his love for them. One day, when he had been preaching to the people of the city of Rimini about repentance and a new life, they stopped their ears and would not hear him; which, St. Anthony seeing, he went to the sea-shore, and stretching forth his hand, he said, "Hear me, ye fishes, for those unbelievers will not listen;" and an infinite number of fishes, both great and small, lifted their heads above the water and listened to the sermon of the saint in praise of their Creator. There is no such simplicity as the simplicity of the saints, and none prize, as the saints prize, the least thing made by the hand of God. I have often seen pretty and modest bunches of fresh and fragrant flowers from the garden, or the fields, or even green-houses, taken away from the altars, or put one side as hardly worthy of a place there, and artificial flowers put in their stead; as if any mortal hand, however skillful, could equal the lovely creations of God's own fingers! The saints understand this difference between the poor imitations of men, and the wonderful works of the Creator, and they would choose, for His altars, the humblest blossom of the field made by Him, to the most cunningly manufactured flower of paper, or muslin, or even wax. Its perfume, they know, will go up to its Creator like sweet incense, and the devout admiration of His beautiful handiwork is, in itself, an act of worship. Therefore, for your own little altars choose the meekest spring violet of the meadows, the wild rose and fragrant clover-tufts of summer, the many-hued asters and golden-rod of the hedges in autumn, instead of the costliest artificial flowers you can ever buy; because these little flowers, although so modest, are the works of God, and are the most worthy of a place on His altars. And, if you are ever allowed the great and sacred privilege of adorning the altars in the church, do not let your first thought be, how the altars will look to the people in the pews; but how the flowers, and the candles, and the garlands, will express your adoration for the Blessed Sacrament, and your veneration for the Blessed Virgin, for St. Joseph, or for the saint in whose honor the altar was raised. Let this be your *first* thought, and then you will be quite sure to put your choicest natural flowers about the Tabernacle; or, at the Benediction, near the Remonstrance; and, on the side altars, you will put a sweet nosegay at the feet of Our Lady, or of St. Joseph, in place of a bunch of staring, scentless, artificial roses; and instead of a heavy garland of muslin buds and leaves, a vine of living ivy will wander gracefully among the delicate carving of the altar niches, beautifying everything, hiding nothing. Do not be afraid of, sometimes, spending a little more money than people who like artificial flowers will approve of; for, before the year ends, they will spend more money at the milliner's than you will at the gardener's or the florist's; and if you really love the altar, you will raise some plants for it yourself, so that on great feast-days you can lend them to the altar; or, when a pretty plant blooms out, you can place it on the altar for some pious intention.

St. Anthony died at the early age of thiry-six, after ten years of holy labor in the Order of St. Francis. He died while reciting his favorite hymn to the Blessed Virgin,—"O gloriosa Domina," which, with the Breviary Hymns to St. Anthony and the collects, makes up the Nine Tuesdays Novena.

It is said that the children, on the first news of the death of Anthony, ran through the streets of Padua, crying, "The saint is dead, the saint is dead!" by which we can see how much he was beloved by children in his life time. No wonder, then, that little Mary loved him so well.

So many were the proofs of his sanctity that within a year after his death he was canonized by Pope Gregory IX, and the grateful people of Padua said a church should be built in his honor by the city. The great Niccola Pisano planned and began this church in 1237; but it was not finished for two hundred years, and we are told that "in all Italy there is not a church more rich in works of ancient and modern art than this one of St. Anthony."

Although I have left you to read for yourselves many of the wonders concerning St. Anthony, I have two narratives which have been selected for these pages by the parents of little Mary, and translated by her sister, from the life of St. Anthony by Azevedo, a Jesuit. The first is the account given by him of the miraculous cure of the Infanta, or the daughter of of the Queen of Portugal.

"The Infanta was already in a dying condition, but the Queen, her mother, in the midst of her distress did not cease recommending her to St. Anthony; and when she heard the physicians declare there was no longer any hope, she began to expostulate with the saint, in whom she still confided with as lively a faith as before: "Is it possible," she cried, "that you are so full of kindness to all that have a devotion to you, in every other part of the world, and yet can show yourself so cruel to your own country alone? Do you keep your ears always open to strangers, and do you mean to close them to us, who are your own people? No, no, it cannot be. When, upon the day of your canonization, you struck the bells of Lisbon with an invisible hand, and made them all ring at once, was it not solely for the purpose of inviting *us* in particular to have recourse to you, no longer indeed a living subject of this realm upon earth, but a protector in the heavens as full of love as of power?" Such earnest appeals the good Queen kept continually repeating, more with the heart, to be sure, than with the lips. But at a moment, when, for a short space, the mother had torn herself away from the bedside to give freer course to her tears, the saint appeared to the Infanta, in a halo of light, and asked her: "Dost thou know me?" She raised her eyes and recognized her deliverer; and, with transports of joy, seized with her hand, and kissed with veneration, the cord of St. Francis, which he wore. Whereupon the saint continued: "God sends me to console thee, and to offer thee the choice, which He gives thee to make and me to grant, either to die now and come with me instantly to Paradise, or to live for the consolation of thy father and mother and be instantly cured." The child, either from inconsiderateness, or because she could think of nothing but comforting her disconsolate mother, made her choice to live; and the saint added: "Well, then, rise from thy bed, for thou art already cured." And so it was. She immediately called out aloud for her mother: "My Saint has cured me: look at him, for I am holding him by the cord of his habit." The Queen ran to her daughter; she did not see the saint, because he had already disappeared, but she found that her daughter, so full of joy at having seen St. Anthony, had really been perfectly cured; and she published abroad the grace thus received in every direction."

The second narrative explains the picture of St. Anthony which accompanies this sketch of his life, and I shall give it to you as it has been sent to me, only leaving out what is not necessary for understanding the miracle, and the picture.

"The Order of Friars Minor, at that time, had no house of their own in Padua, and the convent of Arcella, a mile from the city, was an inconvenient residence for our saint. There were many who would have given him a lodging and who would have entreated him to make use of their own. This privilege, however, fell to the lot of a pious burgher, who set apart for the saint a chamber, quite by itself, in which he could abandon himself to his pious exercises without being in any way disturbed. This burgher, Count Tiso, having become the devoted personal friend of Antony, conceived also a profound veneration for his incomparable sanctity. He took careful note of whatever act or word of his holy guest he saw or heard; and he often watched at the door of the chamber, when Anthony had withdrawn to it to pray. One day Count Tiso, having seen some extraordinary rays of light stream forth from the chamber, ran to the door and saw the saint holding in his arms a pretty child, and the child returning his embrace with tender caresses. Tiso stood mute with wonder, and began to reason within himself, by whose agency and in what manner that unknown child had been brought into the chamber, and how the chamber could have come to shine with a light so extraordinary. The wonder grew to be still greater when he observed with what inexpressible majesty the tender caresses of the child were accompanied, and with what sweet ravishment Antony was carried away, as in an ecstacy; from which he finally concluded that the thing was from God, and that it was Jesus Christ who had made himself visible to our saint, in the likeness of a child, in order to refresh and console him with heavenly delights, for the labors and fatigues which he was enduring for His glory. While the count was lost in wondering observation of the heavenly sight, the child disappeared. Presently, Antony roused himself from his ecstacy, and going forth from the chamber, came upon his friend as he stood, and gave him to understand, that he was already aware of his having been a witness of the vision, with the earnest entreaty that he would tell it to no one. So the count promised, and did, (in fact) *keep* his promise, so long as the saint was alive; but after the servant of God had died, the count published the fact, in order to give due honor to his friend; and, as often as he was enquired of about it, he repeated the story with such an abundance of tears, as bore witness to the effect which the vision had wrought upon him.

"Such is the way in which this most wonderful occurrence is related in all the ancient histories of our saint's life, with the addition, however, of certain other particulars, which are in the highest degree worthy of belief and of repetition. One is, that the pious, unseen observer of the vision was made sure that the child was Jesus, by a mass of light which was sent forth by its Divine body, but which, while it sent consolation to his heart, did not dazzle his sight. Another is, that the Child himself revealed to his beloved-one who it was, that was watching him, and pointed towards the aperture through which the sight was taken; and that the saint made no movement towards his friend, in order not to deprive him of this celestial consolation until the vision should have ceased. The *third* is, that the Holy Child appeared upon a book—a circumstance which became so celebrated and characteristic, that the saint began at once to be represented in pictures with the Child standing on his Breviary. The earliest authors observe that these circumstances were never called in question, such regard was had to the character of the burgher, who was noted in those times for probity, for veracity, and for the abundant tears of tenderness and devotion, with which he was accustomed to relate them."

The picture of St. Anthony will seem still more beautiful to you, I hope, after reading this account of the miraculous vision which it commemorates. Murillo, the great Spanish master, painted this charming subject nine times, and one of these pictures is still in the cathedral at Seville. The lilies, which you see in the hand of St. Anthony, belong to him by the common consent of all the artists who have painted him.

Remember that the Feast of St. Anthony of Padua, who was so beloved by little Mary of Philadelphia, as well as by the young princess of Portugal, is on the 13th of June. On that day let your prayers obtain his aid, not only for the recovery of lost treasures, and the precious things of this world, health or the use of maimed limbs, but the infinitely precious treasures of innocence, piety, holy fervor and sincere contrition, for those who may have lost them, either through carelessness or misfortune. By doing this you will honor St. Anthony, and, in proportion to your love for him and confidence in him, will be his love for you, my dear little reader.

SAINT ALOYSIUS.

F all the graces that our Blessed Lord has given to His saints as marks of His peculiar regard, none has ever moved even the worldly, and those who have grown old in sin, to envy and to a secret loathing of their unworthy lives, so much as the grace of youthful sanctity. It has all the endearing loveliness, all the chaste fragrance, of early spring flowers; of those violets and anemonies, and tiny, four-petaled, azure blossoms we call Innocence, that besprinkle the low hillsides and meadows in the month of May. God has so many endearing ways of drawing our hearts that the only wonder is, why all youths are not good, and all maidens are not holy; and the wonder seems still greater, when we read the life of such a saint as St. Aloysius (or Lewis) Gonzaga.

You have heard of boys, perhaps you have seen them, perhaps you have been in the same class with them at school, or they may have been among the boys of your set out of school, who seemed proud of being irreligious, undevout, and even of being boldly profane. How must such unhappy children stand abashed before the life-long contrition of St. Aloysius, who, having repeated, without knowing their meaning, some profane words that had been used before him, never forgave himself, and continued to shed tears of pious sorrow for a fault for which he was not accountable!

There are children, sad to say, there are men and women, who, because they may have wealth or a high position in society, consider themselves above the practices of devotion. If they go to mass on Sundays, and perform in a decent manner the duties that all Catholics must perform, if they hope to be saved, they are contented. They smile at the devotion of those around them, as if such piety was only practiced by the poor, the uneducated, or the weak-minded. They care more for the respect of their miserable, dying fellow-mortals, than for the smile of God or the everlasting joys of Heaven. How contemptible, how short-sighted, is this judgment, compared with the angelic wisdom of Aloysius, who, born to honors and grandeur, the favorite companion of a young prince, found his highest happiness in speaking to God in prayer, and who obtained, after the most affectionate entreaties, the consent of his father, the Marquis of Castiglione, to give up his titles and riches to his younger brother, Ralph, while he entered, as a novice, the Society of Jesus.

If you have no such sacrifices to make, at least offer

the little you have to give to your Maker, your Redeemer; and, instead of fancying that you honor your Church by attending coldly on her beautiful rites, esteem it your highest honor, your noblest privilege, to practice as many of her devotions as your circumstances allow; and, above all, believe that the best proof you can give of your spotless honor, as Christian knights, is to present, from your earliest years, the fealty due from us all to the King of kings, the Lord of lords. This is the true knighthood, the only true nobility of Christendom; and its glorious ranks have been, and are still, filled from every class and position of life—slaves, beggars, servants, artisans, broad landholders, successful military leaders, the learned of all professions, civil rulers, and crowned potentates. The present generation may not always know who are its real heroes; the Church and the ages give a sure verdict.

The virtues most dear to the heart of Aloysius were humility and obedience. His tender humility was the guard of his youthful purity, which he prized, above all the desire of knowledge natural to his age, all the delight in art, all the pleasures of social intercourse. To preserve this, he was ready to be blind to all that youth admires, to keep a guard over his ears, his every sense. Beautiful innocence, which made him a fit companion for angels, and won for him a speedy entrance into their blissful society!

His devotion to our Blessed Lady was inspired by his love for his Divine Master. With Jesus he loved to converse before all others; and to the Mother of Jesus he rendered that affection, and veneration, which the love of Jesus must always kindle; for who can know and love Jesus, and not wish to know, to love, and be loved in return by, His Mother?

Aloysius brought on his death-sickness by attending upon the victims of a fearful epidemic in Rome; for, although he recovered from the epidemic, he never regained his strength. Permitted by God to have a fore-knowledge of his death, he received with joy, on the octave of Corpus Christi, the last sacraments, and entered, in a few hours, on the eternal vision of Him, whom he had so often received under the veil of the Blessed Sacrament with ecstacies of pious joy. He expired at midnight, between the 20th and 21st of June, 1591, being a little more than twenty-three years of age.

Among the beautiful groves of an Institution devoted to the education of youth, are several small chapels, placed there with the wisely directed intention of arousing and keeping alive those religious affections that are so easily discovered in the young, and only need to be cultivated to become fruitful in all manly virtues. In these groves one is led along walks named after the incidents that marked the passion of our Redeemer, to the foot of a tall cross, and then down by a winding path to a grotto, which is a copy of the Holy Sepulchre; not as it is seen at the present day, but as it must have been when the holy women and the disciples visited it on the first Easter morning, more than eighteen hundred years ago. Inside the chapel one sees the reed which this King of kings carried as a sceptre in His humiliation, the sponge soaked in myrrh and vinegar that was laid to His parched lips during those three hours of agony, the gross, cruel nail that entered His hands and His feet, and the crown of sharp thorns that bound His temples and sent its anguish through His brain*—everything in this narrow grotto speaks of His sorrowful passion and cruel death; now, indeed, forever past, yet forever present to the faithful hearts that try to make Him some reparation for all His woes.

It was a lovely summer morning when I took this walk through the winding paths, in company with a Sister of the Holy Cross, whose *compassion*ate hand had eased the pain of many a wounded soldier, had smoothed his dying pillow, and, better still, had prepared him for his great change. The sister turning into a by-path, we found ourselves in a dense part of the wood, and at the entrance of one of the plainest of the chapels. The door stood open, but, to preserve its privacy a curtain of purple cambric fell before it. The sister held it softly aside, and we kneeled down in a place of wonderful, tender solemnity. I had no thought, at first, as to the means by which this effect was produced; the impulse was to yield to it without a question. Everything, even to the altar and its

*Not the same sponge, reed, crown of thorns or gross nail, but similar to them, to bring back to us the reality of His sufferings. The nail, however, is exactly after the size and shape of the one found, by the Empress Helena, with the *True Cross.*

decorations, was plain almost to poverty; but from above the altar came a soft stream of purple light, and amid the violet-tinted, misty radiance, like a vision, white as moonlight, was the image of our Blessed Lady! I did not realize until we were quite outside the chapel, that this was the only light admitted. Then there came over me another recollection—I had seen, just outside the altar-rail on the left, a mere bit of a shrine, hung, as it were, on the wall, and on it a statue of my favorite, St. Aloysius. This, then, was the Chapel of St. Aloysius! and, although we had walked on a few paces, I begged the sister to return with me: I could not leave it without daguerreotyping, forever, on my memory, the profoundly religious solemnity of this simple interior, and (shall I add?) without kneeling again, for a few minutes, before this humble shrine of the innocent penitent, Aloysius, to engage his prayers for certain little ones, for whom the world is waiting, it may be, to harm their tender innocence. I will trust that the lingering moment won its pleaded grace.

St. Aloysius has always been a favorite with artists. The figure of the angelic youth, bending over his crucifix with a look of love that vainly tries to express itself, of love that is also reparation, of innocence bathed in tears of contrition, is one of the triumphs of religious art.

The learned and holy confessors of St. Aloysius, among whom was Cardinal Bellarmin, declared after his death their firm belief that he had never offended

God, mortally, in his whole life; yet, my dear children, while a child, youth, and young man, he never ceased to bewail his offences against his good God. What then shall we, who have so often and so grievously offended, who have done so little, hitherto, to atone for our offences, what must we think of our unfeeling indifference to our past sins, our short sorrow, if we have, indeed, sorrowed at all, and our unwillingness to make any reparation for them? Let us repeat, with all the contrition possible, the collect used by the Church on the feast of this innocent penitent to obtain the grace of an abiding, habitual sorrow for all our sins:

"O God, the giver of heavenly gifts, who in the angelic youth, Aloysius, didst unite a marvellous innocence of life with equally marvellous penance; grant that through his merits and prayers, we, who have failed to follow the pattern of his innocence, may imitate him in his penance."

Another prayer, in the Office for the feast of St. Aloysius, is too remarkable not to be familiar to all of us:

"Grant us, O Lord, to sit down at the heavenly banquet clothed in the wedding-garment; which the pious preparation and continual tears of blessed Aloysius, adorned with inestimable pearls."

Let me beg of you, my young readers, not to think lightly of, what older people may call, your *little* sins. Aloysius mourned for sins committed before he was seven years old. Pray often in the words of the Psalmist David, "From the sins of my youth deliver me, O Lord."

SAINT VINCENT DE PAUL.

EVERY child who reads these pages has heard of St. Vincent de Paul. The Society of St. Vincent for the relief of the poor, the sick, the needy of all sorts, as it is found in nearly every parish in America, has made you familiar with the spirit of charity, of tender compassion, and of lively sympathy with the sorrows and misfortunes of all mankind, which set its shining mark upon Vincent as a saint, and is fixed, like a seal, upon the Orders that sprang from his root. In one sense all the saints of God are happy. There is no real happiness out of the service of God, inasmuch as we have been created expressly for His service; and no man, no woman, no child, no, not even an animal, can be happy unless doing what he has been created to do. The saints of God are doing precisely what they were created to do, loving and serving God, even when they seemed to be quite taken up with loving and serving their fellow beings; and they are, of all men, the most truly happy.

The lives of many of the saints have been so full of painful mortifications, grievances, persecutions, calumnies, and sorrows of every sort, that it would be hard for girls and boys to call them happy, but I think any of you would call St. Vincent a happy man, notwithstanding the troubles that overtook him; for he bore them all with so sweet a spirit, such an air of cheerfulness surrounds him even while a slave, and under unjust suspicions, that we almost forget how painful those trials must have been; and then the religious Orders founded by St. Vincent of Paul have a peculiar cheerfulness about them, which we may suppose was one of the holy charms of their model and founder.

I wish you, dear children, to understand what really makes a saint, and to judge the saints, and their actions, not by the rule of this world, but by the rule of God as made known by His Church. Thus, while one saint may be leading a silent life in his monastery, spending his time in meditation and prayer, or even like St. Simon Stylites—who lived seven years on the top of a pillar without shelter from sun or storm, thus preaching a perpetual sermon to the luxurious generation around him, upon the meanness of the body and its comforts compared with the soul and its eternal rewards—another saint is living in the world, mixing in its affairs, its governments, wearing the same dress as his neighbors, hardly differing, to a common observer, from those around him, appearing to be occupied with the duties of his trade, his profession, his business, serving his neighbors with readiness and amiability, judging their actions with charity, relieving, without noise or parade, the poor, the sick, the afflicted, unwearied in praying for sinners, in converting the erring, and protecting the innocent. Both, my dear children, are saints, for both pray and work from one motive, the love of God; seasoning all prayer, all work, all recreation, by this ejaculation, this arrow of love sent from the heart of the creature to the heart of the Creator, and which is like a perpetual holocaust of that heart to God, "All for thee, my Jesus, my Jesus, all for thee! My Lord and my God, my God and my all!"

Protestants very often prefer one saint to another, and praise, almost always, those saints who do outward works of mercy, and even think lightly of the merits of the meditative saints. Catholics, however, if they pay any attention to the mind of the Church in these things, passing, as she does, a perfect and just judgment upon the virtues of her children, will never, in this sense, prefer one saint to another; but will rather adore God in the different graces and virtues of His saints, and try to imitate them by performing all the duties of their station, however lofty, or however humble, from the same motive which governed them, *the supreme love of God.*

Vincent was born in the year 1576, in the village of Pouii, near Acqs in Gascony, France, not far from the Pyrenees mountains. His parents, William de Paul and Bertranda de Morass, lived on a very small farm, and on the produce of this farm they brought up four sons and two daughters, innocent, ignorant of the follies of the great world, and taught to perform all the labors falling to their lot with cheerfulness. The third son, Vincent, spent a great part of his time in the field, tending cattle, and this time he also used for prayer and meditation; for from his earliest years he had shown a seriousness, and an affection for prayer, beyond his age. In this humble life he also found those for whose comfort he could sacrifice some of his own; for, from his good parents, he had learned the secret of Christian charity.

In this quiet and laborious life, too, with so little to excite intellectual taste, he showed so much relish for learning, and so much quickness in acquiring it, that his father determined to place him where his piety and learning would serve, not only to his own advantage, but to the glory of God.

He was first put under the Franciscan friars, at Acqs, and had been four years in their school when a gentleman chose him as assistant-preceptor to his children, thus enabling him to go on with his studies without taxing his hard-working parents. At twenty years of age Vincent entered the University of Toulouse, where he studied divinity and was raised to the priesthood.

In 1605, two years before the settlement of Jamestown, Virginia, as Vincent was returning from Marseilles to Toulouse in a boat, he was captured by Mahometans, and by them sold into slavery—for sale like "cattle at a fair," to use Vincent's own words, "making us open our mouths and show our teeth, pinching our sides and making us walk, trot, lift burdens and wrestle to show our strength, beside a thousand other brutalities." He fell from the hands of one master to those of another, and at last became the property of an apostate Christian. St. Vincent never regretted the hardships of his life as a slave, for, by his example he won a soul to God. His master, sorry for his apostacy, not only helped Vincent to escape to Italy, but went with him, leaving behind him the riches he had made by forsaking the faith of Christ.

In Italy, Vincent could have satisfied his devotion—Italy, where the relics of so many martyrs, and the shrines raised in honor of so many of the great saints, declare the virtues possible, by the grace of God in His sacraments, to mortals like ourselves. Still he did not linger in Rome, but hastened to France, where his sense of obedience told him his duties lay, and on his return was charged by Cardinal d'Ossat to deliver a message, too important to be trusted in writing, to the king, Henry IV. He performed this errand with care and fidelity, and then returned, with sincere contentment, to his own obscure manner of living.

At this time, as if no humiliation could be spared in his education as a saint, he was accused by a magistrate, who shared his room, of stealing a large sum of money, and was even charged with this disgraceful sin before a number of distinguished persons. Under this mortifying accusation the serenity of Vincent never failed him, his only reply, being, "God knows the truth." He bore this slander for six years, when the true thief was taken up at Bourdeaux for another crime, and, to quiet his own conscience and to clear the innocent Vincent, he sent for the magistrate, and owned his crime. The magistrate, ashamed of his insulting treatment of Vincent, begged, in the most humble and contrite manner, his forgiveness. It was thus that St. Vincent tried to copy his Divine Master, who bore in silence the malignant accusations of the Jews.

If I should name all the charitable institutions founded by St. Vincent I should fill many pages; and if I added to these the many beautiful acts of his life, so well known to you all, I should fill a volume; but some of these are so remarkable, and seem so little known, that I will give them here.

In France, the galley-slaves were men condemned to the most severe labor, in the most loathsome prisons, cut off from hope and from their fellow men. To these prisons St. Vincent gained admittance, not only to relieve some of their dreadful sufferings, but to help them in gaining merit by them, so that all their punishment should be in this world. He was met by these poor creatures with curses and blasphemies; but he did not shrink, he did not despair. Jesus died for them and therefore Vincent loved them. Yes *loved* them. He did not *pretend* to love them, but really and actually loved them with the same love that Jesus felt for sinners. Loving them, he tried to gain their love. With sweet words, and gentle winning ways, he went among them. He kissed their chains, he embraced them; he listened to all their complaints; he used prayers, and entreaties, to those who had the care of them, to deal more kindly, more forbearingly with them. These gentle looks, words, actions, at length overcame them. He had pierced, with the arrow of saintly sweetness, the hard habit of sin. They learned to weep like children, to pray, to do penance. Their life of terrible punishment was now one of humble expiation, and the sting and the bitterness were gone. But St. Vincent did still more. Seeing one day a man sadder than usual even among these unhappy galley-slaves, he asked the cause of his dejection. The poor man replied, that by his imprisonment a good wife and several little ones were thrown on the charity of the world, and he groaned, not for his own sufferings, but for theirs. The tender heart of Vincent was touched; the courageous, self-forgetful heart was nerved for the sacrifice. Can you imagine it, my dear children? Yet, it is true, that St. Vincent actually took the place of this unhappy man, with the consent of the jailor, and lived, for months, the life of a galley-slave, until he was discovered by his friends, and, against his will, *forcibly* released! The marks of the chains never left his ankles, and the galling of those dreadful irons gave him pain to the end of his life.

Here is a story that rebukes the pride of the rich in their riches, and especially of those rich people who are ashamed of their early poverty.

As St. Vincent grew old and infirm, and the lameness that was brought on by the chains in the galley-prisons, increased, a distinguished lady sent him a carriage and horses, that he might visit his charitable houses. He utterly refused to accept this gift, until obliged to do so under obedience to the archbishop of Paris. The humble Vincent, who would neither allow himself, nor others, to forget that he was the son of a peasant, was ashamed to be seen in what he considered a style above his station. He called his carriage and horses "his shame and disgrace," and said to the Fathers of the Oratory, whom he one day visited, "See, my fathers, see how the son of a peasant has the audacity to ride through the streets in a carriage!"

In our own country, where no distinctions of rank are handed down from father to son, but where the son of the humblest may rise to the highest position of honor or wealth, we may not see the full force of Vincent's humility; but let us copy his spirit, and remember that real greatness is never ashamed of an humble birth, nor does it crave marks of outward rank.

The priory of St. Lazarus, a magnificent building, with a grand chapel, and with an estate around it such as would make a paradise, was, in 1630, given to St. Vincent by the one who had been its prior. From this priory were named the Lazarist Fathers, the spiritual sons of St. Vincent, whom he sent as missionaries throughout France. We are told, that when a claim to this noble property had been made by some other party, and while the question was still under consideration, St. Vincent was found in the chapel, on his knees; and, that the only pain he felt in the prospect of leaving this new home, was, the necessity of parting with three or four poor idiots, whom he found at St. Lazarus, and to whom he had given the most affectionate attention. In the priory of St. Lazarus was the theological school for the training of those who wished to be priests, for the need of good and useful priests lay close to the heart of St. Vincent; there was also an asylum for his old favorites, the idiots; and, besides this, a refuge for those young men who were found in a state of intoxication, or in dens of vice. Many of these unfortunate inebriates were gentlemen by birth; indeed most of them were so, for the poor have no time to indulge in such dreadful dissipation, no money to spend in costly poison. These young men were taken up, while in a state of insensibility, and carried to the priory of St. Lazarus. On their arrival each one was taken to a solitary room, no one, but the superior, knowing his name or rank; and in this solitary chamber, while every care was taken of him, he was left alone with his own sad thoughts and upbraiding conscience. The sudden change from the sinful orgies of saloons to the quiet of this holy place, from boisterous, profane companions to the peaceful society of the monk who attended them, all produced an awe, a solemnity, not to be described; and however angry they might be at first, they yielded by degrees to the sacred influences around them, and

20*

sighed, not after the worldly and wicked pleasures from which they had been taken, but for the innocent and heavenly pleasures of the people of God. After a time the beautiful gardens of the priory were thrown open to these unhappy prodigals, and the freshness and loveliness of nature, the pure joys of an innocent life amid the works of God, helped them to return to their own "Father's house;" they would then throw themselves at the feet of St. Vincent, make an humble confession of their sins, desiring, like good sons of the Church, to practice their Christian duties. When these spiritually sick ones were really strong and well in mind, they were allowed to go out into the world, not to fall again and again, but to show a real conversion and a holy strength to resist temptation. When St. Vincent lay dead, and his remains were visited by princes and peasants, these young men, then among the flower of the French nobility, did not forget him, but came to pay their tribute of love and respect to their kind jailor at the priory of St. Lazarus.

When you have read this short sketch of the life of St. Vincent de Paul, I hope you will take the first opportunity to read the full life, as it has been written several times, and can be found in almost any Catholic library. You will then read about those royal charities—royal because kings might be proud to have it in their power to do so much for the relief of suffering—which Vincent, the son of a peasant in Gascony, was so happy as to distribute among his countrymen in all parts of France. When the little kingdom of

Lorraine had been ruined by the march and counter-march of armies, which fed like locusts on her beautiful fields, famine and pestilence came in to add to the horrors of her terrified people. Parents even fed upon their own children, and Lorraine was like Jerusalem during that siege which makes one's blood run cold as one reads of its unnatural horrors. But the cry of Lorraine came to the ears of St. Vincent; and then flowed, from the supernatural treasures of the heart of our saint, such consolations, such benedictions, as changed Lorraine into a kingdom of peace and joy. It is not until we read such a history as the life of St. Vincent, that we know how readily the heart of man answers to the call of charity, or how rich we are when the heart is inspired to make a generous sacrifice.

You will also read, in the full life of St. Vincent, of the Hospital of Hotel-Dieu; and of the Foundling Hospital for those little ones disowned by unhappy parents. You will also read of the Sisters of Charity, whom you all know and love, and who are sometimes called the "Daughters of St. Vincent." Had St. Vincent done but the one work of giving to the world this noble Order of "The Sisters of Charity," how much should we not all owe to him? "Their name," we may say, "is gone out to all the earth, and their sound to the ends of the world." Their hospitals for the sick, the insane, for armies and navies; their asylums for orphans, for foundlings; their schools and sodalities; and, lastly, that brave army of corneted sisters on the other side of the globe, who take the little infants, left on the rivers of China to a cruel death, and give them the saving sacrament of baptism, waiting for these tiny victims of heathenism to drift down to them, more patiently than merchants watch for their ships from India, loaded with spices and sweet gums —all these wonders of our own day bear the seal of St. Vincent de Paul, while the blessed cheerfulness of his life of charity followed him to the last, and his humility grew with his holiness.

How often do we see worldly people, knowing, very well, that death is near them, yet making no preparations for it! If they were starting in a few months on a long voyage, how careful they would be to put all their affairs in order; so careful that it would seem as if they expected to die before their return. But, when the voyage of death is before them, they make no preparation for it. Age may have set in, their ripe years are passing into decay, yet the things of this world take up all their thoughts. One would fancy they had forgotten that they, too, must die. Behold St. Vincent, after a whole life spent as a preparation for death, renewing every day this preparation for the coming of his Lord and Master, to whom he must render an account of all the graces he had received. Every morning he repeated the prayers of the Church for those in their last agony, and often said to those around him, "One of these days the miserable body of this old sinner will be laid in the ground; it will turn to dust, and you will tread it underfoot." When the hand of death was indeed upon him, and he had received Extreme Unction, he fell at times into a doze; but the sweet name of Jesus, in which he had performed such miracles of charity, would instantly rouse him. He died in his chair, bowing his head while in the act of pronouncing a promise of benediction on his dear children in God. On his tomb is inscribed, "Here lies that venerable man, Vincent de Paul, priest, founder and first superior of the Congregation of the Mission, and also of the Sisters of Charity. He died on the 27th of September, 1660, in the 85th year of his age."

The feast of St. Vincent de Paul is celebrated on the 19th of July. In 1863 a magnificent hospital was opened on the little farm tilled by Vincent's father, and where Vincent himself had tended the flocks and herds. The small cabin in which they lived is still standing under the shadow of the great hospital, that is his best monument, and a tree, under which the boy Vincent often meditated, is still green and flourishing. Many of our dear Sisters of Charity carry crucifixes made from the branches of this tree. They will also show pictures to you of the humble birth-place and of the hospital of St. Vincent. The pride of the Sisters of Charity, we may say, is the humility of their founder.

While I have been writing these pages, a venerable "Daughter of Vincent de Paul," has given up her account as stewardess of many a flourishing house of charity. Seldom does it fall to the lot of any one to do all the good that our noble-minded, noble-hearted Sister O—— was privileged to do. As was said of her by one who knew her well, "even when age allowed her, by the rules of her Order, to retire to St. Joseph's, the beloved home of the Sisters of Charity in America, she chose labor rather than rest;" and came to within a stone's throw of the room in which I am writing, to attend to the sick poor of our large parish. The undertaking grew under her hands, and the result was, under the blessing of God, the patronage of St. Vincent, of our pastor, and the co-operation of the "Ladies of Charity," that she founded the first "House of Providence" in the United States, naming it, as she promised to do if successful, St. Vincent's House of Providence. No one but the sick poor, and their families, know the good that has been done by the visits of these daughters of St. Vincent in the homes of the humble. Not only have the many wants of the sick and aged poor been relieved, but they have found their souls aided as well, and the dying prepared for a happy passage out of this world—proving how the wise rule of St. Vincent de Paul suits itself to the needs of all times, and of all countries.

Among the pictures in my black leather portfolio, are two of St. Vincent de Paul. One represents him with an orphan in his arms, while he leads by the hand another orphan, a dear little girl, through the snowy streets. In the other picture a wretched woman, sinful but penitent, is embracing the feet of her crucified Saviour; beside her lies a little foundling; close to this group stands our Saint, and near him one of those noble women of France who aided Vincent in his gigantic charities. He is pointing out to her this sinful woman, and the innocent foundling, as if saying, "They must be your charge. Your wealth, your position, must provide for them a shelter and protect them from temptation."

O, all ye rich and powerful ones, let the voice of St. Vincent de Paul reach your hearts as it did the hearts of the women of the French nobility! Remember that the noblest privilege of wealth is to relieve the poor, of the virtuous to raise the fallen, of the powerful to protect the innocent from danger, and give a home to the homeless, the orphan and the foundling. By doing such works of charity in the spirit of St. Vincent, we may share in the merits, though our state of life may not allow us to wear the grey habit and the white cornet of the beloved and venerated Sisters of Charity.

Holy Vincent de Paul, pray for us!

SAINT LAURENCE.

SAINT LAURENCE.

SEVERAL years ago there was an exhibition of very rare pictures in Chicago, and among them was one claiming special admiration and respect, for it was said to be "A genuine Titian;" that is, the picture was painted by Titian, that great master of painting, one of the greatest, indeed, that ever lived.

Some persons could not believe it possible that a picture painted by Titian should have found its way to Chicago; but, as I had seen it many years before in a famous collection in Philadelphia, where its genuineness was admitted, and, later still, in the parlor of the gentleman who had come into peaceable possession of it by way of inheritance, I never had any doubt or question as to its being all that it claimed to be, and enjoyed, with my whole heart, the opportunity of seeing, and studying again, in a good light, this masterpiece of art, this triumph of religion.

How heavenly was the face, how ecstatic the joy, in every part of that youthful figure! How lovely the

SAINT LAURENCE.

carnations of that virgin flesh, how exquisite the sensibility of the quivering fingers! Will it not delight every one of my young readers to be told that this master-piece of the great Titian was no other than the martyrdom of St. Laurence? St. Laurence, that youthful deacon, who was so devoted to the venerable Pope, St. Xystus, that when this aged pontiff was led forth to martyrdom, St. Laurence cried out to him, in tears, "Father, whither are you going without your son? Whither are you going, O holy priest, without your deacon?" The holy pontiff, bent and trembling with age, consoled his dear son in Christ, by saying, "Thou art younger, my son, than I, and God keeps thee back for a still harder combat; but take heart; in three days thou shalt follow me."

Sweet promise! Hard, indeed, to be understood by the children of the world, who hear nothing with so much pain, as that they are soon to leave this world and go to God; to God, whom they know not, whom they love not, whom they never sigh to see or to be near; but a most sweet and consoling promise, understood by the young St. Laurence, and more enchanting, and delightful, than any promise of worldly happiness, or of the longest life of prosperity.

St. Laurence lived in an age of dreadful persecution; but it is in such times that we learn to value, as it deserves, our holy religion. It is not in the midst of ease, and softness, that Catholics really prize the glorious old faith for which so many popes and bishops and priests and deacons and virgins and fathers and mothers and even tender children have cheerfully laid down their lives. O, no! it is not in prosperous times, when fathers of families are thinking how they can make money the fastest, and the soonest lay by a fortune, and build spacious houses, and fill them with magnificent furniture and load their tables with silver and gold and delicate glass and costly porcelain; and when mothers are thinking how splendidly they can dress themselves and their children, what showy accomplishments will make them most attractive, or what grand parties and expensive entertainments they can give to secure the admiration of their worldly friends, and the flattery, even, of their enemies. No, my dear children, it is not in such times, as I have just described, that Catholics know, or even take the trouble to consider, how blessed they are in their holy faith. They are too much taken up by the vanity of riches, and the dreams of this world, to think of their souls, or how soon they will need their religion to help them die a safe death, saying nothing of a happy one.

But God often allows the most worldly Catholics to be roused from this miserable, degrading worship of Mammon. He allows them to be stripped of all these dear possessions, all this false grandeur, all this flattery of a deceitful world, and makes them, again, the disciples of the despised Nazarene. Again, it is "Jesus," and "Jesus crucified," "crucified between two thieves," jeered at by the worldly Pharisee, the learned scribe, the unbelieving Saducee, and mocked and insulted by the ignorant rabble, whom they lovingly call "Master"

Yes my dear children, God sometimes allows this; and, indeed, in some part or another of the world, this persecution of Catholics is going on continually, even to the shedding of blood and the most cruel torments. Thus, in truth, God keeps fresh the seed of faith in the hearts of His children, and reminds them that this faith is the only food by which they can live so as to gain eternal bliss, the only riches they can lay up for eternity, the only honor that will outlast crumbling tombstones. and falling monuments, the only joy a wise man will ever covet.

During that fearful persecution, under the Emperor Valerian, that began in the year 257, and in the midst of which St. Laurence lived, Catholics, instead of hoarding up money until they grudged it even for the charities of the Church, brought all their goods, all their gold, silver and precious jewels, all the money for which they sold their vast estates, and put them into the hands of the deacons; through them to be distributed among the poor, or to assist the Church in her necessities. There were no misers, then, among Christians; no worldly people who were trying to serve God and mammon at the same time. It was this knowledge which made the pagans seize St. Laurence, the deacon, hoping to discover by him the treasures of the Church. But St. Laurence had distributed these treasures as freely as they had been given; and in answer to the questions of his persecutors about the place where they were hidden, he pointed to the poor, the sick, the lame, the blind, saying: "Here are our treasures." Yes, dear children, the sick, the poor, the lame, the blind, are, indeed, the *treasures* of the Church; as such she esteems them, claims them, glories in them. Our Lord has said, "The poor ye have always with you," and this, like all His promises to His Church never fails.

We see, then, how easy it was for the Catholics of those days to die, as to their money. They had no long wills to make; they had only to choose between pagan robbery and the charities of the Church, and one need not be a very courageous lover of holy poverty to choose under such circumstances. Having given up their property, with all its cares and anxieties; having given up all ambition in a pagan society, where *a Christian* was another name for an outcast; having, in many cases, given up all the sweet ties of family and home, since the Christian was liable to be exposed to the torture, even by the nearest of pagan friends; and, at all times, living detached lives, persecution having made them realize that God is more to us than any and all friends, however dear—having made all these sacrifices, how easy it was to die! How easy, even, to be a martyr, and die a death of torment for God's sake, since, the short suffering over, Heaven was near —Heaven without an hour of purgatory—Heaven with its Beatific Vision, its torrent of delights, its eternity of good! What a glorious thing, you will say, to be a Catholic in those days! Rather, let us say, what a holy, what a noble, what an unspeakably precious privilege, to be a Catholic, a faithful Catholic, in any age of the Church! There is no such privilege, no such honor, no such happiness, as this.

When the answer of St. Laurence was reported to the prefect, and he found that, instead of heaps of gold and silver, he was shown only a crowd of disgusting lepers, lame, and blind, and ragged beings, to whom these treasures had been given out—he was so enraged that he resolved to be revenged upon St. Laurence, the deacon, for his disappointment, and ordered him to be stretched on an immense gridiron, with fire enough under it to burn, without immediately killing, the holy and intrepid young Christian.

It was upon this bed of fearful tortures, while his skin was slowly cracking over the hot coals, and his flesh roasting inch by inch, that St. Laurence learned how Jesus Christ rewards the love of those who are ready to die for Him. So far from sinking under his tortures, he seems to have been more than insensible to them, for they became sources of the most ravishing joy and exultation. The flames became a bed of refreshment to his soul, and he could say, with a gay smile, to his unfeeling attendants, "Let my body be turned now; one side is broiled enough." He was turned, by the order of the prefect, giving, as he supposed, inconceivable torment; but St. Laurence said, "It is dressed enough. You may eat." The prefect insulted him, hoping to disturb this miraculous peace, this celestial joy; but he continued in fervent prayer for the conversion of Rome, which was still pagan Rome, although it contained the tombs of SS. Peter and Paul. His prayer was, in a manner, answered upon the spot, for several senators, who were present at his death, were so moved by his holy fortitude, his devout exultation, that they became Christians beside the crisped body of St. Laurence on his gridiron. After the pure soul of the young deacon had left the body, these same noble senators took the martyr's relics on their shoulders and gave them honorable burial. All this happened on the 10th of August, 258.

It was St. Laurence on the infamous gridiron of his persecutors, the cruel executioners feeding the flames so as to torment, not immediately kill, their victim, that was represented by the master-piece of Titian in the exhibition of pictures in Chicago. Many persons turned away with a shudder, declaring they could not endure to look at such a scene of torment; while others would linger for hours over the joy, the triumph, on the face of the martyr, whose eyes turned heavenward, as if catching a glimpse of his waiting crown and palm. For us, it is not enough to shudder at the torment, or to admire the triumph. Another step remains for us; humbly, at a far off distance, to imitate St. Laurence on his fiery bed.

There is a notion among children that mortifications are only for grown-up people, who can fast. Grown-up people, too, have a notion that mortifications, beyond the fasts of the Church, were for the days of the martyrs and old-fashioned saints. Leaving the grown-up people to their good pastors, I will tell you, my dear children, how to practice a mortification that is not beyond your age nor your strength—a *real mortification;* for children often long to know of some real mortification which they can practice.

We are very likely to have hot weather the 10th of August, which is the feast of St. Laurence, the day on which he lay on his fiery bed, and smiled from it, calling it his "bed of roses." Now, let every child try, on that day, not to complain, quite as much as usual, of the heat; not to beg and tease your mother, all day, for ice-water, nor to be dressed in your very thinnest frock or pants. Do not say very much about the heat, and especially try not to consider youself privileged to be cross that day, simply, because, "*it is hot.*" To do as I have said, in the spirit of a loving imitation of St. Laurence, is to perform an act of mortification; and Father Faber tells us, exactly what every saint would tell us, that to practice mortification, is a sure way to be very happy, very cheerful, and even gay. It is not having everything that we want, that makes us happy; but the doing without, for the love of God, what we might have if we wished. I repeat, doing without for the *love of God*—remember, it is not doing without to save money, nor to gain one pleasure by giving up another, that will make us happy; but giving it up for the love of God.

I have reminded you, many times, that it is the love of God that makes saints; let me add, that it was this love of God that made the martyrs joyful in their sufferings, made St. Laurence radiant as an angel on his gridiron.

You will often see a poor father and mother working hard, year after year, and so patiently, too, early and late, summer and winter, even when they are ill and their bones aching and their heads throbbing; and they will tell you that it is because they *love* their children, because they wish to give them a comfortable, happy home, and a good education, that they endure this life of labor and privation.

A few doors from me, a dear old lady is lying very ill. She needs to be turned in her bed, to be tended night and day. She is very old, and helpless, and heavy with age. Do you think her children, her good, faithful children, ever complain, ever grudge this good mother their lifting and tending of her? O, no! no! They say it is their happiness, for they *love* their mother. They remember how she carried them as bone of her bone, flesh of her flesh, the very core of her heart, dearer than the apple of her eye; and they love her so well, that they think they can never do enough for her. Yes, my dear children, it is love that makes all hard things easy, all labors pleasant, all privations joyful; and the love of God so filled the hearts of the martyrs, that they grudged Him no labors, no hardships, no torments, that He might ask from them. They remembered how God had loved them, had created and preserved them, and had, finally, redeemed them by a death of such torture as no martyr ever suffered. Therefore they said, "We can never do enough for God, nor, in any way, show Him how much we love Him. O, that we could suffer something for Him, who has suffered all for us!" It is this same love of God that, in all ages, makes mortification easy and sweet; and this sort of mortification will obtain for us an ever increasing love of God, and all the merit of a true martyrdom.

In the church of the Jesuits in Venice, Italy, a church that excites the admiration of all travelers by the beauty of its marbles, there is another picture, also by Titian, of the martyrdom of St. Laurence. I have a large photograph of the High Altar of this church, and it is pleasant, as I look at it, to remember that in one of the side chapels is a picture of this favorite saint.

Fra Angelico painted a series of five pictures, representing St. Laurence. In one of these we see him giving alms to the poor, and sick, and lame, the widowed and orphaned. He is dressed as a deacon, and his dalmatic is covered with little flames, some may think of the fire that consumed his flesh, but I should say, of that fire of the love of God that was stronger to console, than the mortal fire of wood was to torture.

The picture which I have chosen for this volume, however, is from the pious School of Sienna; and no picture could give a lovelier idea of the youthful deacon, clothed in his embroidered dalmatic, the book of the Gospels in one hand, in the other the palm he so nobly won. Everything in this youthful figure breathes of peace, of candor, of innocence; and when we see the gridiron at his side, we understand that his triumph was not that of the strong man, who bites down the cry of pain, but the celestial triumph of love, and faith, over the powers of this world. This is the true triumph of a Christian—the only triumph that deserves the name—and this triumph remember, was gained by the youth, St. Laurence.

Be in the habit of asking God, especially in the person of the Holy Ghost, to "kindle in your hearts the fire of Divine love." The hymn to the Holy Ghost should be committed to memory by every child, and those beautiful invocations to the Holy Ghost, found in the Office of Whit Sunday, or Pentecost, in your "Roman Missal for the Laity," will furnish you with prayers that will grow dearer to you every year of your life. These prayers to the Holy Spirit, which is the Spirit of Love, will take, and more than take, the place of many exhortations to those whom you wish to have attend to their duty, or to avoid temptation. You may not always be able to warn those you love of the dangers around them, or you may not be able to rouse them from their indifference to heavenly things; but you can always pray to the Holy Spirit to kindle in their hearts the "fire of Divine love," and this prayer answered, all your wishes are answered.

Constantly beg of the Blessed Virgin, of St. Joseph, and of all the saints, and, on the 10th of August especially of St. Laurence, to obtain for you this love of God, and I promise you that you will never be a lukewarm Catholic, nor any thing but a very faithful, very happy, and even a very joyful Catholic.

SAINT DOMINIC.

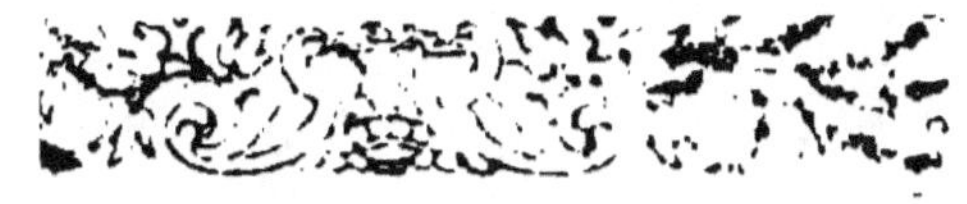

SAINT DOMIN[illegible]

all our waking hours [illegible]
e an idle one as th[illegible] twilight
he labors and [illegible]
e day are over. [illegible]
lightful new [illegible]
ruin your eyes [illegible] twilight;"
er unwillingly she [illegible] other in
every letter, even [illegible]
net. The only [illegible] at this
kitten, and [illegible], even of
ul and frolicksome [illegible]. Nellie turns
on her half-read [illegible], and finishes it in
. If it is [illegible] clouds of
not help her to build [illegible] castles in
l if it is [illegible] castles appear
the bright coals and dancing flames of the
kor[illegible] or anthracite.
no difference then, whether it is [illegible]
twilight hour is [illegible] likely to be [illegible]
ladies who knit, and [illegible]

SAINT DOMINIC.

F all our waking hours not one is so likely to be an idle one as that of the evening twilight. The labors and the active, noisy sports of the day are over. Nellie has been told to lay down her delightful new story-book, "for," says Mamma, "it will ruin your eyes to read by this twilight;" and, however unwillingly she may obey, another moment makes every letter, even to her keen young sight, quite indistinct. The only pet in lively humor at this hour is the kitten, and one tires, sometimes, even of kitty, graceful and frolicksome as she is. Nellie turns dreamily from her half-read story, and finishes it in imagination. If it is summer, the tinted clouds of the long sunset help her to build gorgeous castles in the air; and if it is winter, dozens of castles appear suddenly in the bright coals and dancing flames of the burning hickory or anthracite.

It makes no difference, then, whether it is winter or summer, the twilight hour is very likely to be an idle one. The ladies who knit, and certainly Grandmamma knits, take out their long bright needles at this hour, and many a pretty, red baby-sock has been shaped "between sunset and dark." But although I like my knitting-needles I seldom use them at twilight —that hour so calm, so sacred to thought, so favorable to meditation. Years of custom have made it a second habit to me to say my rosary just at this time, and my idle fingers, released from pencil and pen, instinctively go to the depths of my pocket for my well-worn beads. The habit of monks and nuns, duly observed from age to age, has, perhaps, made it a habit with people living in the world to say the rosary at evening; or, a universal sentiment may have made this devotion, what it really is, a *vesper* devotion; but however this may be, almost every person has the same habit of saying the rosary at evening, before night. It takes the place of castle-building and twilight dreaming, with the young, and sends their active imaginations, not to fairy land, but far, far beyond it—sends them far beyond the lightest arrow of fancy ever sped from the bow of poet, or musician, far beyond the deepening blue of the sky, to the mysteries and glories above it—the mystery of the Incarnation of the Second Person of the Most Holy Trinity, the mystery of His nativity, of His hidden, suffering, and glorified life on earth, and the unutterable glory of His life in Heaven after his ascension—all these mysteries, and glories, invite the imagination of the child that quietly takes up its beads at twilight: and as the shadows deepen, and the colors fade from the changing clouds, and the birds sing their last carol, and the stars come out, one by one, in the solemn sky, the heart of the child has dilated and taken in both Heaven and earth, both God and man! You can well afford, my dear little child, to lay down your very prettiest story-book for an enjoyment that has been prepared to meet this very want of something to do, something to think of, during the one idle hour of the whole day.

Every morning, at church, I see a dear old lady who says her beads all through the mass, excepting at the most solemn parts of it. Catholics often do this. It is not my own way of assisting at mass, for, better than any "Prayers to be said during mass," I like the "Ordinary of the Mass," with the special prayers in the Office of the day, as it is said by the priest who celebrates. Nothing so fills my soul, so excites my devotion, as the grand composure, the solemn joyfulness, and the adoring ecstacy of the "Mass Prayers," as I find them translated in my "Roman Missal for the Laity." I try never to lose sight of what the priest is doing and saying; for, as a wise man once said to me, "The mass is intended for the eye as well as for the ear," and by this way of using both my eyes and my ears in following the action of the priest, my mass is, generally, a recollected one.

But, although this is my favorite way of assisting at the Holy Sacrifice of the mass, there are persons, who, as I have said, always say their beads during mass; and we are not to conclude, from this, that they cannot read their prayers. More than one gallant officer during the late war, was in the habit of saying his rosary on horseback, as he waited for his troops to defile before him for the night. Haydn never found himself hesitating over his musical sentences, or failing to express some devout conception in sacred composition, without having recourse to his rosary; and only the other day I read how Gluck, another musical composer, was in the habit of withdrawing from the gay circles of the imperial palace, to which he was often invited, to say his rosary. The rosary has, very aptly, been called "The book of the ignorant," because the mysteries meditated upon, while saying it, are the great mysteries of the Christian religion; and, because, by meditating upon these mysteries, the heart is kindled to devotion in the same way as the quiet reading of pious books may assist us to meditate, with unction, upon these mysteries. Still the universal use of the rosary, proves that it is not only the book of the ignorant, but the book daily handled, and affectionately conned, by the most learned, and the most theologically pious, of all the faithful children of the Catholic Church. No one says his beads more devoutly than the Holy Father, Pius IX.; and St. Francis de Sales, that accomplished author and learned bishop, never failed, during the last half of his life, to recite, daily, the fifteen decades of the rosary.

I could fill a book with examples of extraordinary faith in the devotion of the rosary, gathered from the lives of popes, cardinals, bishops and doctors of divinity, who have found in their rosary a book of wisdom as well as of piety; but I have said enough to prove to you that you will learn Christian doctrine, as well as true devotion, by a daily recital of your rosary. No child who can read this book, or who can understand it when hearing it read, should fail to recite every day, one decade of his rosary, *i. e.*, one "Our Father," ten "Hail Maries" and one "Glory."

But what, you may say, has all this to do with St. Dominic, whose life we are reading? So much to do with him that one can never say the rosary without being a friend and disciple of St. Dominic, for to St. Dominic we owe the devotion of the rosary. We cannot say that St. Dominic invented the beads, as people speak of things out of the Catholic Church. I cannot remember that anything has been invented by the Church, or by her saints, *i. e.*, as a Church or as saints. Catholics have invented printing, a very great number of wonderful instruments, such as the clock, the mariner's compass, guns and gunpowder, besides discovering the country we live in and the whole of this western continent; but I have yet to learn that the Church or her saints have ever invented, or even discovered, a dogma or a devotion. The reason of this, is, that dogmas and devotions are directly revealed by God, or grow, indirectly, out of what He has already revealed. Thus, the rosary was not invented by St. Dominic, but, under the impulse of a vision, as we are told, he arranged the prayers, already in use among Catholics, in such a way as to unite meditation on the revealed mysteries to vocal prayers (prayers made by the voice or lips), and from this arrangement we have our rosary. It is even said that the use of the beads was not the invention of our saint. Ages before St. Dominic lived, the hermits, or Fathers of the desert, used to count their prayers by using little stones, very much as we use our beads. You see, therefore, that there was nothing new about the rosary, that it was no invention, but only a skillful using of the old, old treasures of the Church of God. You are now prepared, I hope, to feel a deep interest in this sketch of the life of St. Dominic.

It was in the year 1170, while Alexander III. was seated in the chair of St. Peter as Pope of Rome, that Dominic Guzman was born at his father's castle of Calaroga in Old Castile, Spain. St. Dominic was descended from a long and chivalrous line of ancestors, and it is said that his father's family was a family of saints. Both his mother, Joanna of Aza, and Manez, her second son, received the solemn beatification of the Church; and Antonio, the eldest son, was no unworthy member of this devout family; for, becoming a secular priest and in a position to expect the highest ecclesiastical honors, he turned aside from all of them, and chose a state of holy poverty, which he secured by distributing his whole property to the poor and retiring to a hospital, where he spent his life in attending upon the sick. The mother of these two good sons was to be still further rewarded, for her own devoted piety, by the sanctity of her third son, our beloved Dominic. To prepare her to receive this rare treasure, and to guard it suitably, his greatness was revealed to her in a special manner before his birth, for she saw, in a mysterious vision, a dog bearing in his mouth a lighted torch. This vision is hinted at in the pictures in which we see St. Dominic accompanied by a dog with a lighted torch. The noble lady who held him at the font, saw, as the water was poured over his head, a brilliant star on the infant's forehead. It is this star which you see in the picture of St. Dominic that I have chosen to illustrate this sketch of his life, and which is taken from the "Coronation of the Blessed Virgin," as painted by Fra Angelico of Fiesole, and still one of the treasures of the Gallery of the Louvre in Paris. This star on his forehead distinguishes him among the multitudes of saints surrounding the Throne of Heaven in this delightful picture.

When seven years old, Dominic was put under the care of his uncle, the Arch-priest of Gumiel di Izan, a town not far from Calaroga. Here he grew up in the service of the altar, learning to recite the Divine Office, singing hymns, serving at mass and at other public ceremonies, and fulfilling those numberless little duties, which make the lives of so many Catholic boys fragrant with the incense of the sanctuary. Alas! how many of these favored little boys can say that they have improved all these special privileges and graces, and have been better men for having stood so near to our Lord? We will hope, however, that every altar-boy corresponds to some of these graces, and is really better than he would have been if he had never worn the dress, and performed the angelic service, of an acolyte. At the age of fourteen, the young Dominic left his holy uncle, and was sent to the university of Palencia, then one of the most celebrated in Spain. During the ten years he lived in Palencia, he was distinguished for his application as a student, and for his angelic innocence of life. He devoted four years to the most profound study of philosophy and sacred letters, often spending the nights, as well as the days, over his books. "It was a thing most marvellous and lovely to behold," says the one who wrote his life, Theodoric of Apoldia; "this man, a boy in years but a sage in wisdom; superior to the pleasures of his age, he thirsted only after justice; and, not to lose time, he preferred the bosom of his mother, the Church, to the aimless life of the foolish world around him. The sacred repose of her tabernacle was his resting place; his time was divided equally between study and prayer, and God rewarded the fervent love with which he kept His commandments, by bestowing on him such a spirit of wisdom and understanding as made it easy for him to solve the most difficult questions." We can understand, by this devotion of St. Dominic to his studies, how precious in his eyes must have been the books from which he drew such coveted treasures. I hope you have already learned, from these lives of the saints, how dear to these ancient scholars, were their books; not only on account of the difficulty of obtaining them, but for the value placed upon learning itself. Yet we find this lover of learning, this noble-born Dominic

Guzman, during a terrible famine which desolated Spain, so touched by the sufferings of his countrymen that he not only gave all the money he had to give in alms, selling even his clothes in order to buy food for the poor, but he set a still nobler example to his fellow-students by selling his beloved and precious books, that the price of them might be distributed among the starving people. When one of his companions expressed his surprise that Dominic should thus deprive himself of the means of pursuing his studies, he replied, "Would you have me studying off those dead parchments while there are men dying of hunger?" On another occasion, finding a poor woman in great distress because her only son had been taken captive by the Moors, Dominic, having no money to offer for his ransom, begged her to take him, sell him and use the money thus obtained to ransom her son. Such was the tender pity of the self-denying Dominic for the sufferings and sorrows of others.

Dominic was twenty-five years old when he became a priest, ripe for its duties, both in learning and sanctity. He received the habit of the Canons Regular of the Order of St. Augustine, and afterwards spent nine years at Osma, where he was sub-prior of the convent to which he belonged. He won the confidence of every one around him, and laid, deeper and deeper, the foundations of a holiness that was to edify the world.

In 1203 the bishop of Osma was appointed, by Alfonzo VIII, king of Castile, to arrange a marriage between his eldest son and a princess of Denmark;

and the bishop selected Dominic to accompany him. On their way to Denmark they passed through Languedoc, a province in the south of France, which was then overrun with the false doctrines of the Albigenses. The faith of the person with whom they lodged had been unsettled by these doctrines, and Dominic, pierced to the heart by the unhappy delusions of this man, spent the whole night in unravelling its falsehoods to him, and, in that one night, made him a perfect and persevering believer in the blessed truths of the Church.

The death of the princess on the very eve of her marriage, changed all the plans of the ecclesiastics in the royal train, and Dominic was one of those who asked to be allowed to remain where so many laborers were needed in the vineyard of the Church. From this time we see Dominic given up to the conversion of souls. It is said that the rosary was his peculiar weapon in the conversion of Languedoc, and it is certain that prayer, and the preaching of the truth, made up his armor. To assist him in his holy design God allowed him to work wonderful miracles, and many credible witnesses, who had no reason to be partial to Dominic, gave in their testimony to the truth of these miracles. On one occasion, after a long conversation with the Albigenses, Dominic wrote out a short explanation of the Catholic faith, with proofs of each article of belief from the New Testament. This paper he gave to them to look over carefully. After a great deal of disputing among themselves, the leaders of the Albigenses agreed to throw it into the fire, saying,

"If it burns we shall know the doctrine it defends is false." But the paper, instead of burning, was thrown into the fire three times, and was each time taken from it without having been scorched. Yet only one person was converted by this miracle. Sometime after the same miracle was wrought for the same end, to save souls, and many yielded to this proof, so kindly repeated by God to fix their wavering faith in his servant, and faithful priest, Dominic. This miracle has been told by every one who has written the life of St. Dominic, because the testimony to its truth has always been believed.

During all the years spent with such heroic charity among the Albigenses, Dominic never complained of any injuries or affronts which he received, and only studied how to do good to those who persecuted him. One day an Albigensis, unknown to our saint, offered to be his guide; but instead of leading him by the nearest and easiest path, led him through rough ways, over stones and briars, so that Dominic's feet were terribly cut and bruised, for he always walked barefoot. The meekness with which Dominic received this treatment and the joyfulness with which he tried to console his unkind guide, when he saw his regret, calling "My blood is the mark of my success," so shook the wicked intention of the unhappy man, that he confessed his malice and actually became a Catholic.

These deluded people amused themselves by treating this humble, barefooted friar, who was to be seen about their streets, as a fool. They would follow him, throwing dirt at him and spitting in his face, tying straws to his hat and cloak, and running at him with shouts and mocking laughter. Sometimes to these insults were added threats of death, but the meek son of the chivalrous old lord of Castile was never disturbed; he seldom noticed them, or, if he answered, it was only to say, "I am not worthy of martyrdom." Once he was warned that a party of Albigenses were lying in wait at a certain place to kill him. He treated this information with his usual indifference, and passed the place singing hymns with a most joyful countenance. These men, who very likely wished to frighten him rather than to kill him, insultingly asked him: "What would *you* have done if you had fallen into *our* hands?" Then the great and courageous spirit of a Christian martyr spoke out in the barefoooted friar, a spirit superior in courage and more lofty in its sentiment than even the chivalry of his noblest ancestor—"I would have prayed you," he said, "not to have taken my life at a single blow, but little by little, cutting off each member of my body one by one; when you had done that you should have plucked out my eyes, and then have left me, so as to prolong my torments and gain me a richer crown." It is said that this reply so confounded his enemies that for sometime after they left him quite unmolested, being convinced that to persecute such a man was to give him the only consolation he desired.

Two or three of those many wonderful facts related of him have too delicate a charm about them not to be told to my young readers. You will remember the love with which our Dominic regarded his books while a student, and the noble sacrifice he made of them for what was dearer still in his eyes, his fellow-men. During his journeys on foot over the rough ways of Languedoc we still find him accompanied by his beloved tomes. One time, as he was fording the river Ariege on foot, he dropped some of his precious volumes. Three days after, his books were taken from the water by a fisherman, dry, and quite uninjured. Another time he was crossing this same river in a little boat, and being landed on the opposite shore he found he had no money to pay the boatman. The boatman angrily insisted on his fare; "I am," said Dominic, "a follower of Jesus Christ; I carry neither gold nor silver; God will pay you the price of my passage." But the boatman, still more angry, took hold of his cloak, saying, "Leave your cloak with me or pay me my money." Dominic raised his eyes to heaven and stood, for a moment, in prayer; then, looking on the ground, he showed the man a piece of silver lying there which Providence had sent, and said kindly to him, "My brother, there is what you ask; take it and suffer me to go my way."

But the time had come for Dominic to enter in earnest upon the work that was to leave his own mark on the Christian ages. Already he had founded the first house of Dominican nuns, to meet the wants of a distracted, heart-broken neighborhood among the Albigenses. This was at Prouille, a small village near Montréal, at the foot of the Pyrenees mountains. Their habit was white with a tawny mantle. This house, founded Dec. 27th, 1206, was afterwards associated to the Order of St. Dominic. These ladies were engaged in teaching children, spending a certain number of hours every day in such labor with the hands, as spinning. It became the mother-house of twelve other convents, and among the prioresses, or superiors, are numbered several of the royal house of Bourbon. It was at Toulouse that Dominic made his own humble beginnings of the Order of Preaching Friars, an Order which to this day is sending forth noble preachers to the old cities of Christendom.

Nothing helps us to realize how wisely the saints planned, and how thorough and lasting was their work, as to try to count up, and remember, how long such Orders as the Benedictine, the Dominican, and Franciscan Orders, have been in existence; to remember, also, how many strong governments have been shattered while they survive and flourish; survive and flourish, too, not only in the countries and among the people where they were first planted, but transplanted to our own new country, among a people ignorant, often, of their claims to peculiar veneration. And this is not a mere chance, nor is it because of fortunate circumstances. St. Dominic intended to have his Order do exactly what it has done, and began in a way to make sure of the very success, which we, more than six hundred years after, can see it has earned.

Peter Cellani offered his own house, in Toulouse,

to Dominic and the six companions who had joined him in his great work. In after years Peter used to say, that he had not been received into the Order, but that he had received the Order into his own house.

With these six companions, Dominic began a community life of poverty and prayer, under rules of religious discipline. But this simple community life was not all that he had planned for himself and his followers. Besides this, he had a strong wish at his heart, and this was the salvation of souls. The means he chose for saving the souls that he valued so much, was, such a preaching of the word of God as could only come from a knowledge of theology, deep enough, and wide enough, and lofty enough, to defend the doctrines of Christianity against all the attacks of unbelievers. He explained to his followers that in order to teach the truth they must first learn it. It so happened that a celebrated doctor of theology, named Alexander, lived at this very time in Toulouse. To him Dominic resolved to entrust his little company of followers. The same morning on which Dominic made this resolve Alexander had risen very early, and while in his room, engaged in study, was overcome by an irresistible need of sleep. His book dropped from his hand and he sank into a deep slumber. As he slept he saw before him seven stars, at first small and scarcely visible, but which increased in size and brightness, until they enlightened the whole world. As day broke he started from his dream and hastened to the school where he was to deliver his usual lecture.

Scarcely had he entered the room when Dominic and his six companions presented themselves before him. They were all dressed alike, in the white habit and surplice, and they announced themselves as "poor brothers who were about to preach the Gospel of Christ in Toulouse," and who desired, first of all, to profit by his instructions. Alexander understood that he saw before his eyes the seven stars of his morning dream, and, years after, when Europe was ringing with the learning of the Order of Preaching Friars, Alexander, who was at the English court, related the whole circumstance with fatherly pride at having been the first master of the Preaching Friars.

I must ask you, my young friends, to look at the picture of St. Dominic that I have copied for you, and to count the stars on the lower edge of the border. I think you will say, with me, that the person who designed this border, had heard of Alexander, and his seven pupils, the Preaching Friars.

This name of *Preaching Friars* was very dear to St. Dominic. It was the name first given to them by himself, and I will tell you how it was confirmed to them as their true name. The great Pope, Innocent III., was in the chair of St. Peter, when Dominic applied to him, as the head of the Church, for a formal recognition of his young Order; and this far-sighted Pope, although he did not live to grant to it all the privileges necessary, showed a marked affection for Dominic and his brethren. Shortly after giving a favorable answer to Dominic, he had occasion to write to him on some affairs connected with the Order, and desired one of his secretaries to send the necessary instructions. When the note was finished, the secretary asked, to whom it should be addressed. "To Brother Dominic and his companions," he answered; then, after a moment's pause, he added, "No, do not write that; let it be, 'To Brother Dominic and those who preach with him in Toulouse;'" then stopping the secretary a third time, he said, "Write this: 'To Master Dominic and the Brothers Preachers.'"

In these days of palace-cars, and of every luxurious invention to cheat the traveler of the sense of weariness, I think my young friends will enjoy the variety of picturing to themselves the good friar, Dominic, on his long journeys from France to Rome; for a more cheery pedestrian never lived than St. Dominic. He always traveled on foot, with a small bundle on his shoulder and a stick in his hand. As soon as he was a little out of the towns and villages, he would stop and take off his shoes, performing the journey barefoot, however rough the roads might be. He would never let his companions carry his bundle, nor even help him to carry it, although they often begged for the privilege. When his winding and rocky way led him to some height overlooking the country or city below him, he would often pause, looking earnestly at it, and weeping for the miseries suffered, and for the sins committed, within it. Then he would put on his shoes so as not to appear too singular, and kneeling down, would pray that no sin of his might bring a chastisement upon the place. If a river lay before him on the road, he would make the sign of the cross and then enter it without hesitation, being always the first to ford it. If it rained, or any other discomfort occurred, he would encourage his companions, and then begin singing, in a joyful tone, his favorite hymn, the *Ave Maris Stella*, or the *Veni Creator*. In reading his life, one is struck by the frequent mention of his singing psalms, and canticles of joy, while climbing over the rough mountains, and through the dark ravines, that lay in his way. St. Dominic is described as having fair auburn hair and a most beaming smile, with a disposition so gentle and so joyous, that this picture of St. Dominic, singing over the mountain passes of the rugged Swiss Alps, is full of the spirit of the charming traditions that have come down to us about him. He would often stop at the towns and villages, on his way, to preach. One day a young man said to him, "What books have you studied, father, that your sermons are so full of the learning of the Holy Scriptures?" "I have studied the book of charity, my son, more than any other," he replied; "it is the book that teaches us all things."

One more of those delightful events in the life of our saint, so delightful that they read like legends, must adorn these pages, to be laid up in your minds for the coming days of prosperity, it may be, when you will be tempted to forget the Giver of all your blessings, or it may be, for your days of adversity and straightness, when your hearts will cry out, perhaps, to your fellow-men in vain, and when you may almost fancy, in the bitterness of your desolation, that God has forgotten you, has forgotten His promises to those who trust in Him.

After the Pope, Honorius III., had given to the Order of Preaching Friars all the privileges necessary to their success, he allowed St. Dominic to choose a convent for his community. St. Dominic chose one that was, even at that day, full of interest for its religious associations. Among the old churches on the Appian Way, leading from Rome, is one in honor of St. Sixtus, pope and martyr. If an English, Irish, or American traveler should visit this church now, on one of the days when it is open for the devotion of the faithful, he would still find the door opened by a white-robed religious of the Order of St. Dominic; and, what will interest my young readers, is the fact that these good Dominicans speak English. The church of St. Sixtus, the first one occupied by St. Dominic and his followers in the Eternal City, is the property of the Irish Dominicans of St. Clement. This church, with all the buildings attached to it, was granted by Honorius III. to our saint. "When the friars living at St. Sixtus were about one hundred in number, on a certain day the blessed Dominic commanded Brother John of Calabria and Brother Albert of Rome, to go into the city and beg alms. They did so, without success, from morning even until the third hour of the day. Therefore they returned to the convent, and they were already hard by the church of St. Anastasia, when they were met by a certain woman who had a great devotion to the Order; and, seeing that they had nothing with them, she gave them a loaf of bread; "For I would not," she said, "that you should go back quite empty handed." As they went on a little further, they met a man who asked them, very importunately, for charity. They excused themselves, saying they had nothing for themselves; but the man only begged them the more earnestly. Then they said one to another, "What can we do with only one loaf? Let us give it to him for the love of God." So they gave him the loaf, and immediately they lost sight of him. Now, when they were come to the convent, the blessed father to whom the Holy Spirit had, meanwhile, revealed all that had passed, came out to meet them, saying to them with a joyful air, "Children, you have nothing?" They replied, "No father," and they told him all that had happened, and how they had given the loaf to the poor man. Then, said he, "It was an angel of the Lord: the Lord will know how to provide for His own; let us go and pray." Thereupon he entered the church, and, having come out again after a little space, he bade the brethren call the community to the refectory. They replied to him, "But, holy father, how is it you would have us call them, seeing there is nothing to give them to eat?" And they, purposely, delayed obeying the order which they had received. Therefore the blessed father caused Brother Roger, the cellarer, to be summoned, and commanded him to assemble the brethren to dinner, for the Lord would provide for their wants. Thus they prepared the tables, and placed the cups, and at a given signal all the community entered the refectory. The blessed father gave the benediction, and every one being seated, Brother Henry, the Roman, began to read. Meanwhile the blessed Dominic was praying, his hands being joined together on the table, and, lo! suddenly, even as he had promised them by the inspiration of the Holy Ghost, two beautiful young men, ministers of the Divine Providence, appeared in the midst of the refectory, carrying loaves in two white cloths which hung from their shoulders, before and behind. They began to distribute the bread, beginning at the lower rows, one at the right hand, the other at the left, placing before each brother, one whole loaf of admirable beauty. Then when they were come to the blessed Dominic, and had in like manner placed an entire loaf before him, they bowed their heads and disappeared, without anyone knowing, even to this day, whence they came or whither they went. And the blessed Dominic said to his brethren, "My brethren, eat the bread which the Lord has sent you." Then he told the servers to pour out some wine. But they replied, "Holy father, there is none." Then the blessed Dominic, full of the spirit of prophecy, said to them, "Go to the vessel, and pour out to the brethren the wine which the Lord has sent them." They went there, and found, indeed, that the vessel was filled up to the brim with an excellent wine, which they hastened to bring. And Dominic said, "Drink, my brethren, of the wine which the Lord has sent you." They ate, therefore, and drank, as much as they desired, both that day, and the next, and the day after that. But after the meal of the third day, he caused them to give what remained to the poor, and would not allow that any more of it should be kept in the house. During these three days no one went to seek alms, because God had sent them bread and wine in abundance. Then the blessed father made a beautiful discourse to his brethren, never to distrust the Divine goodness, even in time of greatest want. Brother Tancred, the prior of the convent, Brother Odo of Rome, and Brother Henry of the same place, Brother Laurence of England, Brother Gandion, and Brother John, of Rome, and many others who were present at this miracle, related it to Sister Cecilia, and to the other sisters who were then still living on the other side of the Tiber." It is to Sister Cecilia that we owe this beautiful narration, and so highly was the memory of this miracle prized by the Order, that, from that time to the present, the lowest tables are the first served.

It is this "Visit of the Angels" which is still to be seen on the "Ark of St. Dominic," as sculptured by the hand of the great artist, Niccola Pisano, and the beauty of the two angels continues to excite the admiration of the most refined critics on religious art.

So fascinating is the life of St. Dominic, so tender a grace lingers around his least acts and his most casual words, that it is with difficulty I cut short the narrative of his labors and of his death. But something remains to be said, even here, beyond the mere story of the life of St. Dominic. I have said that the visit of the angels to give food to the brethren in a time of sharp necessity, had been commemorated in the beautiful bas-relief on the "Ark of St. Dominic" (as the shrine is called which contained his beloved and venerated relics), and this is only one of several exquisite designs on that wonderful work of art, still to be seen at Bologna. These designs illustrate several of the miracles worked by St. Dominic; viz., the miracle of restoring to life a young lord, named Napoleone; the fiery ordeal in Languedoc, when the flames refused to consume the writings of St. Dominic; the vision of St. Dominic, when the holy apostles, SS. Peter and Paul, appeared to him, presenting to him the staff of a missionary and the book of the Holy Scriptures; both the Staff and the Book being, ever after, the companions of his journeys. The scene is also represented in which St. Dominic gives the Holy Scriptures to his own Friars Preachers, before sending them to proclaim that Divine Word, of which he had said, "The seed will bear fruit if it is sown; it will but moulder if you hoard it up." Between these pictured legends is an exquisite statue of the Madonna with her Divine Son in her arms, as if to express the love of St. Dominic for this "Mother of fair love, of fear, of knowledge, and of holy hope." This Ark of St. Dominic, the pride not only of the city of Bologna, but of entire Christendom, was erected to contain the body of the saint, and shows how the ages crown the humble with just honors. When St. Dominic was dying, his disciples, knowing an affectionate strife would arise for the possession of his relics, asked him, where he would be buried. He replied, "Under the feet of my brethren." Now, that sanctified body is known to have inspired its own sepulchre, and to have thus added another proof to those already existing, of the holy connection between religion and art.

The Dominican Order, founded, as we have seen, by an enthusiastic and accomplished scholar, has been the nurse, not only of sacred letters and pulpit eloquence, but of religious art. There is no one who travels, intelligently, through the beautiful cities of Italy, who does not search out the works of the lay Brother, "Fra Angelico da Fiesole," or the Angelical Brother, also called the *Blessed* Angelico; and the eye turns from the master-pieces of Raphael himself to the celestial visions of the Dominican friar, fixed on the panel or the wall. Fra Angelico illuminated the choral books of the monastery, in which he lived, in a manner to excite the admiration of all succeeding ages, and he also decorated with his inspired pencil, dipped, one might say, in the very colors of paradise, the tabernacles and the altars, the chapter-room of the Order, and the cells of the religious. The favored brethren in that Florentine convent walked, daily, among those seraphic pictures that seem, even in copies and engravings, to bring Heaven to earth. One of these pictures

I find described in a way to quicken the most ardent desire in every soul, not only to see this picture, but to behold, and participate in, the joys it represents. As the object of this book is to rouse a lively interest, not only in sacred literature, but also in sacred art, I do not hesitate to copy out for you this description by one who, himself a Dominican, has written two choice volumes on the Painters, Sculptors, and Architects, of his noble Order. The writer says that this picture which he is describing, is really made up of three, the *Last Judgment* occupying the middle and largest of the three arches. On the left of the Last Judgment, Fra Angelico painted Hell; yet the gentle spirit of the good friar could not bring itself to express the casting away of the wicked by their Omnipotent Judge, in any other way than by a wave of the hand, and a face turned forever away from those whose hearts had been turned away from Him; from Him who was alone worthy to be their joy. But, "where this painter triumphs, and establishes his title to the name of Angelico, with which the people honored him, is on the right side of the picture, where we behold the elect. Who can see these graceful little figures and not be enamored of virtue? Who is it that does not yearn to taste the holy and ineffable joys of these blessed beings, who, having fought the good fight, and completed the term of their exile, are now approaching their true country to enjoy that reward for which they have longed, and for the sake of which they have suffered so many afflictions? They all have their eyes and arms turned towards their Redeemer, and they seem to bless and thank Him for having placed them among His elect. But more charming than even this, are the kisses and embraces which the elect interchange with the angels who protected and guided them on the path of peril, as, kneeling, they clasp each other in heavenly affection. These greetings ended, we see them linking hands and gracefully dancing on a sweet meadow, enameled with the most beauteous flowers. Their garments glisten with innumerable little stars; the head of each is wreathed with a garland of white and red roses, whilst a brilliant little flame burns on the forehead of each angel. Then, light, airy, graceful; and, even during the dance, absorbed in ecstatic contemplation, carolling and singing, they advance toward the celestial Jerusalem; and the nearer they approach to it, the more ethereal and luminous do their bodies become; till at last, arrived at the gates of the holy city, they appear to be transmuted into the most subtile and resplendent spirits; and then, two by two, holding each other's hand, they are introduced into eternal beatitude." Is there a little heart, on the whole round world, that would not follow in that train of angels and saints, and enter with them the gates to eternal bliss?

I have already spoken of another picture by Fra Angelico, the Coronation of the Blessed Virgin Mary, into which he introduced the likeness of St. Dominic and of many others. He painted this subject, "The

Coronation," several times, and always with the most entrancing beauty of expression.

Fra Bartolommeo, another religious painter of great merit, is claimed by the Dominicans. He was not only a friar, but a *preaching* friar, and we read in the Dominican annals that he was the pastor of a parish, and often laid down his palette and brushes to attend to the wants of his people. But besides this Fra Bartolommeo, there was another, called Fra Bartolommeo della Porta, and this last is the one most generally known, and spoken of. To him we owe the St. Stephen which illustrates this volume. In my portfolio is a large photograph from Fra Bartolommeo's sketch of the evangelist, St. Mark, from the very drawing made by his own hand. It brings the great painters very near to us when we can see a perfect sun-picture of their sketches. The pictures of Fra Bartolommeo are eagerly sought for, both in colors and engravings.

But it is not by paintings and sculptures, alone, that the Order of St. Dominic has helped to civilize the most polished nations. To the Dominican architects we owe some of the noblest edifices in Italy, besides those famous bridges that from age to age, one after another, have spanned the river Arno, at Florence; and, so long as the beautiful church of San Maria Novella is the pride of Florence, the names of the Florentine Dominicans, Fra Sisto and Fra Ristoro, will prove how much the world of art and of beauty is indebted to the Order of St. Dominic.

There is still another debt of gratitude which we,

as Americans, owe to St. Dominic and to his Order, a debt specially our own.

After the discovery of America by that saintly navigator, Christopher Columbus, great pains was taken by Columbus, and by the ecclesiastical authorities of Spain, to fulfill the highest wish of the heart of the pious discoverer; which was, to carry the knowledge of Christ to the nations sitting in darkness. If you open any good history of America, you will see the name of Father Bartholomew Las Casas; you will also read how much he did for the poor Indians, who, to the horror and grief of Columbus, were actually made slaves by the avaricious cruelty of those stronger and and more civilized races who came to the Islands after they were discovered. Las Casas did not hesitate to protest against this monstrous injustice, this perfidy and bad faith, on the part of the whites. He made four voyages to Spain in behalf of the oppressed Indians, pleaded their cause before courts and monarchs, and brought this crying wrong to the notice of Cardinal Ximenes; and all these things coming to the ears of the Pope, Paul III., he pronounced "a sentence of excommunication against all those who should make slaves of the Indians, or deprive them of their goods." For sixty years Las Casas labored for their rights as men, for their souls as heirs of heaven; and, to this day, we, as Americans, owe to Las Casas, the Dominican friar, that the curse of the enslaved Indian is not resting upon us.

St. Dominic is honored, in the Office of the Church,

on the 4th of August. He died at Bologna, on the 6th of August, the feast of the Transfiguration of our Lord, 1221; but as he promised to his friars, he has done more for them since his death than during his life; full as that life was of labor and of prayer, every line of it fragrant with the "odor of sanctity," and beaming, like the star on his infant forehead, with the "beauty of holiness."

The next time you say your rosary, will you not remember St. Dominic? Remember, also, to thank him for having left behind him this pleasant way of saying your prayers; asking him, from your heart, to pray for you, that you may be worthy of his protection, and may, at last, enter into his exceeding great reward.

SAINT JEROME.

F you run your eye carefully over the Calendar, or list of saints, for September, you will see, at the very last day of the month, a name which may not be familiar to you, but which is a great and shining name in the Church of God. Sometimes there is a special devotion, for years and even generations, to some one saint, and parents give the name of that saint to their children. I do not know one child who has been baptized Jerome, yet this is the name of the great saint that I shall tell you about to-day.

A certain nun used to say of her patron, St. John Baptist, that he was "a very old-fashioned saint." St. Jerome is one of the old-fashioned saints; but, I confess, I am partial to them, and it is, perhaps, for this very reason, that I admire so much this ancient doctor and confessor.

St. Jerome is one of the Four Latin Fathers; and, as such, we see him, in magnificent old pictures, among these Four Fathers, grouped around the Madonna and

Infant Christ, or the glorified Redeemer, dressed in the rich scarlet hat and robes of a cardinal; and he is venerated like St. Ambrose, St. Augustine and St. Gregory. St. Jerome lived more than a thousand years ago, and, all through these ages, he has been looked up to by popes, cardinals, bishops, doctors, and priests—for the Church never outgrows her saints.

Before God, "a thousand years is as one day;" but for us, mortals, to know that a fellow-mortal has been a saint more than a thousand years, has, for more than a thousand years, received the veneration of the whole Church, and has been, all that time, named in her Sacred Office, and all that time has had one day set apart for his honor, to know that this fellow-mortal has been more than a thousand years in the immediate presence of God, is to gain a wonderful idea of the glory it is to be a saint.

St. Jerome, then, is our patron for September. He was born so early as 342 years after the birth of Our Lord, or about one thousand five hundred years ago. A long time to look back, yet St. Jerome tells us, how, when a young student in Rome, he used to visit, with his school-fellows, the cemeteries of the martyrs, or, what we call, the Catacombs.

We must remember that the history of these martyrs, in the time of St. Jerome, was still as fresh in the minds of Christians as the history of the heroes of the "Revolution of '76," is to us; for, less than a hundred years before, less than fifty years before, such martyrs as St. Agnes, St. Sebastian and St. Pancratius, and hundreds of others, all dear to the hearts of the people of God, had been seen giving up their lives for Christ, and leaving their bodies to find their way, by the hands of pious and courageous Christians, to the Catacombs. It cannot be supposed that an intelligent youth, like St. Jerome, living so near the time of these lights, shining, as they did, amid the dark night of pagan persecution, did not know what that faith was for which they died, or that his own faith did not seem all the more precious for knowing that it was the very same for which so many noble souls had joyfully given up friends, wealth, pleasure, good name, and life itself. As I have said again and again in these pages, there is no way of learning to love and prize our dear old religion, like that of reflecting upon the sacrifices, which the saints, of all ages, have esteemed themselves happy in making for its sake. And, to this remark, so often repeated, I will now add another, that I wish you to remember; which is, that those who suffered for the Christian faith, and suffered in such a manner as to be obliged to answer the questions of their pagan judges, and to make very nice distinctions as to what they were bound to believe and what they were not bound to believe, have a right to be looked upon as well instructed Christians, and their faith to be regarded as the one approved by Christ and by His Church; and, therefore, as the faith which Christ and His true Church still desire us to believe. As I have said above, it is not to be supposed that St. Jerome, living so near the time at which these martyrs confessed to the faith of

Christ by their deaths, did not know what that faith was. We must, therefore, look upon St. Jerome as one of those saints whose testimony should be taken as to what the martyrs really believed, and suffered for; and, knowing this, we have a short way of deciding what we are to believe ourselves; for I have never seen any sincere Christian who did not wish to believe exactly what those early saints and martyrs believed, who lived so near to the time of Christ, and of His apostles, as to be in no danger of misunderstanding the Christian doctrine. You can now see why St. Jerome has this distinguished rank among the Four Latin Fathers and the great doctors of the Church.

St. Jerome's native place was Stridonium, a small town upon the borders of Pannonia, Dalmatia and Italy, near Aquileia. His father, whose name was Eusebius, and who was of good family and had a large estate, knowing that a sound education was the most precious of all the advantages he could give to his children, took great care to have his son instructed in the first principles of piety and literature at home, and then sent him to Rome. In this city he became master of both the Latin and the Greek languages, and was so eloquent that he pleaded at the Roman bar. But, although he was making such progress in worldly learning, he not only made no progress in heavenly things, but he forgot the lessons of piety learned in his youth. The elegant scholar left this pagan school without being soiled by any gross vices, but he had lost the spirit and temper of a Christian, and he afterwards confessed and lamented the vanity and the worldliness of his life at that time.

Although he had left the school, he was still anxious to improve, and resolved to travel. The wise Thomas à Kempis, says, that "those who travel much are seldom holy;" and the mere visiting of celebrated shrines, does not make a person devout. It depends upon the spirit in which we visit holy places, whether we are made better or worse by travel. Almighty God, who saw the soul of the young Jerome, as not even his good father could see it, had designs of mercy towards him, and, by the Divine Providence, his travels, undertaken only out of a desire for learning, became the means of his returning to the piety of his earlier years. The Romans had founded several famous schools in ancient Gaul, now France, and especially at Marseilles, Toulouse, Bordeaux, Autun, Lyons and Triers. It was Triers that drew the attention of young Jerome. It had been his greatest pleasure, at Rome, to collect a choice library, and to read all the best authors, and such was his enjoyment of these books, that he forgot to eat or drink. He bought a great many books, copied several, and had his friends copy for him. It was in the midst of this same studious life at Triers, about the year 370, that the grace of God so touched his heart that he recovered his youthful fervor, gave up all the vanity of his life, and resolved to devote himself to the service of Jesus Christ in a life of continence. From this time his ardor for virtue was even greater than any he had before felt for worldly learning, and he turned the course of his studies into the new, and far more delightful, channels, which Christianity had opened to her devout scholars. Being still intent on adding treasures to his library, he copied at Triers, St. Hilary's book on the Psalms; those "Psalms of David," which Jerome afterwards translated with such zeal. His travels, from this time, were directed by his love for Christian learning, his friendships were made with Christian scholars, and when he returned to Rome, it was to devote himself to his studies in a holy retirement.

But he soon found that he could not lead this life of retirement in his own country, nor even in Rome; and, being in earnest to do something for God, and knowing that he must first sanctify his own soul, he sought to do so after the manner of many pious persons in those ages. He visited holy hermits, going from one desert, or wilderness, to another, to gain from their conversation the secret of a perfect life. After these visits to the hermits he spent some time in Antioch, studying and writing, and from Antioch went into a hideous desert, where he passed four years in solitary study and in the exercises of a most fervent piety. After this he visited Palestine or the Holy Land, and, if even worldly people are deeply moved by visiting the sacred places where Our Lord walked upon earth, with what devotion must not this great saint have kneeled upon the very spots where Jesus Christ lived and suffered for us! He made Bethlehem his home; Bethlehem, that "little one among the princes of Judah," where the Eternal Wisdom lived, Incarnate, under the form of a feeble infant, and where the greatest intellect was continually in a school of humility. But as it was not to gratify a devout sentiment, nor even to secure his own salvation alone, that St. Jerome lived, he began to study everything around him which could throw any light on the Holy Scripture; putting himself under Jewish doctors to learn the Hebrew language, and faithfully seeking out every particular concerning the places named in sacred history.

About the year 380, our saint went to Constantinople, there to study the Holy Scriptures under St. Gregory Nazianzen, who was then bishop of Constantinople. When St. Gregory left that city, St. Jerome returned to Palestine; but the Pope, Damasus, called him to Rome, and kept him near his own person as his secretary. At Rome, among other duties, St. Jerome was the spiritual director of such holy women as St. Paula, Eustochium, Ascella and her sister Marcella, and Fabiola, and we have volumes of letters, in our Catholic libraries, written by this saint, directing the education of children and the pursuits of Christian women.

Very tender are the teachings of St. Jerome in behalf of these daughters of good mothers. "As soon as she can speak," he writes, "let her learn some part of the Psalms. Let her have little letters, made of boxwood or ivory, the names of which she must know, that she may play with them, and that learning may be a diversion. When a little older, let her form each letter in wax with her finger, guided by another's hand; then let her be invited, by prizes and presents, to join syllables together, and to write the names of the patriarchs down from Adam."

You will think, by these instructions quoted from St. Jerome, that the little Roman girls in his time, needed very much the same help as the little girls who are, to day, learning to read in some quiet school in the United States; and we should go far, I think, before we should find any ladies in modern society more zealous in learning, or more patient in teaching, Christian doctrine, than these holy ladies who were trained by St. Jerome. He tells us that Paula, Marcella, Blesilla and Eustochium, spoke, wrote, and recited the Psalms in the Hebrew, as perfectly as in the Greek and Latin tongues.

The history of these noble Roman ladies is one that every child, every girl, should know by heart; and there is nothing more beautiful in Christian friendships than the regard cherished by St. Jerome for these devout Christian women, and the veneration cherished by them for their saintly director.

From Rome St. Jerome went to Egypt, to improve still more in sacred learning; from Egypt to Palestine again, and to Bethlehem, which seemed to draw him, as a magnet draws steel. From this birthplace of our dear Lord his good deeds ran, like clear waters from a pure fountain, to bless the whole world. But the work which he there completed, after years of devout study, and which the Church has crowned with more than approbation—with her gratitude—was the translation of the Holy Scriptures into Latin, the language most generally spoken among Christians at that time and which may still be called the language of the Church. To this translation St. Jerome added such explanations of the Sacred Books as a knowledge of the languages in which they were written, and of the people among whom they were composed, fitted him, above any one living at that time, to give. And, so far is the world and its scholars from having outgrown this translation by St. Jerome, that no one, whether Catholic or Protestant, would think of translating the Bible into any language, without making himself familiar with the "Vulgate," as that translation of the Bible, is called which was made by St. Jerome. Those priests who study to make the meaning of the Holy Scripture more easily understood by their people, or who attempt the great labor of translating them to suit our way of speaking at the present day, always feel a special devotion to St. Jerome. Within a few years an archbishop of the United States, the late Most Reverend Francis Patrick Kenrick, D. D., translated the whole Bible into our English tongue, with very full notes of explanation; and St. Jerome was one of his patrons, as well as authorities, in this great work.

Those people who find the silly, and, too often, the profane poetry and stories of newspapers and magazines more entertaining than the wonderful history and sublime poetry of the Scriptures, can hardly understand the ardent love of these scholars and saints for the inspired Word of God; for, so far from grudging their study and labor, they offered, as a sacrifice of love, the fairest and most fruitful years of their life to this work. Indeed, with most of the saintly translators and commentators of the Bible, as with St. Jerome, St. Bede, and our own beloved Archbishop Kenrick, this work seemed to be the crowning glory of their lives, the last and the most perfect, from which they soon passed to their most sweet reward.

Let the example of this shining saint of olden time, and the saints of our own, inspire you, my young friends, with an admiration, as well as a religious respect, for the Holy Scripture. Never weary of its wonderful story of God's dealings with his people, nor of the touching story of "the Word made flesh," and of the apostles who succeeded our Redeemer as the teachers of His truth. The veneration and love that will grow out of this admiring study of the Bible, will save you from the error of those who rashly presume to judge of its meaning, and, too often, to despise its authority. Remember the learned men who have submitted their life-long researches upon the Bible and its meaning to the decision of the Church, divinely inspired to interpret its most hidden sense, and, imitating their humility, read the Holy Scriptures so as to grow more and more in charity, in hope, and in a steadfast, courageous faith in God, and in the Church which has so faithfully preserved this record of His divine promises, and also their fulfillment.

St. Jerome has always been as much in favor with artists as with theologians. Mrs. Jameson says, "There is scarcely a collection of pictures in which we do not find a St. Jerome, either doing penance in the desert, or writing his famous translation, or meditating on the mystery of the Incarnation," and she asks us to "dwell for a moment on his own description of his solitary life, that we may understand with what a literal and circumstantial truth the painters have expressed it in their pictures." His "companions," he tells us, "were scorpions and wild beasts;" his "home, a recess among caves and precipices;" his "limbs were rough with sackcloth, and his skin so burned and so squalid that he might have been taken for an Ethiopian;" but, Mrs. Jameson adds, "neither his great sorrows, nor his four years of solitude and penance in the desert, could destroy the burning enthusiasm of this celebrated man" for virtue and for learning.

The picture which I have selected to grace this sketch of the life of St. Jerome, is by Titian (the same artist that painted the martyrdom of St. Laurence), and it shows how the soul of this noble artist was inspired by the life of St. Jerome in his rocky solitude, absorbed in contrite meditation upon that Redeemer whose sufferings were so plainly to be seen in the crucifix, which the holy recluse had suspended among the branches of the trees overhanging his cave.

In this, as in all the pictures of St. Jerome, the lion

is seen at his side, and the legend that has given to the king of the desert this distinguished place, is worthy to be read and remembered.

One evening as St. Jerome sat within the gates of his monastery at Bethlehem, a lion entered, limping as if in pain; and all the brethren, when they saw the lion, fled in great terror; but St. Jerome arose and went forward to meet him, receiving him as a guest. Then the king of all the beasts, the terror of men as well as of animals, lifted up his paw, with one blow of which he could have destroyed any man on earth, holding it towards St. Jerome with all the docility and gentleness of a child; and, on examining it, our great doctor and scholar found a cruel thorn fixed in the lion's paw, which he skillfully drew out, and afterwards tended the lion until the wound was quite healed. The grateful beast became so attached to our saint that he chose to stay with him rather than to go back to his native desert and to his natural companions, and he also found out ways to return to St. Jerome the care that he had given to him. In one picture of the death of St. Jerome, the lion is represented as roaring with grief, and in another he is holding his paw to St. Jerome; but usually, as in this picture by Titian, he lies beside his beloved friend, in that majesty of repose suitable in a dumb companion of one whose contemplations were of God, and of eternity.

During all the General Councils that have been held by the Roman Pontiffs as successors of St. Peter, like the Council, which, as I write, is assembling in Rome at the call and under the care of Pius IX., we find them turning over the writings of St. Jerome and the other "Fathers," not only to learn the opinions of these wise scholars on matters of Christian doctrine, but to know what was really the belief of the Christian people in those ages. The faith, once given in charge to the apostles, and by them given in charge to the popes, bishops, and priests of later generations, was garnered up by the fathers and doctors of the Church in their heavy folio volumes of parchment, like the honey of bees in so many richly stored hives, to be read by the faithful in all ages. And, if all cannot be learned, if all cannot gather such treasures for the present or future generations, if all cannot read them in the languages in which they were written, it is still consoling to remember, that God never allows us to be ignorant of anything necessary to salvation, if we, on our part, are careful to use all the opportunities given us to know the truth, and to be instructed in matters of faith and practices of devotion; and, especially, if we listen, faithfully, to the sermons and instructions of our pastors, who have been instructed for the very purpose of instructing us. At least, let us follow the footsteps of St. Jerome at the lowly distance of those, who, to all mere worldly learning, prefer that which makes the learned and the ignorant, alike, wise unto salvation; or, of those who use their learning to build up faith, not to pull down.

Towards the end of his life St. Jerome was interrupted in his studies by roving barbarians, who found their way through Egypt into Palestine; and after this, some of his enemies, who hated him for his defence of the truth, sent a band of robbers to attack the helpless monks and nuns at Bethlehem. They set fire to all the monasteries, and our saint, who was then very old, with great difficulty escaped from their fury to a strong castle. After this storm had passed by, he returned to his books and to his writing, until a fever released his soul from the prison of his mortal body on the 30th of September, in the year 420. He was buried in a vault among the ruins of his own monastery, at Bethlehem, but his relics lie, at present, in the church of St. Mary Major, at Rome.

St. Jerome made it his chief employment in his solitude to meditate upon death, and the Divine Judgment; and it is to St. Jerome that we owe this impressive sentence; "Whether I eat or drink, or whatever else I do, the dreadful trumpet of the last day seems always sounding in my ears! Arise, ye dead, and come to judgment!"

The fear of St. Jerome, which had so much to do with his being a saint, was the fear that springs from the love of God; for how dreadful does it seem, to a saint, to be forever banished from the presence of God! No one need be ashamed of this fear, and we are told, by Thomas à Kempis, that this fear will cast out all other fear from our souls," so that those who fear God are the only brave people in the world.

Ask St. Jerome, on his feast day, to obtain for you

this holy fear of God, and then the trump of the Last Day will have, for your ears, a sound, not of terror, but of holy joy.

SAINT LIOBA.

IT would not surprise me to find that not ten of my young readers had ever heard of St. Lioba; but some of you may remember having seen her name on the list of saints, or, in reading Butler's "Lives," you may have been struck by something which made you linger over the columns devoted to "St. Lioba, Abbess." If so, you will be glad to meet her again; and to me she comes out of the mists of ages to take her place on these pages, with a grace so fresh, with a simple naturalness of feeling, sanctified, not crushed out, by her supernatural devotion, so much in harmony with the races to which many of us belong, that I choose her, as I have already chosen St. Bede and St. Dunstan, to represent us among the nations, and to show how the peculiarities of race and clime may sometimes give a peculiar charm even to a saint.

In a small collection of historical sketches, like this one of Patron Saints, there must be some limit to one's wishes; I have not, therefore, attempted to bring forward the lives of many saints well known, and very dear, both to you and to me. There is a brilliant constellation of Irish saints which I hope to bring out at some future time, in a way to give you a new interest in them; and there are Welsh and Scotch saints, German and African saints, so woven in with the history, and poetry, and the beautiful traditions, of the early Christian ages, that one turns with difficulty from the charming narratives that have come down to us concerning them, rich in the association of some of the fairest ages of the world. There are, also, American saints, and these I have passed over still more unwillingly; but it has been necessary to do so, if I would keep to my first plan; and this plan is one that will allow me, at any time, to continue our sketches.

It would sometimes seem as if one out of every two saint, in any collection of lives, was either French or Italian, so often do we find these nations honored by the choicest gifts of heaven in the persons of saints. Yet it is by our fault that we know so little of our own saints. If one-half the trouble that is taken to read the annals of other nations, were spent upon reading our own, we should find examples of holiness beautifying our national history, like the jewels on an embroidered chasuble, whose lustre has a double claim upon our love and veneration. We see crowds of people following the beaten track of guides and hand-books in their travels, who visit every shrine in France and Italy, but never turn to the holy Isle of Iona, to see where St. Columba lived with his monks, like a father among his devoted children, with a patriarchal simplicity of authority, of affection and pathos, such as the world can never hope to see again; who can scale every crag of the Alps, but stand suddenly aghast, before the prospect of a wild voyage to that northern island whose mutilated crosses, and ruined abbey, tell where the most poetic of all the sons of the Island of Saints passed his voluntary exile. We hope to see the picturesque saints of the north taking their just place in the affections of the youth of coming generations. To study the saints of our own race is to learn how God expects us to become saints. It is to give you some hints as to the way in which Celts, and Anglo-Saxons, and Americans, may serve God with a saintly perfection, that I have chosen St. Lioba as one of the patrons for September. There is many a girl who would shrink, appalled, from the austerities of a St. Catherine of Sienna, or a St. Theresa, who will see, in St. Lioba, a type of sanctity fitted to her own mental and physical habits; and, before she knows it, she will be on the way to a solid, practical, and well-balanced sanctity. Half of the piety in the world is lost, so far as its fitness to the every day necessities is concerned, by these very causes. Our good American girls try to be like Italian and French saints, instead of trying to be, simply, saints of God; of God, who created them, in whatever country He has seen fit to place them, with the intention of having them become types of their race in the order of sanctity, and benefiting their race by the exercise of natural virtues in a supernatural degree. I wish you all to think about this, and believe that sanctity is the same in all nations; as the soul of man is the same among all nations; but, like that soul, clothed upon by the peculiarities of race and clime, which peculiarities are not to be forced upon other races in other climes, any more than dress and social habits.

A charming example of what I wish to make you understand about this occurs to me as I write, and I shall give you the story with its real names.

On one of the warmest days of this last summer, coming into my little parlor, I saw two women seated there, dressed in black serge gowns and cloaks, and in bonnets exactly like the cape-bonnets that many little girls still wear, made of a straight piece of black barège, with narrow strips of pasteboard run in, to make them stand out from the face. You have all seen these cape-bonnets made of pretty colored cambric. Those worn by the two women in black dresses and cloaks, as I have said, were of black barège, and they gave an air of the most rustic humility to their costume. I welcomed them as "Sisters," of some Order unknown to me, and found that only the youngest one could speak English; but a letter in choice French, from Rev. Father P—— of Robinsonville, near Green Bay, in Wisconsin, gave me a clue to the mystery before me. It introduced to me Sister Adèle, a humble Belgian woman, to whom had been granted, undoubtedly, an apparition of Our Blessed Lady, leaving her to tell me, through her young interpreter, the story of her graces and of her labors.

Twelve years ago, Sister Adèle, living in the same neighborhood as now, was in the habit of going to mass every Sunday, though she could do this only by walking eleven miles to the place where mass was celebrated. One summer day as she was returning through the dense woods from mass, she saw a bright, luminous atmosphere in the woods around her, and from this luminous atmosphere there came forth the figure of a most lovely lady, white and shining, her face covered with a veil, her robe falling over her feet, and her hands joined, as one sees the Blessed Virgin represented in pictures of the Immaculate Conception. Our good, humble sister Adèle, recognized the Virgin Mother, and full of joy, kept the vision in her heart, telling no one of the heavenly consolation given to her. A few weeks after, as she was on her way to mass, the same lovely apparition made her step light and her heart joyful; and that same afternoon before sunset, as she was returning, the same white and shining figure stood before her. This time, encouraged by its repeated appearance, she spoke in her humble way, to the veiled Vision, saying, "Dear Mistress, what do you wish me to do?" Good Sister Adèle did not think that the Blessed Virgin was thus appearing to her, repeatedly, for her spiritual consolation, alone; she knew that something was wanted of her. Our Blessed Lady's reply was, "Gather around you the neglected children in this wild country, running idle about the woods, and teach them what they should know for salvation." "Gladly would I gather them in, dear Mistress," said Sister Adèle, "but how shall I teach them, who know so little myself?" "Teach them," said the radiant visitor, "their catechism, how to sign themselves with the sign of the cross, and how to approach the sacraments. This is what I wish you to do;" and the beautiful vision, with its luminous atmosphere, disappeared, and left the dense woods as solemn as before, while dear Sister Adèle walked on to her own humble home with her heavenly commission in her heart. You may believe that Sister Adèle did not put off doing what our Blessed Lady had asked of her, but began to collect the children running wild about the woods and living in the log cabins of the neighborhood. Sister Adèle had no "price," for teaching, no tuition bills to make out to her pupils, even at the end of a whole year; and their parents, finding the school a free school, were glad to send their children. Once started, there was no lack of scholars; and very soon, Sister Adèle found that her room was too small for her school. Then this courageous woman undertook to beg, from more favored communities, the money necessary for building a large school-house, then a chapel, and, finally, to raise a home for the religious, whom she hoped to persuade to assist her in her great work. It was on this errand that she had come to our city, where churches, and schools, and sisterhoods, flourish, and there were few hearts on which her appeal fell unheeded. Every year, on the Feast of the Assumption of Our Lady, a religious procession celebrates the appearance of the Blessed Virgin to Sister Adèle; thus keeping in mind the origin of her humble school of instruction for these wandering lambs of the fold of Christ, which has changed this wilderness into a garden of delights to the Saviour of souls. Sister Adèle does not yet belong to any religious Order, but if she ever does, I hope she will wear her simple cape-bonnet, as a memorial of the rustic garb in which she met the Queen of angels and of saints, and received her commission to teach the little ones of the 'household of faith.'

Sister Adèle's vocation is one very liberally distributed among the Catholic women of America; and if not always attended by such impressive circumstances, the same zeal, courage and cheerfulness, are the dispositions required in fulfilling it. And these very dispositions we shall find in St. Lioba, who may, very aptly, be chosen as the patron of teachers, for she was, ages ago, chosen by the great St. Boniface to assist him in his missionary labors, by teaching the sisters and daughters of, at that time, the barbarous Germans.

Her biographer tells us that she was descended from an illustrious English-Saxon family, and born at Wimbourne, which name signifies, *Fountain of wine.* Ebba, her pious mother, was very nearly related to St. Boniface of Mentz, and as we often see in pious families what seems an inherited inclination to sanctity, vocations to the priesthood and a religious life, so the good Ebba gave proof that she was a spiritual cousin of the heroic St. Boniface. She had lived long in wedlock without being blessed with children, yet, when this lovely little daughter was given to her, she offered her to God from her birth, and trained her up to value the world as it deserves to be valued by the children of God, and the heirs of heaven. Ebba placed her, while still young, in the great convent of Wimbourne, in her native country. She was called Lioba, or the *Beloved One*, because of her exceeding beauty; and her accomplishments were such as fitted her to teach others, and even to rouse our admiration for "a nun, living in the middle of the eighth century in a distant abbey of a half barbarous country." There is a letter, written by St. Lioba to the German apostle, St. Boniface, that gives her history better than it can be given for her. This letter is written from Wimbourne, where Cuthburga, the sister of Ina, the king, was established by him in a convent belonging to their race and country. It was situated in a fertile tract near the royal residence of the kings of Wessex, one of the kingdoms of Britain according to its ancient division, and occupying the southwest portion of what is now England. The abbess, Cuthburga, formerly queen of Northumbria, a kingdom in the extreme north of England, and who had served her novitiate in the noble and learned convent of Barking on the Thames, brought with her, to her own house, the spirit and habits of her first monastic home, and

Wimbourne soon became still more celebrated than Barking, for its literary studies. Here, then, we find our St. Lioba, developed by a course of sound study while she practised the most sublime lessons in piety, and, unconsciously, preparing herself to carry to other regions the blessings of her own religious lot. It was under the good Abbess Tetta, who was governing a community of five hundred nuns, that St. Lioba wrote the following letter to her kinsman, St. Boniface.

"To the most reverend lord and bishop, Boniface, most dear to me in Christ, and, further, united to me by the ties of blood, Leobgitha, the last of the handmaids of Christ, health and salvation.

"I beg your clemency to deign to recollect the friendship which united you to my father, Tinne, an inhabitant of Wessex, who departed from this world eight years ago, that you may pray for the repose of his soul. I also recommend to you my mother Ebba, your kinswoman, as you know better than me, who still lives in great suffering and has been for a long time overwhelmed with her infirmities. I am their only daughter; and God grant, that unworthy as I am, I may have the honor of claiming you as my brother, for no man of our kindred inspires me with the same confidence that you do. I have taken care to send you this little present, not as being worthy of your greatness, but that it may remind you of my littleness, and that you may not forget me on account of the distance that separates us. What I chiefly ask of you, dearest brother, is, that you will defend me, by the buckler of your prayers, from the hidden snares of the enemy. I beg you to excuse the rustic style of this letter, and that your courtesy will not refuse the few words of answer that I so much desire. You will find below some lines, which I have attempted to compose according to the rules of poetic art, not from self-confidence, but to exercise the weak little genius that God has given me, and to ask the help of your elegant mind. I have learned all that I know from Eadburga, my mistress, who gives herself to the profound study of the divine law. Farewell; live a long and happy life; and pray for me.

"May the Almighty Judge, who made the earth,
And glorious in His Father's kingdom reigns,
Preserve your chaste fire, warm as at its birth,
Till time for you shall lose its rights and pains."

St. Boniface responded very heartily to this appeal of his amiable kinswoman, and a correspondence was at once opened between them which resulted in the call, afterwards made upon her, to assist him in the mission to which he at last fell a martyr.

My young friends, especially the girls, may like to know what sort of learning was pursued, so ardently, by this young nun, educated by the studious Eadburga, and we copy, for their gratification, this list of her accomplishments. "Instructed from her childhood in grammar, poetry, and the liberal arts, she increased her treasures of learning by assiduous reading. She studied, attentively, the Old and New Testaments, and committed a great part of them to memory. She was familiar with the writings of the Fathers, and with the decrees and canons of the Church. As we have seen, she could write the Latin tongue with a graceful simplicity, both in prose and verse. When not engaged in study, she worked with her hands, as was enjoined by the rule, but she greatly preferred reading or hearing others read, to any other employment. Indeed it was not easy to satisfy her in this respect. After she became abbess she insisted upon all those under her charge taking that mid-day repose allowed by the rule of St. Benedict, chiefly, as she said, because the want of sleep takes away the love of reading. But when she herself lay down at these times to rest, she had some of her pupils to read the Scriptures by the side of her couch, and they could not omit or mispronounce a word without her correcting it, though apparently she might be asleep. Yet all this learning was accompanied with a modesty, and humility, that made her seek in all things to be regarded as the least in the house. There was nothing of arrogance in her behavior, nothing of bitterness in her words. She was admirable in her understanding as she was boundless in her charity. She liked to wash the feet of her spiritual children, and to serve them at table, and she did this when she herself was fasting. Her countenance was truly angelic, always sweet and joyful, though she never indulged in laughter. No one ever saw her angry, and her aspect agreed with her name, which in Saxon means Beloved, and in Greek, Philomena."

It was in 748 that the letters from St. Boniface reached the quiet cloisters of Wimbourne, requesting that Lioba and her cousin Thecla, and Walburga, sister to the two companions of St. Boniface, Winibald and Wilibald, might be sent over to him, together with as many of their companions as might be willing to share in their enterprise. Thirty nuns at once offered themselves, and the little colony, after a stormy passage across the sea to Antwerp, was met, at Mentz, by St. Boniface. He immediately proceeded to establish Lioba in a monastery he had built for her at Bischoffsheim, where she very soon collected around her a large community of virgins, consecrated to the service of God in Germany.

If I did not hope to write for you, at some future time, the life of St. Boniface, I should be tempted to put some of the picturesque incidents of his career into this sketch of St. Lioba; but as I hope to give them to you more at length, I will only go out of my way to tell you something of her companion, St. Walburga. This brave company of zealous nuns stopped at Antwerp several days, and a grotto is still shown in the ancient church of that city dedicated to St. Walburga, where she is said to have prayed. Walburga did not remain with Lioba, but went on to Thuringia, that favored country, blessed, centuries afterwards, by the presence of St. Elizabeth of Hungary. Here her brother, Winibald, was superior of seven houses of monks, having "converted the wild pagan forest into a smiling land of woods and pastures, where all the arts of civilized life were taught and practiced, and over which the good abbot was allowed a paternal sway."

Walburga and her nuns cultivated letters as diligently in their new forest home, as they had been accustomed to do in the dear old abbey of Wimbourne. The travels of her brother, St. Wilibald, in the Holy Land, and his pilgrimage to Jerusalem, which he had often related to her and to her nuns, were afterwards written by them; and St. Walburga wrote, also, the "Life of St. Wilibald." The taste for literature among the German nuns of the tenth century may thus be traced back to our St. Lioba and her friend St. Walburga. Mabillon, who wrote about the time of the settlement of the American colonies, 1680, and who became one of the most learned of the Benedictines of St. Maur, praises the early German nuns for "Devoting themselves to study and the transcription of books with no less energy than the monks; and his praise is given in particular to those nuns of Eiken, who gave their time to reading, meditating, transcribing and painting, and to their two abbesses, Harlinda and Renilda, who wrote out the Psalter, the Four Gospels, and many other books of Holy Scripture, adorning them with liquid gold, gems and pearls."

But St. Lioba did not forget her duty to her neighbor in her books, because both the book and the neighbor were loved for God's sake, and she turned from one to the other most willingly, as God's interests required. We often feel like grudging our time for certain acts of devotion, or of charity, or even of civility and good neighborhood. The thought which cures this feeling is, that our time is God's; when spent for Him and in His service it is well spent; and, if well spent, we certainly need not grudge it. God, whose servants we are, as rightfully as the angels in heaven, can easily make good to us all the time spent for Him, or for His poor ones. We must carefully lay out the hours of the day and evening; but, in laying them out, let us be sure to give God His share. It was in the spirit of giving to God his share of her time, that we see St. Lioba rejoicing in every opportunity to exercise hospitality and charity to the poor. Kings and princes respected and honored her, especially Pepin, king of the French, and his two sons, Charles, or the great Charlemagne, and Carloman. Charlemagne, who reigned alone after the death of his brother, often sent for St. Lioba to his court at Aix-la-Chapelle, and treated her with the highest veneration. His queen, Hildegardis, loved her as her own soul, and took her advice in the most important matters. She would have been glad to keep our beloved saint always near her, to be assisted in her own efforts to lead a pious life by the example, and instruction, of St. Lioba; but our saint knew, too well, the dangers of living among the great ones of this world, and always hastened back to her own convent, and to the safe, and dear society of her beloved sisters in religion. Bishops often sought out St. Lioba in her peaceful retreat, and listened to her counsels.

St. Boniface never forgot her, and a little while before he started on his mission into Friesland, where he met death as a martyr, he recommended her, most earnestly, to his friend St. Lullus, and to his monks at Fulda; entreating them to care for her with great respect and honor; declaring it to be his desire, that after her death she should be buried by his bones, that thus they might together await the resurrection, and be raised in glory to meet the Lord and be forever united in the kingdom of Divine love. After the martyrdom of St. Boniface she frequently visited Fulda, and was allowed to enter the church, by a singular privilege, in company with two older sisters, and thus assist at the Holy Mass and at the instructions; after which she would return to her cell with her companions; and when she had continued a few days in the atmosphere of the monastery of her saintly kinsman and friend, she would return to her own nunnery.

St. Lioba lived to be very old, and, by the advice of St. Lullus, she resigned the care of her large nunneries and retired to a new one, where she devoted herself with fresh ardor to all pious exercises. Queen Hildegardis invited her so pressingly to Aix-la-Chapelle, that she could not refuse this dear friend, who, under the gorgeous robe of the sovereigns of that age, kept a heart formed for the most holy and faithful friendship. After some days, St. Lioba could not be persuaded to remain any longer from her dear solitude. On taking leave of the queen, she embraced her more affectionately than usual, and kissing her garment, her forehead, and mouth, she said, "Farewell, precious part of my soul; may Christ, our Creator and Redeemer, grant that we may see each other without confusion in the day of judgment." She died about the year 779, and was buried at Fulda, on the north side of the high altar. Her tomb was honored with miracles, and, to several, her historian, Ralph of Fulda, assures us that he was an eye-witness.

The feast of St. Lioba is kept on the 28th day of September. I have never seen a picture of St. Lioba. The portrait of this beautiful, amiable woman, enriched by so many rare gifts of mind and of heart, and finally crowned by the grace of actual sanctity, is only found traced by the pens of those who had seen her, loved her, and rejoiced in the sunshine of her holy life, her most beautiful and winning example. How many do we see in the world, who seem born to be loved and admired, born to attract others and to draw them to heaven, falling short of the peculiar grace of their vocation by reason—of what? Simply because they use these gifts only for themselves, not for God. Lovely in their own homes, faultless, as might seem at first sight, in the discharge of all domestic and social duties, yet they never win one soul to God or to the *love* of *truth*. Their own families, even, cannot remember one, of all their charming acts, that could be said to have had a supernatural motive; and thus, while possessing the beauty of a St. Lioba, her power of pleasing, her charm of poetic fancy, and her intellectual tastes, they have never used these gifts for the benefit of their fellow-beings, or for the glory of God.

Let my young girl-readers ponder this difference between St. Lioba and, perhaps, themselves; and, pondering upon this difference, as great as between the world and heaven, let them determine to set the seal of divine love upon every natural endowment, dedicating to the service of God the fairest blossoms and the choicest fruits, which the grace of God so often produces in the sheltered paradise of a happy Christian home, as well as among the holy retreats of religion; and if, by any of those providential events that change the currents of human life you are called to teach your accomplishments, whether in or out of the convent walls, to others, remember what the civilization of Europe still owes to her Anglo-Saxon *nuns*, and believe, that from your teaching, may yet spring a race of heroes, of great historians, poets, painters, sculptors, architects, and even of saints, since by your teaching will be modeled the mothers of generations to come. You can never tell which of the countless mustard seeds of wise precept, or noble sentiment sown by you, may take root, and send forth branches for the delight of the nations. It was in this sublime spirit, we must suppose, that St. Lioba and her companions studied, wrote, and taught; and this is why the perfume of their acts has come down to us through these ages of wars and revolutions, attracting our love, and stirring up in our own souls a holy emulation of their serene courage, and their persevering labors.

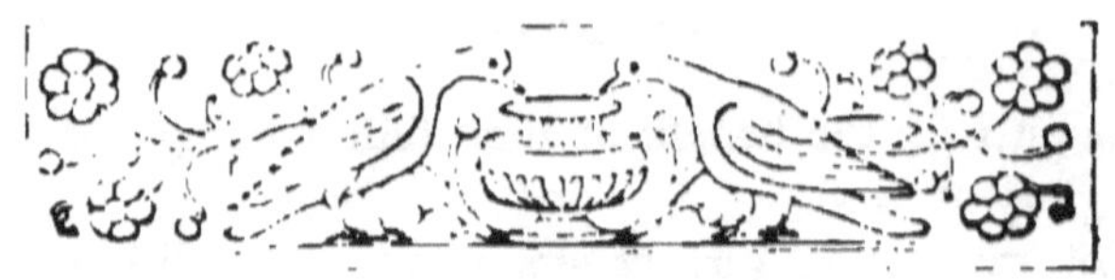

SAINT LUKE.

ISAIAH was, above all others, the prophet of the Holy Infancy. St. Jerome was its recluse and devotee; but St. Luke may be called the evangelist, poet, artist, and cantor, of the Holy Infancy, of Nazareth, and of that Bethlehem of Juda, of which it was written, "And thou Bethlehem of Juda, that art a little one among the princes of Juda, out of thee shall come the leader that shall rule my people Israel." (Mich. v. ii.) St. Matthew invites us to join the train of the three kings—the holy Magi—and by the light of that miraculous star we come to the stable of Bethlehem, where the young Virgin Mother is found, with her Divine Infant "wrapped in His swaddling clothes and lying in a manger." But St. Matthew only gives us time enough to offer our gold, frankincense, and myrrh, with the three wise men, and then leads us from Bethlehem "by another way," never to return to its Infant King. It is St. Luke who takes the Holy Infancy directly to his

SAINT LUKE.

SAINT LUKE.

heart, who goes to Nazareth and listens to the wonderful message of the archangel, Gabriel, catches the light of his celestial smile as he utters the first "*Ave Maria*," the first "Hail Mary, full of grace, the Lord is with thee," that ever gladdened the world; watches, as only the artist of the Holy Infancy could watch, the virginal hesitation that overshadowed, like the wing of a dove, the face of Mary when she heard the salutation of the angel, and "was troubled;" and then, the shadow lifted, sees the first streak of the dawn of Redemption breaking over her face, with that meek, yet most powerful consent—powerful, since without this consent we should have had no Nazareth and no Bethlehem—"Behold the handmaid of the Lord, be it done unto me according thy word;" and, that consent of Mary's free will having been given, without which God would not have come down to us, since He would not force Himself on His own creatures, it is our evangelist, poet, artist, and cantor, who stands in the solemn light of that mystical eclipse of the Eternal Word at the moment of His Incarnation, when the Dove of the Holy Spirit brooded over the Immaculate Virgin, and Mary held in her womb the "Word made flesh." It is St. Luke who goes with the Holy Virgin, in her happy haste, over the steep ways of the "hill country of Judea," with that step lighter than an angel's, yet far more careful than an angel's, since no angel could ever be a mother—goes with Mary over those stony paths to her cousin, St. Elizabeth, whose unborn babe, St. John Baptist, leaps in her womb for joy when he hears the voice of our Blessed Lady; it is St. Luke who hears the congratulation of the aged but joyful Elizabeth, chiming in with the angelical salutation like the second phrase of some strain of heavenly music, "Blessed art thou among women, and blessed is the fruit of thy womb;" and then hears, with his memory inspired to repeat it for us, the sublime response of Mary, in her own anthem of the 'Magnificat,' in which Mary prophecies that "all nations shall call her blessed;" and by the solemn chanting of which the Church celebrates the exaltation of Mary as the Mother of God. It is St. Luke who gives us, after three months of joyful waiting, the 'Benedictus' of St. Zachary at the birth of John the Baptist, and, after this event, returns with Mary to that humble, but holy house, where St. Joseph lived chastely with his most chaste spouse, until the time came for that long, wintry journey to Bethlehem. It is St. Luke who travels, with faithful step, beside these meek spouses, these spotless guardians of the "Word made flesh," along the inhospitable streets of Bethlehem, every door closed upon them in their great straight; and, night coming on, takes, with them, shelter in that poor, but most blissful stable—contemptible in the eyes of men, but radiant and beauteous to the eye of faith and love—where Mary brings forth, not with sighs and tears like the daughters of Eve, but in an ecstacy of rapture, adoration, and thanksgiving, Jesus, the fruit of her womb. It is St. Luke whose dilated ear catches that one strain of the angel's song heard by mortals, "*Gloria in excelsis Deo; et in terra pax hominibus bonae voluntatis*," "Glory be to God on high, and on earth peace to men of good will," which the Church repeats in her solemn Office on all days but those of mourning, and it is St. Luke who brings the shepherds from their flocks on the frosty hillsides, out of the clear, cold starlight of the December night, into the tender brightness of that atmosphere radiating from and surrounding, the new-born "Lamb of God, who takes away the sin of the world." It is St. Luke who leads us to the beautiful courts of the temple, points out to us the holy Simeon and the devout Anna, and invites us to draw near when the aged Hebrew, taking the young Messias into his arms, breaks forth into that hymn of adoring satisfaction, "*Nunc dimittis*," "Now let thy servant, O Lord, depart in peace for mine eyes have seen thy salvation." It is St. Luke who returns once more to Nazareth with the Holy Family, and, after twelve years, gives us one more glimpse of the humble carpenter, St. Joseph, and of Mary, his virgin spouse, in company with "the boy, Jesus," going up to the Temple at Jerusalem; the cruel loss of Him during three days, and the joyful finding of Him, at length, in the Temple, where He sat with the doctors of the Jewish Sanhedrim, "both hearing them and asking them questions." It is in this way that St. Luke has garnered up, in his beautiful gospel, a rich legacy of pictures in words, and of songs without musical notes, for the artists, poets, musicians of all generations, to be used by them for the ever new delight of the young and the old, the joyful and the sorrowful. Well may St. Luke be called the evangelist, artist, poet, cantor of the Holy Infancy, of Bethlehem, and of Nazareth! The tender grace of the Holy Infancy, its gentleness and simplicity, have been stamped upon his writings, and it is in the company of Jesus, Mary, and Joseph, that we are to look for St. Luke, until in later years—when the Rod of Jesse had not only budded, blossomed, but had borne its fruit, and the tree of the cross had been bathed all over with the Precious Blood—we find him beside the fervid apostle, St. Paul, as his constant companion, his steadfast friend, and his faithful biographer. It is with St. Paul, standing to him in all these beautiful relations, that we hear of St. Luke in the See of Peter, in the old city of Rome, that Eternal City of perfect beauty to the eye of faith, where the aged and worn pilgrim of the Holy Infancy, of Bethlehem, and Nazareth, can, to this day, lay down his palmer's staff, and don his scallop-shell, before the successor of the Fisherman, and the Vicegerent of the Babe of Bethlehem.

St. Luke is thus the evangelist, poet, artist and cantor of the Holy Infancy; but the artists have claimed him for their special patron, and this choice is founded on a tradition which the worldly-wise seek in vain to destroy.

The picture that accompanies this sketch of St. Luke, represents the evangelist painting Our Blessed Lady with her Divine Son in her arms, and this is no mere fancy of the great Italian artist, Raphael; for, "Theodorus Lector, who lived in 518, relates, that a picture of the Blessed Virgin, painted by St. Luke, was sent from Jerusalem to the Empress Pulcheria, who placed it in the church of Hodegorum, which she built in Constantinople. Moreover, a very ancient inscription was found in a vault near the church of St. Mary *in via lata* at Rome, in which it is said of a picture of the Blessed Virgin Mary, discovered there, that it is "One of the seven painted by St. Luke." Three or four such pictures are still in being; the principal one is that placed by Pope Paul V., in the Burghesian chapel in St. Mary Major at Rome." We have copied this account of St. Luke's pictures of the Blessed Virgin Mary, from the Rev. Alban Butler's Lives of the Saints, a work written with most admirable regard to sober, well authenticated facts. It is not "an article of faith" that St. Luke painted the Blessed Virgin Mary, but we need not be ashamed to believe it on the word of witnesses so worthy of confidence. It is also an evidence in favor of this tradition, that a part of the relics of St. Luke the Evangelist, were kept at Mount Athos, in Greece; for we know that in this monastery there has existed an art school, without interruption, since the fifth century; and there can be no doubt that the veneration of the monks for St. Luke, and for the Madonnas painted by him, had a great deal to do with the style of art which they held to for ages, with almost superstitious obstinacy, but which the world has long since outgrown. But it was not at Mount Athos alone that St. Luke was venerated as the friend of artists. In Italy, so long ago as 1350, a confraternity of painters was formed and placed under the immediate protection of St. Luke. Their intention, in thus banding together, "was not to communicate to each other discoveries, or to advise with each other on new methods, but simply to offer up thanks and praises to God."

The pictures painted at that time were all Christian pictures, and the artist depicted to the eye what the priests of God endeavored to impress on the minds and hearts of men through the ear. Buffalmacco, one of the scholars of Giotto, and who died 1340, says; "We painters occupy ourselves entirely in tracing saints on the walls, and on the altars, in order that by this means, men, to the great despite of the demons, may be more drawn to virtue and piety." As M. Rio adds, after quoting these words, "Amid these pious pre-occupations the studio of the painter became an oratory."

It was by this spirit of ardent devotion that the painters of that, and of succeeding ages, were able to express in their pictures such a divine grandeur, such a supernatural majesty, with the most tender modesty, unaffected humility, and a rapturous enjoyment of celestial delights, as, to this day, have never been exceeded, indeed we must own, have not since been equalled. They lived nearer heaven than earth, and sought, not only to please men, but to offer up their works as hymns of praise and acts of adoration, to the majesty of God. The people, too, for whom these works were executed, had the same devout tastes. It was not, in those days of Christian simplicity, their own countenances that they desired to perpetuate, but the celestial countenances of Christ and of His Blessed Mother, of the saints and beloved friends of God. It was not so much the scenery and abodes of this perishable world that they wish to behold, as the scenery of heaven, the abode of the angels and saints, the true native land and eternal home of every child of God. Therefore it was, that the artists were so beloved by the people, and no artist was obliged to pander to perverted or wicked tastes, in order to gain praise, or to earn his bread. No artist, indeed, of any age of the world, is obliged to do this; but in these days the unhappy artist finds, very often, that his heavenly pictures are not the ones most praised, nor even his innocent ones; and he yields to the temptation to please men rather than God, and employs his pencil to adorn the haunts of pleasure rather than the house of prayer, until, debased by such unworthy labors, he brings to the adornment of the church and the altar, the unhallowed tastes and the bedizened splendors of a corrupt generation. If we would have pious painters we must have a pious generation for them to paint for. There are very few artists who do not begin with a holy sense of their high vocation, and who do not lose it with keen remorse and bitter loathing.

An artist who paints the Madonna and her Divine Son, so as to touch the hearts of men and win the praise of God, must paint, as we see St. Luke painting in this picture before us, on his knees; at least in the spirit of one whose dear privilege it is often to hold converse with his Heavenly Father and his celestial friends. It was thus that painting, and the pursuit of all art, became most noble in the eyes of the people of those days, and to devote a son to an artistic career was to devote him to God and the service of the altar. We read of painters who never began a work without practising special devotions, even retiring from the world for a season, and frequenting the sacraments as the sources of their inspiration. The altar and the sacraments are the same now as in the thirteenth and fourteenth centuries, and one has only to live, as the old painters lived, in the spirit of faith and in the atmosphere of faith, to revive all the glories of that religious art which claimed St. Luke for its patron. How happy should I be, if, to the reading of these few pages about St. Luke, some boy or girl should date a resolve to use for God, and for His most holy service, any skill in the art of design that either may possess, or may hereafter acquire! Let not this child be discouraged, as if all the subjects of art were exhausted, as if the world were tired of Madonnas and of saints. The world is never tired of sincerely devout pictures; and though some people may try to prove that the pagan works of Raphael are more admirable than his religious ones, the heart of the world, long ago, decided that question. Raphael lives in the affections of his fellow men through his religious pictures; and so long as the heart of one Christian is stirred to devotion by his Virgins and Madonnas, so long will Raphael live as the favorite and delight of Christendom; and no longer; for although the critics might crown him with their garlands, they could never compel the world to love him, as it does now.

It is not, then, in Schools of Design, and Academies of Art, that the secret of the great religious picture is learned, but in some moment of devotion, some practice of piety, some habit, it may be, of devotion to the Mother of God, when the heart, the soul, the sense, kindled by love, eagerly portrays what it sees with the eye of faith, and longs for with all the ardor of devout aspiration. Study, if you would paint well, but pray far more; and the inspiration that flies from the mere student will come to the one that "waits on the Mother of wisdom and knocketh at the posts of her door."

It sometimes takes ages for the world to find out what it really likes best, to sift out the wheat from the chaff, separate the gold from the dross of base ores around it; but the decision is, at last, always on the side of virtue and of God. Even in ancient pagan art, the works most prized to day are those in which the soul of man recognizes some fragment of a divine idea; and the scorn of the Apollo Belvidere is not so much the scorn of the glorious youth for the dead "python," as the scorn of the immortal soul for the monster sin. So, in Christian art, the ages will winnow the wheat from the chaff, smelt the gold from the ore, and God and His truth will be justified, and the true artist will be crowned with an honor that will be a promise of the far greater honor awaiting him, at the last day, in the eyes of the assembled nations; for then, the smallest picture painted for the love of God, will be rewarded as faithfully, as the cup of water given to the thirsty traveler for Christ's sake.

But it is not as the patron of artists, alone, that St. Luke is venerated; he is also claimed as the patron of physicians; and this reminds me that I must give you the history of St. Luke as it has been handed down from age to age. When we see into how short a space the life of such a man as St. Luke, is crowded in the libraries of a world which he served with such singular zeal, such purity of motive, and with so many accomplishments to grace his career, we sigh that so little has been written of him, so little preserved. But it is not the number of pages written, so much as the noble and supernatural acts and graces recorded, that make a rich biography; and we also know that the life of St. Luke was offered as a holocaust, a *whole* burnt offering to God. It is when we forget ourselves, have no desire to leave after us what will make us distinguished, that God remembers us, that the Church remembers us, and writes upon tablets, more enduring than tablets of fine brass, the acts of those whose ambition has been all for her.

St. Luke was born at Antioch, the metropolis of Syria, a city noted for its delightful situation, the riches of its traffic, its vast extent, and the number of its inhabitants, and also for their politeness of manners, learning, and wisdom. In her schools, the most renowned in all Asia, St. Luke acquired an education, at once solid and brilliant, and this he improved still further by his travels in Greece and Egypt. St. Jerome says that St. Luke was more skilled in Greek than in Hebrew, and his style is one of uncommon elegance. He was converted to Christianity after the ascension of Our Lord, but by whose preaching is uncertain. He does not claim to have written his gospel as an eye-witness, like St. John, to the events in the life of Our Lord, but from the narratives of those "who from the beginning were eye-witnesses and ministers of the word." There can be no doubt that St. Luke received from the lips of the Blessed Virgin herself, the account of the Annunciation, of the Incarnation, and of the visit of the Blessed Virgin to St. Elizabeth, which are related only in his gospel; and this probability adds another charm to his beautiful narrative, which is worthy of having been dictated by the Virgin Mother. The parable of the Prodigal Son, is found only in St. Luke's gospel, and it would seem as if St. Luke had a predilection for every circumstance that could set forth the tender compassion of the Redeemer for poor, unhappy sinners.

St. Luke wrote the Acts of the Apostles, a sacred history compiled at Rome by Divine inspiration, as an appendix to his gospel, to prevent any false accounts of the great events which he had related, and also to leave an authentic record of the manner in which God planted His infant Church, and replenished it with all needful graces. In the first twelve chapters he relates the actions of the principal apostles after the ascension of Our Lord, especially of St. Peter, Prince of the Apostles, including that wonderful description of the conversion of St. Paul which can never be read without a thrill of awe and a throb of thanksgiving. From the thirteenth chapter, however, he speaks of little besides the history of St. Paul, his preaching and his miracles, which he heard and saw for himself, and could therefore correct the false repprts that had been given of them. It is in his account of the voyage of St. Paul from Troas to Macedon, after St. Barnabas left him, that St. Luke first speaks of himself as the companion of St. Paul; and although before that time he had been his devoted disciple, he appears never afterwards to have left him, unless to fulfill his commissions. He shared the toils, dangers, and sufferings, of the great "Apostle to the Gentiles." St. Paul calls him, his "fellow laborer," and, "Luke, the beloved physician." St. Jerome tells us that St. Luke was eminent in his profession, and from the testimony of St. Paul it appears that he did not lay aside its practice while performing the labors of a missionary and an apostle. We can readily understand how he may have used his healing art on his long and varied journeys; for, after the priestly office, there is no profession that so commends itself to the heart of the humane as that of the Christian physician. How often is he the only one present to assist the dying to make those acts of faith, of hope, and of charity, so necessary at the last awful moment, and to raise their sinking courage under the pains of their mortal agony! How often, also, may not the prayers of the pious and believing physician do more than all human remedies, by inspiring in the mind of the sick person a calm faith in God's power and goodness, that puts even the body into a state of repose, and allows the medicine to do its work. How often, alas! is the sacrament of baptism lost to the new-born infant, because no one sees the danger of the little one, but the physician, who may despise this sacrament of regeneration; or, on the contrary, how often does the Christian physician pour the saving waters of baptism on the head of the dying babe, when others are forgetful of its rights as a child of God! Well may we rejoice in this powerful patron of physicians, and heartily should we pray that they may never act otherwise, in the practice of their noble profession, than St. Luke would have done while in full possession of his sacred office as an evangelist, and a teacher of the truth of God.

St. Luke attended St. Paul when he was sent to Rome as a prisoner, from Jerusalem, in the year 61; and had the happiness of seeing him set at liberty in 63, the year in which he finished writing his Acts of the Apostles. He continued with St. Paul after his release, and the great apostle, during his last imprisonment, writes that his other friends had all left him, only Luke was with him.

From these circumstances, we may conclude that the gentle and refined nature of St. Luke was capable of the most faithful friendship, a capacity far less common than is supposed. It is not every one who knows how to be a friend; it seems, indeed, to be a special grace, reserved for some, and withheld from others who may be very good people, but the sacred quality of friendship is beyond their grasp. We must not, then, complain if those who seem to be our friends do not show an heroic friendship towards us when their own interests stand between them and us, or when our misfortunes may try all but those supernaturally devoted to us. Let us be ready to overlook any such imperfections in others, while, for ourselves, we try to live out that golden rule of love to our neighbor, which is the secret of that true and noble friendship manifested for St. Paul by St. Luke, increased as it must have been, in this instance, by his veneration for the "Apostle and doctor of the Gentiles."

After the martyrdom of St. Paul, St. Luke is said to have preached in Italy, Gaul, Dalmatia and Macedon. Some say that he traveled into Egypt, and preached in Thebais. St. Hippolitus says that St. Luke was crucified in Peloponnesus, near Achaia, in Greece, and the modern Greeks tell us that he was crucified on an olive tree. His relics were distributed among many churches, and St. Gregory is said to have brought the head of St. Luke from Constantinople to Rome, and to have deposited it in the church of his monastery of St. Andrew. The ancient picture of St. Luke, together with all the instruments formerly used in writing, is copied from old manuscript books of his gospel. As I have said, some of his relics are kept in the great Grecian monastery on Mount Athos.

The pictures of St. Luke in his character of evangelist, represent him with his gospel in his hand, and beside him the ox, with or without wings; and by this mark he may always be known from the other evangelists. There are four round pictures, called "Lunettes," in the cathedral at Parma, Italy, painted by Correggio, representing the Four Evangelists, as if seated, St. John on the eagle, St. Mark on the winged lion, St. Luke on the winged ox, while St. Matthew is borne up on clouds supported by a youth. There is a noble inspiration about these figures, as we have seen them copied in large photographs suitable for framing, and the recollection of these sublime personages, as given by the Christian painter, might well prove a shield against many a shaft of unbelief aimed at the Four Gospels.

The symbols in these lunettes, and in all pictures of the evangelists, are taken from the first chapter in Ezekiel, in which the prophet describes the "Four living creatures," in a way that applies to the Four Evangelists; and we find them distinguished from each other by these symbols in the earliest Christian pictures, whether in the Greek and Latin mosaics, or on the stained glass of Gothic windows, or on the rich vellum pages of the illuminated missals in the ancient monasteries; and even on the delicately carved wood, and ivory, and engraved precious metals, that beautify the covers of those venerated copies of the gospels used on the great festival days, in many an abbey church or grand cathedral, amid the flare of the tall wax candles held by the acolytes, and the fuming of the incense from the censors; and held then, as now, in a manner so picturesque, that few groups during the Holy Sacrifice of the mass, as it is solemnly celebrated on great feasts, are so strikingly beautiful as the one called together at the singing of the gospel by the deacon. I remember seeing, for the first time, this grouping at the chanting of the gospel. The book was solemnly taken from the altar by the deacon, who kneeled for the blessing of the celebrating priest; and well do I remember the recollected air of that youthful deacon, worthy of a St. Stephen or a St. Laurence, as he moved with the sub-deacon and the acolytes, with the lights and the incense, to the gospel side of the sanctuary, and there adjusted the book so that it would be held by the hands of the sub-deacon, and rest against his forehead. When he had signed the book and himself, most solemnly, three times, he gave forth, in the clear tones of the old Gregorian Chant, the gospel of the day, after which the book was taken to the celebrating priest, who devoutly kissed the gospel just sung, saying, "By the words of this gospel may all our sins be blotted out."

And well do I remember how there flashed across my mind, this thought: could the Church, thus venerating the gospels, ever have been guilty of cutting off the people of God from these sacred fountains? "It must be a calumny," I said to myself, and whenever this calumny was repeated in my presence, that solemn group, so full of artistic as well as of religious beauty, rose up to my mind as a testimony against the slander. To this day, the most moving instances on record of a sincere and affectionate reverence for the Four Gospels, are to be found among the scholars and monks of that Church, which so many, honestly, suppose, has made it a sealed book to her children; whereas, it is one of the glories of the Catholic Church, that not only were the writers of the Four Gospels and of the New Testament among her most honored founders, but that the preservation of their inspired writings has been the object of her unceasing care, has furnished the motive for her most profound learning, and has inspired some of her most sublime works of art.

In this generation, when so many pens and tongues are directed against the authority of the Holy Gospels, let us address not only St. Luke, but, in the well known invocation of the Litany of the Saints, cry out,

"O all ye holy Evangelists, pray for us!"

Especially let us do so on the 18th of October, the day on which the Church claims for St. Luke, the veneration, honor, and devotion of entire Christendom.

SAINT CECILIA.

ONE Sunday morning, as we were leaving the church of the Holy Name, we saw that our pastor had a surprise for his congregation. The organ had been put very quietly into a new case, as appropriate as beautiful; for, above all the architectural forms and ornamentation rose the cross, and, on either side, in the shadow of the grand arches, with here and there a fleck of colored light from the stained glass of the windows on their draperies, were two statues, carved in wood, and of very nearly life size.

One of the statues represented David, the sweet Psalmist of Israel, who not only wrote those inspired hymns, called "The Psalms," but sang them to the music of his harp. There he stood, with his noble and regal countenance turned to heaven, from whence he derived the spirit of his divine melodies, while his fingers touched the strings of his sacred instrument. On the other side of the cross stood a majestic figure, her face, also, turned upward, and irradiated with that light of joy and love which heaven alone can give to human or angelic forms, and in her hands were the organ pipes, which she is said to have invented at the suggestion of an angel. Could any subjects have been chosen more likely to inspire those who were to make the responses to the celebrating priest, to do so according to the intention of the Holy Sacrifice of the mass; or, more fitted to remind them of the noble obligations resting on those whose vocation it is to sing, not in the presence of any earthly dignitaries, however great, not to gain their applause and patronage, but, to sing in His presence who sits between the cherubim in glory, and, also, in a hidden, yet most perfect, manner, upon our altars—to sing in His presence, and, as an act of worship, such canticles, and such notes, as are a fitting response to the eternal alleluias of Heaven?

What sensible devotion, what adoration, may not be raised by the music of a religious choir! The music of the Church has, always, been regarded as one of those aids to devotion which no priest will allow to decline from its sacred intention of praising God. St. Gregory the Great, a pope who lived in such stirring times that one would think he might have been excused from paying any particular attention to music, nevertheless, expressed the mind of the Church in this matter, by working a perfect reformation in the sacred music of his age; a reformation, which succeeding generations, so far from outgrowing, or despising, can never enough admire.

To this day, the, so called, Gregorian chants, are those which the Church selects for her greatest feasts; and during Holy week she confines herself to their grand and impressive strains. Later compositions, even of the most religious character, are laid aside, and the language of the mournful Office of the Tenebræ, all that is sung on Good Friday and on Holy Saturday, is set to these majestic measures. In vain will any human genius hope to improve such musical phrases as the priestly, "*Ave sanctum Oleum*," of Holy Thursday; the refrain "*O Jerusalem, Jerusalem*," of the Tenebræ; the "*Respondit Jesus*," of Good Friday; or that hymn of divine joy, issuing from the shadows of the grave, the "*Exultet*," of Holy Saturday! The heart of Christendom has, for centuries, found her faith, her hope, her love, her sorrow and her joy, expressed by these holy cadences; and these centuries have not only consecrated them to the ear of the Church, but have proved their perfection.

But I have not told you, dear children, who is represented by the second statue; the one, I mean, with the organ pipes in her hand. Some of you may have guessed, already, from having seen pictures of this patroness of sacred music, or from hearing of some musical festival in her honor; for it is no less a person than the St. Cecilia of the third century of the Christian era, that noble Roman lady, who knew how to consecrate her genius to God, and to honor Him with His own celestial gifts.

There is no history of the early saints more authentic than that of St. Cecilia, who is honored as a virgin and martyr, and whose name adorns, not only the Litany of the Saints, but the holy Canon of the Mass. Although sketches of her life are found in every work giving a poetical history of music, yet it has never suffered, like so many others, from the gross misrepresentations of unbelief, and she stands forth, in the simplicity of Christian heroism, untainted by any surroundings, secular, or even profane; and many, who would smile at the idea of asking her aid in their musical compositions or performances, still claim her as their gentle patroness, and honor her by producing their noblest strains to grace her festival.

St. Cecilia was born about the year 214. Her parents were of noble Roman families, and their house was built upon the famous Campus Martius, an immense tract of ground set aside for the military exercises of the imperial army. By degrees, temples, and public edifices, and the houses of the nobles, were allowed to be built there, and, among others, the palace of the family of Cecilia. Here, surrounded by all the splendor of the Roman nobility, and by the crowns and trophies of her ancestors, this beautiful young girl, despising the pomps and vanities of the heathen society to which she belonged, practiced, with perfect fidelity, the maxims of Christianity.

We often hear persons excuse themselves for any carelessness in the practice of their duties, because it is, they say, "so hard to act differently from the world around us." Let such persons blush at the example set by this young girl; and let any one, who is placed in circumstances somewhat like Cecilia, take courage, remembering her fidelity among pagans.

It is not certain whether the little Cecilia learned Christianity from her parents, who might have been obliged to practice their religion in secret, or, from her nurse. The circumstances of her marriage make it probable that her parents were pagans, but, however this may have been, there were dangers, she knew, in store for her as a Christian, and she devoted herself to her religion as those do who are preparing to suffer for it. She carried, night and day, a copy of the gospels hidden in the folds of her robe. She also made a secret, but solemn, vow to her Divine Spouse, and, in the spirit of this promise, shunned the pleasures and vanities of the world. She excelled in music; and this charming gift she consecrated to God by composing hymns in His honor, which she sang with such ravishing sweetness that the very angels are said to have descended from heaven to listen to her, and also to join their voices with hers. She played, skillfully, upon all the instruments used in those luxurious days of Roman civilization; but through none of them was she able to express the sublime harmonies that flooded her soul, and she was inspired to invent the organ, thereby to worship God through the sweetness of terrestrial sounds. To this day, the organ is used only for sacred music, so perfectly do we see the intention of its saintly author carried out.

When Cecilia was sixteen, her parents married her

to a young Roman noble, who possessed uncommon natural goodness; but he was still in the darkness of paganism. No doubt, God, who saw that his ignorance of Christianity alone prevented his belief in its saving truths, moved Cecilia's father and mother to act as they did in this matter. Cecilia obeyed her parents, accepting the husband thus chosen for her; but beneath her white bridal robe, she wore the hair skirt of the penitent, praying, as she walked to the altar, that she might receive help from above to persevere in her solemn vow of virginity.

Her mortifications, her prayers, her acts of filial obedience were not in vain; for she not only persuaded her husband, Valerian, to respect her promise, but converted him to the true faith.

How wonderful are the graces that come to the assistance of those who put their whole trust in God! How wonderful, yet how silent! yet not more wonderful nor more silent, than the souls, who, leaving to God the manner of their deliverance, are satisfied to offer themselves as victims to His adorable will.

When the festivities of the marriage day were over, and Cecilia was left alone with her husband, she told him of the solemn promise she had made to preserve her virginity, and of the glorious angel who was ever at her side to protect her in this promise, asking him to respect what had been dedicated to God. Valerian wished to see this angel, visible only to her. She told him that he must be instructed in her religion, before he could have this privilege; and when she saw him so mild and so candid, so ready to hear, so ready to believe all that she said to him, she knew that God had heard her prayers, and had, by His divine grace, prepared the mind of her young husband to be a Christian, like herself, and to respect her vow, and she sent him to the good Pope, Urban, for instruction. The instructions of the holy old man were not lost on the willing mind of Valerian, and before he left him he was baptized by St. Urban. He returned to his wife in the white garments of his baptismal innocence, and, as he entered her room, heard the most enchanting music and saw the angel standing near her, in his hand two crowns of lilies and roses, gathered in Paradise, and immortal in their freshness and perfume, with which he crowned these two young spouses, so chaste in their mutual affection.

Valerian had a brother, dearly beloved by him. It was in answer to the wish he expressed to the angel for the conversion of his brother, that Tiburtius, when he came to their house, was allowed to perceive the fragrance of these celestial flowers; and not only were his bodily senses quickened, but his mind was prepared to see the truth of the Christian doctrine, as explained to him by the seraphic Cecilia; and he, also, hastened to St. Urban to be baptized.

Happy haste, holy fervor, most prudent impatience of these elected ones! Celestial ardor, which flew along the path of perfection, and seized, as its natural food, what could alone satisfy the hunger of an immortal child of God! The happy trio now went about doing all sorts of good works, giving alms of their great riches, encouraging those who were to suffer for Christ, and burying, honorably, those who were put to death for his sake. The Roman prefect, seeing this joyful exercise of charity, sent for the young nobles, Valerian, and Tiburtius, and commanded them to cease these works of faith and love; but they made this sublime answer: "How can we cease from this which is our duty, for anything that man can do to us?" The two brothers, gave the most courageous answers to all the questions of the prefect, Almachius, and at last, Tiburtius, having been first scourgéd, they were led to prison, and put under the care of the centurion, Maximus. By the eloquence of their piety and their chains, they converted Maximus, so that when they were called upon to offer a libation to Jupiter, he, also, had the grace to refuse, and to follow them in their holy death.

Cecilia herself, was afterwards brought before the cruel Almachius, and commanded to sacrifice to the idols of Rome. But one who had overcome the temptations of a heart most tender in its affections, choosing to preserve for God what He had created to love, serve and enjoy Him forever, could not hesitate to refuse this grossly impious request, and she was condemned to suffer death in a dry bath, or a closed bath with fire under it. This cruel sentence was immediately carried out in her own magnificent house, to which she had been taken, only a few months before, as the bride of one of the flowers of the

Roman nobility. Yet the fearful heat seemed only to refresh the celestial maiden, and an executioner was sent to dispatch her with the sword; but, although he made three attempts with his keen blade, he could not sever her head from her body. The Roman law forbade a fourth trial, and she was suffered to linger in this state for three days, using them to encourage the Christians who came to see her, until, at the end of that time, God released her pure and heroic soul from the prison of her mortal body, it being the 22nd of November, 230.

The feast of SS. Valerian and Tiburtius and of St. Maximus, is celebrated on the 14th of April, that of St. Cecilia on the 22d of November, and on her feast day, in the church of St. Cecilia-in-Trastevere, (or beyond the Tiber), one hears all the noblest choirs of the Eternal City uniting their canticles to those of the angels and of St. Cecilia.

A church called St. Cecilia de Domo was built, very early, on the ground formerly occupied by the palace in which St. Cecilia was born. This church was rebuilt in the last century by Pope Benedict XIII., and an ancient inscription was taken from the old church to the new, "*This is the house where Saint Cecilia prayed.*" The house where she resided with her husband, and where she met her death, was, at her request, consecrated by St. Urban as a church, the chamber in which she suffered being regarded as a spot of peculiar sanctity. Pope Symmachus held a council in the church of St. Cecilia in the year 500.

Falling into ruins, it was rebuilt by Pope Paschal I., in the ninth century, and, while he was engaged in this pious work, the saint appeared to him in a dream, discovering to him the place of her burial. Searching for her body as she instructed him to do, he found it in the Cemetery of St. Calixtus, clothed in the rich robe of silk, and gold tissue, which she had worn at her martyrdom, and at her feet a linen cloth dipped in her blood. It was then removed, with the bodies of SS. Valerian and Tiburtius and St. Maximus, to her church of "*St. Cecilia-in-Trastevere.*"

In 1599 this church was again repaired, and richly embellished by the order of Clement VIII. The body of St. Cecilia was taken from its vault and examined in the presence of the assembled dignitaries of the Church, among whom was Cardinal Baronius, who has given us a description of its appearance. "She was lying within a coffin of cypress-wood, enclosed in a marble sarcophagus, not in the manner of one dead and buried, that is, on her back, but on her right side, as one asleep; in a very modest attitude, covered with a simple stuff of taffety, having her head bound with cloth, and at her feet the remains of the cloth of gold and silk, which Pope Paschal had found in her tomb." Clement VIII. ordered that the relics should not be touched, and the cypress coffin was enclosed in a silver shrine. Stefano Maderno, a sculptor, was then in the employment of the cardinal who presided on this occasion, and he modelled, and afterward executed in marble, by the order of the cardinal, the celebrated statue of "St. Cecilia lying dead," which has been called one of the most perfect in modern times.

Every one who goes to Rome visits this church of St. Cecilia, and obtains a photograph, at least, of this statue, that will tell, so long as marble endures, the story of the miraculous preservation of the body of the saint. Nothing can exceed the grace and tenderness of this figure, as it comes to us, in America, in books upon art, in small *terra cotta* copies, and in photographs. Though we do not see the face of the Roman maiden, the chastely disposed limbs, the hands softly locked, the neck, turned without violence, but, still, so as to show the triple martyrdom of the sword —the whole attitude of the virgin and martyr, appeals to the most insensible heart. "It lies as no living body could lie, and yet correctly, as the dead when left to expire."

Happy martyr! Glorious saint! The horrors of that prolonged trial, by which the tenderness of the girl was changed to more than womanly heroism, are still commemorated in the remains of the room in which she suffered; and those who fancy, in the cowardice of their self-love, that the gifted, and the gently reared, should be excused from suffering, as too sensitive to bear the cross of the Christian, may well pause before this statue of Cecilia in the sweet sleep of martyrdom. The world may boast of her singing men and singing women; the songsters of the opera and the ballad; but the world's inmost heart pays the tribute of its admiration, of its love, and of its sympathy, at the shrine of Cecilia, the Roman virgin and martyr, who knew how to turn from the smiles of time, and the delusions of sense, to plunge into the flood of glory streaming down from the Eternal; and, losing her finite self, to find, forever, the living, infinite God.

St. Cecilia inspired one of Raphael's most sublime pictures. In this, she stands robed in the rich garments of a Roman patrician, surrounded by saints, the organ pipes in her hands and musical instruments on the ground at her feet, with her virginal face turned in an ecstacy to heaven, where one sees a choir of angels, singing; and their song seems to have inspired her to reproduce, on earth, their harmonious worship. Carlo Dolce, also, painted a picture of St. Cecilia seated in a dim organ loft, a look of holy recollection on her face, the rich stuffs in which she is dressed showing the nobility of her rank, the lily blooming at her side expressing her voluntary virginity; while the beautiful hands touch the keys with a grace so full of worship that we can almost hear the "*Sanctus, Sanctus*," of the angelic hosts, which we feel sure must surround her.

We might mention pictures of St. Cecilia by so early an artist as Cimabue, so accomplished an one as Domenichino, and so pious an one as Lucas von Leyden; but we will pass over these to one of our own day and generation, painted by Ary Scheffer. In this St. Cecilia is sitting in a Roman chair, and, two angels, kneeling, present to her the organ-pipes. It is a very lovely picture, and shows that the artists of to-day have not forgotten her.

The most eminent of all the composers of sacred music in modern times, is Palestrina, so called, because he was born in a town of that name near Rome. It is to Palestrina that we owe the pleasure of hearing the choir in church; for, in his time, musical composers had so far forgotten the end of church music, that the Pope and cardinals resolved to banish choirs, unless some one should compose a mass expressing the divine end of sacred melody. Palestrina was the chapel-master, or leader of the music, of the church of St. John Lateran, that cathedral of the whole world, as the inscription over its ancient portal declares, and whose canons, or ecclesiastics, take the place of honor before those of St. Peter's itself; and it was Palestrina who was honored by this august commission from the Father of the faithful. He wrote three masses, each to be sung by six voices. The two first were highly approved, but the third was heard with the most enthusiastic admiration for the grandeur of its devotion, and the purity of its harmonies. It was the triumph of religion in the world of music; and God and the Church again claimed music for the handmaid of piety and the nurse of devotion.

Palestrina lived to see several popes in the chair of St. Peter at Rome; but every one of these popes was his friend, and encouraged him to continue writing such masses as those which decided the Pope and cardinals to allow music to form a part of the worship in the Pontifical Chapel, and in all churches, Catholic, Apostolic and Roman. When he found his end approaching, he called to him his son, and said to him in these words, worthy of so true an artist, "My son, I leave to you a great number of unpublished works; thanks to the Abbé de Baume, to the Cardinal Aldobrandini, and to the Grand Duke of Tuscany, I also leave to you what is necessary to get them printed; I charge you to do this for the glory of God and for the honorable celebration of the worship in His temples."

In the Music Hall in Boston is a bust of Palestrina, giving us a face, grave, religious, and exalted in its expression. The bust stands on a bracket, and the shelf of this bracket is supported by a figure of St. Cecilia attended by angels. She holds a book of music on her hands, to which one angel points while he looks at St. Cecilia as if instructing her; and the hands of the other angel, joined in worship, express the sacredness of their musical studies. Back of this group, which seems to be floating down from heaven with its calm brightness on their heads, crowd numbers of angelic faces, the far off hosts of heaven lying under the deep shadow of the bracket like soft summer clouds. Nothing could be imagined more lovely in its effect. The whole is a tribute of this present age to the grandeur of religious music, to the genius and piety of Palestrina, and, to that Virgin Martyr, who is still one of the glories of the Church of the Catacombs, St. Cecilia of Rome.

On my table lies a book giving a curious and interesting account of the musical celebrations, held in

England in honor of St. Cecilia, during the sixteenth, seventeenth, and eighteenth centuries. To this is added a collection of the Odes written in her praise, and, among the Catholic poets who have thus consecrated their muse, are Alexander Pope and John Dryden.

I have taken pains to speak of these facts to show you how attractive, even to the eyes of the worldly, may become, in the course of ages, those who have been willing to forget the world, to do without its approbation, and have been contented to please God. In the exquisite language of King Solomon, in his *Book of Wisdom*, which the Church uses in her lesson for the feasts of her martyrs, "We fools esteemed their life madness and their end without honor. Behold how they are numbered among the children of God, and their lot is among the saints."

Little child, youth, maiden, if God has given you a sweet voice with which to sing His praise, can you stand in sight of St. Cecilia, as she seems to have alighted, for a moment, on the fair organ case which I have described to you, and grudge that voice when the decorum of the church service may need its aid; or, can you sacrifice to the idle song, much less the enticing one, the gift that won, for St. Cecilia, some of the fairest of the lilies and roses in her virgin's crown? Hang over your piano-forte, over your harp, over your music stand, some print of St. Cecilia, be it ever so small, and she will help you to consecrate to God one of the most endearing of His gifts.

SAINT STANISLAUS.

YOU may know Catholic families who have a habit of "Drawing a saint," for each member, and, perhaps, for some dear friend outside their own little circle, every month in the year. It is in the same spirit, and with a similar intention, that I have selected the saints for our book; for I wish you to look upon the saints as your friends, and as we all have one or two friends who are especially dear to us, and to whom we go when we need any help or consolation, so I wish you to have special friends among the saints, *intimate* friends, if you please, whom you will not hesitate to ask to pray for you, and to whom you will turn in all your little difficulties. This is, really, what is meant by a *Patron Saint*. When you were baptized, your good parents chose a name for you, perhaps two or three names, and, all of them names of saints. They chose these names to secure for you so many holy patrons, or friends, in heaven; friends who would feel themselves bound to look after your interests, and who will rejoice to do so, so long as you show a proper regard for them. Besides these patrons, secured for you at your baptism, every one of you has an opportnnity, at your confirmation, to take a patron of your own choosing, and you can also bear, his, or her, name. Still more; as you grow older, and feel a particular affection for some saint, you can express this affection by asking him, or her, to be one of your patrons. It is in the way I have mentioned last, that cities, and nations, have their Patron Saints, who are always particularly honored by these cities and nations, their pictures and statues being seen everywhere, and churches being named for them. This choice is always founded upon some particular affection for these saints, and this affection has grown out of the favors which these saints have obtained for them in times of distress, or, from some visible manifestation of good will during the history of these cities and nations. St. Patrick is thus the Patron Saint of Ireland, St. Andrew of Scotland, St. George of England, St. Louis of France, St. Boniface of Germany; and the Blessed Virgin Mary, under her title, *Conceived without sin*, is the Patroness of the United States. If you have seen pictures of Venice, you may have noticed the *winged lion*, figuring every where; on the top of one of the beautiful pillars near her Ducal-palace, on her churches, and worked into all their decorations. This winged lion is the symbol of St. Mark, Evangelist, the Patron Saint of the city of Venice, and his symbol finds an honored place, even where the statue of St. Mark could not, with propriety, be put. The protection of St. Mark is relied upon by all the Venetians, and noble pictures have been painted, commemorating his interference in their behalf.

Besides these examples of patrons, honored from age to age, through all the existence of great and powerful nations, and by individuals, like yourselves, from their baptism to their death, there are, as I have said, other patrons, whom we choose as we do our associates in study or in work, for the time being; or like persons whom we meet on our travels, and, for a month, are almost constantly beside us, adding to our enjoyment and doing us a great many favors. It is in this way, precisely, that the saint drawn every month, or the saints whose feasts gladden the several months of the year, do us so much good. They give us variety, and are to the soul what society is to the mind; and I dwell upon this, because I wish you to realize how near the saints are to you; how easy it is to get acquainted with them; how familiar may be your intercourse with them.

We will, then, look over the Calendar for November, and see whom we are to have for a friend during this month. As I look over it, my eye falls upon a very, very dear name. The 14th of November, how pleasant a feast is that of its youthful confessor! I will not tell you his name, however, until I have told you of a small picture, not, this time, in the black portfolio, but for many a year nestled in my Roman Missal. The picture is not larger than your Angel

Guardian medal, but it has a flowery border in the shape of a vase. It was given to me—let me think—fifteen years ago, by a pious, lovely boy, now a student in the American College, at Rome, preparing to be a priest. The little picture was a favorite with him. It cost him, I know, many a pang to give it to me, but when he found how lovely it was in my eyes, how its loveliness was enhanced by my devotion to the saint, he insisted upon my taking it. It has often come near destruction, for the border is very frail, and careless people sometimes take up and lay down the book; but I have glued bits of tissue paper under the broken parts, and it still remains one of the chosen few allowed in my missal. I believe the picture had something to do with the vocation of my young friend; certainly, his devotion to this saint had very much to do with it, for the saint is no other than St. Stanislaus Kostka, our saint for the 14th of November, the lovely boy-saint, who has been the favorite of painters and poets, the darling model and beloved patron of many an innocent school-boy. Happy will be those of my young readers who take St. Stanislaus Kostka for their model.

We have had so many ancient saints that it may be pleasant to you—may seem a little more possible for you to be like him—if you know that St. Stanislaus was not only a boy in years, but that he lived no longer than three hundred years ago; more than a thousand years after some of the saints whose lives you have been reading. He was born in the castle of

Rostkou, on the 28th of October, 1550, of one of the most ancient and most illustrious families in Poland. Both his father and his mother added to the nobility of their position the crowning glory of a devoted attachment to the Catholic faith. The infant Stanislaus gave an example, not only of early piety, but, of angelic innocence. His face was radiant with a more than infantine beauty, and the sweetness, truthfulness, and peacefulness of his disposition, were such as no parent could too much admire. In his tender piety, and habitual love of retirement, he was often seen on his young knees, his small hands clasped, and his eyes raised to Heaven, invoking the sweet names of Jesus and Mary. He was, indeed, a child in whom Jesus and Mary could delight, and on whom they could bestow their choicest favors.

When the time came for him to study he was sent to a school in Vienna, conducted by the Society of Jesus. Here he gave an example, not only as a diligent pupil, but as a follower of the Lamb of God, since no insult, no injury, could move him to revenge. The teasing, even the cruel, and wanton, treatment of his brother Paul, and his companions, who, sharing his room, were impatient at his piety, never ruffled the angelic sweetness of his amiable soul. At Vienna he fell very ill; and as the boys had lodgings, not with the Fathers, but with a Lutheran gentleman, Stanislaus was in danger of dying without the sacraments.

Behold! dear children, and imitate, the anxiety of this holy youth for his salvation. Seeing his own danger, he prayed fervently to the martyr, St. Barbara (who has often been known to assist those in danger of dying without the aid of the Blessed Sacrament), and, immediately St. Barbara appeared, attended by two angels, who communicated to the languishing boy, far from parents and friends, the adorable Body of his Lord and Saviour. Scarcely had St. Barbara vanished, when the Blessed Virgin appeared to him, bearing in her arms her Divine Son as a most lovely infant, whom she laid into the arms of our Stanislaus; thus prolonging, and as it were beatifying, the communion he had made by the hands of St. Barbara and the angels. It is this lovely scene, the Divine Infant in the arms of Stanislaus, who is almost swooning with happiness, which is represented by the little picture in my missal. Could you help loving such a picture?

These great favors, my dear children, were the blissful rewards of the daily virtues practiced by Stanislaus. He was most diligent in prayer, rising even at night to recite the praises of God, or to shed tears of contrition for his imperfections; he bore harassing contradictions and ridicule with heroic patience, and from his earliest years guarded his mind from every temptation against the virtue of purity. No indelicate word or jest ever came from the lips of Stanislaus; no unguarded moment betrayed the secrets of a heart careless of its thoughts, of its eyes and of its ears. The candid mind of St. Stanislaus was like a clear lakelet, such as one finds in some sheltered glen, where the stream leaps from rock to rock, falling into tiny basins in which one sees every pebble, and vein of rock, through the same water that reflects the blue of summer skies.

It was while he was at Vienna that our young saint was called by God to the mysterious, and holy joys of a religious life. He left Vienna secretly, to escape the obstacles which his high birth would put between him and the dear wish of his heart. Clad in the coarse garment of a pilgrim, a cord for his girdle, with only his rosary and a staff, he set out for Rome—to travel 1200 miles, bare-footed, solitary and unknown, there to put on the humble garb of a novice in the Society of Jesus, and to perform all those menial services by which the proudest hearts are won from their dainty love of themselves, and are taught the humility of the saints and the sanctity of labor. Here we see no proud, ambitious boy, impatient of a rival, envious of the success of a companion, but a holy youth sighing only for neglect and hardship.

Dear little reader, are you poor, are you compelled to labor every day with your small hands, perhaps to sweep the streets, or to knock at the back gates of grand houses for the dry crusts, and are you shabbily clothed because you are too poor to be dressed otherwise? Remember the holy Stanislaus, a novice in the Society of Jesus, courting the most humiliating labors, and the most uncomfortable clothes, that his superiors would allow him, and try to love that state of poverty which has been embraced, voluntarily, by so many saints.

Or, my little reader, are you rich, do you eat dainty food from exquisite dishes of the most elegant forms and painted by skillful artists; do you wear fashionabe clothing; more than this, do you judge of your companions by their dress, or by the street and house they live in, more than by their conduct? If so, my unfortunate rich child, remember, with shame, the nobly-born Stanislaus, who was of too lofty a soul to prize any such trifles. Like him, ask God for a mind capable of loving better things, and for a spirit of heroic self-denial, with that grace of holy purity which is always in danger amid luxury.

Claudio Aquaviva, the famous general of the Society, often mentioned, with tears, a circumstance which occurred while they were both in the novitiate, and which will show you the sort of obedience practiced by the saints. "We were one day," said the general, "appointed to help in the kitchen; the cook ordered us to bring some wood, and told us how many sticks each of us was to carry. I believed that I could carry more, and said so to Stanislaus; but he answered, smiling, 'No, you remember we must now obey the cook;' and he would carry exactly the number of sticks that he had been told to carry—no more and no less."

Stanislaus had not been quite ten months in the novitiate, when he received a forewarning of his death. To how many of you would not this be a cause of grievous lamentation, and of prayer to God to avert your unhappy fate? Our angelic young saint poured forth his soul in petitions—but, for what? To be allowed to celebrate the feast of Our Lady's Assumption in heaven, and, so earnestly did he ask for this favor, that she gave him a promise on the 10th of August, the feast of St. Laurence, who was his saint for the month, that his wish should be gratified. On that very day he was seized with a slight fever which his superior thought should put him in bed. Hearing this, he made over it the sign of the cross and said, aloud; "O can I any longer doubt that my wishes have been heard in heaven; never shall I rise from here!" His thoughts dwelt, unceasingly, upon the approaching solemnity of the Assumption, of which he spoke with exceeding tenderness. Still his sickness continued to be very slight until the 14th, when at midnight he swooned, and the assistant called out, "He has spoken too truly; we shall lose him."

Stanislaus, who had led a life of miraculous innocence, had no other thought than to die like a penitent, and he asked to receive the last sacraments prostrate upon the ground. He thanked his superiors for all their kindness to him, begging pardon for any ill example that he might have given. From this time he spoke only with God. Kissing, often, an image of the Blessed Virgin that he held in his hand, and keeping his beads twined around his arm; "A buckler," he said, "by which the Mother of God defends me from the arrows of hell."

The sun had just risen to announce the glorious

festival of Mary's triumph, when the countenance of the seraphic youth suddenly beamed with a brilliant, and serene joy. One moment after, he calmly expired. This happy death took place on the 15th of August, 1568, towards the close of his eighteenth year.

Can any of my young readers forget the feast of St. Stanislaus Kostka, on the 14th of November, or, can any child's heart resist the holy, lovely example of this youthful saint? Fervently beg of him, on that day, to obtain for you those solid virtues of faith, hope, charity, humility and purity, which made him a saint so admirable, even among the most venerable of the saints of God.

SAINT STEPHEN.

SAINT STEPHEN.

WHAT saint could we choose for the month of December, dear children, more interesting than St. Stephen; the first, of all that multitude of disciples who crowded around our Blessed Lord, to lay down his life, and shed his blood, for Christ? The apostles, and many a zealous follower of the crucified Jesus of Nazareth, lingered on through the summer, and autumn, and into the bleak winter, of a long life of hardships, earning their martyr's crown, as men earn the glory of a great name, when life had become a burden easy to lay down; while St. Stephen, was called, in the first freshness of the paschal joy, with the light of that Resurrection morning still kindling the fervors of his youthful soul, and making sacrifice more than easy—a joy, a triumph!

There is no doubt that St. Stephen was one of the seventy-two disciples of our Lord; for, immediately after the descent of the Holy Ghost, we find him perfectly instructed in the law of Christianity, and with the power to work miracles, while he preached with an earnestness that excited the fear of the Jews, and, their hatred. It was not, in that day, the first thought of a Christian to smooth down the rough and sharp edges of the doctrines of Christ. It was not supposed to be the best way of making converts to the new faith, to tell people that they could be "saved as well out of the Church as in it, if only they were honest in their detestation of it, if only they thought themselves safe." The first Christians were wholly given up to the glorious work of making Christ known as the Redeemer of men, and they were too much in earnest to flatter men into the belief that they could get to heaven in their own way; which would have been the same as to say, that their way was as good as God's way, and that Jesus Christ had been born, had suffered, and had died, all for no purpose.

This very easy way of taking care of one's own salvation, or of instructing others how to do so, was not, certainly, the way of the apostles, or of St. Stephen. They, certainly, did not tell people that it was really of very little importance what they believed, if they were only good, honest, well behaved, people. If they had done this, who, among the Jews, would ever have taken much thought or trouble about them? Instead of this we find them preaching, everywhere, the necessity to salvation of a belief in Jesus Christ, and of baptism in His name. I suspect that if St. Stephen should appear among us now, he would not be among the liberal sort of Christians, or the liberal sort of Catholics, who are ready to say anything which they think will flatter their neighbors, and make them good friends, and companions.

In those first days of Christian charity, when every Christian was known to every other Christian, there was a holy strife, as to who should be most ready to part with his own, special, privileges, for the good of the whole. Such was the zeal of their charity, that the apostles found it impossible for them to preach the gospel, and, at the same time, give out the alms put into their hands. Seven deacons were, therefore, appointed to this work, and the first one named was "Stephen, a man full of faith and of the Holy Ghost."

But the duty of a deacon also included teaching, and St. Stephen was attacked by the Jews who wished to dispute with him. When they found that they could not withstand his arguments, they bribed witnesses, as in the case of Our Lord Himself, to charge him with blasphemy against Moses and against God. Upon this false charge he was dragged before the Sanhedrim, or the highest Jewish court, and, after the accusation had been read, Caiphas, the high priest, ordered him to make his defence.

It was now that St. Stephen showed all the supernatural wisdom of one upon whom the Holy Ghost had descended, and, also, all the courage and constancy, which, like heavenly wisdom, are the fruits of the Holy Spirit.

With all the fiery eloquence of the Prophet Isaiah, he reminded them of the prophecies, beginning with the books of Moses, concerning the Messiah; and also reminded them how the very sacrifices of the temple were a figure which was well understood by the Jewish doctors of the law, of a better and more perfect Sacrifice, which he showed to have been completed in the Sacrifice of Jesus on the cross. Then, seeing, no doubt, the unbelief of their hearts written on their countenances, he accused them, in burning words, of having rejected and slain those prophets "who foretold the Just One; of whom," he said, "you are now the betrayers and murderers."

St. Luke tells us, while giving this account of St. Stephen, that "All who sat in the council, looking on him, saw his face as if it had been the face of an angel;" yet, with this shining face before them, bright with the holy indignation of a St. Michael, they no sooner heard this truth concerning themselves, than, as St. Luke says, they were "cut to the heart, and gnashed upon him with their teeth." But St. Stephen, nowise frightened by these signs of raging hate, "looking up steadfastly into heaven saw the glory of God, and Jesus standing on the right hand of God. And he said: Behold I see the heavens opened, and the Son of Man standing on the right hand of God." No longer able to contain themselves for fury and revenge, "Crying out with a loud voice, and stopping their ears," as if to shut out their own yells, worthy of the demons, "with one accord they ran violently upon him. And casting him forth without the city they stoned him." But our holy deacon, Stephen, had no resentment towards his cruel murderers. His indignation was not against them, but against their sin—their sin of unbelief; that sin which is now thought so little of that people are not ashamed of it, are even proud of it, and seem to think it a mark of superiority—it was against their sin, and not against them, that St. Stephen had uttered such burning words; and therefore, while the heavy stones were hurled upon him from all sides, he could say, with a just confidence in his Divine Master, "Lord Jesus, into thy hands I commend my spirit." Then, "Falling on his knees he cried with a loud voice, saying; Lord, lay not this sin to their charge. And when he had said this he fell asleep in the Lord."

Such was the death of the first martyr, "the protomartyr," as he is called, the model of all martyrs, so long as Christ shall ask the testimony of Christian blood for His truth. However you may look at this martyrdom, from whatever side you may approach it, it is still the same; and, after eighteen hundred years, almost nineteen hundred, we still go back to it to learn how to confess Christ, and how to suffer for him.

In the course of this narrative, at its very close, St. Luke tells us that "the witnesses laid down their garments at the feet of a young man whose name was Saul;" and again, that "Saul was consenting unto his death."

This, my dear children, is the first mention made in the Bible of Saul of Tarsus. Afterwards we hear of him as going to the chief priest, for letters to the synagogues of Damascus; still "breathing out," as St. Luke tells us, "threatening and slaughter against the disciples of the Lord," and intending to bring the men and women he might find, who were of this way, to Jerusalem, bound.

How little did Saul imagine when he set out, with his armed guard, for Damascus, what was really before him! He remembered, no doubt, the martyr, Stephen; but he remembered him to despise him; remembered him as another reason for persecuting every Christian he should meet. How is it, we say to ourselves, that this martyrdom, of which we cannot read the barest account without making acts of veneration, should not have sent one arrow of remorse into the conscience of Saul, should, indeed, only have increased his hatred of the Christians?

We can never give an answer to such questions, but, we do know, that not one drop of a martyr's blood is ever shed in vain; and, the martyr's prayer—what shall we say of that? St. Stephen had been one month dead; the blood of the martyr still clung to the stones lying on that waste field outside the city, and some poor Hebrew, perhaps, shuddered, as he remembered the awful scene of murder that went on there, but without courage enough to express his horror, even to himself when alone. There had been no rising from the dead with St. Stephen, and the prayer he uttered in behalf of his persecutors was heard with derision by his enemies, and was scarcely remembered after these few weeks. But the prayer which men could afford to despise, forget, had never been forgotten by that Jesus who knows how to reward those who suffer for Him. St. Stephen had asked a favor of his Master at the very moment he was dying for Him. Do you think Jesus Christ would refuse it?

If the others, who had persecuted St. Stephen, were very guilty, how much more this young man, Saul, at whose feet the witnesses laid their garments and who, so ostentatiously, consented to his death! Therefore this most guilty one, according to some law in the mind of God, was the one in whom the prayer of St. Stephen was to find its answer; find it, too, when we should say it was least to be expected, when it was the least merited by the one who profited by it. For it was on this very journey to Damascus, that the same Lord Jesus, who had appeared to St. Stephen standing on the right hand of God while his poor disciple was standing before the judgment seat of his persecutors, who now appeared, in all the blinding splendor of His Heavenly glory, to Saul of Tarsus, on his way to ill-use others of his disciples, and followers; and, calling out from the midst of the intolerable brightness to the terror-stricken Saul, said; "Saul, Saul, why persecutest thou me?"

Saul could sneer at the deacon, Stephen, falling dead under the shower of stones; but he could not laugh, or sneer, or cavil, when our Lord thus called him to an account for this cruel treatment of His followers. There was but one word for Saul to speak, and he spoke it, prostrate on the ground, his mouth in the dust; "Who art thou, Lord?" And the glorious vision answered Saul; "I am Jesus, whom thou persecutest: it is hard for thee to kick against the goad." Saul has always been called an honest persecutor; and yet, Our Lord seems to say that he has resisted some grace, has "kicked against" some "goad" of conscience. But now there is no resisting of graces, no despising of opportunities. If Saul is admitted to have been the most honest of persecutors, how poor indeed is the shelter for the honesty of others when they must meet our Lord, face to face, and answer His question, "Why persecutest thou me?" The most honest persecutor will then be glad to say with Saul, "Lord, what wilt thou have me to do?"

We have already followed, in the life of St. Paul, the wonderful story of Saul of Tarsus; but we can well afford to look over it again, in the Acts of the Apostles, while the prayer of St. Stephen is fresh in our minds. It has always been the belief of the Church, that the conversion of St. Paul was in answer to the prayer of the dying St. Stephen; and, to this day, the only sure means of converting the unbelieving, or those in any way gone astray from the path of safety, is—prayer. Prayer is our catechism, prayer is our logic, prayer is the one arrow which can pierce the shield that unbelief holds up to ward off the unwelcome conviction of the truth of Christ, and the truth of His Church. Jesus has promised that the prayer of faith shall not go unheard, shall not go unanswered; and, day and night, the incense of these prevailing prayers is going up before Him whose "arm is not shortened that it cannot save." How strange that we should ever doubt, ever waver in our confidence, our perfect confidence, in prayer! How strange that we must go back to the first martyr, St. Stephen, to be convinced of the might of prayer! How strange that we will go on, trying everything else, before we try prayer!

There is one more lesson to be learned as we stand by the side of the proto-martyr. It is very hard, sometimes, to suffer for our faith, without feeling resentment towards those who are thus loading us with injuries; but the prayer of St. Stephen tells us the true character of such resentment. If St. Stephen had resented the ill treatment of the Jews, he would not have been a martyr, would not have been what he was, a saint. Neither is it for us to distinguish between what we suffer for our faith, and what we suffer from the ill-temper, or imperfections of others. Not one, nor two, nor three, sorts of injuries are to be forgiven, but every sort of injury is to be forgiven so as never to be in any way avenged, if we would be like St. Stephen. No one can have injured us so deeply that we cannot pray for him, that we cannot serve him, if it is ever in our power to do so; and, above all, serve him in his spiritual necessities, which we can do without ostentation and without remark; and this, will, in itself, disarm every feeling of resentment or of revenge.

When beset by temptations to resentment, remember St. Stephen, and let this collect, which the Church recites every year on the feast of St. Stephen, be so familiar to you that you can, any time, repeat it, and thus ward off every feeling of bitterness:

"Grant us grace, O Lord, we beseech thee, so to imitate what we revere, that we may love even our enemies; as we now celebrate the birthday to immortality of him who knew to ask forgiveness, even for his persecutors, of thy Son, our Lord Jesus Christ."

The picture which I have copied for you, is by Fra Bartolommeo, a Dominican friar, and represents St. Stephen standing in a niche, young, and clothed in the embroidered vestment, or dalmatic of a deacon. In his hand, is the palm of martyrdom and of victory, and beside him lie the heavy stones with which the infuriated people of his own nation bruised him to death, setting free his gentle, forgiving, and heroic spirit. Who can look on that uplifted face, which shone, even to the eyes of his persecutors, like the face of an angel, without saying: Holy St. Stephen, pray for us!

SAINT LUCY.

A FEW blocks from the place where I am writing is a hospital, not for the blind, but for those who are likely to become so. The light comes into the rooms through soft green shades, and everything is done to keep its inmates cheerful. On the walls are prints and lithographs, pictures that soothe the anxious mind, and give a ray of heavenly hope to the most desponding. One of the pictures has a peculiar fitness for this place. Indeed the saint whom it represents, the gentle patroness and friend of the blind, is no other than St. Lucy, whose name in Latin, *Lucia*, means light, and one of whose sufferings, during her long martyrdom, was to lose her eyes.

St. Lucy was born in the city of Syracuse, in the Island of Sicily. Her parents were wealthy and honorable. She was educated, from her cradle, as a Christian, and so early did this tender seed blossom, and bear fruit in her heart, that when, at the age of fourteen, she was betrothed by her parents to a young nobleman, she had already dedicated herself to God, in the secrecy of her own heart.

Strange to say, these parents, who had taken such care to instruct their little daughter in the love of Christian truth, and in the practice of every virtue, did not hesitate to betroth her to one who was a pagan, because he was noble and very rich. St. Lucy put every obstacle between herself and her marriage, and at length her mother was attacked by a very grievous disease, under which, for four years, she languished in a state beyond the power of any physician to help her.

Lucy now urged her mother to visit the tomb of St. Agatha (in Catania on their own Island of Sicily), who, in 251, suffered a most cruel martyrdom for her Divine Spouse. Lucy accompanied her mother to Catania, and there, before the tomb of St. Agatha, obtained by her prayers, and the prayers of St. Agatha, the cure of her mother. After this miraculous cure, St. Lucy told her mother of the promise which she had made, and entreated her to be allowed to fulfill it; and, at the same time, to sell all her possessions in order to give them to the poor in alms. Eutychia, her mother, was very unwilling to consent to this request, and, especially, to her giving away all her vast fortune; but at last, seeing Lucy's great importunity, and somewhat softened, it may be, by the cure of her disease, she consented, saying: "My child, I am content; do with all my riches as you will; only let me die first, lest during my lifetime I become a beggar."

To this Lucy answered with a smile, "Of a certainty, O my mother, God hath little care for that which a man dedicates to His service only when he can no longer enjoy it himself. What doth it profit to leave behind that which we cannot carry away?" Her mother was convinced, by these words, of her mistake, and said, "Do as thou wilt, my daughter." So Lucia, with great gladness of heart, sold all their possessions and gave the money to the poor and the sick, to the widows and the orphans.

Now when the young nobleman to whom she was betrothed, heard of this, he was greatly enraged. He was very glad to marry Lucy with all her vast treasures, although he knew her to be a Christian; but when he found that her treasures were not to be his, that he could not profit by this marriage with a portionless Christian, he very soon found out how little he really loved Lucy, for he went immediately to the governor and *denounced* her as a Christian. Like the lover of St. Dorothea, his affection was of that false sort, which is changed to hate by contradiction; like base metals, such as copper and brass, which change their color when long exposed to the air, or if touched by acid, while the pure gold never grows dim.

The governor, Pascasius, ordered her to be brought before him, commanding her to sacrifice to the gods. When she refused, he ordered her to be taken to a place of shame, treated with indignity, and humbled to his will. But this pagan governor, who knew what value a Christian maiden sets upon her virtue and therefore threatened her with its loss, knew not that the God of the Christian maiden, and her Divine Spouse, could protect what she cherished for His sake; for behold! when these wicked men attempted to seize her and drag her away by force, the maiden suddenly became, by the power of God, immovable. They brought ropes, fastening them to her waist, but the more they tried to move her, the more firmly she stood there. Then Pascasius sent for magicians and enchanters; but their spells and incantations failed also. Then, in his rage, he ordered a fire to be kindled around her; but she prayed that the fire might not harm her, and that her enemies might be confounded. After this, one of the servants of the governor, seeing that his fury was gratified by any torture of her innocent body, thrust a poignard into her throat, and of this wound God was pleased to let her die. The Christians took her body and buried it on the very spot where she had suffered with such constancy, and there a church was afterwards built and called by her name.

It is not told in her acts how, or exactly at what time, she suffered the loss of her eyes; but her most careful historians speak of this as one of her grievous torments, and, in commemoration of it, she is invoked by those who are anxiously trying every means to preserve the precious gift of sight.

In pictures, St. Lucy is known, either by her eyes laid upon a dish which she carries in her hand, as if they had been plucked out with cruel violence, referring to this tradition concerning her martyrdom; or by a lighted lamp in her hand, referring to her name, Lucia, which, as I have said, means light. In both cases she carries the blessed palm of a martyr. Our beloved monk, Fra Angelico, has painted her with her lamp in her hand, beautiful, with fair hair and in pale green drapery. In a picture by another painter, St. Lucy is giving her palm to Our Lady, while an angel holds her eyes in a cup. Sometimes she is painted with a wound in her neck, from which beam rays of light, in allusion to her name, as the one by Carlo Dolce in the Florence Gallery. At Padua, where St. Anthony lived, there is an ancient fresco, representing her with ropes about her waist, her neck, her arms; and men, and even oxen, are trying, in vain, to move her, standing as she does, not in her own strength, but in the Almighty power of God, and with a confidence full of Christian meekness.

The great Italian poet, Dante, must have had, what we should call, a special devotion to St. Lucy, for he has introduced her into each of the three parts of his immortal poem. In one of his scenes in Hell, he calls upon her as

"Lucia, of all cruelty the foe;"

In his Purgatory, these lovely lines celebrate her gentle praises:

"Ere the dawn
Ushered the daylight, when thy wearied soul
Slept in thee, o'er the flowery vale beneath

> A lady came, and thus bespake me: 'I
> Am Lucia. Suffer me to take this man,
> Who slumbers. Easier so his way shall speed.'
> Here did she place thee. First her lovely eyes
> That open entrance showed me; then at once
> She vanished with thy sleep;"

and in his Paradise, he says,

> "Lucia, at whose hest thy lady sped."

After this we cannot doubt that St. Lucy has been very dear both to the artists and poets of Christendom, and neither can we doubt that she has deserved this admiring affection. It is for us to hold fast to the holy and beautiful traditions of the early Church, which are always fresh, always living, like the immortal flowers of Paradise, and not to be treated by us like the dry, scentless flowers collected in our herbariums.

St. Lucia suffered martyrdom on the 13th of December, in the year 304, the same year in which St. Agnes gave up her young life for Christ; and these virgin martyrs have come down together through the long, and often troubled, and blood-stained, ages, both in the Canon of the Mass, in which they are invoked by name, and, also, in the Litany of the Saints, where with St. Cecilia, St. Catherine, and St. Agatha, they shine as the five wise virgins, who took the oil of divine love in their lamps and went joyfully forth to meet their celestial Bridegroom.

How can any little girl, after reading the lives of such charming virgins and heroic martyrs, ever consent to be worldly, fond of dress, careless of her soul? Never let their holy examples fade from your memory, and, on the feast of St. Lucy, while asking, perhaps, for her powerful prayers in behalf of some dear friend whose blinded eyes are not yet wholly dark, ask her prayers, also, to obtain for yourself the light of that heavenly wisdom of which she is the symbol.

APPENDIX.

PATRON SAINTS was already in the hands of the type-setters and the electrotypers, when the news came across the stormy ocean that the Holy Father, Pius IX., had, on the feast of the Immaculate Conception of the Blessed Virgin Mary, proclaimed St. Joseph the Patron of the Universal Church. I was therefore obliged, however unwillingly, to let the life of St. Joseph stand, just as it had been written. But I have decided to put into an appendix, an account of this act of justice toward so great and so humble a saint, and thus, make it quite sure that all my young friends understand, that devotion to St. Joseph is not only allowed by the Church, approved by the Church, but encouraged and urged upon us by the Church. We can, therefore, feel no hesitation about the honors we are to pay to St. Joseph, and if some one should say that we are inclined to dress his altar too much, put too many flowers upon it, such as lilies and roses and choice pansies, or too many lighted wax-candles, we can defend ourselves by saying, "Do you not remember that the Holy Father, Pius IX., has declared him to be the Patron of the Universal Church, and did he not mean, by this, that he wished us to give special honor to St. Joseph, in return for his protection of the Church, and the blessings he will obtain for us?"

The best way to give you the confidence which I wish you all to have in St. Joseph, is to copy, word for word as it has been translated from Latin into English, the decree by which this new honor, paid to St. Joseph, was proclaimed to the whole Christian world. That you may not waste your time puzzling over old Latin words, I will tell you that the title, "*Decretum Urbis et Orbis*," would read in English, "Decree for the City and the World." Here, then, is a copy of the Decree:

DECRETUM URBIS ET ORBIS.

"As Almighty God appointed Joseph, son of the Patriarch Jacob, over all the land of Egypt, to save corn for the people, so when the fullness of time was come, and He was about to send on earth His only-begotten Son, the Saviour of the World, He chose another Joseph, of whom the first Joseph had been the type, and whom He made the lord and chief of His household, and possessor and guardian of His choicest treasures. So, also, He espoused to Himself the Immaculate Virgin Mary, of whom was born, by the Holy Ghost, Jesus Christ our Lord, who, as before men, deigned to be reputed the son of Joseph, and was subject unto him. And He whom so many kings and prophets had desired to see, Joseph not only saw, but conversed with and embraced with paternal affection, and kissed, and most sedulously nourished, even Him whom the faithful were to receive as the Bread that came down from Heaven, that they might obtain eternal life. On account of this sublime dignity which God conferred on His most faithful servant, the Church has always most highly honored and praised the most Blessed Joseph, next to his spouse, the Virgin Mother of God, and has besought his intercession in times of trouble. And now that in these most troublous times the Church is beset by enemies on every side, and is weighed down by heavy calamities, so that ungodly men imagine the gates of hell to have at length prevailed against her, therefore the Venerable Prelates of the Catholic world have presented to the Sovereign Pontiff their own petitions and those of the Faithful committed to their charge, praying that he would vouchsafe to constitute St. Joseph, Patron of the Catholic Church. They, also, renewed still more earnestly this their prayer and desire at the Sacred Æcumenical Council of the Vatican. Therefore our most Holy Lord, Pius IX., Pope, being moved by the recent mournful events, has been pleased to comply with the desires of the Prelates, and to commit to St. Joseph's most powerful patronage, Himself and all the Faithful, and has declared St. Joseph, ***Patron of the Catholic Church;*** and has commanded his festival, occurring on the 19th day of

March, to be celebrated for the future as a Double of the First Class, but yet without an Octave on account of Lent.

Finally, he has ordained that on this day, sacred to the Blessed Virgin, Mother of God, and her most chaste spouse St. Joseph, a declaration to that effect by this present Decree of the Sacred Congregation of Rites be then published. All things to the contrary notwithstanding.

The 8th day of December, 1870.

CONSTANTINE,

Bishop of Ostia and Velletri; CARDINAL PATRIZI, Prefect of the Sacred College.

Loco ✠ Signi.

D. BARTOLINI, *Sec.*

If you were climbing a very steep hill, and should see before you, places steeper and harder to climb than any you had yet climbed over, and if, while clambering up this steep path with all your might, and while feeling the loose stones giving way at every step under your feet or cutting them with their sharp edges, you should see several branches hanging down within your reach, you would not only seize one of the branches to help you up the steep mountain-side, but you would take care to seize the very longest and strongest one within your reach; the very one, indeed, which looked the most able to help you.

This seizing of the longest and strongest branch, is precisely what the Holy Father, Pius IX., has done by declaring St. Joseph to be the Patron, or the protector and friend, of the Universal Church.

Very likely you may have thought of St. Joseph as one whose vocation was accomplished, whose career was over, when he had taken care of the Blessed Virgin Mary, and had watched over the infancy, childhood and youth of her Divine Son. It was, certainly, a vocation and a career sublime enough to have taken up all St. Joseph's thoughts, and, also, to have excused him from all further duties; the wonder, too, which you may sometimes have felt, that St. Joseph did not stay on earth to protect the Blessed Virgin during the terrible passion of our Lord, may have inclined you to think that his work was over when Jesus became a man; and all this would be probable if the saints were not very different from most of us. When we have finished an important piece of work, we feel that we have a right to rest upon it; like the officers in the army or navy, who are excused, after living to a certain age, from the active labors of their rank. But the saints have a much more noble way of working than this. As they do every thing for the love of God, and as their love of God not only never ceases, but is always increasing, their labors and their prayers never cease; and, if we look a little longer at St. Joseph, we shall see why his work would not, could not end, except with the end of the world.

If we turn back to Nazareth, after the Archangel Gabriel had announced to Mary the greatness of her dignity as the Mother of the Messias, and before the birth of our Divine Lord, how wonderful a life was our humble friend, Joseph the carpenter, living! It was not to Mary alone that he found himself the protector, but to the Hope and the Expectation of Israel; and it is almost impossible to imagine the veneration with which St. Joseph attended upon Mary, supplied all her necessities, saved her from dangers and fatigues, and, in every way possible, ministered to her happiness. No one outside that humble home could tell why it seemed such a holy as well as a happy home; but some wonderful beauty shone forth in its low rooms that was more than summer and more than sunshine; for Jesus was there, hidden, but still always present, as He is upon our altars to-day.

When they left their cottage on the hill-side of the little city of Nazareth, one cold morning in December, and started on their wintry journey to Bethlehem—when they reached Bethlehem to find all the doors of its houses, large and small, rich and poor, shut against them—when they were glad to find a rude stable on the edge of the town, used only by the ox and the ass, which were willing to share it with them, and went in to wait, there, for His coming who had created all things—it was not for himself that St. Joseph was in the least anxious. He could bear heat and cold, wet and dry; he could, for himself, have slept soundly on the bare earth like the shepherds, at that very time keeping watch over their flocks on the hills; but his soul melted with pity for the tender virgin given into his care to whom the world was showing so rude a manner and so unkind a face; and, even more than for Mary, for the little Omnipotent One, who had chosen for Himself so cheerless a birth-place. There is no way to sound the deep and tender compassion of St. Joseph, that night, for the shivering Infant, and His adoring Mother. On Christmas night, if you have ever been at a midnight mass, you may have tried to realize it, but you only felt how very far it was above you and below you, and you felt as if you could sink down, forever, into the deep, tender, compassionate heart of St. Joseph.

Again: when St. Joseph had been visited in his sleep by the angel whose voice he knew so well, and, without a question or a minute's delay, rose from his hard couch, roused, very gently, the Blessed Virgin, setting her, with her little infant, on the meek ass which had shared the stable with them, and started, while it was yet deep night, on the long weary journey to Egypt —it was not for himself that St. Joseph felt so keenly all the discomforts of that journey, even when compared with their life in the stable, but it was for the Virgin Mother and the Divine Child. Perhaps he thought more than once, that meek and gentle husband of Mary, of their pleasant cottage at Nazareth and of the summer they had spent there; but he never lingered, never hesitated; and when he found himself in a strange country, among dark faces with fierce eyes, and hideous idols on every side, it was not for himself that he shuddered, but for Jesus, insulted by the presence of these idols and their worshippers, as he bore Him in his arms with a love which was also adoration. We can never sound the desire which St. Joseph had, at this time, to make reparation for the gross sins of idolatrous generations, any more than we could sound his compassion in the stable of Bethlehem. Perhaps we may try to do this when we see Jesus despised in the Holy Sacrament of the Altar, but we know that we must always fall very far short of St. Joseph even in our moments of most ardent devotion.

From this review of the life of St. Joseph, we see how every thing was done for Jesus, either to protect Him from dangers, and to give Him a quiet home, or to help Jesus carry out His plans for the salvation of men. Much as St. Joseph loved Mary, it was for "Mary the mother of Jesus," that he undertook such great labors and forgot all his own affairs and interests. And this lets us, at once, into the secret of this calling upon St. Joseph, by the Holy Father, to be the Patron of the Universal Church. There is work to be done for Jesus now, and who so ready to do that work, who so used to doing that work, as St. Joseph? Jesus is to be protected now, in the person of His Vicar, the head of the Church, Pius IX., and who will be more alive to the danger of the Church and of the Vicar of Jesus Christ, than he who "took the young child and his mother," into a place of safety — distant as that place of safety was? Jesus is to be served and borne in the arms now, by His faithful priests, and at the risk of life even, not only in pagan lands but in the countries and beautiful cities of civilized, Christian Europe; and who will be so ready to teach these priests how they are to serve Him, and bear Him in their arms, and give Him to His sheep, scattered and desponding, as St. Joseph, who carried Him with so steadfast and prudent a courage through the high-ways and by-ways, and across the stretches of desert sand on the flight into Egypt? Jesus is to be protected and honored now, in the persons of holy monks and of holy nuns, who have given up the world to live in their consecrated homes as in so many Nazareths, but whom rulers, who call themselves Christians, are driving from these sacred retreats of peace, and of prayer, into the noisy and wicked world again, compelling them to fly before their unpitying persecutors; and who so able, or so willing, to protect them as St. Joseph, who was willing to live in Egypt, that land of darkness and of the most disgusting idolatry, in order to protect Jesus, driven even from the stable of Bethlehem by the murderous Herod, and afterwards bringing Him back, with most glad heart, to Nazareth, and to all the peace of its humble cottage?

After spending even these few minutes in recalling the meek goodness of St. Joseph, his unassuming fidelity and perfect singleness of mind, contented with pleasing Jesus, as he was appointed to serve Him, without having any regard to the way in which his service would be looked upon or esteemed by the people around him, how beautiful seems the honor now paid to St. Joseph by the whole Christian world, from the Holy Father himself, cardinals, bishops, priests, down to the very poorest and humblest child of the Catholic Church, who pins up a little picture of St. Joseph on the wall beside his bed, asking St. Joseph, when he kneels to say his morning and evening prayers, to pray for him, to be *his* protector and friend, as he is the protector and friend of the whole Church! How beautiful, as I have said, does all this seem, and *how just!* Our Lord said, "He that humbleth himself shall be exalted." St. Joseph was the most humble of men, as our Blessed Lady was the most humble of all creatures; now, he is the most honored of all men, and held in esteem next to the Blessed Virgin herself.

Remember, my dear children, it is not enough for us that the Church honors St. Joseph. She honors him in order that *we* may honor him, and thus win for ourselves, and for the Church, his favor, his friendship, and his protection. Let us, then, follow the example of our Holy Mother, the Catholic Church, each and all of us choosing St. Joseph as our dear patron in life and in death; the patron of our homes, of our families, of all we hold dear. We may thus expect our riches to be turned into the eternal riches of the children of God, and our poverty will be the *holy poverty* which has always been so dear to the saints of God, especially to St. Joseph. We shall feel contented with our lot in life, whatever it may be, and we shall be contented to die whenever God may call us, for we shall have one for our friend, in every event, so kind, so powerful, as to be chosen by the Church as her Universal Patron; and we shall say with the Church, "Blessed Joseph is the helper in trouble, and the protector of all those who piously call upon him in danger."

Feast of the Patronage of St. Joseph, 1871.

www.ingramcontent.com/pod-product-compliance
Lightning Source LLC
Chambersburg PA
CBHW021338110726
47900CB00005B/1525